PRAISE FOR

THE HEIR AFFAIR

Named a Best Book of 2020 by *Glamour* ∗ Kobo

Named a Best Romance Novel of 2020 by *Vanity Fair* ∗ *Cosmopolitan* ∗ OprahMag.com ∗ Insider

Recommended by *USA Today* ∗ *InStyle* ∗ *The Hollywood Reporter* ∗ PopSugar ∗ Literary Hub ∗ Bitch Media ∗ She Reads ∗ Refinery29 ∗ *Serendipity*

"With an unintentional knack for paralleling the lives of the real British royal family, Heather Cocks and Jessica Morgan deliver up their highly anticipated sequel with all the pomp, circumstance (and gossip!) of a royal wedding. God save the queen? More like God save these books."

—*Entertainment Weekly*

"Those in need of smart escapism will find just what they're looking for here: a plucky American taking the monarchy by storm; an imperious queen who's gradually won over by her charms; a devastating family secret; not one, but two royal love triangles."

—*Vanity Fair*

"If you're obsessed with Prince Harry, Meghan Markle, and generally all things royal, this series is the escapist dream you need."

—*Cosmopolitan*

"Heather and Jessica have done it again! *The Heir Affair* is the perfect sequel to *The Royal We*. It is just as fun, charming, and delightful as the first—now with even more complexity and wisdom as we grow to know and love these characters even more. A timely and positively delicious story. I loved it."   —Taylor Jenkins Reid, bestselling author of
Daisy Jones & The Six

"This book is like a long, juicy, satisfying gossip over a glass of wine with your best friend, if your best friend just happened to be married to the heir to the throne. I enjoyed this book from the intriguing beginning to the delightful end."   —Jasmine Guillory, bestselling author of
The Wedding Date

"If you're a royals fan, *The Heir Affair* is absolutely a must-read. It's the perfect remedy if you need a break from *the times*."   —*Glamour*

"Can't get enough real-life royal scandal? Pick up this breezy sequel to the 2015 bestseller *The Royal We*."   —*Town & Country*

"If you loved *The Royal We*, get your British romance fix with this scandalous sequel."   —*Good Housekeeping*

"The highly anticipated sequel to *The Royal We* is coming out just when we need it most."   —TODAY.com

"*The Heir Affair* is finally on shelves—and it's even more fun and feel-good than [*The Royal We*]."   —HelloGiggles

"Irresistibly fun [...] there's real heart in this escapist romp, and royal watchers and romance fans alike will be left hungry for another sequel."
—*Publishers Weekly*

"Royal watchers and tabloid devotees will devour this juicy look behind the gilded curtain of palace life."   —*Kirkus*

"[A] fast-paced, funny, enjoyable read."   —*Booklist*

"Cocks and Morgan, the masterminds behind the screamingly funny fashion website Go Fug Yourself, are royal whisperers of a sort... [T]he characters remain utterly charming, particularly the young couple's circle of friends, and the book is ultimately a sweet referendum on love's ability to conquer all."   —*Seattle Times*

"[R]oyal-lovers will love *The Heir Affair* and its predecessor."
            —*New York Journal of Books*

"*The Heir Affair* is filled with details about life among the (fictional) royals, with enough based-on-real events and details to satisfy the most dedicated Anglophile... [T]his wickedly good tale shouldn't be missed!"
            —*Washington Independent Review of Books*

"Funny yet poignant, *The Heir Affair* has much more depth than might be expected... The dramatic details that Cocks and Morgan unfold make *The Heir Affair* a timely and perfect escape for royalty lovers and romance readers alike."   —*Shelf Awareness*

"A must for anyone who loves the royals!"   —*The/Thirty*

"We've been patiently waiting for this sequel since [Cocks and Morgan] published *The Royal We* way back in 2015... As clever and dishy as the first, this one's a right royal romp."   —*The Kit*

"*The Heir Affair* is an enjoyable romp through royal succession in its own right, but it certainly will be most appreciated by those who loved *The Royal We* and are looking forward to reconnecting with its characters."
            —*BookReporter*

"Cocks and Morgan have crafted a delicious story of complicated families, it's just that this one happens to be royal... Read if you're into: royals.

Gossip. Drama. Complicated families. Compulsively readable books. This has literally everything!"
— *Alma*

PRAISE FOR *THE ROYAL WE*

"The authors hit all the right notes in this funny, smart, emotional tale."
—*Library Journal*, starred review

"Cute, well-written, and perfect for summer...I loved it."
—BuzzFeed.com

"Smart, funny...[Cocks and Morgan] write like the pros they've become."
—Janet Maslin, *New York Times*

"The characters should all be familiar: the heir to the British throne, his mischievous younger brother, his granny and the pretty commoner he meets in college. But in this version by bloggers Cocks and Morgan (a.k.a. the Fug Girls), the girl is American. Nick and Bex's love story is so fun and dishy, you'll hope for a sequel—with royal babies."
—*People*

"Real life inspirations loom large and small and Cocks and Morgan cleverly poke fun at the more ridiculous elements of British high society."
—*Washington Post*

"An entertaining read—but also a sharp critique of how we treat celebrities and what happens to people always in the paparazzi glare...Cocks and Morgan also know that daydreams should stay daydreams because the reality is much harsher. That's what elevates *The Royal We* from just a good beach book to a beach book with a message—while remaining entertaining enough to keep your butt in your beach chair."
—*Philadelphia Inquirer*

"The perfect summer read...a confection of a tale, but a satisfying one, a romantic romp carried by Cocks and Morgan's storytelling."

—*Metro* (Canada)

"A joy from start to finish. *The Royal We* is that rare novel that makes you think, makes you cry, and is such fun to read that you'll want to clear your schedule until you've turned the final page. But be warned—Cocks and Morgan have created a world so rich, a romance so compelling, and characters so funny and alive that you'll be terribly sad to see them go."

—J. Courtney Sullivan, *New York Times* bestselling author of *The Engagements, Maine,* and *Commencement*

"*The Royal We* is full of love and humor, and delicious in too many ways to mention in one little blurb. I read this novel as quickly as I could, relishing any few minutes I had to turn back to its pages. An absolute delight."

—Emma Straub, *New York Times* bestselling author of *The Vacationers*

"*The Royal We* is as engrossing and deeply satisfying as any royal wedding documentary, and it's a thousand times more fun, from the fairy tale to the inevitable foibles. You will want Bex Porter to be your best friend. You will feel the same way about Cocks and Morgan, who are warm, witty, hilarious, and moving in their depiction of a very complicated relationship indeed."

—Jen Doll, author of *Save the Date*

"A heartfelt exploration of a life lived in the spotlight, *The Royal We* balances dishy decadence with an honest look at the sacrifices required to stay princess to Prince Charming."

—Courtney Maum, author of *I Am Having So Much Fun Here Without You*

"Royal watchers and chick-lit fans alike will delight in this sparkling tale. Pure fun."

—*Publishers Weekly*

THE
HEIR AFFAIR

HEATHER COCKS
AND
JESSICA MORGAN

GRAND CENTRAL
PUBLISHING

NEW YORK   BOSTON

Grand Central Publishing
Hachette Book Group
1290 Avenue of the Americas, New York, NY 10104
grandcentralpublishing.com
twitter.com/grandcentralpub

Originally published in hardcover and ebook by Grand Central Publishing in July 2020
First Trade Paperback Edition: July 2021

Grand Central Publishing is a division of Hachette Book Group, Inc. The Grand Central Publishing name and logo is a trademark of Hachette Book Group, Inc.

The publisher is not responsible for websites (or their content) that are not owned by the publisher.

The Hachette Speakers Bureau provides a wide range of authors for speaking events. To find out more, go to www.hachettespeakersbureau.com or call (866) 376-6591.

Library of Congress Control Number: 2020933671

ISBN: 978-1-5387-1591-8 (hardcover), 978-1-5387-1592-5 (ebook), 978-1-5387-5394-1 (Can. pbk.), 978-1-5387-1593-2 (trade paperback)

Printed in the United States of America

LSC-C

Printing 1, 2021

To our mothers,
for their strength, their wisdom, and their love

THE HOUSE OF LYONS
(c. 2015)

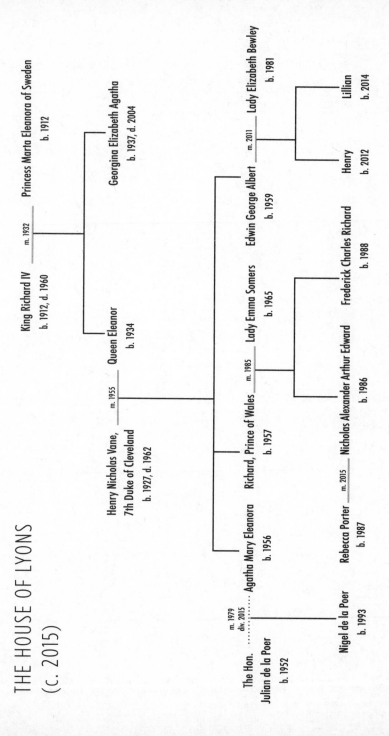

ACT ONE

A clear and innocent conscience fears nothing.
—Queen Elizabeth

CHAPTER ONE

Pardon me, lass, but could you help me with a wee spot of murder?"

I jumped. I hadn't heard anyone enter the store. The peeling P. G. Wodehouse hardbacks I'd been alphabetizing tumbled onto the floor.

"Absolutely, just one second," I said over my shoulder. Could I help with murder? Please. It had become my specialty. P. G. could wait.

I knelt, ostensibly to reorganize my pile of books so that I could return to it easily, but mostly to take a stabilizing breath. That had become my pattern: Whenever I had to interact with someone for longer than a moment, I caught myself pausing first, wondering whether that second of anonymity was my last. All it would take to blow my cover was one keen eye or ear. One person whose tabloid habit meant they'd recognize the contours of my face, one person to hear through the shaky upper-crust British accent I'd adopted. Assuming a new identity was thrilling, but the accompanying dread never fully went away.

My customer turned out to be a stooped older gent in a thin beige cotton cardigan, his hand wobbling on a cane, light age spots making a mosaic of his balding pate. Not the archetype of a *Hello!* addict, though if there's anything I've learned over the last eight years, it's that you can never tell. But from what I could see through my own (fake) glasses, there was no spark of recognition behind his.

"What precise kind of murder do you fancy?" I asked. "Real, or fictional?"

"I've always been a fan of the truth," he said with a thump of his cane.

"Who isn't?" I squawked, too loudly. MI6 was missing out on a once-in-a-generation talent. But his face was calm and open. No traces of double meaning. I smiled and added, "Follow me."

The back of the bookstore was a tight warren of blond-wood shelves, and smelled invitingly of yellowed pages and sixty years of shopkeepers making themselves a cup of tea. Right now, we had ample secondhand Agatha Christies, and I'd spent my first day here working on an intricate window display paying tribute to her lesser works; a day later, after that engendered some buyer interest, I'd enlisted Nick to help me rearrange the whole Mysteries and Crimes section. I'd become an expert in every flavor of murder we had to offer.

"Have you read this?" I said, handing him Ann Rule's *The Stranger Beside Me*. "She worked with—"

"Ted Bundy," he said, scoffing mildly. "Everyone's read that one, love."

"So I assume you've also read *Helter Skelter*, and *In Cold Blood*," I said, poring through the shelves. We were in the section Nick called Enormously Famous American Murders (Brutal). He'd insisted on re-organizing the books first by where the murder happened, then by exceptionally specific genre, and then alphabetically. It had been a long night that nearly ended in Small-Town Royal Murder (Justified).

"Here's a good one," I said, scuttling past Assassinations and into Bloodless Crimes. "*The Gardner Heist*. No one dies, but there is a massive unsolved art theft."

He chewed his lip, then nodded. "The wife *does* think I need a break from slashers." He chuckled and zipped his cane through the air for emphasis.

I left him browsing the stacks, the book tucked under his arm, and took the long way back to finish up with my Wodehouse. Nick and I had gotten unbelievably lucky with this Airbnb, which allowed its tenants to live in a flat above the bookstore and run the business for the duration of their stay. It was typically full up years in advance—there are a lot of people in the world itching to play bookseller for a week—but there had been a last-minute cancellation. So after three weeks of skipping like pebbles across England, putting as much distance as we could between ourselves and the mess we'd left behind in London, we'd found a sanctuary: a short-term rental of what our lives might have been like if he'd been born plain old Nick, lover of bad snacks and worse TV, rather than Prince Nicholas, future king.

I ran my fingers idly across the spines of the books I passed. My twin sister, Lacey, had always hated used books; she wanted everything brand new, born into this world for her alone to make her mark on it. I'd never minded a little scruff. I liked that used books brought with them their own history—every dog-ear, every stain, every crease. Maybe a book was slightly faded because someone had left it in the sun on their honeymoon. Maybe page ninety-eight was turned at the corner because it contained a glorious insult, or the perfect romantic turn of phrase. Maybe the person who'd highlighted nearly every line had graduated at the top of her class. Secondhand books could have lived in tiny walk-ups or hotel rooms or the White House—or, here, even in Balmoral Castle itself. Each book was a mystery, its secrets hidden in plain sight.

Kind of like me.

Most shoppers in Wigtown, known officially as Scotland's National Book Town, were so immersed in its bookstores that they barely looked at the human beings working in them. No one appeared to notice the beauty mark that to me seemed so obviously to be made of eyeliner; the fact that I could see the register better if I looked over, rather than through, the lenses in my matronly frames; or that I was, appropriately, wearing an actual wig. And whenever Nick joked that there might be a village somewhere called Booktown that specialized in wigs—which was often—no one realized they were laughing politely with the second in line to the throne. The store itself was part of our disguise.

My elderly murder aficionado eventually met me at the register with my recommendation and a couple of grim offerings from Creepy French Murders (Historical). I rang him up with the promise to set aside anything else obscure that came our way.

"Much obliged, Miss...?" He peered at me expectantly.

"Margot," I said.

He touched his hat. "Name's Duncan," he said. "Remember me

to your husband. He helped me find a very naughty bodice ripper yesterday for the wife. Best recommendation of the year so far."

"Ah, so you're a regular here," I said.

"Too right. This shop is like a telly program! New every week," he said. "You wouldn't believe the variety. Just last month we had a Danish lass who'd left her fourth husband when she found him shagging her second husband." He wiggled the twin thickets above his eyes in gossipy glee.

"Sounds like this place is a book in itself," I said. "Maybe you should write it."

"Not enough murder, lass." He studied me. "What brings you here? Don't suppose *you're* on the lam?"

I held a neutral expression amid a flutter of nerves. We'd sketched out a story, but this was the first time anyone had looked me square in the face and asked.

"Steve left his job," I said. "We've been traveling. He's looking for inspiration, and I'm..."

Duncan cocked his head and waited.

"I guess I'm looking for inspiration, too." I shrugged apologetically. "I hope our chapter in your book isn't too boring."

"Nonsense," Duncan said. "No one is boring." He hooked a thumb back toward the bowels of the shop. "There's stacks of inspiration right here. You'll find it soon enough."

He left with a ding of the bell over the door. From my perch behind the cash register, I watched as he touched the brim of his hat in the direction of the owner of the café across the street. The sun didn't fully set in Scotland at this time of year until late, but around closing time every night, I would glance out the window, and my hand would itch to sketch its slow descent. Nick had joked that the soft light of the Scottish evenings made his face more luminous, like the lead actress on *Outlander*—which he'd been binge-watching—and I had laughed, but he was right about its effect, both on his face and on everything else. The Bookmark wasn't even on Wigtown's most picturesque stretch of road, but the waning rays still suffused a singular glow onto its buildings, and the street took on a gentle quality, as if it were easing you into its arms for a good-night hug.

The woman across the street finished sweeping the patio and leaned on her broom in a moment of fatigue. She was winding down for the night; with a swell of satisfaction, I too locked the door of the shop. Our shop. For now, anyway.

I flipped the sign on the door to CLOSED, and then my body took over, instinctively tensing my muscles to brace me for what it knew was coming. Right on cue, the church bells clanged, and I was no longer in Scotland. They ceased being the bells of Wigtown and became those of Westminster Abbey, ripping through the temperate London air in a celebratory aria I will never forget—because nobody was celebrating with them. The crowd, which practically screamed off the roofs when I'd arrived, was quiet. No cheering. Not even any booing. Just staring, either at us or at the devices in their hands, in icy silence.

For six sonorous clangs, I was back in front of that church. Exposed. Loathed. Ashamed.

The church bells made it hard to forget.

I trudged up our narrow staircase toward the smell of something burnt, as usual. The flat above the shop was, in many ways, an echo of the books below: tattered, torn in parts, but well loved. The ancient appliances were tricky to regulate even for an experienced chef, which Nick was not, and so the aromas wafting from his general direction come dinnertime were always just left of tempting. Nick had been raised in a place where chores were done before he would ever realize they needed doing, and in these few weeks on our own, I think he'd enjoyed playacting as a civilian—running to the market, doing laundry, scrubbing down the kitchen counters. What was a drudge for most people was a novelty for him, as was the concept of cooking dinner for us every night.

"Evening, Margot," Nick said, greeting me at the door in an apron with a sketch of a carrot on it, his sandy hair sticking up haphazardly. "How's the shop?"

"Hi, Steve," I said, kissing him deeply. "You taste like butter."

"All good cooks sample their ingredients."

I wiped a smudge off his face. "But you're technically not a good cook."

"Not yet," Nick said. "But I've come a long way from burning lasagna." He made a *voila* gesture at the dining table, where two charred circles sat on mismatched, chipped dishes. "Now I'm burning meat pies."

"These look almost edible!" I said.

"See?" Nick clapped adorably. "I'm really improving."

I tossed my glasses onto the table, where they landed next to a copy of the *Mirror*. I didn't look. Instead, I poked at one of the pies. Black flakes matching the ones on Nick's cheek came away on my finger.

"Yes, unfortunately, they are indeed only almost edible. The second lot are in the oven now." He frowned. "They look a bit better. Maybe? I keep wanting to text Gaz a photo, but..."

He didn't need to finish.

"I missed you in the shop today," I said. "You and your saucy new mustache."

Nick wrapped his arms around me from behind. "I took my mustache into town for a bit," he said. "Steve had a lot of advice for the butcher's assistant about her rude girlfriend who deletes everything prematurely from the DVR. And then Steve popped round the off-license for a new box of wine and ran into Keith from the betting shop. You will not *believe* what his landlord is trying to pull."

"Hang on," I said, swiveling in his arms to face him. "We've only been here a few days. How do you know all these people already?"

He grinned. "I have always wanted to be some village's busybody," he said. He dipped his head and kissed me. "Isn't it sexy?"

My laughter was lost in the clash of our mouths. Both our pulses quickened. So did my breathing.

"Margot," he said, pulling away. "I approve of where you're going with this, but if I ruin this second lot of pies, I might pull off your wig and weep into it."

I nipped at his lip one last time. "Fine. I'll go collect myself elsewhere."

"Send my wife Bex out in about fifteen minutes for her pie, please," he said, hurrying over to the oven. "These are going to blow her mind."

Grinning, I headed into our tiny bedroom and pulled off my blond hair, plopping it onto the top of the dresser next to a pile of romance novels Nick had bought downstairs. One of them was called *Fancy Ladies*, and I itched to take a picture and send it to Freddie, who could spin it into a solid month of brotherly teasing.

But I couldn't. We weren't telling Freddie, or anybody else, a thing. After our wedding-day fiasco, Nick and I went off the grid, hoping to start our married life anywhere other than amid the ashes of a tabloid tire fire. It had been hard. I missed my sister, my mother, our friends. I even missed Marj, the boys' personal secretary, and the way she would hiss through her front teeth whenever one of them ticked her off (which was often). I especially missed Freddie. But missing Freddie was more complicated, because Freddie's feelings for me didn't stop at friendship. He and I had once crashed impulsively into a kiss; we'd agreed it was a careless, confused mistake, and I'd believed it. He apparently hadn't been so sure, and now, thanks to a combination of betrayals both accidental and chillingly deliberate, everybody knew it.

Nick and I had both decided we couldn't draw anyone else into our escape. It was better for them to know nothing, and safer for us to keep it that way. No texts, no emails, no check-ins, nothing that risked getting leaked to the media and threatening the peace of mind that we had found by hitting the road incognito, ambling sociably through small country towns, and now selling books to people who had no idea they were passing their bills to a royal cuckold and his faithless wife—the most hated person in Great Britain, if not the world.

Stop it, I told myself. *The whole point is to get away from all that.* But the damn bells had really thrown me off tonight. I shoved aside my feelings and dragged a hairbrush roughly through my own brown hair, matted and tragic from a day of being shoved into Margot's flaxen disguise. With every night that Nick and I climbed into someone else's lumpy old bed, our adrenaline surging from another day of going undetected and our hormones rising to match it, the shitshow that had erupted in London felt farther away. The ruse was working—both for us and on us.

With a tug of the brush, one of my hair extensions got caught in the bristles and came free. One more vestige of Duchess Rebecca that I could leave behind. I tossed it into the wastebasket and followed my nose back out into the kitchen, where Nick was taking two faintly less charred objects out of the oven. He set a pie in front of me with a flourish.

"This one might even be mediocre," he said.

"High praise," I said, and with a grateful sniff, sank into a dining chair. It did at least smell like meat. Of some kind. "Oh, our last customer of the evening sent his regards. It's a good sign that he's met us both and didn't twig to anything. Your mustache is really effective."

"We're also not front and center in as many papers anymore," he said. "Or at least our faces aren't."

He nodded toward the *Mirror* as he joined me at the table. I stabbed through the lid of my pie, and as it belched steam, I reluctantly pulled the paper toward my plate. The lead story was about an MP being found passed out in a shrub, but at the bottom, there I was. Allegedly. It was really a random brunette in one of the royal Range Rovers, her face obscured by giant sunglasses and a copy of the *Times*. I wondered how much she knew. And how much her silence cost.

The teaser next to it caught my attention. "Yikes, Freddie and Richard did an event together *again*? What's that, six now?"

"Seven." Nick shuddered. "Better him than me. That's a lot of Dick."

I nearly choked on a piece of what seemed like chicken.

"Imagine having to spend so many days in a row with Father, talking about God knows what," Nick continued, not noticing. "I can think of no worse punishment."

I couldn't tear my eyes from Freddie's face, which smiled up at me underneath the headline, APOLOGY (TOUR) NOT ACCEPTED. I searched it for a sign of what he was really feeling, whether his smile was real, or—as was so often the case when the brothers were around the Prince of Wales—wilting at the edges, merely pasted on top of a lifetime of resentment. Suddenly, I burned to know if he was okay.

I forced myself to push the paper aside. "So. What's on for this evening?"

"I thought I might get my hands all over some dirty dishes," Nick said. "Then, I don't know, coffee and biscuits, perhaps a quiz show?"

"Wow, we're really starting our married life with a bang," I teased.

"This is, in fact, a perfect start to our married life," he said with a contented sigh. "I had a long chat with the greengrocer today about courgette, and then walked to the chemist to buy dandruff shampoo. In *person*. I've *never* been able to do that."

I grinned. "And your nearly adequate food is far superior to anything I've ever made."

"Don't sell yourself short," Nick said, raising a piece of pie on his fork. "Your toast is exquisite."

We clinked forks. It was quiet again for a bit, interrupted only by the sounds of my chewing. I noticed Nick was spearing the same pea over and over again, so I fixed him with an expectant look and waited for him to meet my gaze.

"Bex," he began, staring at the table.

"Nick," I said. Then I lowered my voice. "*Steve.*"

He giggled. "I do love the way you say that," he said. "It makes me feel like I'm my own evil twin." He looked up at me. "We need to talk about what happens when our week here is up."

"It's so unfair. We just got here." Every tick of the walnut carriage clock on the bookshop desk, its glass so fogged that the sound was our only proof it still told time, reminded me that this domesticity had an expiration date. "On to the next, I guess?"

"That's just it." Nick leaned toward me, a flush in his cheeks. "Maybe not. Maybe we don't even have to go *anywhere*," he said. "Picture it: you, me, a thatched roof, a garden in the back with tomatoes and plenty of room for you and an easel, me and my knitting…"

"You're *knitting* now?" I asked.

"I read a very interesting book about it yesterday at the shop," Nick said defensively. "How hard can it be?"

"Okay, well, that aside, this all sounds idyllic," I said, "but how is it going to work?"

He scooted to the left and strained to grab his laptop from the nearby counter, then woke it up and turned it to face me. There it was:

a thatched roof, a garden, a modest bedroom with a surprisingly big lead-paned window, a warmly shabby kitchen, a sitting room with a TV nook. I leaned closer.

"Is that an antenna on that thing?" I asked. "Can you live without satellite TV?"

"No," Nick said. "I shall attend to that. But as for the rest...what do you think? It's down the road near the edge of town. The owner hares off to Lisbon every year and it's wide open." He pushed the laptop away and took my hands. "We've been on the go for weeks, Bex. What if we just...stop?"

"Stop," I echoed, turning the word over in my mouth and the concept over in my mind. We hadn't stopped since we'd left the palace. This flat was the first time we'd even bothered to unpack our suitcases. A moving target would be harder for Queen Eleanor to hit, and the weight of her fury had been so crushing that I wasn't keen to relive it. "Stopping feels like a mistake. Like we're going to be found out."

"I don't think so. Certainly not now that I'm planning to let myself go." He patted his stomach. "No one looks twice at us here. If they do, it's to wonder how that crispy blonde snagged such a foxy continental toy boy."

I snorted. "Be serious."

"I seriously am," Nick deadpanned. "Look, we've pulled it off, Bex. We've spent weeks being whomever we like, with no one the wiser. And now that we've managed to get lost up here, I want to relax for a bit. I want a slow pace and a kitchen full of groceries and a routine. I love you, and us, and *this*, and I want to focus on that. Don't you want that, too?"

As I searched his face, considering what he'd said, suddenly I was back at Nick's long-ago birthday party at Buckingham Palace—an event where he'd backed out of introducing me publicly as his girlfriend—and I was looking into the eyes of my father. *I really do love him, Dad*, I'd said then, my way of promising that the pain of loving Nick in secret was made right by the sincere depth of our feelings, and that the oddities of his life, of *this* life, were worth bringing into mine. My dad died before I got the chance to prove it. He'd missed my happiest hour, but also my lowest—the day I let myself get so lost that I nearly turned that promise into a lie.

The bizarre turns of the last few weeks had in so many ways brought me and Nick closer, both to each other and to the seeds of ourselves that wanted to grow outside the confines of the palace walls. If our former friend Clive hadn't become the kind of reporter he'd always taught me to mistrust, if he hadn't dug until he found a half-truth about me and Freddie that he spun into what I could only classify as an international sex scandal, then Nick and I would have had a week in paradise and then gone right back behind the curtain. I wasn't glad for Clive's betrayal, but I could still find optimism in the wreckage.

I half stood and shifted into Nick's lap, cupping his face in my hands and then kissing him slow and soft.

"I really do love you," I said. The echo was deliberate. I wanted this to be a new promise—a fresh one to Nick, to my dad, to myself. "And I love this idea. Let's stay. Steve and Margot can make it work."

"In life, as in the kitchen," Nick said, then popped a triumphant piece of pie crust into his mouth. "Please note that Steve's pastry did not have a soggy bottom." His hand slid down my back. "And how's your bottom today? I'd better check that, too."

I looped my arms around his neck. "You are getting cornier every day."

He shrugged. "Steve is a very basic man with very basic urges."

"I said *cornier*, not *hornier*, but apparently both are true."

Nick wound his hands in my hair. "It turns out Scotland is a much more convenient aphrodisiac than the Seychelles," he said. "My only problem is finding bedsprings that can stand up to our needs."

I ran a finger down his neck to where his shirt buttoned and flicked one open. "That's why God invented floors." Another button. "And showers." A third. I moved again so that I was straddling him. "And dining room tables and chairs, and..."

"Mmm," Nick said, running his hands around me and pulling my face to his. "God is good," he murmured between kisses. "Very, very good."

CHAPTER TWO

I could hear Nick even through the juddering of the bathroom pipes, which complained every time I used the old chrome hand shower. His whistling always got more elaborate when he was in a good mood, and he was apparently feeling extra carefree this morning, because his rendition of the Pointer Sisters' "Jump" was note perfect and flashy.

"Need any help out there?" I called to Nick as I heaved myself out of the yellow porcelain tub and wrapped my hair in one of the cottage's thin, rough white towels.

Between the whistling and clanking noises emanating from the kitchen, Nick didn't seem to hear me, which I decided to take as a no. Smiling, I crossed the slim hallway from our bathroom to our bedroom, pulled on shorts and a T-shirt, and curled up with my laptop on the bed. An email from my mother waited, updating me on various shenanigans with the Iowa Business Council—Mom had taken over my late father's fridge-furniture enterprise—and passing along the hometown gossip that Laundry Bill from Bill's Laundry had caused a scandal when he had an affair with Diner Sue from Sue's Diner, who was married to Cowboy Lou, who owned a hair salon. We'd been on the lam for almost two months now, and I'd decided a few weeks ago that my mother at the very least deserved occasional proof of life, even if it lacked specifics. She tiptoed around the situation via politely vague statements like "I hope married life is treating you well," which didn't beg for answers, and my replies were nothing more than benign confirmation that we still existed. I dashed one off and then wound my hair into a bun as I scanned the longer list of unread messages and spam that I hadn't touched. An all-caps subject line from two weeks ago jumped out at me: CARE TO COMMENT?

The sender: Clive.

I almost cried out, but caught myself. Bile rose in my throat. In the other room, "Jump" had segued into "We Didn't Start the Fire," so I knew Nick was still occupied. Shaking, I hesitated, then opened the email. All it said was, Your Royal Highness: We've been through a lot together, and you've had a trying month. If you'd like the world to hear your side of the story, I'd be pleased to give my old friend the chance to tell it. Best, Clive Fitzwilliam, Royals Columnist, The Sun.

"You have got to be shitting me," I hissed at my laptop. *Been through a lot together? A trying month?* As if he hadn't been the architect of it all? His email said he worked for *The Sun*, and not his dream employer the *Daily Mail*, but that was small consolation for the fact that selling out his friends had given this infected wart of a human (nearly) everything he'd ever wanted.

I closed my eyes and inhaled. The morning of my Abbey wedding, my best friend Cilla had suggested maybe Clive would loom less scary to me if I reduced him to something more human, more fallible, by picturing him as he was before: Nick's childhood friend, the kind and flirty guy I'd met at Oxford who'd been a hapless but hungry local reporter, writing about Tube station loos and the nun who claimed to see the Virgin Mary in a pancake, rather than a person who'd attempted to blackmail me.

But my mind's eye couldn't see that Clive anymore; all I could conjure was the bitter, twisted Clive who'd vibrated with spite when he confronted me and Nick about his claims that Freddie and I were having an affair. He was fueled by a lifetime of buried resentment and throttled hate. What did that Clive, the only Clive who would ever exist for me now, think he was doing emailing me?

My worst impulses won out, and I Googled him. He had tucked into his new gig with vigor: THE CHEAT, THE CAD, AND THE CUCKOLD, one of his headlines read, as if he were telling a bad joke over a whiskey. I snorted derisively.

I knew I should stop reading. But on the internet, you are only ever a few easy clicks from a horror show, and I could not turn away from mine. One story about Freddie at the opening of a distillery had me studying his face again for signs of stress, and that led me to an older one theorizing that he was drowning his sorrows in socialites. Another click took me to a report that Queen Eleanor might exile us. The tabloids had pulled whatever photos they had of me and Freddie and turned their body-language experts loose to find proof that he was checking me out, or vice versa. I fell further and further down the wormhole, all the way back to those grainy early morning photos of Freddie leaving my apartment, which Clive had used to bolster his claim of an affair. Eventually, I landed on the BBC's video of my entire wedding—right down to its abysmal end. I'd never seen it. Why would I have? I'd lived it.

I hit play.

Everything started out brilliantly. The commentators lapped up the décor, swooned over my dress, and—in a twist of dramatic irony I would find delicious if it were on one of my soap operas—extolled me as a perfect future queen.

"She looks stunning," the BBC lip-reader caught Freddie saying to Nick as I came up the aisle. "You're a lucky man."

(That explained the headline of one of Clive's pieces from the aftermath, 'LUCKY NICK,' SAYS TRICKY PRICK.)

You could pinpoint the second the news broke, even before the lead commentator's sharp intake of breath. Nick and I had emerged from signing the register behind the altar when, amid the choir's gorgeous elegy to our love, a light murmur started to creep through the Abbey.

"Ladies and gentlemen," the commentator said, "we've received word of the most astonishing story…"

As I curtsied to the Queen, you could see from above how many people had ignored the directive to switch off their cell phones. Their screens lit up one after the other, sweeping like fire all the way down the pews of the church, apace with the realization I remembered washing over me with every step toward the Abbey door: Clive had called our bluff. Or maybe we'd called his.

Reflexively, I hit mute to see, rather than hear, the next part. Incredibly, our veneer never visibly faltered. If you had somehow missed the headline OPEN-DOOR DUCHESS: BEX SCANDAL BLINDSIDES BUCKINGHAM, or slept on the *Mirror*'s poetic FREDDIE NICKS NICK'S BRIDE, then you'd have assumed our happy ending was delivered on schedule. The newly minted duke and duchess, who seemed a lifetime removed from me and Nick even though it had been only about six weeks, emerged into the soundless streets of London as if nothing were the matter. We waved. We held hands. As we climbed into the carriage and began the journey to Buckingham Palace through what were meant to be adoring crowds, Nick even held mine aloft and kissed it. He had suffered the most in all this and yet he'd been the perfect gentleman. As a silent film, it was flawless.

But with the sound on...

Nick poked his head into the bedroom, and I stabbed at the pause button. "Ready yet? I've got the picnic packed." He studied my face. "You look pale. Are you feeling all right?"

"Nothing a little vitamin D won't fix," I said, smiling as brightly as I could. "I'm finishing up a note to Mom."

"Ah. Tell Nancy about those muffins I accidentally set on fire. She'll like that," he said, and then off he went, whistling anew.

Don't do it. This is insane. Do not.

My lip trembled. I didn't need to hear this again; it was seared into me already. I could just follow Nick into the living room and forget this whole thing. But my disobedient hands were already rewinding the video and unmuting it. And there it was, clear as a bell. The woman right opposite the Abbey doors—sporting a Union Jack top hat and caricature of my face on her T-shirt—had started it, her face purple and contorted with rage.

"Slut!"

Her loud, angry braying had spread like a virus through the crowd. Until that day, I'd never personally experienced real booing outside of a baseball stadium. The verbal battery, fully audible on this worldwide TV broadcast, was exactly as I'd remembered it—every sound, every screed, every epithet spit at me from a frothing spectator, a wave of furious words crashing together amid the clip-clop of the horses drawing our carriage. Anyone not booing us just looked broken. Confused. Betrayed. A nation's worth of what I'd seen on Nick's face one day prior.

I sat back on the bed and hugged my knees to my chest. The truth was so much more nuanced than Clive or anyone else cared to communicate. But nuance wasn't worth a damn. No one cares if a future duchess feels isolated by her new global notoriety or about the loss of personal liberty that comes with it. They would hardly cry me a river over how badly I'd missed Nick while he was on his Naval deployments, or the way my relationship with Lacey had been poisoned by the chokehold my love life put on my family. I'd spun out, and Freddie— the spare, adrift in his own way—had caught me, and tried to offer an answer. Running away together would save us both, he promised. But the tug of my love for Freddie was outmatched by the pull of being *in* love with Nick. Freddie had slunk out of my apartment, our tryst over before it ever began, unwittingly giving a waiting Clive the photographic ammo he needed.

As far as the public was concerned, however, the picture was clear: The Duchess of Clarence had cheated on her duke with his beloved baby brother. The fairy tale was a falsehood. The people had been sold a bill of goods, and they wanted their money back.

"Bex? Are you coming?"

"One sec," I managed.

I clicked back over to Clive's email. Without me and Nick on full display, the media hadn't moved on; instead, everyone filled in the blanks themselves, conjuring up screaming matches, ongoing trysts, legal confabs, and whispers of divorce. One of the papers assured its readers that I was being deported and our marriage annulled; another claimed I was already pregnant and that the baby's paternity was a big old question mark. It read like a contest to come up with the most plausibly dire headline. I felt another wave of disgust. Clive had emailed because he needed me and Nick. He couldn't keep winning this game without his pawns, and knowing me as he unfortunately did, he probably figured he'd provoke a rude response from the unruly American that he could release to the world.

I hit delete. As far as that asshole was concerned, I was a ghost.

"Success!"

I nearly knocked over the jar of murky water I was using to clean my brushes.

"Sorry, I didn't mean to startle you," Nick said, materializing by my side. "That's looking marvelous."

"Gotta keep my skills fresh," I said. "I don't know what we're going to do with all these paintings of ruined castles, though. They're starting to pile up."

"We'll frame them and hang them in the Hall of Castles, which is a thing I've just made up that we should absolutely have." Nick tugged down the brim of his baseball cap and knelt on the large plaid blanket I'd stretched over the grass. "I saw a baby lapwing inside the keep," he said.

"Amazing!" I said. "I assume? I have no idea what that is."

"It's a bird," he said, tossing his copy of *Birding: A Life* on the ground. "With a thingy on its head. You know. Like...a head thingy."

"You're really getting the hang of the terminology," I teased.

Nick laughed, and swung his binoculars off from around his neck.

"Uncle Edwin is obsessed with birds, and Father loves shooting at Balmoral," he said. "I thought birding might be in my DNA, but perhaps I'll stick to cooking." He rubbed his hands together. "On that note, I do think it's time for lunch."

"Amen," I said, wiping my hands clean on a towel. "What did you pack for us today?"

Nick plunged a hand into the wicker picnic basket and withdrew two cold ham sandwiches—the meat cut thick, the bread heavy with salted butter, a beautiful calorie bomb—a pair of apples, a Thermos that I suspected contained clandestine Pimm's Cups, and some hard-boiled eggs.

"Surely there's a baked good in there somewhere," I said. "You weren't bashing around the kitchen for no reason this morning."

"Guilty as charged," Nick said. "Jam tarts."

He pulled them out with a flourish. They had cracked in half.

"You're making progress," I said, taking an exploratory bite. "It's...apricot?"

"Spot on!" Nick looked delighted. He stretched out next to me, long and lean, with his head on a crumpled-up sweater, a sandwich in one hand, and *Birding: A Life* in the other. "This entire book is gibberish," he said, squinting at it. "If Father had ever bothered to take me hunting with him, maybe it would be different, but Mum was always the one who wanted to take us outside. She was never afraid to get grubby. Father would always come back immaculate from shooting grouse, and we'd be on the lawns rolling about in the mud after a rain looking for earthworms. He told her off about it once, said we were being improper, and she walked right up to him and grabbed his face and kissed him, and left two giant muddy handprints on his cheeks."

I laughed. "I would have paid good money to see that."

"Mum could be very funny, when she wanted to be."

His smile faltered. Nick didn't have many memories like that of his mother, because mental illness had overcome her when he was still young. Emma, Princess of Wales, spent most of her days now in a seaside retreat in Cornwall, which had hidden her from the world's prying eyes both before and after everyone learned the truth about her condition.

I leaned over and gave him a peck. "Her spirit lives on in you, Steve," I said. "God knows you didn't get your sense of humor from Richard."

He grinned around a mouthful of ham and then lifted the book back to his face.

I returned to my project. Like Nick, I'd been dabbling, though in my case it was only to expand my artistic horizons to paints from my usual sketching; today I'd managed a mediocre watercolor of the triangular Caerlaverock Castle, which rose from a dirty brown pond that wouldn't have offered much protection back in the day—which probably explained why the castle had been brutalized by siege warfare

between the English and the Scots. Since landing in Wigtown, we'd
spent countless days touring Scotland's many remote and ruined castles,
which for me was a kicky diversion and an excuse for fresh air but
carried a little more personal weight for Nick.

"I wonder if any of my lot are responsible for this one," he'd say,
touching a crumbling wall in a building that had, once upon a time,
been sacked and burned. Another day, we'd taken a rowboat to Threave
Castle, and he'd opined, "I suspect this moat was meant to keep my
family out. If Archibald the Grim's grave is here, he's spinning in it."

It seemed that, while our decision to run had been spontaneous,
visiting the various trappings (or crime scenes) of the institution we'd
left behind was reinforcing Nick's desire to stay away. And how ironic
that, in the end, I *had* run off in order to save myself. Just not with
Freddie, the way he'd hoped. I wondered idly if he'd thought of that,
too. Or what he was thinking at all. Over the last several weeks, I'd
written a hundred texts to Freddie that I'd deleted instead of sending—
partly because I'd waited too long to know what to say. *Hey, we saw a
sausage roll that looks exactly like Cousin Nigel* didn't seem to cut it after
all this time.

A burst of raucous laughter carried across the lawn.

"You're off your head," a girl cackled from several yards behind us.

"I am not! Look at him in that uniform! And now he's all heartbroken, and needy, which makes him even sexier," her friend said.

"Give that here," said the first girl, and I heard the flutter of what
sounded like a magazine being tossed from one to the next. "No, sorry,
you're mad. His wife went off and shagged his brother! He can't know
what he's doing in there."

"It's not his fault she's rubbish," her friend said. "Imagine getting to
have it off with them both, though, eh? And she did pick Nick, so he
must not be totally useless."

"Nah, love. Nick will be king in the streets, but Freddie is king in
the sheets," the girl said. This sent them into gales of laughter.

"Please have *not totally useless* put on my headstone."

My eyes clicked back into focus. Nick was peering over my shoulder
at the source of the chatter.

"I don't know what you're talking about," I lied. "I'm just reveling in how lucky we are to picnic in this perfect field and paint medieval ruins."

Nick rolled onto his stomach, facing the castle. "I wish I knew how to explain the effect these places have on me without sounding like a total prat," he said. "It's not like we don't have oodles of stupendous old things in England. In London alone."

"Well, *these* stupendous old things are new to you," I said. "Of course they feel different."

"They make me feel small. In a good way." He picked a blade of grass and stretched it between his fingers. "Standing on top of centuries of history reminds me that being the future king is a fragment of it. I am not a big deal. In the scheme of things, I'm a blip. And maybe so is . . ."

He stopped himself. I took a deep breath. "Nick," I said. "We should probably—"

"Don't say it." He turned onto his side, his long, lean form stretched fully out on the blanket. "I'm not ready."

I tapped my brush. "I'm wondering if we'll ever be."

"I feel so free here," he said. "No one pays me any mind. I'm like any other bloke, looking at birds and eating a ham sandwich on a blanket with his wife. I can do whatever I want. *We* can do whatever we want, with no gossip and no papers chasing us. I've never had that, Bex, not really."

"It *is* chasing us, though, Nick," I said, gesturing at the girls behind us. "You know it is."

"We're still ahead of it. Please don't take this from me. Not yet."

"We can't run forever."

"Please."

He searched my face, and I felt myself nod.

But the mood had shifted. Nick pulled his cap brim lower over his face and plucked his binoculars off the blanket.

"I'd like to go bang around the castle again," he said, and without a backward glance, he trudged up to Caerlaverock.

The outside world had found its way in.

CHAPTER THREE

If Nick's refuge was in ancient ruins, mine was in running. Every day before my morning coffee, I would hit the roads, reveling in working up a fresh-air sweat the way I did before I'd gotten engaged and been consigned to a treadmill. My route took me out of town and along the river, where no one gave me a passing glance other than the odd motorist who honked for my safety; I could easily hide under my new Sheffield Wednesday baseball cap, which I'd bought because I've always thought Sheffield Wednesday sounded less like a football club than a heroine in a novel who'd be described as "formidable" and "whip smart" and who'd constantly get the better of condescending men. I wish I could have used her as my alias.

At first these runs were just one more welcome sliver of normalcy, but lately, that daily hour or so had become meditative. The rhythmic pounding of my feet had a metronome effect on my thoughts. They didn't tangle up in each other the way they sometimes did when I was sitting on our couch; they simply came in an orderly way, one after the other, check, check, check.

Today, I'd needed that order: I had to come to grips with the fact that we were close to the end in Wigtown.

You can't unburst a bubble.

The longer Nick and I had lived like ostriches, the easier it had become, to the point where I had been astonished to look at a calendar and see we were deep into June. Nobody had asked us to come home, but the complete silence we'd once found to be a relief suddenly felt unnerving. Hearing those girls giggle about us proved nothing had changed as much as we might have imagined. Even now, as I jogged, I wondered where our rotating cabal of personal protection officers was. I knew intellectually that Stout, Twiggy, Popeye, and Furrow—so christened by Nick and Freddie years ago because they hadn't been given their real names—were experts at creating the illusion of privacy, and that escaping royal life didn't mean escaping royal security, but it wasn't until this past Tuesday that I'd started to look for them in my periphery. Surely Eleanor had deployed them. There's no way we were as alone as we pretended to be. I'd tricked myself into obliviousness, but it wasn't working anymore. I had to talk to Nick.

But I didn't know how. We were here, in the global sense, because my secrets had hurt him. Loving Nick had meant giving him whatever agency he could find in this, for as long as was feasible, but hiding out had just been a convenient illusion for us both. Ever since our afternoon at Caerlaverock, any time Nick left the room, I'd sneak online to gauge public opinion, and the news wasn't good. Nothing had been forgiven, or forgotten. I tried to take it as a compliment that the entire country now believed me to be some kind of sexual sorceress (in addition to a gold-digging tramp), while Freddie was alternately a predatory jerk and a lovelorn moron, and Nick was a hero, a martyr, or an unbearable wuss for not having me burned at the stake. *Vanity Fair* even made a *Game of Thrones* comparison chart. I was Cersei.

I slowed to a walk, panting, at our battered front door and let myself inside. I found Nick in the garden poking morosely at a tomato.

"Another one bites the dust?" I asked, picking up his coffee from the patio table and taking a sip. "Ugh, too much sugar."

"I don't know what's wrong with these tomatoes. Maybe they need a pep talk," he said, squinting at one limp-looking vine.

"You look more like you do."

His gaze stayed fixed on the veggies for a long while. Then he lifted his other hand to reveal a rolled-up newspaper, which he handed to me.

I unfurled it and was met with the headline FAITHLESS FREDDIE AND NERVELESS NICK.

"As you can see, I haven't entirely quit the papers," he said.

I scanned the article, which suggested that while Freddie had done him a grievous wrong, Nick was the bigger loser here for not jettisoning his evil wife. Inside were shots of Freddie at various recent appearances, both with Richard and without, accompanied by captions praising his busy schedule.

"I hate this," Nick said. "I don't know what I thought would happen when we left, but it wasn't being made the villain, and it definitely wasn't my brother being hailed as a hero for doing actual work for once in his life." He stuffed his hands in his pockets. "Makes me glad we're gone, if that's how they feel."

"See, it makes *me* think we need to go back," I said softly. "I haven't wanted to bring this up, because I didn't want to be the one to say it. We've always been good in a bubble. But…"

"But staying in the bubble too long has historically been bad for us," Nick finished. "I know."

"I'll grant you that a bit of a bubble is important," I said. "This bubble gave us a chance to ground ourselves. And I learned a ton about you. Like, for example, that you will need ten more years to finish knitting that scarf—"

"It's a sock," he said defensively.

"And that you overcook chicken on purpose because it freaks you out."

"And you are an even worse cook than I am," he said, "but are getting very adept at watercolors, and I can't wait to hang some of your pieces from Wigtown in our house."

"But that house is in London," I said. "Whether we want it to be or not. And unless we show up soon, what's in the papers is only going to get worse. We can't pretend that whole other part of our lives doesn't exist."

"Why not?" he asked. "It's worked so far."

"Has it? Because I'm starting to think we've been fooling ourselves."

The silence between us stretched and expanded, and I let it, having learned not to rush Nick into his feelings. He walked away from me and fussed with some of the other vegetables in the garden, then kicked the grass and looked at the cottage.

"They say nothing good can last," he said.

"We can last," I said, coming up next to him and sliding an arm around his waist. "I think we're pretty good."

"I feel like I'm about to say goodbye to a friend I'll never see again," he said. "And I don't only mean Steve and Margot, although she was a proper vixen."

I let my head fall against him. "Margot will never really leave. She'll just start plucking her eyebrows again."

He took my hand and rubbed at the spot where my ring should be. We'd left the famed Lyons Emerald back at Kensington Palace for safekeeping.

"I don't want this," he said. "I understand what you're saying, but I still don't want to do it."

"Neither do I, but I don't think it matters," I replied. "I think we have to deal with a lot of stuff we don't want to, including—"

A bracing knock came at the door, followed a second later by Nick's cell phone blaring Taylor Swift on the nearby patio table.

"I'll get the door, you get Taylor," I said.

I marched back inside as I heard Nick answer the phone. With one glance through the peephole, I gasped audibly, and pulled open the door.

"Greetings, Your Royal Highness," said PPO Stout, an apologetic look on his face. "You really shouldn't open the door without your wig on."

"What are you doing here?" I asked, waving him inside and closing the door. "I mean, I knew you were here, probably, but not *here* here..."

"I believe the duke may have some intel on that," Stout said.

Nick appeared and shook Stout's hand, but his face was white as a sheet.

"Gran's had a heart attack," he said. "It doesn't look good."

Eleanor tended to dash off to her home in the northeastern Scottish countryside more than was reasonable, given its distance from the monarchy's official seat in London. Balmoral had been a royal refuge dating all the way back to the reign of Victoria I, whose husband Albert purchased it in the 1800s and built it up into a sprawling granite fairy-tale castle. Eleanor claimed to find it a welcome hideout from the honking, touristy bustle of London, but Nick suspected part of the appeal was that Balmoral was entirely hers: It was not owned by the Crown, and nothing but the majestic old ballroom was open to the public. That she'd fallen ill there meant we only had to drive four hours to her bedside, but it's still agony to spend four hours driving toward a family you stormed away from, after learning its most important member is dying.

I stared out the window but saw none of the scenery. My heart pounded, echoing the memory of Eleanor's heels clacking on the Buckingham Palace floors. After the disastrous procession out of Westminster Abbey on my wedding day, we had tumbled out of our carriages and hustled to the Balcony Room, per the schedule—which of course had not included a clause for what to do if a sex scandal broke during the ceremony. We'd huddled like cornered prey and listened as Eleanor's steps grew louder, faster, closer. Unbidden, the *Jaws* theme had popped into my head.

And then she had appeared, resplendent in cerulean, her simple cake-shaped hat still pinned immaculately in place despite the fury on her face underneath it. My nervous laugh had died in my throat.

Everyone else filed in behind her: Nick's father, Richard, his jaw so clenched and angular, you could use it to file metal; my ashen mother, arm in arm with Nick's aunt Agatha; his uncle Edwin guiding his wife, Elizabeth, five months pregnant but moving like it was five years (which in a way it had been; this was their third child in about that much time), and Nick's centenarian great-grandmother Marta. Nick's wretched cousin Nigel was nowhere to be found, which was a relief. If anyone was likely to broadcast the fallout live on Instagram, it was him.

"Bex, my God. I had no idea," murmured Elizabeth, drifting past to take a heavy seat in one of the silk-upholstered love seats. "Aren't you a minx."

"It's not what you think."

"Isn't it?" This was Eleanor. "Perhaps you should educate me on what it is that I think."

The contempt on her face was so complete, so hard and fast. If it wasn't pure hatred, it was incestuously close. Fresh shame pounded my chest.

"It's rich that you're trusting the *Mail*, when it's printed rubbish about every single person in this room," Nick said. "We were duped. Clive lay in wait for years until he found a lie that was plausible."

"A lie," Eleanor echoed. "Frederick did not, then, make a pass at Rebecca."

"Well..." Freddie began.

"And Rebecca's sister did not provide voice recordings detailing what she saw of the affair, and Frederick's infatuation, and there is no proof of her calling Rebecca—what was the catchy little phrase, dear?"

Lacey's mouth opened but no sound came out.

"The exact wording was 'She is a cheating trashbag sex addict who won't be happy unless she gets all the attention.'" Our heads swiveled toward the Queen Mother, who waggled her phone. "It's all over Twitter."

"What a charming new way you've found to make a mockery of the monarchy, Rebecca," Eleanor said. "I'm thrilled to be shepherding us through the lowest point in our history."

"Hardly in *history*," Freddie said.

"Didn't one of your lot die by a hot poker thrust up his bum?" piped up Elizabeth.

"Not to mention all the questionable Henrys," Edwin added.

"Arthur the Second was a massive prat," Marta said plainly.

"It's not as black and white as Clive makes it sound," Nick added. "It was a misunderstanding."

"No," Eleanor said.

Lacey took a stab. "Clive drugged me. He—"

"*No*," Eleanor thundered. "No excuses."

"They're not excuses," Nick spat back, his voice jumping an octave. "It is complicated. Clive didn't get it exactly wrong, but he also didn't get it right. You cannot lay blame at any one person's feet, certainly not without bloody listening."

"Nick, don't yell," I said. "You'll make it worse."

"Worse?" Eleanor trilled with a frosty, mirthless laugh. "How could it be worse? The entire world saw those meaningless vows. We are a laughingstock."

Richard glowered. "It seems to me that the common denominator in every embarrassment of the last few years is Rebecca," he said. "Eliminate her from the equation and none of this happens."

"And that's exactly what we're going to do," Eleanor concluded.

"You can't," Nick said. "We saw to that."

Eleanor cocked her head, as if unclear whether her ears were working.

"This wedding was for ceremony," Nick said. "Everything's already been signed and sealed and witnessed, and, yes—er, cover your ears, Nancy—it's been consummated. You can't undo it without making it worse. It's done."

Eleanor's eyes hardened into sapphires. "You knew this was coming?"

"Er, yes, but only barely," Nick said, flustered. "Clive sneaked into the rehearsal dinner to torture us. After that confrontation, the plan just sort of came together."

"And then you were simply too busy *consummating* to warn me that an unprecedented fiasco was about to drop in my lap?"

"Ooh, *The Sun* called her the Whore of Bexylon," Marta said, poking at her phone. "That's clever."

"Shush, Granny," whispered Edwin. "Although, can I just see?"

"'The Princess Is a Porter-stitute' is a bit of a reach," Marta said, turning the screen to Edwin. "She's not an actual princess."

"Your Majesty, we didn't intend to disrespect you," I told Eleanor. "We just…didn't think he'd go through with it."

Eleanor snapped her head toward me. "Lies. Your secret little wedding was because you knew he very well might. You may be an absolute idiot, Rebecca, but I am not."

Mom put her hand on my shoulder. "Do not speak to my daughter that way."

"The audacity!" Eleanor scoffed. "You come in here with your squalid furniture company and your loud husband and your unruly off-spring, and trample the dignity of this institution, and then you show no remorse for having raised an unrepentant trollop."

My mother marched right up into Eleanor's face. "I said not to speak to, or about, my daughter that way," she said in a low staccato. "Earl Porter was worth ten times you people. He loved his children for who they are, not for what they could do for him. I haven't heard you say the word *family* once. Monarchy, institution, history—never family. But this *is* a family, or it's supposed to be. Stop acting like a mob boss, and start acting like a grandmother."

Every living being in the room, and possibly some of the painted ones, seemed gobsmacked by this outburst—Mom included. Her confidence visibly ebbed the longer Eleanor remained mute, and she backed away until she was standing between me and Lacey, taking each of our hands. Eleanor's were clenched, her body all but quaking from the effort it took to retain her composure.

"I have reigned for nearly six decades," she finally said. "Without a whiff of scandal. Every lid stays on every pot. Richard's wife went mad, and no one had any idea until *we* decided it was time. And then this promiscuous weakling waltzes in here and—"

I held out one arm to block my mother, and another to block Nick. "But we can fight back, Your Majesty," I said. "We can discredit him."

"I recorded what he said to them," Lacey added. "It's hateful." She proffered her cell phone to Eleanor, who looked down at it like Lacey was trying to give her a used tampon. Lacey slowly withdrew her hand.

"Which part of his story can you prove was inaccurate, Rebecca?" Eleanor asked, crossing her arms over her chest.

I cleared my throat. "On the recording he makes it very clear that revenge was his driving force, and he, er, he talks a lot about resenting being a good little royal foot soldier..."

Eleanor's tone was caked in sarcasm. "So your grand plan is to reveal that a man who lived close to the monarchy for his whole life, with access most people only dream of, finds it to be oppressive."

I couldn't find the right words. Eleanor had twisted our logic until it cracked and broke.

"You are correct that it's our word against his, ma'am," I conceded.

"And your word is worth what in this scenario?" Eleanor asked. "No, don't answer that, you'll only embarrass yourself. And *you* will say nothing," she said, flicking her hand in the direction of my mother, whose blood pressure was clearly still on the boil.

"Gran, I won't stand for—" Nick began.

"YOU WILL ALL BE SILENT." Eleanor's voice exploded through the room as if she'd barked into a megaphone. "This family"—she paused for emphasis—"answers to something greater than bonds of blood. Our priorities cannot be so quaint. We maintain control. Never complain, never explain." She straightened, as if her posture were not already immaculate. "Nicholas and Rebecca, you will cancel your honeymoon and work at the pleasure of your queen until I am satisfied you have deflected public attention from Rebecca's indiscretions."

"Don't punish Nick for my—" Freddie began.

"I'll deal with you later," she said. "But right now, we shall go out onto that balcony. Whether there are a hundred people or a hundred thousand people, whether they are scornful or celebrating, we will wave and smile and play the parts our birthright demands. And then we will grit our teeth and do our jobs, and prove that everything within the House of Lyons is humming along as it should be." She narrowed her eyes at me and Nick. "But Rebecca is on borrowed time. She must earn every minute she gets, or so help me God, I will void this union and exile her to purgatory. I will not allow this harlot to be our undoing. Have I made myself clear?"

Nick stared at his grandmother for what felt like a year. "Crystal," he said.

Eleanor's tone brightened. "Now. Shall we to the balcony?"

Everyone tried to settle into the masks they'd developed for public consumption. The balcony door had magically opened despite my not being aware of any staffers in the room, and as we glided toward it, I saw Eleanor pluck Lacey's phone from her hand.

"One more point of business," she said.

And she smashed it under the heel of her signature sensible pump.

"What the *hell*," Lacey blurted out.

Eleanor brushed her hands together in a "that's that" gesture that reminded me, ridiculously, of Mary Poppins. "Be a dear, Edwin, and scoop that up."

Nick's grip on my hand tightened. He exhaled hard through his nose, then slid a look on his face that even I couldn't read.

"Do you trust me?" he breathed.

I nodded, and we stepped outside. The crowd had dissipated by about half, and those that remained were too far away for us to hear— but we could see the sea of smartphones, and feel their almost scientific interest in what the next act of this drama would be.

And then Nick dipped me into the most passionate, lengthy kiss that balcony had ever seen, as if we'd decided our wedding night should begin as publicly as our marriage. When we broke apart, I realized no one else had followed us outside. Edwin was gawking at us from halfway behind a curtain.

"Now what?" I breathed. "Do the people need to see me climb you like a tree?"

"Rebecca, Duchess of Clarence," he said. "If I may be so bold: Fuck all of this. I want to take my wife on a honeymoon. Are you in?"

I grinned. "Damn straight, Your Highness."

And with a jaunty wave to the masses that remained, Nick and I had turned on our heels and marched straight through the Balcony Room, down the stairs, and out to our waiting car. We'd said not a word to the people we left behind.

Not even to Her Majesty the Queen.

"What if the stress of our running away did this to her?" Nick fretted now, turning to me. "I can't believe the last thing she saw me do was paw at you. I was so angry. I really hated her that day. And now..."

My stomach flipped. "I can't pretend that wasn't bad," I told him.

"But it also wasn't the only thing that ever happened between you. There are more good memories than bad."

"Are there?"

"She told me how special she thought you were," I said, leaving off the bit where she had done so in the context of implying that I was unworthy of him.

Nick leaned his head against the leather back seat of the Range Rover. "She's the only monarch most of the country has ever known," he said. "What will we do?"

There was nothing to say to that. My mind was a whirl of images of Eleanor, and worry for Nick. We'd only been the Duke and Duchess of Clarence—or, since we were in Scotland, technically Baron and Baroness Inverclyde—for about a nanosecond. The next step up, which had weighed on Nick his whole life, had felt forever away, and yet suddenly we were on the brink. It didn't feel real. *I haven't even showered*, I thought absurdly.

By the time Balmoral's portly clock tower and leaf-covered façade slid into view, Nick's body must have burned a million calories from tensing every muscle. The car careened up the drive and parked next to five others that had been left haphazardly on the gravel. It was eerily tranquil. Nick and I were ushered inside a side door and up a red-carpeted staircase that felt like a mini-version of Buckingham Palace's, although the overall vibe of this residence was more that of an expensive hunting lodge, all rugged wood beams, tartan accents, and aggressive taxidermy. That none of the imposing buck heads hanging above us as we ascended the stairs took that moment to drop off and impale us, I interpreted as an encouraging sign that Eleanor herself was not yet haunting the place.

A wordless staffer led us to Eleanor's private quarters, then bowed and withdrew. Nick took my hand. Then dropped it. Then took it again.

"I don't know what we're going to see," he said, as much to himself as to me.

"Want me to go first?"

"No," he said, taking a deep breath. "I can do it."

He pushed open the door. As we crept through Eleanor's sitting room toward her bedroom, we heard a clutch of voices getting louder and louder.

"Nicholas," barked an unmistakable one when we came into view. "You need a haircut."

Eleanor wasn't dead.

Eleanor wasn't even unconscious.

Eleanor, in fact, looked absolutely fine.

CHAPTER FOUR

ell, well. Clearly two months of playing peasant stimulates the follicles."

The Queen was in bed, but propped up on a pile of silk pillows, a rosy glow in her cheeks. Her hair was done. She was wearing lipstick. Someone had even had the presence of mind to pin a starburst-shaped diamond brooch to her blue bed jacket.

I'd been in Eleanor's chambers in Buckingham Palace, and by comparison, these looked exactly like what they were: the bedroom of a glorified summer cottage, sparsely decorated, with a no-frills bedframe and a dated green floral bedspread that mirrored the one my aunt Kitty had at her actual cottage in Michigan. To Eleanor's right was a brown leather Eames chair—clearly an original—in which her mother, Marta, napped, snoring lightly; to her left stood Richard, wearing what I assumed was his hunting outfit. (My first clue was his actual rifle, which he was leaning on, barrel end down, like a cane.) The whole tableau was so surreal—the opposite of what we'd braced ourselves for—that Nick and I could only gape.

I felt rather than saw Nick's fury. The temperature around him seemed to rise ten degrees.

"Protocol, Nicholas," Richard said, his lips compressed into a pale white line.

Nick obliged with a bow, something I wasn't even aware a person could do sarcastically until I saw it, and I stumbled through the most dignified curtsy I could manage. It's hard to be graceful when you're simultaneously shocked, relieved, enraged, and still in your running clothes.

"I wish I could say the life of a fugitive suited you," Eleanor said. "But now that you've come to your senses, we can repair this mess, including that hair situation on your face."

"Come…to my senses?" Nick choked. "We're talking about *my* senses here?" He started to wipe at his eyes with his T-shirt sleeve. "You let us think you were dying. I can't believe this."

He turned to hide his face from them and started tugging at his hair. "We came back because you were fucking *dying*," he repeated.

"Language," Richard snapped. Eleanor might have been fine, but Richard looked like he was about to have a rage aneurysm.

"I cannot believe you faked a heart attack to call us to heel," Nick spat over his shoulder.

"I did no such thing," Eleanor said. "There was…a flutter. Fortunately, the doctors believe it's not significant. They'll sort out my pharmaceutical cocktail and I'll be back to work." She shrugged. "Perhaps my condition may have been exaggerated to you, but I cannot control that."

"That's bollocks and you know it," Nick said, turning back to face them.

"What's 'bollocks' is you two running off like petulant children," Richard snarled.

"This entire exercise was unnecessary," Eleanor said. "Honestly, Nicholas. *Wigtown*?" She said the word as if it hurt the inside of her mouth.

"And to think, we were about to come back of our own accord," Nick said. "Now I can't fathom why."

Eleanor raised one penciled brow. "I know Richard didn't raise you to think abdication of duty was acceptable," she said. "Frederick has been doing yeoman's work in your absence."

Her eyes went to another corner of the room. It was only when I followed her gaze that I noticed another person had been sitting there the whole time, tucked in a tufted leather wing chair as if he wished to disappear into it.

Freddie.

I had missed him, but precisely how much didn't hit me until I saw his face. His thicket of red-brown hair was still barely this side of unkempt, and he had the rosy cheeks of a very pale person who'd been spending more time than usual outside. His roguish handsomeness was still potent—doubly impressive because he was dressed in an outfit that matched Richard's exactly: green hunting jacket, sturdy loafers, socks over trousers. I wanted to run over and hug him, but if he had any urge to approach us, he was suppressing it, so I did, too.

Nick turned and they looked at each other for a beat longer than seemed natural. "You could've warned us," Nick finally said.

"I assumed you'd chucked your phone, since you never used it," Freddie said airily.

"This was beneath you all," Nick said, to Richard this time, as if it were easier to blame the person he already disliked the most.

"You can hardly get on your high horse about false pretenses when you've been living under them for the past two months," Richard said. "This farce ends today. Start acting like a man and do your duty by the rest of this family."

"You cannot expect us to snap back to business as usual after all this," Nick said.

"None of *us* was to blame for business being *unusual*," Eleanor said, with a cold glare in my direction. "Even with Frederick's dedication, we cannot get past this until the three of you reestablish the appearance of family normalcy. It is well past time for the papers to see your faces again, together and apart."

Richard cleared his throat. "We'll convene a Conclave tomorrow in London to hammer out next steps." He referred to all high-level family meetings as "Conclaves," which made them sound considerably fancier than the sibling bickerfests they actually were. "We fly tonight."

Eleanor laughed insincerely, a tinkling noise that sounded like an assortment of crystal being smashed in a velvet bag. "*We* fly," she emphasized to us. "Since you two so enjoy a good road trip, you may drive yourselves home." She checked the slim Cartier watch on her wrist. "Technically, you'll arrive tomorrow, but I imagine you shall cope." She leaned back. "All of you may leave. The doctors insist that I not be aggravated."

Richard turned and actually made a shooing motion to usher us out, before he and Freddie followed us through the adjoining sitting room and out into the hallway. The door closed behind us with a gentle click, and then Richard turned on us. Even his argyle tie looked angry.

"I assume this has been an amusing experiment for you," he said to me, his voice low but pregnant with rage. I tried not to look at the rifle whose butt was not that far from my own. "I hope you're grateful for Her Majesty's benevolence in the face of your selfishness. If it were me, I would have had the army after you." He snapped his fingers in Freddie's direction. "Outside in ten."

He turned on his heel and took off down the hallway.

"Prince Dick, still living up to his name," I said as soon as he was out of earshot. I turned and gave Freddie a hug. "Hey, Fred. It's so good to see you."

Freddie tensed, then patted me on the back before untangling himself. "Father's just anxious," he said. "She's never caught so much as a cold before." He stuffed his hands into his pockets. "Listen, Gran apparently came up because she knew you were banging around Scotland, and then Father invited me up for a grouse shoot, but I'd no idea..." He shrugged helplessly. "I wouldn't have supported it."

"I can't believe you're up here voluntarily after being stuck with them for so long," Nick said to Freddie, reaching out for a handshake that did not, as it normally did, turn into a bro-hug. "Time got away from us."

"I understand. Things happen. It's been fine!" Freddie said. "Your decoys did a great job. No one seemed to notice that yours was almost bald."

"Fantastic," Nick muttered.

"How are you?" I asked. "What have we missed?"

"Gosh, I'm fine," Freddie said. "I've been very busy. Everything is fine!"

Nick furrowed his brow. "I find that hard to believe."

"It's been more fun than having my rib cage flayed open, and less fun than the time Gaz ate forty-five flaming hot chicken wings in fifteen minutes. How's that?" Freddie chirped.

Nick and I exchanged a look.

"The headlines...they were..." I couldn't even finish the thought. We'd seen them. He'd lived them. We'd run; he stayed. I felt, suddenly, like human garbage.

"We just felt like we needed to—" Nick started.

"Absolutely fine," Freddie interrupted. "You had to do what's best for your team. Father was in a right state. But he's fine now! We're all fine."

Fine, fine, fine. It felt like Freddie had been replaced by a clone who'd been poorly briefed on the gig.

"Right, you two have a long drive ahead, and I've got to meet Father, so I won't keep you," Freddie added, starting toward the stairs Richard had taken.

"Wait, Freddie," Nick called after him.

"Hmm?" Freddie turned to face us, but continued walking away backwards.

"Let's have dinner tomorrow night, the three of us," Nick said. "It's hard to catch up here, this way."

"That is a great idea," I said. "I've missed your chef's Scotch eggs."

Freddie pulled a sad face. "Ooh, he's gone," he said. "One of the Euros pilfered him. Paid his way to Sweden and everything."

"Oh," I said. "I didn't know."

"How could you?" Freddie said. "Dinner sounds great. Really great! But I've got plans tomorrow night. I couldn't have guessed that you'd be coming back, obviously. Super sorry to miss it. But it'd be great to touch base later!"

"Great," Nick echoed oddly.

Freddie ate up the rest of the distance to the stairs in three bounding strides, and was gone.

"Fine," I said. "*Great.*"

Nick tugged on his hair. "Since when does Freddie voluntarily spend time with Prince Dick?"

"Since when does Freddie say things like *super sorry?*" I asked.

Nick stared thoughtfully at the painting hanging across from us. It was a giant, gilt-trimmed portrait of Eleanor and her younger sister Georgina as children. The words JOYOVSS SISTERHOODE were scrawled across the top of the frame in a florid, old-fashioned script.

"And why is that spelled like they painted this in medieval times?" I asked.

Nick shook his head like he was trying to knock something out of his ears. "Because apparently nothing makes sense anymore," he said. "Come on. Let's go home."

We were waved back into Kensington Palace at 3:00 a.m. as if we'd merely been out for the night at a bar—and we felt like it. We were punch-drunk, and our ears rang from hours of loud music keeping us alert. Being folded into the car for so long made our knees creaky, and Nick was wired from pints of coffee, because my inaugural attempts at driving on the left side of the road had been spectacular failures and resulted in his spending the majority of the trip at the wheel. We were sticky and pale and smelled like bad breath and grease, because all the food we ate on the road came from bags we'd torn open with our teeth and consisted primarily of flavor powder. We had not showered in nearly thirty-six hours, which included my final morning run in Scotland. The fug between my ears felt like jet lag.

"We're back," Nick said.

His voice echoed in the palace halls. We were not in Wigtown anymore.

Nick's room was neat but for one corner in which the clothes and effects from my Chelsea flat had been packed and stacked, waiting for me. How sobering to see my entire pre-wedding life boiled down to a couple of crates of picture frames and jeans, and one pathetically small box marked KITCHEN. Everything felt wrong—a tad too immaculate, a tad too organized, a tad too perfect. Any posters or photos Nick had put up over the years had been discreetly tucked away. His quarters showed our abandonment, and now felt like a guest room, cold and strange. I took a running jump and flopped onto the familiar king-size bed, which greeted me with its usual groan of old age. At least one thing remained the same.

Nick must have read my mind. "I guess they had the cleaners in," he said. "It's like I was never even here. Where's my signed Ginger Spice postcard?"

"Maybe the ghost got bored and decided to redecorate."

Nick lay down next to me and buried his face in my neck. "Maybe the ghost can give me a haircut," he mumbled.

"Or a club sandwich," I lamented. "Today is probably my last hurrah before your grandmother puts me back on a diet."

Nick rubbed my hip. "Feels just right to me," he said. "But Night Nick and Night Bex cannot win. Our dignified daytime selves have to be at the Conclave in..." He checked his watch and groaned. "Six hours."

"I'm sorry, Nick," I said. "We wouldn't be in this situation if it weren't for me."

Nick opened his mouth and I placed my hand over it. "No," I said. "Admit it. We'd be coming back from the Seychelles all tan and fancy-free and with seven new recipes for cocktails you can drink out of a hollowed pineapple, but I fucked up, and *ow!*"

He had nipped at my hand, which I yanked away, freeing his mouth. "I will admit nothing," he said. "Besides, we need sleep. We don't need to do this now."

"At least let me say that I love you," I said. "Even though your grandmother hates my guts, and might disown us both and we'll end up sleeping in the park."

He kissed me firmly. "Thank you, and I love you, too."

"Even if we're sleeping in the park?"

"Especially then," he said. "I'll need your body heat, for starters. You're a furnace."

He snuggled up closer, and the edges of the world blurred. But as we slipped toward a contented, united sleep, I knew that we hadn't even begun to unravel the knot that Freddie kissing me—and the world finding out—had created.

'WHERE'S THE HEIR?'

Steady Freddie Steps Up as Nick Is a No-Show, Says XANDRA DEANE

Since the airing of his dirty laundry stained the monarchy, Prince Freddie has been hard at work doing his washing up. But have his wayward brother and erstwhile lover done the same?

Exclusive sources tell me palace insiders are frustrated with the Duke and Duchess of Clarence's refusal to be seen in public, stemming—they say—from Rebecca's ego having taken a hit when her tawdry affair was revealed.

"She's furious," the source said. "And he does whatever she says, and right now that's to run away from their jobs. All on the taxpayers' dime."

Nick cast a bleary glare at the empty place setting that had been left for Freddie, and then tossed the *Mail* facedown onto the floor. "Remind me to tell Marj to cancel all our subscriptions," he said.

The two of us had managed four hours of rock-hard slumber before being awoken by the arrival of a rack of clothing for me, put forth by my stylist Donna so that I could look appropriate for our appearance at the Conclave—and, vitally, the drive over to the palace, which Marj had made sure would be photographed so that our actual faces made the news. We had about ten minutes to wolf down breakfast before getting ready, and the morning papers hadn't made them especially pleasant. Xandra Deane was the Wizard of Oz of royal reporters: great and powerful, and no one had ever met her. Even before the wedding, she regularly churned out stories that painted me as conniving and unstable, and Nick as my patsy. The twist was in her growing support for Freddie, when most of the country still thought we were shagging in dark corners. There was no mention—from her, or anyone—about the Queen's heart flutter; The Firm, apparently, still had some things on lockdown.

I muddled through my ablutions as competently as I could, but I was so far out of practice that I burned two fingers and part of my earlobe while flat-ironing my hair. I selected a gray polka-dot belted shirtdress with matching heels and my sartorial nemesis: pantyhose. Nick and I had to look scrupulously appropriate, and even though the paparazzi wouldn't be able to see my legs, deferring to Eleanor's nylon preferences was a goodwill gesture with the added benefit of ensuring that my duchess persona—which didn't fit as neatly after so many weeks on the shelf—wouldn't slip. I was about to leave when something winked at me from atop the dresser: a pin, in the form of the Union Jack and the Stars and Stripes, crossed at the poles. It had been a friendly gift from Nick back when we were pretending we didn't have feelings for each other, and for years, I'd worn it—often secretly—as a talisman of our love. The last time had been pinned to my underwear on our wedding day. On a whim, I opened the top buttons on my dress and affixed it to the center of my bra. It felt right to have it on again, known only to me, as if to drive home that I was still myself no matter what lay ahead.

Nick had caved to only one of his father's demands, shaving his mustache but leaving his longish hair on the unruly side. But if he was trying to pick a fight with Richard via his grooming choices, he didn't get one. When we arrived outside the Chinese Dining Room in the east wing of Buckingham Palace—Richard's favorite place to have a Conclave outside of Clarence House; Freddie once theorized that his father must identify with the dragon painted on the ceiling—Richard ignored Nick, but held up a hand in front of me, like a posh bouncer at a very uptight nightclub.

"Not you," he said. "Her Majesty has requested your presence in her chambers."

Nick turned to me with a flummoxed look on his face. I'd only been in Eleanor's room once before, when she'd dazzled me with tiaras before essentially threatening me into renouncing my American citizenship. The idea of facing her now that she had real cause to loathe me made me queasy, but I wasn't about to let Richard see me falter, so I put a reassuring hand on Nick's arm.

"It's all good," I said. "I've got this."

"There's that American can-do spirit," Lady Elizabeth sang, pushing past us, her pregnant belly having swollen to a truly impressive girth over the last two months. She was technically a duchess now, as Edwin had been given his father's dukedom, but to me and the press and everyone else she would always be Lady Elizabeth—much like how, to most people, I would always be Bex. We both liked it that way.

. "Hang on, is Elizabeth taking Edwin's place now?" Nick asked his father. "I can't believe you allowed that."

Elizabeth chortled. "Pet, it's easier if I do this bit! Eddy's no good at linear thinking, we all know that." She gave me a rushed hug. "Welcome back. I've been wanting to ask: Where *did* you consummate it? Eddybear and I have tried all over St. James's and there were never any closets that could—"

"We'd better begin," Richard interrupted. "Nicholas, take a seat. You, wait here for Marj."

And then he closed the door in my face.

"No problem," I said to the door, which didn't seem impressed by my false confidence.

The barren hallway was peaceful, with just the ticking of the hand-carved walnut grandfather clock to keep me company. I would've loved to take off and explore on my own en route to Eleanor, but Buckingham Palace had 775 rooms, and I could barely make my way through the ones that were on the public tour, much less find the Queen from a dining room I'd never seen before today. Instead, I wandered to the large window overlooking the private park that stretched out behind the palace. The last time I was out on the lawn, Clive's threats were closing in around me, and it seemed possible that I'd never return to it. I looked down at the Lyons Emerald, sparkling once more on my left hand. At least we'd gotten this far, even if the route had been ugly.

"Fond memories?"

Marj had appeared behind me, as comforting and grandmotherly as always in her light shawl and the half-moon glasses she wore hooked to a thin gold chain.

"Memories, anyway," I said. "It's good to see you, Marj."

She smiled, but did not offer a hug. "Let me walk you to Her Majesty's quarters. I've got a few items to discuss on the way."

"Thank you for having Donna send me something to wear," I said, falling in step with her. "I'm so fried from yesterday that I could not have done it on my own."

"As we suspected," she said. "Everything you and Nicholas left in Scotland will be delivered tomorrow, including your art pieces and some very odd lumps of wool." She frowned. "Are they blankets?"

"Nick claims they're socks."

Marj looked astonished. "For whom? A giant?" She shook her head, then made a mark on her clipboard. "You've seen your other belongings are at Kensington Palace already. The Queen has ear-marked her sister Georgina's former residence on the grounds there for you and the duke, and we were going to start discussing renovations during the honeymoon, but...as you know, other issues took precedence."

I stopped in front of another picture window, this one overlooking the less-scenic London morning rush-hour traffic. It was, aptly for my situation, a total clusterfuck.

Marj took my pause for something other than what it was. "Apartment 1A is highly desirable," she said. "Yes, it needs updating, and hasn't been lived in since the princess died. But I'm sure twenty-six rooms will be more than enough for your needs."

"Oh, I'm sure it's gorgeous!" I said. "It's extremely generous of Her Majesty, especially after...everything."

"Indeed," Marj said tightly.

"Marj," I said, touching her arm. "I owe you an apology. I cannot imagine what a disaster we left in our wake, and we—I—feel awful about how our behavior has impacted you."

Marj's face relaxed. "Thank you, my dear. I appreciate that," she said. "But I'm the one who convinced you to roll the dice in the first place. I can't believe how badly I misjudged it."

"In your defense, it was the middle of the night when we called," I said.

"Nonetheless, I didn't think Clive would detonate his family's entire relationship with the Crown over some silly vendetta," she said. "Frederick tried to keep me out of the blowback, and I appreciate it, but I'm not sure I deserve it. I should have gotten in front of it instead of crossing my fingers that there would be nothing to get in front of, but…" She shook her head. "It's done now. How are you?"

The cars outside had barely moved at all.

"My body is here, but my brain is still adjusting," I said. "Yesterday, we thought the Queen was nearly dead, and today you're giving me a mansion."

Marj touched my arm. "My dear, if there is one thing to know about The Firm, it is this: Things move terribly quickly, and also not at all, often at the same time."

We started walking again.

"The apartment is a bit of a shambles, but I thought you and Nicholas might want to move in anyway," she continued. "Unless you'd prefer to stay where you are? But as newlyweds, living so near Frederick…?"

"This morning you'd never have known Freddie was there," I said.

"He wasn't. He slept here," Marj said. "I could continue having him do that, I suppose."

I thought about the strange sensation we'd experienced in Nick's old room last night—how it felt like the remnant of a life that didn't fit us anymore.

"We can't evict Freddie from his own home," I said. "I wish he felt like he could stay there with us, but since he doesn't, we should be the ones to go."

"I will arrange it," Marj said.

We rounded a corner, and I chased her up a flight of stairs before she came to a halt in front of a familiar gilt-trimmed door. "And this is where I leave you," she said.

I nervously fluffed my hair, and Marj clearly saw the tremor in my hand.

"I cannot pretend you and the duke didn't leave us in a pickle," she said, tucking a strand of hair behind my ear. "Most people are allowed several moments of massive immaturity in their lives. Frederick, in fact, is overdrawn on that account." She looked me right in the eyes. "But Nicholas, because of what he will one day be, hasn't been afforded much space for that. He gets one. He's earned one. But *only* one."

She swung open the door for me. "I'll have a footman run over the keys to 1A." She winked. "Chin up. She didn't call for a firing squad today."

Walking into Eleanor's dark, quiet quarters felt like breaking and entering, and even though I was there by invitation, I couldn't help but tiptoe. I was so fixated on the door of her actual bedroom sitting ajar, and at the swath of carpet that would lead me there without knocking over anything expensive, that I didn't even look at the rest of the sitting room. I certainly didn't expect to feel a light whack at the back of my calves.

"Since you're up," Marta's voice said, "my mobile's done charging."

I turned to see the Queen Mum, hair in tight white curls, sitting on the couch with a frown, her cane innocently propped up next to her as if she hadn't just used it to prod me. She waved in the direction of an end table across the room, and I obligingly went over and unplugged her phone.

"Ah," she said. "Edwin's made a move at Scrabble." She peered at it. "*Cat.* What a twit."

"How are you this morning, Your Majesty?"

Marta's eyes flashed. "I've spent the morning in a Twitter fight with a berk who thinks we've killed you in secret," she said.

I glanced at her screen. Her handle was @KingIdrisElba and she'd kept the default egg avatar.

"He'd weep if he knew the call was coming from inside the house," she added. "I feel quite alive." Then she nodded toward Eleanor's room. "Don't speak until spoken to. My daughter does love her rules."

The bedroom loomed dead silent before me. For a harrowing second, I wondered if Eleanor had suffered another flutter and all this dead silence would prove to be literal. But once again Eleanor was sitting up in bed, backed by a pile of pillows, and sporting a silk bed jacket—today's was pink, with a stupendous oval ruby pinned to it. She did not look up from the paper when I walked in, and my curtsy went unacknowledged. I knew that "don't speak until spoken to" also meant "do nothing at all without permission," so I stood and waited.

Eleanor read the entire *Times*. When she finished it, she folded it and laid it on her bed tray. Then she picked up *The Guardian* and raised it to her face without ever looking at me. Occasionally, she emitted a light *mmph* of interest, but nothing that could be interpreted as speaking to me.

My phone buzzed in my pocket. Eleanor lowered the newspaper and stared straight ahead with a look of supreme irritation until I turned it off. When her head vanished behind the paper again, I began glancing around the room. I'd seen the picture beside her bed of her late husband Henry, the Duke of Cleveland, but the mantel was littered with other snaps I hadn't noticed before. One was Richard at his investiture as Prince of Wales, standing between Eleanor and Marta, whose garish feathered hat was the color of a yellow highlighter. The most interesting one looked as if it had been snapped aboard the royal yacht sometime in the late '70s—Eleanor and her three children, in sunglasses, smiling. I wondered who took the photo. I wondered what had made them so happy. And I couldn't ask.

Eleanor heaved a weighty sigh and cast aside *The Guardian* in favor of the *Daily Mail*. She glanced at the front-page story about Freddie and pulled it closer with an overly obvious show of interest. When she finished that one, she turned to the *International Herald Tribune*. And so it went. The ticking clock on her mantel chimed. My balance wavered, and the balls of my feet complained—I hadn't worn heels since the wedding—so I shifted my weight back and forth and tried not to lock my knees. This was either a punishment or a power play. Probably both. And although I was dying to sit down, there was something admirably petty about the Queen calling me into her bedroom specifically to ignore me.

My savior arrived in the form of a nurse rolling a cart covered in medical paraphernalia. She dipped into a low curtsy.

"Good morning, Olivia," Eleanor said.

"Good morning, Your Majesty. It's time for me to take your vital signs." Olivia turned to me with an apologetic smile. "Good morning, Your Royal Highness."

"Rebecca was just leaving," Eleanor said.

I did not miss that this wasn't explicitly spoken to me. With a dip of my aching knees, I speed-staggered out of Eleanor's chambers without our having exchanged a single word.

In the sitting room, Marta was laughing.

"Does she do that to people often?" I asked.

Marta looked puzzled, then turned her phone toward me. "*Orange Is the New Black*," she said. "American prison looks amusing. Have you been?"

"Not yet," I said.

"Don't give up hope," Marta said. "Life is long. I'm proof."

I excused myself and collapsed into an antique chair in the hallway. Nick had apparently been very busy on his own cell while mine was off.

You're lucky to miss this

Dick just said how much harm we could have done to Scotland through our "book lies" wtf

He called Freddie a hero

The agenda for this meeting is 46 pages so I live here now

I am texting under the table

Hiding my phone under the table not sitting under the table

REBECCA, THIS IS AGATHA. WE HAVE CONFISCATED NICHOLAS'S PHONE.

I put my mobile in my bag and stood. Then I sat again. Nick had the keys to the Range Rover, not that I trusted myself to drive one without accidentally mowing down a bunch of tourists. I could call Stout or Popeye to drive me home, wherever that was now—neither Nick's place nor 1A fit that title. I fidgeted. Innumerable people would die for the chance to be trapped unsupervised in Buckingham Palace, but all I wanted was out, and yet I had nowhere welcoming to go.

I retrieved my phone again and scrolled through my contacts, hovering over Cilla's name. She had first been one of Nick's closest friends, then one of mine, to the point where I'd hired her as my assistant in the run-up to the wedding so that I had someone of my own on the team. But Cilla and I hadn't talked since Nick and I fled. I'd told myself that was because she might get in trouble for withholding information about us from her palace overlords, but Nick and I had also been pretty far up our own asses in Scotland. We may have needed to be alone, but we'd left the rest of our family and friends holding the bag while we did it. My apology tour of London would be prolonged.

Hi, I wrote to Cilla. I miss you.

The word *read* appeared underneath my message. But there was no reply.

We're back and supposed to move into 1A. Want to come poke around?

Three little dots immediately appeared on my screen. They winked at me, one at a time, for an interminable stretch. And then the dots disappeared.

That didn't seem like a good sign.

Marj says it's a mess. Loads of antiques. Probably some stolen objects from your ancestors.

More dots.

And then, finally: Got the key from Marj. Meet you there.

CHAPTER FIVE

Cilla did not come to Kensington Palace alone. By the time PPO Popeye pulled the Range Rover into the courtyard, the steps of Apartment 1A held not only her but also her husband, Gaz, and the illustrious snob and skeptic Lady Beatrix Larchmont-Kent-Smythe, whom we privately referred to as Lady Bollocks (both due to her initials and the unnecessarily snooty first—and second, and tenth—impression she tended to make). Cilla and Gaz were bickering, as they'd done for years at Oxford in what proved to be their version of foreplay, while Bea stood away from them as if they'd all merely arrived in the same place by accident. My nerves at how they'd receive me were completely overpowered by relief at seeing them again, and in my excitement, I nearly fell out of the car.

"Appalling," Bea said, elegant in a navy shirtdress and pearls, her style as sharp as her features. "Have you forgotten everything I taught you?"

"Hush up and hug me," I told her.

"I will not," Bea said. "You're not a hero home from war, you're a—"

If she finished that thought, I didn't hear it, because Gaz sped over and wrapped his arms around me so hard that my ears popped. He pushed a pastry box into my hand.

"Crumpets," he said. "It's a traditional English housewarming gift."

"It is *not*," Cilla huffed.

"It could be," he said. "If you'd open yourself up to it."

Cilla sighed. "If you're trying to use her to win an argument, Garamond, at least tell her," she said, then turned to me. "I told him they were a bit chewy and he didn't believe me."

"Master of curries; servant of baking," Bea said.

"Not half," Gaz said defensively. "I'm just a perfectionist. Unfortunately, so is my wife."

"I don't remember you ever baking before," I said, looping my arm through his, delighting in his familiar shock of red hair and the traces of beard threatening to take root on his cheeks.

"I need a break from my savory cooking," he said. "It's ruining restaurant cuisine for me."

Cilla suppressed a smirk. "His five-star palate is a curse."

"Oh, get off it, so we can get *on* with it," Bea said, snatching a manila envelope from Cilla and ripping it open. An old skeleton key tied to a ribbon plopped into her hand with a satisfying thud.

"That's the first thing we'll change," Bea said, marching to the door. "Any idiot can pick one of these locks."

She jammed it into the keyhole and wiggled. It wouldn't turn. Gaz hurried over to help, leaving Cilla and me to circle each other. She didn't seem angry, but my five-foot firebrand of a friend was holding herself unusually reserved, so I kept my arms to myself.

"You look terrific," I said. "I love your hair like that."

She touched her new side-swept bangs. "I felt a bit cliché going blond, but they say it's more fun, and I needed fun."

Gaz pushed open the door with a holler of triumph.

"Get in here, you lot," he called.

Cilla and I started up the steps, but the crunch of tires stopped me. I turned around to see a coupe I didn't recognize creep past the arch toward the entrance to Freddie and Nick's current apartment. The driver appeared to be a woman, and by the way she was working her accelerator—which is to say, barely—it seemed as if she was afraid that anything above a crawl would get her in trouble. She paused and squinted at us before looking down at a paper in her hand.

"Who is that?" I asked.

"Hmm," Cilla said. "Probably someone Freddie knows."

Her tone was way too casual. "Is he seeing someone?" I asked.

Cilla gazed into the middle distance, as if doing math. "*Seeing someone* can mean one thing to one person…"

"Another party planner?" I asked, glancing again at the archway. The woman had apparently read her map correctly and was gone. "Good to know Freddie is back on his game."

Gaz interrupted by tromping down the stairs. "What's the holdup? Aren't you the least bit curious what Great-Auntie Georgina's got in her foyer?"

"Cilla was telling me about Freddie's latest," I said. "Or not telling me."

Gaz brightened. "Hannah? She's a peach. Loved my vindaloo *aaaaah*," he said, wringing a hand that Cilla clearly had just pinched. "But, I have no idea who you're talking about. Fancy a crumpet? I wonder if Georgie Girl's toaster still works."

"I wonder if her dishes are even clean," Cilla said, following him.

I lingered. I'd never known Freddie to be a model of discretion. Had he asked Cilla and Gaz to keep their mouths shut? *Does that mean this is serious? That's kind of soon, right?*

I knew Freddie wasn't mine; I'd chosen Nick, and I loved Nick. But what I had *not* chosen was this new world in which I knew nothing about the inner life of a person who meant so much to me. It had begun to feel like we'd crossed a bridge away from him that had started to crumble and might not hold up long enough for us to get back across.

I shook my head as if to evict the thought and walked into the house. My house.

I'd like to say I was instantly captivated by the enchanted, opulent majesty of Apartment 1A. (My unofficial biographer Aurelia Maupassant would've written exactly that, if she hadn't hung up her pen after my recent behavior all but invalidated her slavishly inaccurate prose salad *The Bexicon*.) In reality, the first thing that greeted me was a stale, musty odor. Georgina had died about a decade ago, and obviously no meaningful efforts had been made to open a window.

"I can still smell her last cigarette," Bea said, scrunching her nose.

Cilla wrestled open a heavy drapery and, with a grunt, got it back under the control of the gold rope whose job it had once been to restrain it. Daylight coursed into the rectangular foyer, illuminating a hallway to my right, and a grand, curving wooden staircase in the far corner of the room. It was shabby—the deep forest-green wallpaper was peeling in places, the checked marble floor was scuffed and dirty—but it was undeniably impressive, from the two gilded cherub sculptures flanking the carved double doors directly ahead of me, to the sweeping crystal chandelier hanging perilously over our heads like the Phantom of the Opera's would-be murder weapon. It was centered over Georgina's monogram, set in gold in the floor, sullied only by a moderate coating of dust.

"I don't understand," Gaz said, poking at the cherubs.

"You're telling me," carped Bea. "Who wallpapers a room *one* color? Just paint it." She whipped out a notebook and started jotting down ideas. "That will be the first to go, after that ghastly logo in the floor."

"Who hired you?" Gaz asked.

Bea shot him a withering look.

I took a fuzzy leopard-print coat out of a front hall closet and held it up against myself.

"No one ever talks about Georgina," I said, looking down at it and wondering where she got it, where she wore it, whether it ever saw the light of day. "I feel rude manhandling all her private stuff."

"She's quite dead. She'll never know," Bea said. "Let's get cracking."

She threw open the double doors to reveal a massive formal living room with a thick, powder-blue fabric covering the walls. The four of us got to work pulling back those draperies, too, exposing enormous windows that looked out onto the park. Though the dimensions of the room were gracious, it felt claustrophobic because Georgina had been, charitably speaking, a bit of a hoarder. It was crammed to the edges with bric-a-brac: a ceremonial plate from the Netherlands; ceramics painted with the vista of a Tuscan village; a didgeridoo propped up in the corner next to a grand piano, both of which Cilla immediately banned Gaz from touching; a ceremonial mask that looked to have been carved out of ivory ("No, no, *no*," Bea tsked at it, scribbling furiously); two enormous Asian urns that came up to my knees; and countless crystal animal figurines, the likes of which you might win at the county fair. The rug was big and Persian, the couches were wood-and-velvet Louis XV–style antiques, and the coffee tables were pocked with drink rings and cigarette burns.

Even the walls hadn't escaped her overdecorating. I noticed a Magritte, several exquisite landscapes, and a small but disturbing Dalí ("She hung this on purpose?" Bea screeched). Presiding over the room: a massive oil portrait of the coronation of Georgina and Eleanor's father, King Richard IV, with "God Save the King" on a plaque on the bottom of the frame. God hadn't listened; Richard fell off a boat and drowned a year later.

"Cor," Cilla breathed, gawking at the sheer number of paperweights and collectibles cluttering an impressive oak desk that sat in one corner near an equally big smoke-stained fireplace. It still had ashes in the grate, as if someone had simply carried Georgina's body out of the building and locked the door. "This whole place is like a badly curated museum. I wonder if any of this was cataloged when she died."

"It must have been, right? Otherwise why would they even let us in here?" I yanked the trunk of an elephant lamp. Nothing happened. "One of you could waltz out of here with this under your coat and no one would be the wiser."

"Including whoever stole it, because that is ghastly," Bea said.

"I think it's neat. All of it," I said protectively, fishing out my phone and snapping some photos of the room for posterity. "I might not want to live in the middle of it forever, but Georgina clearly led an intriguing life."

"For a time," Cilla said. She peered down at a set of carved wood coasters with Georgina's monogram in them. They were obviously handmade. "I don't think she left the house much in the last, oh, twenty years she lived here."

"Probably why everyone bought that bit about Emma being a recluse," Gaz reasoned. "They already had one in the family."

I clambered over a pile of reference books and opened a rolltop desk that was missing a plank. Inside was a jumble of framed photos that was relieved to be free, judging by how quickly it spilled out across the table. One was of Georgina and Eleanor as children, with their grandmother, Queen Victoria II. Eleanor had inherited her gimlet stare; Georgina, her curls and curves. There were other shots of the girls as they grew, and then a time jump to an older Georgina beaming widely on the prow of a motorboat next to a handsome blond man, Georgina blowing a kiss to the camera as she rode a camel, Georgina in what looked like France with a stylish dark-haired man, Georgina smoking coquettishly and nursing a scotch as three younger gents hovered. For the second time that day, I wondered who'd taken these shots—these intimate moments that did not seem to belong to a princess who locked herself in a redbrick tower.

"It occurs to me that Georgina is basically the Freddie of her family," I said, carefully setting down the final photo on top of the pile.

"More or less," Bea said. "Freddie at least grew up knowing his position. Georgina didn't become the spare until her uncle died. She was a lot freer before that than Freddie has ever been." She tapped her notebook. "And a world-class dilettante, for a spell, so they do have that in common."

"I wonder if that ever occurred to him," I said.

"You'd have to ask," Bea replied.

"I would, but I think he's avoiding us."

Bea raised an eyebrow. "I can't imagine why."

"Oooh, a Royal Doulton cabinet!" Gaz said, clapping his hands and rushing to another corner. "Look at all these tiny ladies! Crikey, I think one of these *is* Georgina."

"Bea," I said, ignoring Gaz. "Are *we* okay?"

Bea came over and perused some of the photos with interest.

"I certainly wouldn't have hared off into oblivion the way you did, but you know I try not to judge," she said. I bit back a snort so strong that I had to turn it into a cough. "You and Nick may have been in some sexy life limbo, but we weren't. The PPOs were going back and forth, making sure you two weren't in mortal peril. Freddie took it from the press and from Eleanor. And Cilla..."

"Is doing fine," Cilla called out firmly.

"Cilla got put on Decoy Duty," Bea said. "She had to audition the fake Nick and Bex, and coach them, and arrange all their appearances. Total crap assignment."

"Which I turned into a success," Cilla said.

"I shall miss Fake Nick," called out Gaz as he peered into a giant porcelain bowl. "Terrific bloke. Loved my marmalade muffins. Remind me to send him a basket of my pita bread once I crack that."

"Gaz got hooked on *Ready, Set, Bake*, and now he fancies himself competitive," Cilla explained. "I've never been happier. Or fatter."

"Food is my love language," Gaz said, coming up behind his wife and giving her a peck.

Cilla blushed. "Yes, well, I'm chock-full of adoration, then."

I wrapped my arms around myself. The rapport between us seemed like it was slipping back into place. "I missed you loons."

"All these feelings are exceedingly dull," Bea cut in. "Move along. We've barely started."

The apartment's infamous twenty-six rooms were spread across three floors and a basement. We saw a multitude of guest chambers with chaste twin beds, all sporting once-trendy Laura Ashley floral wallpaper and thin cotton comforters in matching pastels. A few lesser reception rooms were empty, as if they'd already been scraped for everything valuable, or simply never used. The large formal dining room, its display cabinets teeming with silver that hadn't been polished since Georgina died if not before, led into a kitchen too far away to feel particularly useful to the occupant—which, as Bea pointed out, had been immaterial until now because Georgina probably hadn't made so much as a glass of ice water in her entire life. There were countless bathrooms, a small kitchenette on each floor, and even an elevator. The most tempting spots were an unused day nursery for the children Georgina never had, which boasted floor-to-ceiling windows and would make a great art studio; the first-floor library (complete with one of those sliding ladders, which Gaz rode while singing selections from *Beauty and the Beast* in a key best described as "nonmusical"); and a sprawling terrace, whose rotting white plastic loungers faced a magnificent view of London.

Despite not being in the employ of the royal family, Bea had filled her notebook with thoughts and announced I'd receive a report by the end of the week before stomping out to, in her words, "break a very stubborn mare."

"She's so cranky when Gemma is away," I said.

"How can you tell the difference?" wondered Gaz.

Cilla's laugh morphed into a groan when we peeked into a second-floor half bath. "*Why* is this carpeted?" She twisted the faucet for the hot water. The sink answered with a groan and a rust-colored trickle. "Please distract me. How's Lacey getting on at Gemma's place?"

There was a time I'd felt jealous of Gemma Sands, the ex with whom Nick had remained the closest. That was before I'd discovered her true love was actually Bea. Since then Gemma had been as loyal to me as to Nick, and when Clive's story made a public enemy of Lacey, too, Gemma had immediately offered her an escape: a temporary internship at her father's game preserve in Kenya, where nobody cared who Lacey was or what she'd done as long as she pulled her load. Lacey had kept me posted via email, the long-distance relationship we should have tried when I decided to stay in the UK after college—the one we might have had if she hadn't quit medical school to join me here, then lost herself in London, in Freddie, in her resentment of the constraints my relationship put on her freedom, and finally in the attention of a press corps that used to snap her picture at the snap of her fingers.

I feel more myself now than I have in a long time, she'd written two days ago. I'm super unimportant here, obviously, but I like that. They're just happy if I show up on time and work hard, and that's something I can do. My favorite part of med school was always the science, not the actual doctoring, anyway. Also, one of the researchers is hot. (That is NOT my priority . . . but it's a perk.)

To Cilla, I simply said, "She likes having a real job again."

Cilla frowned and leaned against the sink. "Speaking of jobs . . . I need to talk to you." She swallowed. "The decoy scheme worked so well that the Palace offered me a few other opportunities in the, er, official planning arena. Mainly for the Queen and Richard."

I clapped my hands. "Cilla! That's fantastic."

"It's a job I've really earned, you know? I'd nannied for my sister, and then I worked for you..."

"*Also* nannying," I cracked.

She didn't protest, which was fair. "The point is, those were things I did because they were handed to me, not because I was good at them."

"You were great for me," I protested. "But I understand what you mean."

She scraped at a dried splash of pink paint on the sink's white enamel, and looked up at me. "I lied to you earlier," she said. "I *have* been angry at you for disappearing. We'd all been in it together, and then we were frozen out. It made me feel like you were punishing me for not noticing something was amiss, and I thought it was unfair."

"I never thought that," I told her. "It wasn't your job to root out the secrets I was keeping. Honestly, it didn't occur to me that you would take us leaving personally."

"How could we not?" Cilla said. "You stopped speaking to us."

"We couldn't see past the shit we were in," I told her. "It's selfish, but it's the truth. That's all there was to it."

"That's all very well and good now, but it took me a lot of time to realize that, and I had to do it on my own," Cilla said. "I'm not trying to make you feel worse. I'm being honest. It's what friends are supposed to do."

This was a jab, but I saw in her face it was not a malicious one. "It is, and I am really sorry, Cilla," I said. "What can I do?"

Cilla fiddled with the tap. "You can accept my resignation," she said. "I took the job. Started last week. But, you know. Technicalities."

"Done," I said. "And I am so sorry that I hurt you. I convinced myself that you guys needed plausible deniability, but I think that turned into...plausible *dumb*ability." I punctuated this with the classic rim-shot noise that my dad used to love.

Cilla bit her lip, then burst out laughing. "You're barmy," she said. "But I am glad you're back." She moved as if to hug me, then pulled back. "Don't run off like that again, though."

I grinned at her. "I wouldn't dare."

An hour later, I sat cross-legged on the living room floor poring over a yellowing photo album and drinking a flat Orangina someone had left in the fridge, hopefully from this decade. The album consisted of family photos from Osborne House, the Isle of Wight residence where the royals had summered for yonks before it fell out of favor. Most of the pictures were from Georgina's girlhood, well before her father became king. There were several of Queen Victoria II, Marta, and Eleanor being very solemn, while Georgina pulled a silly face, or flashed a smile that looked sweetly like Nick's. Even in her more light-hearted snaps, Eleanor was a petite version of her current self: stern and serious and a little intense. But the sisters did seem close. They often clasped hands, and there were some in which Georgina clearly had elicited a rare giggle, or was hugging Eleanor enthusiastically while she tried and failed to hide her pleasure. In the years since I'd met Nick, his great-aunt's name had come up exactly zero times. But now we'd been instructed to live in her house and, per the memo that came with the key, "preserve the building's historical importance and value while modernizing the interior to suit a young royal family," and I felt a responsibility to at least learn who she was before we swept her aside.

The door slammed, and an exhausted Nick padded into the room and flopped facedown onto the couch. Dust flew everywhere.

"Nmmgsllyphas," he said into the cushions.

"Say what?"

He turned his face. "This couch is not as soft as it looks." He reached under his head and pulled out my nylons. "And this was an unexpected treat."

He tossed them in my direction. They traveled about six inches before floating gracefully down onto the table, where they formed a soft brown puddle.

"Sorry. I could not keep them on a minute longer," I said. "How was the Conclave?"

Nick sat up. "I'm parched. Pass the Orangina?"

"No," I said. "Not because I don't love you, but because I do. It tastes twenty-five years old. It is a *journey*."

He took a swig, then nearly choked on it. "That is murder in a bottle."

"Stop changing the subject," I said. "How did it go?"

"The usual," he said. "Lots of Agatha and Elizabeth gossiping, and Father posturing."

"You and Freddie must have wanted to beat your heads on the table."

"That was the one odd bit," Nick said. "Freddie was being relentlessly agreeable with old Dick. He actually volunteered to do an appearance with him in Wales."

"Whoa," I said. "Are the locusts next?"

"Not if it isn't on Father's agenda," Nick said. "And Freddie said nothing to me at all."

"I think he might be seeing someone on the sly," I said. "A woman drove in here today and Gaz and Cilla seemed to know who she was, but they clammed up when I asked."

Nick rubbed his temples. "That's not like him. None of this is like him. He even said Edwin's laziness needed to be nipped in the bud," he said. "*Freddie* said that. And he backed up Father on not releasing any word of Gran's health to the press." He blew out his cheeks. "I understand that, I suppose, given that she's going to be fine, but this family has told enough lies over the years and now that our wedding turned into one—"

I don't know which he heard first, his own words, or the gasp from me. "I mean, that's how it looked to the public," he insisted.

"Right." I couldn't hide that it stung.

"It's been a long day and it's only teatime," Nick said. "My brother is behaving like a mini-Dick and going on father-son hunting outings that we've never done in the history of our lives, and we're about to get trotted out in public to act like nothing has ever been wrong, so pardon me if I'm not at my diplomatic best."

His voice had hit a thin, loud pitch. I bowed my head and intoned, "Point to the gentleman." I gave that a second. "Things will chill out. It's only our first day."

Nick relaxed visibly. "You're right. Hello." He rolled off the sofa, crawled over to me, and kissed my cheek. "How was your day?" He blinked as if seeing his surroundings for the first time. "Did we get the wrong key? Why are we in a flea market?"

I waved an arm at the room. "Behold our new home. It's a hoarder's paradise. I saved the main master bedroom for us to look at together, if you want to head upstairs with me."

He smiled. "I always want to go upstairs with you."

We padded into the foyer and then up, traversing the threadbare carpet runner that once matched the green walls, all the way to the top of the stairs and to the end of the cream-painted hallway. We stopped at a door with ornate moldings and a huge brass knob smack in the center, like a safe.

"After you," I said, and Nick eagerly pushed it open.

The master suite was a time capsule of hideousness so acute that it almost turned the corner into being perfect. The armchairs in front of the fireplace were a riotous mélange of pinks, the wallpaper was an aggressive selection of purples, the king-size bed was topped with a moth-eaten Marie Antoinette–style canopy in baby yellow, and the dusty hardwood floors were covered with multiple rugs that coordinated with none of it. Not a single floral matched any other one. The en suite bathroom provided no relief: While the giant claw-foot tub looked inviting, the wallpaper—again—was a peeling gold foil, the long heated towel rail was falling off the wall, and one of the double sinks was cracked down the middle so dramatically that I could see the inside of the cupboard beneath it. Every lampshade was stained glass, as if Georgina had once seen a photo of an Italian family restaurant in New Jersey and fallen in love.

"This. Is. Something," Nick said.

"For someone who didn't go out much, she had a huge closet." I crossed to a massive floor-to-ceiling armoire set into the wall at the back of the room. "This is the size of my old bedroom in Shepherd's Bush. We could sublet it."

I yanked it open. Whoever gave up on handling Georgina's belongings also had zero interest in archiving her clothes, because it was stuffed with vintage dresses and suits. The wardrobe was deep enough that I could step in and walk around, which I did, poking my head out between two gowns to make a face at Nick.

"Fetching." He grinned, sitting on the bed and bouncing. "Hmm. We're going to have to swap this out. Also, I think she died in this bed."

"Some of these are still wrapped like they're fresh from the cleaners," I said, squeezing around one of the hangers. My foot hit a pile of the plastic sleeves that had pooled on the floor of the closet, and I skidded and slammed hard into the back wall.

It greeted my weight by swinging open. I tumbled to the ground and found myself lying at the foot of a narrow, steep staircase that led up into darkness.

"Holy shit," I said.

"You're a duchess now, Rebecca," Nick teased. "Watch your language." But I heard him hurry over to check on me, and when he saw the opening, he stopped short.

"Holy shit," he said. "Does that lead to Narnia?"

"The Lyons, the Bitch, and the Wardrobe," I quipped.

"Obviously we're going to investigate," Nick said, helping me to my feet, then scrambling past me up the stairs. There was no railing, so I braced myself with my hands against the smooth walls and slowly ascended behind him.

I alighted into a cozy, completely secret room—windowless, which made it easier to escape notice from the outside. The bulb was dead in the room's only lamp, so Nick and I had to poke around by the lights of our mobile phones. They revealed floor-to-ceiling built-in bookshelves and a wide array of plush, faintly musty lounging pillows. Rudimentary sketches and poems littered a small writing desk, and a hardback copy of *The Unbearable Lightness of Being* sat next to a piece of notepaper onto which someone had copied a quote from the book: *Love is the longing for the half of ourselves we have lost.* The novel was open and overturned to mark a page, and had been thus for so long that when I picked it up, it stayed that way.

"What *is* this place?" Nick wondered, shaking his head.

"She must have wanted a spot where no one could find her." I thought back to the events of the last few days, all of us tromping in and out of Eleanor's sickroom, and then back even further, to the day of the wedding when countless palace employees had borne witness to me trying to pull it together. It made sense that a person might go to extremes for her privacy, even in a palace. Especially in a palace.

I went to set the book back down where I'd found it, and saw that it had been sitting atop a torn corner of paper.

NOT UNTIL THE END OF MY DAYS, it read.

"Do you know what this is about?" I asked Nick, showing it to him.

He shook his head. "Sounds like a juicy feud, but I haven't heard any stories about that."

"It could be a love note," I reasoned.

"I've not heard any stories about her being in love with anyone, either."

I rubbed the scrap with my thumb. "So these are her secrets. How soapy," I said. "I love it."

He sidled up to me and slid his arms around my waist. "It *is* very romantic in here."

"You know, this little den means our house actually has twenty-*seven* rooms." I turned to face him and locked my hands around his neck. "It's going to take us a while to mark our territory. We'd better get started."

He dipped his head to kiss me. "It's the middle of the day," he said, even as he drew me down to the cushioned floor. "What would Georgina say?"

"She had a den of secrets," I murmured. "I think she'd approve."

CHAPTER SIX

She sounds like she's being a total cow."

"Lacey. You're talking about the Queen," my mother said.

"Sorry. A right royal cow," Lacey amended.

My mother snickered. "Much better."

"You guys are terrible influences," I said. "I love it."

This three-way Skype session was the closest to being in the same room that Mom, Lacey, and I had managed since the wedding, and it was good to see their faces, even if they were squeezed into halves of my laptop screen and Lacey's internet connection was spotty. And I'd already said more to my sister and my mother—each on different continents—than I had to my grandmother-in-law, who'd summoned me to her chambers twice more over the last week for more time spent in rigorous quietude. The only use of my voice was with Marta, who was habitually fiddling on her iPhone in her daughter's sitting room, and either sharing internet gossip or dropping tidbits about Eleanor.

"Did you happen to notice the pocket watch?" she'd asked earlier this week. Eleanor had been wearing one around her neck. "Dates from the 1900s. Made in Coventry." Her lip twitched, and I knew why: Being sent to Coventry was a British expression for being iced out. It turned out Eleanor *was* speaking to me. Through her accessories.

To my family, I said, "She at least let me sit down. Or, more accurately, Marta told me Eleanor didn't care for my hovering, and that she said I would get huge ankles if I didn't find a chair."

Lacey whistled. "She's cankle-baiting you. Her evil runs deep."

"Don't let her get to you," Mom said, topping off her coffee with some cream.

"Says the woman who yelled at the Queen in her own home," Lacey said.

"Do as I say, not as I do," Mom said airily. "How are the elephants, dear?"

At the same time, I said, "Have you even brushed your hair, Lace? You look like me."

"You wish," Lacey said. "But I do spend like 70 percent less time on my head here than I ever did in London." She sighed contentedly. "The elephants are so smart. I got to give the baby a bath yesterday and she really likes me. Olly says he's worried she'll try to follow me home."

"*Olly* says that, does he?" I asked. "What else does this *Olly* say? Maybe we should ask Olly how to handle Eleanor."

"Unless you want him to suggest an electronic collar to study her migratory patterns, better leave it alone," Lacey said, but she was blushing. "Push back at her, Bex. Crack her first. What's she going to do? It's not like she can have you killed."

"Debatable."

"I think it's a test of your moxie," Lacey insisted.

"I don't think Eleanor is interested in other people's moxie," I said. "I think I just have to be patient. Except, historically, I'm shitty at it."

"Correct," Mom said. "Which is why Lacey is right."

"Yay!" Lacey pumped her fist.

"It's time to force a reaction out of Eleanor," Mom continued. "As your father used to say, make yourself big and the world can't ignore you."

She hugged herself for a moment, as if basking in a memory too private to share aloud. I gazed at the laptop screen, my entire immediate family in one LCD frame—Mom, with my chin and my hair but Lacey's nose and blue eyes; Lacey, once the fancy twin, suddenly shoving her hair into messy ponytails and looking a lot more like I used to when I was running cross-country through the back roads of Iowa. And me, sporting both hair *and* eyelash extensions, because I was now a person with image architects (though not, thankfully, a person who used the phrase *image architects* with a straight face). It was comforting to know that we could bridge the miles and the time differences to keep our threesome tight. Even as it still broke my heart, one piece every day, that we were no longer four.

"Okay, girls. I've got to shower. Bed Bath and Beyond is taking me to lunch," Mom said, breaking my reverie. She'd been running Coucherator, Inc., to great acclaim since my dad died. "SkyMall closing has led to so many meetings, I cannot even tell you."

"And I have to go meet Ol—uh, Oliver, er, Dr. Omundi about some data entry, and..."

"Please say *slide into some spreadsheets* next," I said.

Lacey rolled her eyes. "Fix your eyebrows," she said.

"I love you guys," I said. "I'll keep you posted. Pray for me."

I closed my computer heavily. Back to the emotional grind. Since returning from Scotland, my primary job (other than being summoned to Eleanor's chamber) had been going through Georgina's old stuff to decide what Nick and I wanted to consign to storage. This was usually interesting, but it was also overwhelming and dusty, and it bummed me out that the contents of Georgina's entire life were the responsibility of someone who'd never met her. I'd done some online digging, too, into the enigmatic woman who'd called this place home before I did, but the results were unsatisfying. Her Wikipedia entry was complete but dry, a long litany of only the most elemental facts. At least the *Daily Mail* had written about a minor scandal in the '70s when Georgina went on a twelve-hour craps marathon in Monte Carlo. A few fashion stories popped up about Georgina's outrageous taste in hats, but were all pegged to the same photo of her at Ascot wearing what looked like a feathered swim cap and gesturing with a bejeweled cigarette holder. And her obituaries painted her as a party girl eliding the last reclusive chunk of her life. None of it helped me know the whole story, or her true self, any better.

The jaunts to Eleanor's bedside fomented equal frustration. I'd looked at every photo in the room, from afar. I knew the contours of every piece of furniture. I could sketch the wallpaper blindfolded. The only excitement was hearing Marta's latest travails on what she persistently referred to in full as the World Wide Web. My dad's beyond-the-grave advice started making sense: Maybe if I made myself big enough, Eleanor would stop ignoring me. *Something* had to change, or I would lose my mind.

So I pushed my limits. First, I did bring in paper and pencils to draw the wallpaper. The next time, while Eleanor read the *Express*'s front-page story about how Freddie had coached a team of adorable five-year-olds to a rugby win, I blew through Jilly Cooper's smut classic *Riders*, the cover of which features a hand groping a shapely rump in breeches. I played countless games of *Candy Crush* with the sound on, ate as much loud snack food as I could, and clicked a pen for five straight minutes. I even brought a tablet to stream Cubs highlights, and treated the bedroom as if it were my living room—language and all. Earl Porter would have been proud.

Eleanor didn't blink. Not even when I called one of our middle relievers a douchecanoe (which I hadn't even done for effect; it was a fact). Her impassiveness was impressive, and it was going to drive me into early insanity.

"It's been two weeks," I marveled to Nick while we were rummaging through the second-floor drawing room. "She's made of iron. I don't think there's anything inside her chest that *could* flutter."

"I don't know what to tell you," Nick said. "She's never been this angry at me before. Today she and Father had me indexing charity names in the back room at Clarence House while Freddie gave the cast of *Worthington Hall* its OBEs."

"I read an entire issue of *Playboy* in front of the Queen."

"Do you know how many charities in Britain begin with *B*?"

"Do you know the word-to-nipple ratio in *Playboy*?"

Nick chuckled. "Please tell me you went to the newsstand and bought it yourself."

"I made Gaz go," I said. "I need to send him a bottle of wine.

I guarantee you he is still blushing." I let out a puff of frustration. "I've tried everything to get her to crack, short of rekindling the Revolution."

"Before you go in muskets blazing, I've got news about a proper job for us," he said.

"Do you think we need a brass magazine rack?" I asked Nick, holding up a metal basket that still had old issues of *People* and *Newsweek* in it. "Wait, what did you say?"

He snatched the rack from me. "I was *about* to say, 'Yes, we absolutely need Nick Nolte's Sexiest Man Alive issue.'"

"No, the other thing—wait, what is this?" I held up a small silver bowl with a snug lid and a small hole in the top.

"I think it's an inkwell," Nick said, "but if we don't know what it is, we don't need it."

"What if later we decide we really need an inkwell?"

Nick rolled up Nick Nolte into a megaphone. "Rebecca," he boomed. "If you change your mind, someone will go into storage and fetch you the inkwell."

"*Antiques Roadshow* has given me anxiety that I'll trash something priceless," I told him. "What's this about a job?"

"It might not help your anxiety," Nick said, "but it seems we're on the docket for an engagement with Freddie. Our first as a trio. We're going to Hampton Court to unveil a new tapestry. Or, I guess, technically an old tapestry that they found in a hole and restored."

"Of course. Nothing says, 'Behold our marital bliss!' like Henry the Eighth," I said.

"Does it make you feel better that this tapestry was commissioned for the wife he liked best?" Nick asked. "Although nine days later she died. Maybe that's why it got chucked in a hole." He sighed. "I haven't been to Hampton Court in ages. Mum took us as kids and I pretended to roast Freddie on the giant spit in the kitchen."

"Gee, I wonder who'll get roasted at this one," I muttered.

I wasn't kidding. We were going to be scrutinized within an inch of our lives, from our body language to whether or not the boys' ties held some kind of hidden message, to how many times I smiled and at whom; I couldn't cling to Nick, but neither could I keep my distance, and I had to maintain a paradoxical friendly disinterest in Freddie—all while pretending the reporters trailing us hadn't just spent weeks calling me Duchess Degenerate. It was a high-wire act with no room for mistakes, especially with suspicion of me and my motives at an all-time high. Everyone knew that we knew that they knew that *we* knew that *they* knew what was at stake. To get through it, I had to believe in it. I had to put my faith in the notion that the sooner Nick and Freddie and I convinced the public that everything was fine—there was that word again—the sooner it actually would be.

The morning of the event, my nervousness had taken root and sprouted thorns. I had meant to stop reading the blogs devoted to covering me, but they're as easy to quit as smoking (and about as hazardous to my health). People mostly fell into two camps: betrayed by my duplicity, or fiercely certain that every word Clive wrote was a lie. Those in the middle—even and often especially the ones with well-reasoned theories skating close to the truth—got shouted down and chased away. And every single one of them was itching to see what I would wear for my first public event since my disastrous wedding. Donna had been making pulls for weeks in anticipation of this exact eventuality, and would later be tasked with passing that information to the Palace's social media director. *Someone* had to make sure reporters found out that my beige suede shoes were Jimmy Choos (pricey, to indicate that I wasn't half-assing this) and my simple pink day dress was from Boden (a high-street brand, to communicate that I hadn't been blowing *all* The Firm's money).

Even so, managing all those outside expectations was practically uncomplicated compared to the other major X factor. I hadn't spoken to Freddie in person since the night we were recalled to Balmoral. I'd seen him out the library window coming and going, and I'd texted him twice to ask if he wanted to come dig through Georgina's junk, or join us for dinner. Both times, he'd been otherwise engaged.

Right before we were meant to leave for Hampton Court, I saw Freddie wander over and sit on our front steps to bury his nose in our dossier for this appearance. My stomach sank. Normally, Freddie wouldn't think twice about walking in and flopping on the couch—hell, the first time we met, it was because he'd snuck into Nick's room as a joke—but now he couldn't even stand to ring the bell. I decided to force a conversation even if it killed him. Apparently, the main duty of the Duchess of Clarence was finagling recalcitrant royals into talking.

I pulled open the door as subtly as I could, poked out my head, and then shouted, "Why didn't you knock?"

Freddie jumped, nearly dropping the dossier. He closed it around his finger to mark his place, and got to his feet. "I, uh, didn't know if you'd be ready," he said.

I eased outside and closed the door, then waved my hand in a ta-da motion. "My duchess costume is a go."

He took a step back against the railing. "You look extremely unscandalous. Where's Nick?"

"On the phone. Probably getting yelled at about something."

"I heard Gran is giving *you* a rough go," Freddie said.

"She is the immovable object and the unstoppable force, all at once," I said. "Lacey's theory is that she's testing my moxie."

"How is Lacey?" Freddie asked, a genuine smile on his face.

"She's great. We Skyped the other day and it's obvious she's happy, even though she's had to become a morning person. The time stamps on her emails are early as hell."

"At least she's finding time to reach out and put things in writing," Freddie said.

A silence, pregnant with meaning, stretched between us.

I nudged him with my foot. "I've seen the woman visiting you."

Freddie turned inward. "I can't, Bex. Not now. Not with you."

"Fred," I began, shifting so that I was next to him. "I started so many texts, Freddie. I wanted to email. But I didn't—"

"You can stop right there. You didn't," he said.

His face had turned pink. My heart simultaneously rose into my throat and sank into my feet.

"I hate that we made you feel alone," I said.

"But you don't hate that you *left* me alone."

I wanted to argue, but I couldn't. Leaving, and hiding, had been easier for me than staying and dealing with the fallout. Maybe we should have stayed. For Freddie, for the family, for The Firm. But I knew I'd make that same decision again. Nick and I had an entire lifetime ahead in which we'd doubtless, and often, surrender our personal needs for family and country, so even in the face of Freddie's anguish, I couldn't rightly say I felt regret.

"I know this was hard for you," I said instead. "But it was hard for us, too, Freddie. That was our wedding day, and it was an epic disaster. I don't think either one of us was in our right mind. Put yourself in Nick's shoes."

"You think I haven't ever put myself in Nick's shoes?" Freddie hissed.

"He would not have gotten his feet back underneath him if we'd stayed here," I pressed on, opting to ignore his implication. "I hate seeing you like this and knowing it's my fault, Freddie. I *hate* it. But staying would have killed us, and . . . we're married. We have to be each other's priority."

"Yes, being cut out was a nasty reminder that we're not three anymore," he said. "We're two and one. Things were already changing, and then they got infinitely worse."

He appeared, for a split second, to check the door for any sign of Nick. "I don't have a right to have expected more from Nick, but it was shitty that *you* abandoned me to deal with this by myself. I'd already been pretending I didn't care that you chose him, that it didn't hurt, that my heart wasn't broken. But when you ran, it was like it happened all over again, only this time I had to go through it in public."

His sad eyes, blue pools so similar to Nick's, cut me to the quick. Then he dipped his head toward me, the better to speak quietly as his voice cracked. "You were there. You are the only other person who really knows how it was. How low we both were. And then the worst thing I've ever done, ever, became public. And you *left*, Bex. And I had to be the face of it alone."

The front door opened. Freddie leapt away from me so fast that the railing actually rattled.

"Hello," said Nick stiffly. His sunglasses made it hard to tell which one of us he was looking at more closely.

"Hello, yes, hi. Bex and I were just catching up," Freddie said, looking anywhere but at either of us.

Nick took this in for a second, and then pointed at the dossier Freddie was still bookmarking. "Bit late to start cramming now."

"I don't need to cram. I read it twice last night," Freddie said. "I'm excited to hear how they were able to tell that the bloke they found with the tapestry had died by choking on a cheese sandwich."

"And I hear congratulations are in order," Nick said. "Father tells me Gran is making you a Counsellor of State. It's an honor, being one of her official proxies." Nick's tone had mounted into one of false joviality. "And to get it before the direct heir does? It's unheard of."

"Father has come to respect what I can contribute. I was touched to know Gran agrees," Freddie said loftily. "I'm sure you'll get there."

"Quite," Nick said coldly. "Well done, you."

"Yes, it's nice to have this one thing, at least," Freddie said.

Both men glanced at me, before we heard the crunch of the Range Rover's tires on gravel.

"I think I'll ride up front," said Freddie, stalking over to the car and disappearing inside.

I reached for Nick's hand. "At least he didn't use the word *fine*?"

Freddie spent the whole ride to Hampton Court chatting with PPO Twiggy about any weightless issue that came to mind—next year's World Cup favorite, compression socks, whether pistachios were worth the trouble. Nick and I were content to flip through our dossiers in the back seat and occasionally murmur commentary to one another.

"I can't believe we've known each other this long and you never took me to see William the Third's toilet," I said.

"And yet you married me anyway," he said.

Unless I was crazy, he said that part a little bit louder.

The redbrick towers of Hampton Court—Henry VIII's favorite residence, and accordingly the scene of a lot of questionable behavior—popped against the azure sky, and a breeze coming off the Thames tickled the leaves on the ancient oaks. It was the kind of idyllic British summer day that graced countless postcards, had inspired two thousand poems about flowers, and made everyone forget how much rain they got the rest of the year. Even the swans looked pleased with their lot in life. I wished there was time to explore the grounds, but there was no sightseeing on the agenda: After a walk-through of the exhibit, Nick was meant to give a speech about his undying passion for the woven arts, after which the three of us would pose for photos, put on a display of unbothered family unity in which everyone was only being sexy in the correct directions, and head home to London. In, out, and on our way.

The rule was that we shouldn't look closely at the press pack, but it was impossible for me not to notice half of the reporters holding up phones, the rest furiously scribbling in notebooks. There was also a sizable pack of civilians, either there solely to eyeball us or gobsmacked to bump into the UK's most notorious trio on their day out. We all exited the car smoothly and without a flashing incident (Bea would be relieved to know my skills on that front hadn't rusted), Nick placing a very pointed hand on the small of my back as we moved toward the awaiting historians and dignitaries. Later, *People* would interpret this to mean our marriage was on solid ground, and the *Daily Mail* would claim Nick was asserting sexual dominance in front of Freddie and the world. According to me, it was both.

Nick reached our hosts first, but it was Freddie who spoke.

"I'm afraid we're keeping some of these fine folks from getting lost in the maze," he quipped to appreciative giggles.

The purpose of the event was to show off our circle of three, but instead, Freddie was dialed in as a solo act. He deployed a well-received joke about sharing ginger genetics with Henry VIII that magically avoided veering into the minefield of how Henry's first wife originally married his older brother. He remembered one of the Hampton Court tour guides from a previous event at a totally different historic royal palace. He fist-bumped a child, then high-fived its parent. (Nick knew better than to try to outdo any of this, so he simply laughed along and exuded calm warmth, even if inside it had to be killing him.) At one point, Nick fumbled the tapestry's country of origin and Freddie loudly corrected him; when Nick asked how long it could withstand the projections of light that illustrated its original splendor before sustaining damage, Freddie piped up, "Six minutes at a time, five times a day, if I remember correctly?" I couldn't ding him for being prepared, but it was disorienting, and disingenuous, because Nick and Freddie both knew Nick was simply asking the second question to engage the computer technicians. The guides moved on to a different subject, oblivious, but I saw Nick angrily tighten his light blue tie as if trying to strangle himself. Freddie's apparent commitment to upstaging us was complete.

As we gathered in a small break room for a sip of water before Nick's speech—out of sight of the reporters trailing us—Nick walked straight past Freddie to the tall blonde in the flowered dress who'd been steering us through the palace with helpful details.

"Annie!" he said, hugging her. "What's it been—fifteen years? I didn't know you were going to be here!"

She beamed. "I wasn't meant to be! But I'm consulting for the facility in Manchester that worked on this, and their regular PR lad got a kidney stone."

"How's Shanghai?" he asked.

"Dubai, and it's lovely, but Artie's liver is acting up, so we're home for a bit," she said.

The two of them slipped into merry, familiar chatter as I stood off to the side, forgotten and craving a Diet Coke.

"Annabelle Farthing," Freddie said in my ear. "Married to some hopeless old marquess with a huge pile in Somerset. Her father's friends with Agatha so we knew each other as kids." He nudged me. "You know that bit in *Bridget Jones* where she played naked in Colin Firth's paddling pool? It's like that."

"Oh, and how often have you seen that movie?"

Freddie fidgeted. "Well, you know, it's Marj's favorite. Ah, they're ready for us," he said. "Let's go play happy families again."

"Right," I said to his back. "Happy families."

So I was already feeling out of sorts when it happened. As we were passing back through the long hallway outside the room where the tapestries lived, I caught sight of something in my periphery and whipped my head around—and felt crushingly sick.

"Are you all right?" Freddie asked, grabbing my elbow.

Nick dropped his conversation with Annabelle and snapped to my side with concern. "You're green," he said.

"You were right in Catherine Howard's path," Annabelle said, nudging in and guiding me to a window seat ten feet away. "That's where she was standing when she found out Henry was sending her to the Tower. I don't really believe in ghosts, but you do hear of people feeling ill here." She studied me. "This is the first time I've ever seen it."

Nick knelt beside me. "Do you need to lie down?" He looked up at Annabelle. "Could someone get her a glass of water?"

"No, she's right, I feel much better over here," I said. But what I couldn't admit, or even know for sure myself, was that it might not have been Catherine Howard's lingering psychic devastation that felled me. Because I could have sworn I saw a face as familiar to me as my own shuffling out with the press pack, bent over a notebook, jotting down details with his poison pen. I thought about the prospect—or threat—of Clive showing up at every event I did for the rest of my life, always only a hundred feet away from me and Nick and our fragile happiness. It suddenly felt as if no matter what show we tried to put on, we'd never escape him.

So yes, maybe I had seen a ghost. Just maybe not the one they meant.

CHAPTER SEVEN

A NEW HEIR-A?

Clive Fitzwilliam on Britain's Tricky Trio

It was meant to be a pretty picture of sibling stability, and the casual observer may have been happily hoodwinked. But take it from me: Yesterday's Hampton Court farce proved the opposite.

The Duke of Clarence takes dynastic precedence, but once again his brother showed nobody can dazzle like he does. Prince Frederick was quick with his quips, charming the crowd and making the future King look dull as dishwater by comparison. Even the darling Duchess, his erstwhile lover, appeared to go weak at the knees just from standing near the magnetic majesty that is Flashy Freddie. The photo outside the palace was as palpably pained as Prince Nicholas's pride, knowing his brother is the spark that lights the fire, and he's the sand that snuffs it.

Perhaps, in the wake of Queen Eleanor's unprecedented passing over of Nicholas to make his younger brother a Counsellor of State, the Duchess of Clarence believes she gambled on the wrong brother.

Reviews of the Great Tapestry Unveiling were not all as negative as Clive's. *The American't*—the most critical of the blogs chronicling my every move—miraculously didn't hate my dress (though the author did write, "Her shoes are the most boring thing to come out of Kensington Palace since her face"), and the *Mirror* gave me a solid three and a half stars, docking marks because I looked peaky in the group photo, which it cited as proof of my romantic indecision about the two brothers. *Heat* debuted a feature called "The Heat Index," in which a motley panel of comics and psychologists analyzed the photos and decided whether Nick and I were still banging. (The verdict: maybe.) In general, it seemed expectations for decorum were so low—and for gossip, so high—that the press was either relieved or disappointed that Freddie hadn't tried to mount me right there on Henry VIII's dining table. But Clive was the worst of it, and he was brutal.

Annabelle Farthing had overseen the press passes and confirmed to Nick that none had been produced in his name. Then again, every detail in his piece could have come from video and wire photos, with the lone exception of Freddie aiding me when I felt faint. But any number of spies could've fed that to him, including whomever *The Sun* did send. We had to accept that Clive was free to hear whatever he liked, and draw whatever conclusions he could, from the comfort of his desk. And if Marj had her way, he'd be doing so all summer long: Her plan was to load us up on group outings to bludgeon Great Britain into believing that there was nothing to believe. Freddie, Nick, and Bex were officially open for business.

"I'll be glad when this crisis management stuff is over," I grumbled to Lacey over the phone. "It's stressful. Let's skip ahead to actual work."

"Hmm, yes, work," Lacey teased. "What is a duchess's job, exactly?"

"That's the problem," I said. "I have no idea. My main responsibility used to be etiquette training, and now it's Look, Everyone, We're Not Acting Awkward. No one has told me what the next phase is."

"Popping out a kid, I assume," she said. "That'll turn the tide. Come to think of it, Marj might also file *that* under Crisis Management."

"My brand is crisis," I sighed. "But hopefully we can keep my uterus out of it for a while. I am nowhere near ready for a baby. Its uncle isn't even speaking to us."

Freddie had seemed energized by ribbing the two of us at Hampton Court, but he'd shut down again as soon as we left. He hadn't set foot inside Apartment 1A, and we'd learned nothing more about the mysterious Hannah beyond what we saw a week later in the papers, after he got papped hustling into Soho House with a brunette in a coat and pulled-down hat.

"Do you think we're ever going to meet her?" I asked Nick one night as we clambered into the Den of Secrets.

"Do you think she'll last long enough?" Nick asked, flopping down on his favorite pillows and pulling out a crossword. He liked doing them up there by candlelight (LED, so as not to burn down the monarchy in a literal sense).

"He's definitely handling this differently, so maybe it's serious."

"That'd be a first," Nick snarked. He rolled onto his stomach. "Can we please leave Freddie and all his bullshit downstairs?"

"But if you need to—"

"I don't, Bex." His forcefulness seemed to surprise even him. He softened. "And Sex Den is our time."

I laughed off the tension. "It's Den of Secrets, not Sex Den."

"That seems like semantics," Nick said. "But we should sort that out before I have the sign made."

I watched him start to work on his crossword, as if the cloud had never passed over us. Since we'd come back, his resistance to discussing anything deeper than Georgina's cavalcade of artifacts had only increased. If I pushed, he might freeze me out completely; if I let it go, I might miss a window. At a loss for answers, I started opening cabinets willy-nilly, as if the solution would fly out at me.

"Oooh, a feather boa." I tossed it at Nick, who wrapped it around his neck without even looking up from his crossword. I picked up a small hardbound book that had fallen out along with two silk scarves and a loafer, and flipped through the pages. It appeared to be a diary.

"Hot damn," I said. "Georgina lives."

I opened to a random page near the middle, and read aloud:

*is SO tiresome. Ellie and I teach ourselves more from reading
the newspapers. And today when we asked to go outside to run
about a bit because it had FINALLY stopped raining, he said that
nice young ladies don't run, and yesterday he told Ellie that princesses don't need opinions which I think is MOST disrespectful.
MY opinion is that he's a cow-faced BORE and so I drew him that
way while his back was turned to do some maths on the board
and Ellie laughed out loud and we both nearly got our ears boxed.
And later Ellie felt really guilty because Granny always tells us
not to speak rudely about people (even though Granny speaks
rudely about people all the time!!!!) but I told her we weren't
<u>speaking</u> about him at all and I think she felt better because she
fell right to sleep. I don't know what Ellie would do without me.
She is still snoring terribly though and it's driving me mad. It's
going to be very embarrassing for her when she gets married.*

Nick burst out laughing. "That is amazing," he said. "It's odd to hear
Gran referred to as Ellie." He gestured for me to throw him the book,
and caught it deftly. He flipped through its pages. "Crikey. She wrote
loads. This book is full up."

"I wonder if there are more of these anywhere," I said. "Maybe
they've all already been sent to the official royal archives."

Nick shook his head. "We'd have heard," he said. He gnawed on his
pen cap. "All my ancestors apparently kept massive diaries. Am I ruining
things for future historians by not doing that? It sounds exhausting to
document every detail of every minute of every day."

"We don't need it," I said. "Historians will have our text messages."

Nick pulled a face. "I hope not," he said, giving me back the journal.
"Some of them are highly inappropriate. I should have sent you proper
love letters."

"It's not too late to start," I said. "I've enjoyed writing to Lacey. We get
a little deeper. When we're texting or talking, it turns into teasing."

"Maybe *you* should be our official diarist," Nick suggested. "When
you put it all on paper, please make sure I come across as very muscular."
He tugged at his hair. "And with more of this, please."

I dropped the journal and stared at Nick. "Put it in writing," I said. "That's it. That is *it*."

Nick looked pleased. "Am I a genius?"

"Don't get cocky," I said. "But you just might be."

The next morning, when I arrived at Eleanor's chambers for what she surely intended to be another day of pretending I was inanimate, I came prepared.

Marta greeted me with her usual poke of the cane. "I don't think I care much for this Clive person," she said.

"Welcome to the team," I said. "What pushed you over the edge?"

She crossed her arms. "He uses too much alliteration. I don't trust it."

"He's a cow-faced bore," I said with a chuckle, mostly to myself, but then I looked up and saw Marta staring at me as if I'd spoken in tongues. "Sorry. That phrase makes me laugh. It's from an old diary of Georgina's that we found last night. She did not like one of her tutors."

Marta stood her cane on one end and tapped it as if considering coming to her feet. "How curious."

"It's super charming," I said. "I've learned more about Georgina from the stuff in that house than even Google can tell me. She seems like she was very feisty."

"She was, for most of her life."

"What changed?" I asked.

"Nothing," Marta said. "She simply turned to a genteel life of quietude and spiritual reflection, as all respectable aristocratic ladies do." She looked down at her buzzing mobile. "Piss it, Edwin just played *bat*. What a git."

I bit back a smirk. "Do you want to read the diary?" I asked. "I can bring it to you."

"Perhaps." She tsked. "Whatever Eleanor paid for Edwin's schooling was highway robbery. He took four days to put down that bloody word."

I continued into Eleanor's room. Her flutter had forced light bed rest for longer than expected due to an issue with keeping her blood pressure down, though I couldn't imagine what it was, given how placid she was every time I saw her. Today was no different: Calmly, she leafed through yesterday's *Globe and Mail* wearing a green bed jacket and a brooch that was a bigger version of the Lyons Emerald. Pulling rank, but more luxuriously than most.

I settled into my usual armchair by the side of the bed and opened my large pad of paper. But instead of doodling, I uncapped a Sharpie and wrote, GOOD MORNING TO YOU, TOO.

Eleanor glanced up.

THE NEW CANADIAN PRIME MINISTER HAS GREAT HAIR, I wrote next.

Eleanor raised a brow and flipped a page. This was the most she'd ever even looked at me during one of these sessions, so I pressed onward.

TECHNICALLY, "SPEAK WHEN SPOKEN TO" DOES NOT APPLY TO WRITING. HOW ARE YOU FEELING?

I heard the newsprint crunch slightly as Eleanor's hand tightened on it. I said a quick prayer that Lacey was even partly correct about Eleanor having a secret appreciation for moxie, and turned to another fresh page.

SOME WOULD ARGUE ETIQUETTE DEMANDS A LADY'S TIMELY RESPONSE TO A WRITTEN MISSIVE FROM A FAMILY MEMBER.

Eleanor lowered the paper and stared at me, stone-faced. Maybe she *would* have me killed. That would solve a lot of her problems.

"Technically," she said, "etiquette only requires a written response. But my stationery is out of reach at the moment."

Holy shit. I did it.

"Would you like me to fetch it for you?" I asked, in as polite a tone as I could manage.

Eleanor folded her paper and set it aside. "No," she said. "Congratulations. You crossed the first hurdle."

"So it *was* a test. I thought maybe you were just being petty!"

"They are not mutually exclusive." Eleanor tapped her tented fingers together like Mr. Burns. "I hadn't thought of the writing loophole. I assumed that eventually you would blurt out something asinine." She raised an eyebrow. "Which of course you did, but about one of your baseball gentlemen."

"I knew you were listening."

"My ears are not the problem," she said. "I've never heard words put together in that order."

When I cracked up, Eleanor glared at me again, and my laugh died almost as fast as it came.

"Do not press your luck," she said. "We have much to discuss, and none of it involves complimenting your vocabulary."

I braced myself for another litany of my faults, and what further penances I had to perform, but Eleanor merely appraised me sharply.

"For a time in my youth, I was the closest approximation to you," she said.

"Me?" I blinked. "How do you mean?"

"Uncle Arthur came to the throne before my father did, but even before that, it was clear he and Ingeborg couldn't have children," Eleanor said. "I was an heir presumptive. A few places removed, certainly, but all eyes were on me."

Comprehension dawned. "As they're on Nick."

"As they're on you." Eleanor folded her hands. "Richard will never remarry. *You* are the next queen this country shall have, and the public knows it."

She said this with such certainty that I was tempted to wonder aloud if *Richard* knew remarriage was off the table.

"You married an unusual man, and thus you shall have an unusual fate. You need to be ready," she continued. "Men are weak, Rebecca. All of them. Richard, Nicholas, Frederick." She held out her hand to stop my protesting. "I know whereof I speak. Men are weak, but women are not. We aren't afforded that luxury. And unfortunately, I will not live forever."

"Nick is solid, Your Majesty," I said. "I know we've made mistakes, but you don't need to worry about him."

"Nicholas has a good heart. But he is not strong, not alone," Eleanor said. "He will wobble. He already did. My patience with that has expired."

"With all due respect," I said, "if the point is to steady him, then why play him against Freddie by making Freddie a Counsellor of State first?"

"Nicholas needed a reminder that being born first may not always mean coming first," Eleanor said sharply. "A title is not entitlement. Frederick erred, but at least he knows it. If your husband would like to be treated as someone who can handle the responsibility of his position, he needs to act like a responsible person."

"I believe in Nick," I said.

"As did I, once. I should like to again," she said. "I have grave concerns about your ability to stabilize him after all the ugliness. But what is it you Americans say? You break it, you buy it? Well, you broke it, and you've bought it, so it must be you who mends it. You will either make or ruin those boys, and it had better be the former, Rebecca. *Soon.*" Her glare ran through me like a knife. "Do not disappoint me again."

CHAPTER EIGHT

"That woman is a conniving genius," Bea announced, stomping into Cilla's postage-stamp-size back garden and dropping her briefcase right into a surprised Cilla's lap.

"The Queen, I presume?" Cilla asked, pointedly putting the bag on the ground.

"No, Bitsy Armbrister-Shayles. *Yes*, the Queen." Bea crossed her arms. "But in point of fact, also Bitsy Armbrister-Shayles. She ran a bidding war for her stallion's sperm knowing full well she'd already sired him out six other places. I've half a mind to neuter him."

She sank hard into one of Cilla's white metal chairs and teetered precariously to one side. She shrieked and struggled to collect herself. It was the first time I'd ever seen Lady Bollocks off-kilter.

"Right, meant to tell you, that one's the wonky one," Cilla said impassively, pouring a cup of tea.

"I thought this was the wonky one," I said, wriggling and feeling my chair clunk unevenly.

"They're all the wonky one," said Gaz as he bustled out with a purple frilly apron around his waist and a plate of petits fours. "Now, get stuck in and tell me what you think. Be kind. But truthful. But mostly kind?" He twiddled his fingers hopefully and then disappeared back into the kitchen.

Bea ignored him. "The sheer nerve of making you try that hard for a crumb of attention," she marveled. "And now she's made you so grateful to be speaking that you'll do whatever she asks. Stay at her knee as long as you can, Bex. You'll be a master manipulator in no time."

"I don't want to be a master manipulator," I protested. "Literally nothing has ever sounded less appealing to me."

"Then you suffer from a shocking lack of imagination," Bea said, pointing firmly at me and then letting that finger fall onto one of Gaz's petits fours. It was beige with a little green ball on top. She studied it suspiciously.

"This is silly." Cilla frowned as she stirred sugar into her tea. "Surely babysitting the brothers isn't your job."

"That's what it feels like," I said. "That, and doing internet deep dives on Georgina. I read an amazing rumor that she had an affair with Elvis Presley, but no one could prove it."

"And why would she have wanted them to? All those jumpsuits." Bea shuddered, then bit into Gaz's confection and gagged. "What have I just put in my mouth?"

Gaz scurried back out, clearly only having pretended to leave. "A surprise savory curry petit four! My greatest strength, wrapped up into a dessert package."

"Who on earth would want a savory curry petit four?" Bea squawked.

Gaz looked offended. "People willing to have their worldview expanded."

"Like, say, the judges on *Ready, Set, Bake*," Cilla said, shooting me a glance that said, *He'd best not quit his day job.*

I nibbled at one. "You know, that's actually good," I said. "Once you aren't expecting it to be sweet, it's less shocking when it tastes like a samosa."

Gaz looked pleased. "Wait until you taste tomorrow's batch," he said. "Pork-pie flavor!"

"You are an affront to my sweet tooth," Bea called after his retreating figure, and he turned to blow a kiss along with an exceedingly rude gesture.

"How's the new gig?" I asked, turning to Cilla.

"Planning this Dutch state visit is giving even my gray hairs gray hairs. We've crammed a year's worth of logistics into half that time," she said. "Spoiler: You'll get to wear a tiara again."

"If Eleanor lets me go. If I fail at this assignment, she might put me on house arrest." I glanced at Bea. "And how about you, what's going on at your...job?"

My voice trailed up in a telltale way that Bea did not miss. She drummed her nails on the table and leveled me with a glare. "What do you think a person with my job might have going on?" she asked.

I looked to Cilla for help. "Lots of...typing," she offered.

"And conference calls," I said. "Many, many calls."

"You've described every office job in the world," Bea said. "Be more specific."

"Er. Making...lists," Cilla offered.

"Checking them twice," I added.

Bea set her lips in a thin line. "So you think I'm Father Christmas."

"But with horses that you teach to do cute walks," I said.

Bea slammed her hand on the table. The petits fours jumped. "You two have no idea what I do for a living," she said. "Nor the finer points of dressage. I knew Bex was a lost cause, but I expected better from you, Cilla."

"My aunt once married a man she thought was a landscape architect, but it turns out he worked for MI5," Cilla said. "Might you be doing something like that?"

"Come on, Bea," I said. "Put us out of our misery."

"No. You can marinate in it," Bea said. "Back to the topic at hand."

"Gaz's baking career?" I asked innocently.

Bea actually snapped her fingers in front of my face. Cilla swatted her hand away.

"Leave it, Bea. She's just been in a sex scandal."

"Please. Everyone has been in a sex scandal," Bea said. "Someday I'll tell you about the time Penelope Eight-Names offered me an antique urn in exchange for a threesome with me and Gemma." She raised a brow. "*After* her wedding."

Gaz poked his head out the patio door. "I'm listening."

"What more could there possibly be to that story?" Cilla said, popping a petit four into her mouth. "Mmm, that one's coffee."

"Well, we don't know if she got the urn," Gaz said.

I rubbed my face with my hands. "Look," I said. "I get that it was insane to think Nick and I could cruise back into town, and that nothing would change. We might look the same on the outside, but on the inside, everything is—"

"A savory curry petit four," Bea said drily.

"Basically," I said. "Freddie clearly doesn't want us all up in his business. But I don't know how to respect his personal space *and* do as I'm told by Eleanor."

"Freddie is a grown man, and he's going to have to learn to deal with you, seeing as you don't appear to be going anywhere," she said.

"That makes me sound so appealing," I said.

Cilla and Bea exchanged unreadable looks. "You're not *meant* to be appealing to him, Bex," Bea said. "You're meant to be an unremarkable part of his day. He needs... to grow accustomed to your face."

"Thanks, Professor Higgins."

"You actually *are* my Eliza Doolittle," Bea said. "But my point is that by keeping yourself scarce, every encounter feels fresh. Remind Freddie of how dull you actually are."

"I wouldn't put it that way," Cilla jumped in, giving Bea a dirty look. "But Bea's right that avoiding each other hasn't fixed anything. Compel him to deal with you, like you did with Eleanor."

"There is nothing less sexy than being tiresome," Bea said.

"I wouldn't be too certain," called Gaz, from inside their sliding door. "Tiresome was my only move, and it got me a goddess."

"It's wearing out its welcome," Cilla said, but as usual, she was smiling. "Either come to tea or don't, Gaz, but hovering makes you look like a nutter."

In a flash—I have never seen Gaz move so fast—he came out and plopped into the fourth chair. It didn't jiggle.

"I thought you said they were all wonky," I said.

"They are," Gaz said. "But so is my bum, so it evens things out." He handed me a petit four with a pink flower on top. "Food for thought."

I bit it. "Tuna casserole?"

Gaz's face fell. "Beef Wellington," he said. "Apparently, we've both got some work to do."

Cilla's and Bea's logic was solid, and the Queen had made it clear that she was sick of the status quo, so during the next few weeks—while Gaz tried to conquer the art of artificial beef Wellington flavoring— I searched for middle ground between "passive" and "aggressive." I'd run over to Freddie's apartments to drop off boxes of whatever Gaz had baked, making brief small talk if he answered the door but always leaving before I was shooed away. I saw his new girlfriend coming and going, but never prodded. When Nick and Freddie and I were called up again for two more events, I drew deep on the well of Lady Bollocks's duchess training about chatting with strangers—Freddie, sadly, increasingly qualified—and began innocuous conversations about subjects I knew they both enjoyed: British craft beers, how Agatha's ex Awful Julian had opened a hookah bar, the likelihood of Roger Federer avenging his Wimbledon loss. Neither of them told me to cut it out, so this peaceful coexistence started to feel only a few steps away from friendship. As we rolled into Nick's birthday near the end of August, I was hopeful.

Prince Dick, in a show of the exact sensitive parenting he'd performed their whole lives, marked his son's birthday with a party for something unrelated. The Royal Geographical Society, to celebrate its twentieth anniversary as the largest group of its kind, had spent all year drumming up cash for a study in Antarctica about the effect of climate change on its ice sheets; with a third of the year to go, the chairman thought a cocktail party with his patron the Prince of Wales would be the best push to loosen some pocketbooks. Nick's birthday took a back seat—both to global warming, and to The Firm's ongoing desire to prove to the posh guests that Freddie and I were not secretly banging in the coat closet. The toffs had a formidable grapevine, and I sensed Richard and Eleanor felt their good opinion could spread farther and wider than that of the average *Mail* reader. One afternoon, she ordered me to bring over pictures of Donna's pulls for Richard's party—actual tangible photographs—and studied them with a magnifying glass.

"The purple one," she said, tapping a sculptural cap-sleeve Roland Mouret. "It's slim cut enough to prevent anyone deciding you're pregnant with Frederick's love child. Which I assume you are not."

"Not unless it was immaculately conceived," I said. "But I think the green one gives me more room to eat the passed apps."

"Which you will not do in any dress," Eleanor said. "Your public mastication still needs work." She looked down at the photo again and added, "You will wear my River Bend brooch. It was given to me in the 1970s by the Spanish king, and the diamonds mimic the curves of the Thames."

"Thank you! What a brilliant idea," I said.

"Of course it is," Eleanor said. "Loaning you jewels will make them think I like you."

The party was on the seventy-second floor of The Shard, a massive glass skyscraper designed to look like its name—as if a huge piece of debris had dropped out of the sky and embedded itself in the South Bank. It was the tallest building in London, and the open-air venue at the top boasted spectacular panoramic views of the city, making it a particularly apt choice for an organization devoted to, in its simplest terms, the layout of the world. The planners had chosen to let said view speak for itself, decorating only with well-placed antique maps of whichever part of the city we happened to be overlooking, all of which were part of the silent auction. We'd given everyone about an hour and a half to get buzzed at the open bar and overbid on a few things before we arrived and did our part: Each of us had a designated area to glad-hand as many would-be donors and society staples as possible in that radius—like zone defense, but for fundraising—and then otherwise pretend we didn't know we were the subject of a mass gawking. Nick always said he felt like a zoo animal at these things, but I didn't realize how dead-on the analogy was until I was in the cage with him. As I talked to each potential donor, it took all my concentration not to get distracted by the people around us craning their necks, leaning toward each other in what looked like a gossipy whisper, or, in one case, snickering in my direction at something that I had to hope wasn't a piece of food in my teeth.

When I finally saw Richard veer from his zone to greet a cluster of his old pals, I recognized my cue to stop mingling with the toffs and start making our family circle look whole. Nick and I found each other near a north-facing window. That high up, London looked tiny and perfect, like a toy. I could have stood there for hours, looking for all the signposts of my life—the spire of Westminster Abbey, the Tower that I kept joking I'd be tossed into, and if I squinted, the part of Chelsea where my flat had been. But instead I let Nick steer me toward our friends, the touch of his hand on my back pointedly visible, and telegraphing, *All is well, nothing to see here. But please, do see the nothing that there is to see.*

"Happy birthday, mate," Gaz said, clapping Nick on the back. "Please thank old Dick for the invitation. It was kind of him."

"Kind would've been scheduling this for tomorrow," I muttered.

"But at least we get to raise a glass together," Cilla soothed me. "And please tell Gaz we don't need to bid four hundred pounds for an artist's rendering of a dirt road."

Nick laughed. "Gaz, in fine form as usual," he said. Then he lowered his voice. "This evening was meant to suck dry the hopelessly rich viscounts of such and such, not people we actually like."

"It's not just any dirt road. It's Knightsbridge, right by our flat!" Gaz said. "Happy memories, my love."

"It says they *think* it's Knightsbridge. It could be any old grubby strip," said Freddie, appearing between them and wrapping an arm around each shoulder. "All ancient dirt roads look a bit the same, don't they?"

Gaz sucked in some air. "Hopefully someone will outbid me, then," he said.

Cilla smacked him in the chest. "You didn't tell me you'd already bid," she exclaimed. "You know, my great-grandfather's cousin was a cartographer. They say he was fired from every job he had because he'd draw all the maps wrong if he had a vendetta against anyone in the area." She grinned. "As you might imagine, that was rather a lot."

The five of us bantered so comfortably even Eleanor would have been fooled into thinking there was no fire where there had once been smoke. But then Cilla got too deep in her cups and developed a competitive urge for Gaz to lock down the Knightsbridge etching, and an old Naval admiral pulled Nick away into a conversation about submarines that I was more than happy to miss. Suddenly, it was just me and Freddie.

"My, won't people talk?" he quipped.

"I think that's the idea," I said. "Try to look like I'm not interesting. Shouldn't be too hard."

He laughed. "But it's been such a stimulating few weeks," he said. "Your endless small talk had me about ready to move out until I realized I'd started to depend on your pastry deliveries." He tried to look nonchalant. "You'll be pleased to know I'd planned for you to meet Hannah tonight."

I brightened. "We're talking about this now?"

"Seemed about time." He tucked his hands into his pockets. "Or maybe you've simply nattered me into submission. For the love of God, either write that Sheffield Wednesday detective series or don't."

I craned my neck as if I'd recognize Hannah in a crowd, or even at all. "Is she here?"

"Alas, no," he said. "She's stuck at work. She's a barrister, a very fancy one, actually. Human rights. Makes me feel like a lazy tosser by comparison."

"Freddie!" I clasped my hands together in what was as subtle a gesture of glee as I could manage. "She sounds…"

"Out of my league?"

"I was going to say cool as hell," I said. "Has she met Richard?"

Freddie shook his head. "I think she'll impress the socks off him, but it's been tricky enough getting me into her datebook," he says. "And I don't want her to feel pressured. It's hard to find the right time to go public, and meeting Father could be even harder."

I nodded. "Tell her your brother married a ne'er-do-well former greeting card artist. Richard will be delighted for someone with a real job to raise the level of discourse."

He grinned at me, the most genuine one I'd seen in far too long. "Wise as ever, Killer."

The sun had dipped below the horizon line, leaving only a last pulse of gold and an electric-blue sky swirled with pink clouds. The light flared with eerily cinematic timing as he said my old nickname, and it felt so good, I almost hugged him. But a halo of space was beginning to form around Richard, which was Freddie's and Nick's cue to join him. They nearly bumped into each other as they arranged themselves on either side of their father; Freddie gave an extra-jovial "after you" gesture. Unusually, I couldn't read Nick's face.

"Thank you for joining us to honor the important work of the Royal Geographical Society, one of my favorite patronages," Richard said. "I'm told we've raised, conservatively, five million pounds towards the Antarctic mission. The anthropological and environmental impact of these grants is immense, and I've learnt more in my close meetings about RGS projects than I ever did at Oxford. Though don't tell Oxford I said that."

The room laughed politely.

"Which is why what I'm about to say is so bittersweet," Richard continued. "Being a young patron of this society was formative for me, and it would be selfish to keep that experience from my own sons. My father held it before he passed, then my mother handed it down to me, and I'm delighted to continue the tradition by passing along this patronage to someone whose professional dedication has recently been on impressive display. So please, a round of applause for the RGS's new patron, Prince Frederick."

Richard put a hand on his younger son's shoulder as he continued to wax proud. Freddie lapped up every word, unable to hide his delight, but all I saw was a mirage. Richard had taken oratorical pains to trace the patronage through the line of succession before skipping Nick—a slight the general public might not notice but Nick obviously would. What can look like a small twist of the knife often does the most harm; while Nick held it together admirably, it was the second time he'd been passed over for Freddie since our return, and I knew by the tension in his jaw that he felt the stab.

As the crowd thinned out, Nick took refuge in a corner of the viewing gallery. I joined him and we stared at the Millennium Wheel in the distance, framed by the last of the pink and purple sky.

"Do you think Father even remembers that my degree is in geography?" Nick asked.

"Probably not," I said.

He closed his eyes. "I've taken every assignment, every crap job, spent hours in the basement filing meaningless papers at Clarence House."

"You've been rock solid," I said. "It's just one patronage."

"It's puppeteering," Nick said. "He couldn't control me after the wedding, and it killed him, so he's finding a way now. By using Freddie." He rubbed the top of his head. "And people love it," he marveled. "That's the magic I apparently don't have. Freddie worked his way out of the doghouse in, what, two months? And I'm still on the leash."

I rubbed his back, trying to look as passively affectionate as possible while our faces were turned firmly away from any amateur lip-readers.

"So what can I do, love?" I asked. "What can we do?"

Nick picked at the railing. "I always knew, my whole life, how I fit in here," he said. "My role was defined for me. But then this all happened, and…" He let out a harsh breath through his nose. "Freddie is the reason Clive had anything to write at all, and somehow he's become the hero in this story, and I don't understand why. *I didn't do this.* I am so confused. I know how I'm *supposed* to fit in here, but do I, anymore? Did we go too far? Is there any coming back from this?"

I had wondered if I'd know a wobble when I saw one, but there was no mistaking it. Nick was metaphorically teetering on the edge of his future, as Eleanor had feared, and I didn't know if I should yank him back to her idea of solid ground or let him fall into whatever fantasy was playing in his mind and see if it caught him. I wanted to be the patient advisor I knew he needed, but if Nick was wobbling, how much of it was because my actions had pushed him to it?

Before I mustered a reply, I spotted a small barnyard animal floating toward us.

"Barnes, incoming, my three o'clock," I said, under my breath. "His toupee is *extra* tonight."

Richard's longtime secretary appeared at our elbows. "Follow me. Now."

His tone was deadly. A switch flipped in me and Nick, and we joined hands and followed Barnes to the staff elevator. His finger trembled as he punched the button for floor sixty-five, and the ten seconds felt like they swelled into ten minutes. When the doors sprang open, we saw a glass conference room with Richard and Freddie pacing white-faced near the windows.

"Go in," Barnes said, and he glided back into the elevator.

My mind raced as I tried to read their expressions. When the door clicked shut behind us, Richard punched a button on his cell phone and placed it in the middle of the table.

"I don't know what could be so important that you'd put me on hold, Dickie," came Agatha's bitter complaint.

"I was playing Maids and Milkmen," Edwin protested, and I assumed this was some weird British children's game that never made it to Iowa until I heard Elizabeth purr, "I'm here to collect your delivery, sir."

Richard appeared to fight the urge to spit bile into the phone, and instead said, "London Bridge may be falling."

Agatha's gasp was guttural. Freddie groped for a chair, while Nick swayed in place. They'd obviously been briefed on the code, though it didn't take a wizard to guess.

"She suffered a severe stroke," Richard said. "She is still with us, but her future is uncertain."

Nick and I had lived this moment once before, wringing ourselves out during four torturous hours in a car, only for it not to be true. Now that it was not a drill, I had no idea how to feel, other than empty. Nick, too, looked hollow, as if the first scare had drained him dry.

Richard drew his mouth into a thin line. "I've called the ministers here. Edwin, you'll need to come at once. No time to change." He paused. "Depending on what you're wearing. I cannot act as a Counsellor of State in this instance, so you and Frederick must be the two who make it official."

I took several shallow breaths. "Make what official?"

Richard looked at me with the closest thing to gentleness I've ever seen in his face. "We cannot be without a monarch," he said. "My mother is incapacitated. The power must be vested in me."

Night rolled over London. As we stood in history's limbo, the city beneath us blazed with its second life—the headlights of black cabs, the warm glow of bars and restaurants bustling with people, and the juxtaposition of mighty landmarks with the absurdly theatrical modern buildings that sit cheek by ancient jowl with them. One by one, three concerned-looking government ministers trundled in sporting a variety of evening wear, Edwin minutes behind them in a pair of overalls. And as I stared out at my adopted homeland, through a backlit window that showed me London through my own reflection, one by one they signed the document that heralded the dawn of Richard's regency.

And maybe of his reign.

CHAPTER NINE

Everything that happened before Eleanor's stroke felt like it existed in another universe—and in a way, I suppose it did. As soon as Richard's regency became official, Barnes alerted the BBC, and journalists countrywide—as half-drunk as the pints they ditched—fled the pubs to try to catch us on the way out of The Shard. Fortunately, we were long gone, hustled home in private cars so no newspaper could lead its coverage with tearstained royal faces. Grief is a normal human impulse, but a monarchy is not a normal human thing, and so its opacity had to remain in place.

The world, however, promptly lost its shit at the idea of Queen Eleanor being on death's gangplank. The news, ironically, achieved the one thing she had wanted most earlier in the summer, when she'd cried wolf: pushing speculation about me and Nick and Freddie onto the back burner. Reporters camped out in front of Buckingham Palace for the first two weeks and stayed there, reporting all day every day, as if they could tap straight into her IV drip.

But every single one of those reports said the same thing: The stroke had left the Queen in what the royal doctors called *a minimally conscious state*, so as to sound slightly more optimistic. The truth was a shade more dire: She had not shown any awareness, so even though six weeks hence she was still with us, they were no closer to knowing when or if she would come out of it. The longer Eleanor remained not dead, but neither wholly alive, the more everyone had been forced to ponder what a different world it would be without her. The country was littered with items that would need rebranding (for lack of a better word) when Richard took the throne for real, from cash to the postboxes with *ER* insignias on them to the pile of mail that arrived every day from well-wishers, covered in stamps bearing Eleanor's profile.

"I'm not remotely ready to be Prince of Wales for real," Nick confessed to me. "I thought we had years to go at our current level. I'd like to just worry about my grandmother, full stop, rather than boning up on all the logistics of what happens when she's gone. It's sickening."

He seemed to have thrown off the hurt feelings that had begun to boil over at The Shard, in favor of devoting himself to whatever duties the new family order demanded of him. Prince Dick's coronation was becoming less theoretical with every passing day, and he was out to remind everyone that Eleanor's direct descendants—all of them, no matter what mind games he'd been putting Nick through before—were solid. It was undoubtedly easier to build Nick back up in this regard if the woman who had allegedly cuckolded him receded from view, so Richard immediately put me on the back burner. As we got deeper into October, the *Daily Mail* wrote a piece complimenting Nick's stepped-up work schedule, and when I did the math, I realized he had caught up to Freddie's pace from earlier in the summer. This felt too specific on Nick's part to be coincidental, and as Freddie responded in kind, his stated resolve to introduce us to his new girlfriend had eroded. We had gotten nowhere. Sometimes in bed at night, Nick's words ran through my head on a loop: *Is there any coming back from this?*

But during the day, I shoved those thoughts aside and tried to focus on what I could control. Nick and I had made a decent dent in our house's clutter, but the overall vibe was still more Grey Gardens than I would have liked. The royal designer sent over plans and mood boards and swatches for the interior makeover, and when I couldn't take any more rugs and L-shaped sofas and chevron accent pillows, I wandered over to the backlog of Georgina articles that I'd bookmarked to try to understand why there was, at heart, so little out there to understand about her later years. I'd tracked down some detailed royal forums dedicated to everyone in The Firm, no matter how obscure. (I was particularly grateful to a librarian in Maryland called Roberta, who had digitized a lot of old newspaper articles during her downtime.) In the early '70s there was an outcry over Georgina's profligate travel spending, complete with photos of her in sunglasses and head scarves, laughing carelessly, like some that I'd seen in her living room. Hermès even named a handbag after her in 1980. But by the end of that decade, it had all just…stopped. She'd pop onto the balcony at royal occasions, always in the back, looking like someone else's edict demanded she be there. Some pieces speculated that Georgina's élan was snuffed out by heartbreak—she'd once caused a stir by telling a reporter at *Spy*, "Men are like the monarchy itself, aren't they? Splendid to look at, occasionally fun to have around, but cruel and pointless to the end"—but no one could agree whether it was the French politician, the dashing matador, the heart surgeon from Canada, or the Welsh toy boy she'd taken to Capri. Nobody, not even Roberta, could connect the dots between the lively life of the party and the lonely lady of the manor. One article even mentioned "quietude and spiritual reflection," as if The Firm had fed reporters that line directly. It reflected the way Nick's mother's condition had been recast as mere reclusiveness, with no further questions asked. But there was no evidence of any buried mental illness here; Georgina's eventual liver cancer did lend credence to the supposition that she'd retreated because her wild life had worn her out and then turned on her, but that theory rang a little hollow to me. Better answers had to be in Apartment 1A somewhere.

I longed to discuss this with Nick, but if he wasn't out glad-handing people for photo ops, he was in endless meetings planning the next few. It was the worst of times, yet The Firm had closed ranks and left me on the outside; our home life was in stasis with no end in sight, and I was loath to speak up in case this was construed as making the Queen's ill health about me. But I couldn't even escape to blow off steam with my friends without it turning into a whole security production. My boredom burgeoned until one day I did get so fed up that I yanked on a floppy hat and sunglasses and snuck out the back gate onto the high street, just to *do* it. My blood was fizzing from the adrenaline. But then a busload of camera-clicking tourists near Royal Albert Hall spooked me, and I'd ducked into the gardens and hidden in a shrub, calling Cilla in a panic to rescue me. I felt ridiculous and embarrassed and *trapped*.

"Ugh, I'm sorry I pulled you away from your job for this," I said once we'd settled down with some snacks back at Apartment 1A. "I was starting to feel like a recluse myself, but I may have overcompensated."

"Believe me, I'm thrilled to be called away for an emergency that involves tea." She tore open a scone. "I'm up to my ears in Dutch state dinner minutiae."

"Do you need an intern? Because I would love to have useful face-to-face conversations with someone, *anyone*, that don't involve whether to turn one corner of the living room into its own walled-off office."

"You should not," Cilla said. "You have too many rooms as it is. Besides, it's your reception room. It has to be grand."

I blinked. "When you put it that way," I said, shoving the renovation binder away. "This stuff is making my eyes cross. Should we paint the hallways Clotted Cream, or Cream Cheese, or Double Cream? They look the same to me, but what if Nick has strong feelings about cream?"

"Only Gaz has strong feelings about cream."

"Or the kitchen. Twisted Goldenrod? Sunshine Martinet?"

She looked taken aback. "Isn't a martinet a torture device?"

"In more ways than one," I grumbled. "These are not real problems. Intellectually I know this. It'd be better if Richard would let me help with family business."

"Small problems can still feel big," she said. "Nick's schedule will slow down in due time, and then you can sort out together what your public role will be. It hasn't even been two months since the Queen's stroke, has it? One of my mother's cousins stole a hat from her sister, and they didn't speak for thirty years. This is nothing."

"Did they eventually make up?" I asked.

"In a sense. One of them died." Cilla peered at the table. "Go with the Sunshine Martinet."

We spent the rest of the afternoon chuckling at paint names, designating bedrooms for my mother and Lacey for when they came to stay, and agreeing that Nick and I should overhaul our own room last so that we could move into suitably modernized guest quarters while it was being put together. With a squeeze and a promise to make dinner plans for the four of us soon, I saw Cilla off at the front door with a happy smile. But as her little car disappeared past the clock tower, her absence hit me sharply, and I realized what I felt was homesickness. Even though I was, technically, at home. I felt so much like myself with Cilla—the Bex Porter of old, a person I knew well, and whose goals and dreams and agenda were not dictated by anyone but herself.

So I called in another old friend: Margot.

I'd made it out of the palace gates once, and it was only my own skittishness that put an end to the mischief. Maybe Margot could go even farther. Her wig and her mole and her retro sunglasses and frumpy taste might be my ticket out of the lavish prison in which I'd found myself, so I boldly signed off on some paint colors and then dug out Margot's hair for some restorative fluffing. There was so much I wanted to do—the Magritte exhibit at the Tate Modern, a stroll through Apsley House to ogle all the Duke of Wellington's expensive stuff, which appealed now that I was living in the home of another person who never threw anything out—but I knew I needed my first attempt to be something simpler. Very basic, very uncool, very much a place where nobody would give me a second glance.

I needed a McDonald's.

Once, when we first started dating, Nick had shown me a door in his and Freddie's quarters that connected to the Kensington Palace museum. Emma used to sneak the kids in there at night and they'd explore; he'd never taken me through it, but I knew it would put me out somewhere near the downstairs public bathrooms. I waited until Freddie's car left his apartment the next morning, and I let myself into Nick's old place with my key. The passage was just off a little-used billiard room at the far end of the flat, looking like nothing more than a bookcase. Nick had told me that pulling out *Martin Chuzzlewit* and Jackie Collins's *Lucky* would reveal it, so I ran my finger over the shelves until I found them both, took a deep breath, and slid them toward me. I heard a click, and saw a subtle release. Success.

I pushed it open to reveal a dark hallway—with a functioning nightlight; apparently even the secret passageways were attended to scrupulously by the staff—and then another door, which let me into a janitorial closet. I slipped into the museum from there and pretended to "discover" that the women's room was across the hall. Nobody was there to see my acting job, so I simply strolled in, washed my hands, smoothed my wig, and then walked right out toward the foyer. Any nearby tourists were all too busy consulting their maps of the palace, or turning over souvenir mugs in their hands, to pay me any mind. (I couldn't help but notice that the gift shop's stock of teacups honoring our wedding had been deeply discounted.) I feigned an interest in some aprons, and then set out into the park, pulling up the collar of my wool coat against the brisk October air.

It was sunny, but crisp; a breeze ruffled what was left on the trees and convinced several leaves to give up the ghost. I strolled toward the high street, then headed into the McDonald's and ordered an Egg McMuffin and a hash brown. The teller looked at me very curiously, and as my heart leapt into my throat, she pointed up at the clock.

"Sorry, love," she said. "We've stopped serving breakfast."

"Oh," I said, nearly forgetting to put on my accent, and sliding into a compromise that sounded vaguely Australian. Okay, then. Margot was from Down Under now. "Right, sorry, lost the plot there. Jet lag. One Big Mac meal, please, mate. Er, g'day."

The woman didn't even look up again; she just took the bill I handed her, my grandmother-in-law glaring officiously up at me from one side. *Oh, hush*, I thought, before guiltily remembering she was hooked up to a heart monitor.

I polished off my burger at a table by the window, pleasing myself with people-watching, and eavesdropping on the patrons who came and went around me. One was discussing Aston Villa's football fortunes; another wanted to write an angry letter to the entire England cricket squad. A mother-daughter duo spoke French to each other and pointed in the general vicinity of the palace, then asked me for directions. I jotted some down on a napkin in a blocky imitation of Cilla's half-capitalized, half-lowercase script.

"*Merci,*" the mother said. "Me, I don't care, but Giselle is hoping the prince will notice her if she walks past the windows."

"You mean Frederick?" I asked, feigning uncertainty.

"No, the other," the mom said dismissively. "The one married to that American whore. Giselle gives them two more months at most."

They packed up and left, and I tried not to laugh into the remaining sliver of my Big Mac. Giselle's mother had no idea she was speaking to the American whore in question. Margot had pulled it off. Margot was *feeling it.*

An hour later, high on my own supply, I'd bought a hideous, scratchy sweater for almost nothing at H&M, picked up croissants at a bakery for next morning's breakfast, tried some free samples at Boots, and pressed my luck by reading a paper out in the open that had an actual photo of me on it. I could have stayed out all day, but the sheer number of smartphones and swelling scrums of shoppers started to make me jumpy, so I decided to count my blessings and go home. This plan fell apart when I realized that I hadn't thought about how I was going to get back inside the palace, but I'd practically brought enough cash to bail myself out of jail, so I bought a ticket like everyone else and skulked back past the gift shop with its crimson signs marked ROYAL WEDDING SOUVENIRS: CLEARANCE SALE, 80% OFF.

I hesitated, then picked up my phone and sent a quick selfie to Lacey. I'm on a field trip, I texted. Then I slid my phone back into my pocket and nonchalantly bought a mug with my own face on it. My phone buzzed as I was heading back out to the bathrooms.

YOU REBEL, Lacey had replied.

The corridor near the bathrooms was busier now. But I couldn't bail and reenter through our main gate, because I'd have to reveal myself—to the guards, and possibly also to the paparazzi that lingered nearby, if not directly outside—and Margot would be exposed. So I hovered near the water fountain until there was a mild slowdown in bathroom traffic, then muttered, "TP empty in stall three—I'm on it" into my collar like some kind of custodial spy, and slipped into the cleaning closet. The next step was more complicated: All Nick had told me about getting back into their apartments was that they'd pulled the fire alarm, which now that I was supposed to do it seemed absurd and also like a felony. Wildly, I looked around the room, clocking the stock of toilet paper and hand sanitizer and the fire alarm itself, plus some mops and buckets and a fire alarm, and…aha, two fire alarms. One by the door, and the other poking out from behind a tall set of metal shelves. It looked substantially older and the plastic around it was cracked, but artfully so, as if to give the impression it was defunct. I could hear voices in the hallway getting nearer, so I took a deep breath, lifted the plastic casing, and pulled.

The door back to Freddie's place sprang open. Biting back a triumphant whoop, I scrambled through and pulled it closed, running back through the tunnel and tumbling out the other side as an elated giggle escaped my lips. I'd done it.

"That's quite a getup you're sporting, Killer."

My giggle turned to a comically deep gasp. "Shit, Freddie, you scared me."

"*I* scared *you*?" he said, leaning his billiard cue against the wall. "Imagine how I felt, coming in for a peaceful game of snooker, only to have a strange blonde fall through my wall."

Sheepishly, I pulled off the wig. "It was an experiment."

"The hair, or the passage?" he asked.

"Both," I said. "This will sound stupid to you, given everything that's happening with Eleanor, but I got sick of staring at fabric samples so I decided to—"

"You don't have to justify it to me," Freddie said. "I used to give my PPOs the slip all the time. I strolled right into that card company you worked for, remember?"

"I do. Because it was the same day Lacey and I led the paparazzi on a wild-goose chase, and Nick got so mad at us for it." I pursed my lips. "He might not be very happy that I went rogue here, either."

"Then don't tell him," Freddie said.

"Keeping secrets from him hasn't worked out that well for us so far," I said.

Freddie picked up his cue and chalked the tip thoughtfully. "You're assuming all secrets are morally equivalent," he said.

"I'm just trying to think like your brother."

"Think like yourself," he said. "If you need to tell him, tell him. But no one got hurt. You needed to feel normal for one second. He understands how that feels. I know I do."

I rubbed the felt on the table. It was pilling. "Everyone else has real responsibilities right now and I'm spinning my wheels. I feel really fucking useless."

He scratched his chin. "Frankly I'm a bit cross I didn't think of doing your trick here myself. Or at least sneaking in a strange blonde or three that way."

"Oh, please, all your strange blondes come in the front," I said.

He smirked.

"*Ew*, that is not what I meant," I said, but I was laughing.

He gave me a more complete once-over. "Speaking of, is this what passes for role play in your house, Killer? You look like Mrs. Doubtfire's niece."

We laughed even harder, and I was overcome with the sensation of having something returned to me, or finding the last missing piece of a jigsaw I'd been doing for weeks.

"I miss you," I blurted out.

Freddie didn't react; he just handed me his snooker cue. "Break?"

"I don't know how to play."

"Easily fixed." Freddie began lining up the red balls in the triangular rack. "Knickers might not like this, either, you know."

"He ought to be past that by now. We all should," I announced boldly. "I want my friend back. And I want to meet your girlfriend."

Freddie pulled a pink ball out of the corner pocket and spun it in his palm before gently setting it on a dot on the felt. "About that," he said. "She's not in the picture anymore." He scooped up other balls and laid them out in their designated spots. "It would seem that dating the third in line to the throne, or the second, or whatever I am right now, is not very appealing to a person who's trying a case against ISIS at the UN next week."

"She broke up with you?"

He nodded ruefully. "Didn't want the publicity," he said. "She told me she'd worked too hard for this job to gamble it on me. Said nobody at work would respect her anymore."

I whistled low and long. "Damn. She didn't exactly let you down easy."

"It seems I am drawn to women who don't pull their punches," Freddie said.

I took the cube of chalk and rubbed it on the tip of my cue. "I'm sorry, Freddie. You seemed to like her."

"I did," he said. "She kept me on my toes. She was brilliant. I liked the idea that maybe, in the view of a person like that, I was worth being with."

"You are," I said. "Of course you are."

"Not to her, apparently," he said, and the sadness gnawing at the edges of his tone also ate away at me.

"Well, she's just one person," I said. "We are not giving up."

"We?" he laughed. "Thanks for the support, Killer, but I'd better sort out my sex life on my own this time." He paused. "I suppose it's too soon to make jokes like that."

"Probably," I said. "But you can have that one for free."

He grinned, and straightened. "Right," he said. "As long as we're in the cone of silence, let me confess that I haven't ever properly learnt how to play this bloody game and I don't understand why they show so much of it on the telly. I was only coming in here earlier because there is a stash of excellent brandy in the bar that Father forgot he left here, and I like to save it for special occasions. Like being dumped."

A bolt of tension passed through us as I wondered, without wanting to, whether he'd come in here on another night, looking for that same brandy.

"I suppose I have you to thank in a way," he added, aiming for lightness. "I never took women or dating particularly seriously before, but I've realized that I want to, and I can." He gave me a tentative smile. "Can we drink to that?"

I glanced at my watch. "It's happy hour somewhere, as they say."

"I'll pour the hooch if you'll Google the snooker rules."

As he turned toward the liquor cabinet, I wrestled my conscience. Deep down I knew that Nick *wouldn't* love this. But Freddie and I weren't the same people we had been that night in my Chelsea flat. He'd found the beginnings of love elsewhere, however briefly, and Nick and I had formed a united front in Scotland. And none of us could hide from each other forever. We had no chance at fixing this if one of us didn't make the first move. With any luck, Nick would understand if that person was me.

CHAPTER TEN

Good morning, Rebecca."

To my great surprise, Agatha—who'd never had much time for me in the past—appeared and perched next to me on a tufted bench outside the locked Chinese Dining Room. As if she were practicing a new social interaction, she patted me awkwardly on the hand.

"How are you getting on with it all?" she said.

Nick's often-persnickety aunt was an inveterate whiner and hand wringer—the outmoded primogeniture laws that passed the throne through her to Richard had bred in Agatha a bone-deep sense that she was always being wronged—and she had doubted me from the start. This, in fact, might have been the first time she initiated a conversation with me.

"We're muddling through," I said. "It's so surreal. I thought she'd be around forever. She's still relatively young."

"Still young?" Agatha blinked. "My dear, you do know that she's dead?"

"Wait," I said, a numbness rolling over me like a cloud. "*Who's* dead?"

"Auntie Georgina," Agatha said. "What did you think, that we hid her in the attic?"

I tipped back my head in relief and grabbed her arm instinctively. "You scared me for a second," I said. "I thought you were referring to the whole Eleanor...situation."

Agatha disentangled her arm with a curl of the lip. "Obviously *that* situation is horrible," she said. "I was merely making polite conversation about your redecorating." She looked around as if hoping for someone to save her. "I assume Georgina's collection is as robust as I remember."

"It is. Maybe even more so," I said. "Were you two close?"

"I was the only one in this family Georgina liked," Agatha announced. "She often went on about how unfair it was that Mummy didn't get primogeniture sorted so that I would be Queen. It infuriated her, actually." Agatha glowed a bit at the memory. "I felt very seen by my auntie for much of her life. Until she stopped seeing any of us at all, anyway."

"Why did she shut herself off?" I asked. "Did she ever tell you?"

Agatha stared up at the ceiling for a moment. "It would have been rude to ask," she said. "Georgina was a capricious woman, so I rather thought that it was just a phase. Perhaps it would have been, but then she got sick." She looked sad. "I was the only person she'd still speak to on the phone, but it was very one-sided. She only wanted to tell the same stories about her boyfriends, and which of them adored her the most. I couldn't get a word in about Nigel. I doubt she even knew his name."

Barnes rounded the corner with a ring of keys in his hand. "And that's enough of that," Agatha said, standing and brushing off her skirt. "No sense in dwelling on the past with so much happening in the present."

At long last, Richard had been forced to include me at a Conclave, and I had the Dutch to thank: My participation in December's state dinner was critical, and he could no longer ice me out for sport. He was begrudging about it, making a big show of thanking Barnes for the extra effort required to make a sixth dossier, but it counted.

Eleanor had put this event on the docket the day after our wedding to, as Richard often reminded us, "wash out the stain from that debacle as quickly as possible." They'd concocted a barely plausible historical hook—an anniversary of a tulip that was named after William of Orange, the Dutch English king who, in the manner of so many of Nick's male relatives, died after his horse tripped in a mole hole.

The truth was much simpler: The Dutch wouldn't make this hard. King Hendrik-Alexander and Queen Lucretia—the press whimsically referred to them as Hax and Lax, and therefore so did everyone else— were low pressure, congenial, and happy to do Eleanor a solid during her time of PR need. And Prince Dick had been waiting to take the reins for a lifetime, so he refused to cancel this, regardless of whether anyone felt weird about ceremonial folderol while the monarch lay unconscious.

He opened the Conclave by distributing to each of us a ream of papers so thick, the staple barely poked through the other side.

"It is imperative that this go off without a hitch," he said. "The public and the press need to be confident that the changeover will be seamless, if indeed any permanent transfer of power is en route."

Only Richard would call death a "permanent transfer of power." I took a bite of my scone instead of my tongue, and resisted the urge to spit it out; it was awful, just as Freddie had always complained. I met his eyes across the table. His expression said, *I told you so.*

"May I ask a question?" I said, half raising my hand. "What exactly happens at a state dinner?"

Richard regarded me like a very stupid child. "Dinner happens," he said.

"And tiaras happen," said Lady Elizabeth. She had gone from "fill-ing in for Edwin" to "taking Edwin's place," to the relief of everyone (including Edwin).

"On that topic, the public always laps up pageantry, and we could use some favorable, frivolous press," Richard said. "Accordingly, Rebecca, we'll be loaning you the Lover's Knot tiara."

The Lover's Knot was famously Emma's. She'd worn it in her official portrait, so even though her illness meant she hadn't donned it herself in a quarter century, the public had seen it about a million times in the papers and on racks of cheap postcards. It was her most iconic accessory as the Princess of Wales.

"Dickie, don't you think that's extreme?" Agatha said. "You don't even like her!"

"She's sitting *right here*," Nick said.

"I don't have to like her to see the symbolism," Richard said. "She will ascend to Emma's position someday. This will be viewed as a clear endorsement."

I put a steadying hand on Nick's leg. "I will try to do it justice."

"I think it's a very smart move, Father," Freddie piped up.

Nick made a noise next to me that was not useful. I flicked his thigh.

"As the de facto heir, Nicholas will handle certain ceremonial duties that once fell to me, such as walking the Dutch king through the morning inspection at Horse Guards," Richard barreled on. "He will then ride over with Queen Lucretia." He looked at his notes. "Frederick, you'll be escorting Princess Daphne."

Freddie made a face. "But she's so boring," he said.

"She's just shy," Nick said.

"Is she the one who got kidnapped?" Elizabeth asked.

"You'd think a person who got kidnapped might be more interesting," Freddie said.

"Have a heart," Nick said. "She was trapped in a car for six hours while held at knifepoint."

"It was only a speed-skate blade," Freddie protested.

"*You* try to tell the difference with a blindfold on," Nick snapped back.

"Wouldn't I be of more use with the queen?" Freddie pushed. "She and I know each other better than she knows Nick. We had a very long chat at his rehearsal dinner."

"I could go with Daphne," I suggested. "It'll look good for Freddie and Nick to be working together. And if she's so shy, I might be less...intimidating to her than Freddie, right off the bat."

Richard drummed his fingers on the meeting's sixty-seven-page agenda. I felt my phone buzz in my lap and snuck a look. It was Freddie.

Intimidating?!!

I'm trying to help, I pecked back.

"That would be acceptable," Richard concluded. "Frederick, you will therefore escort her at dinner, where you will be charming and courteous. Unintimidatingly." He waited a beat. "Daphne is an important assignment. She is the crown princess, after all. The catch of Europe, some might say."

Freddie raised an eyebrow. As Richard moved on to other logistical details, my phone buzzed again.

Is my father pimping me out?

I grinned and looked up at Freddie, who smirked back at me.

"Bex?" Nick said. My head swung over to find that he and Richard were waiting on me to say something. "You can do that, yes?"

"Um, of course," I said. "I'd love to."

"Did you even hear what I said?" Richard looked cross.

"Yesssss," I said unconvincingly, hoping I hadn't just agreed to sing the Dutch national anthem in their native tongue.

"Bex will schedule the tiara test," Nick said smoothly, but I didn't miss that his glance darted between me and Freddie.

Richard turned back to his pile of papers, but I had been addressed directly, and I decided I shouldn't miss my chance. "Is there anything else I can do to help?" I asked.

His lips curled coldly. "How are you at napkin folding?"

"I meant...in general. During this horrible time," I said. Nothing. "I am proud to be part of your family, and I'd really like to help shoulder the load." Silence. Agatha cleared her throat. "Anyway...keep me in mind, I guess, if it would make anything easier for...anyone."

"It would certainly be the first time." Richard pointedly turned the page on his packet. The staple immediately came out with it and flew across the room. He looked pained. "Now, let us start with a brief primer on the dignitaries in attendance..."

"That was sweet, dear," Elizabeth murmured, looking as if she felt sorry for me.

Nick pressed his thigh to mine. "I'll see what I can do," he whispered under Richard's droning.

And when he got home, much later that night, I was waiting for him on the stairs, wearing nothing but the Lyons Emerald and a diaphanous robe.

"*Hello.* To what do I owe the honor?" he asked, bemused.

"Yourself," I said. "And your hot, hot awesomeness."

He dropped everything he'd been holding and pawed at the knot in his tie. "This cannot be just because I'm full of irresistible trivia about clogs now."

"That's part of it," I said. "But I also got a phone call this afternoon from Marj. I'm off the bench. And I am . . ." I tugged at the belt on my robe. ". . . *really* happy about it."

Richard had tasked Nick and Freddie and me with unveiling a new portrait of Eleanor—well, technically, an old portrait of a young Eleanor—that had been donated to the National Portrait Gallery by the dead artist's family. Apropos to my warm welcome, the painting in question had once been considered scandalous: Eleanor, my age but already a mother of three, was seated with her back to the viewer, wearing a strapless gown partially unzipped and shooting what could only be called a come-hither gaze over her shoulder. She'd commissioned it for her husband, but it had hung in his dressing room for merely a month before his untimely death—at which point Eleanor shipped it back to the artist with a letter blessing him to do with it what he chose. He'd plonked it over his own dining room table until he died, and then when Eleanor had her stroke, his family decided it had a higher calling. I was thrilled, both to be part of its public debut and to have something to do that didn't involve wallpaper samples.

"The prince feels your presence will draw a direct line between Eleanor and your position as the future queen," Marj had said when she called.

"Interesting," I said. "Considering he's been openly hostile to the concept of me as queen ever since I've known him."

Marj coughed lightly. "Far be it from me to question the prince's reasoning," she said. "But I suppose I did hear him discussing the event with Nicholas, and the duke used, shall we say, strong tones when they talked about whether or not you ought to be present."

Bless my beautiful husband, who had now given up on his tie in favor of trying to kick off his tightly laced oxfords.

"I can't believe you turned the tide in one afternoon," I said. "You work fast."

His second shoe flew across the foyer and hit a table. "You would know," he purred. Then he paused. "Wait, I think I just insulted myself."

"Think of it as sexual efficiency." I dropped the robe. "It means we can fit in twice as much in the same amount of time."

"Goodness," he said, yanking anew at his tie. "If I'd known it meant this much to you, I'd have talked to Father ages ago, and why the bloody hell is this knot refusing to come undone?"

"Leave it on," I said, slinking over and tearing open his dress shirt. "It's not in the way."

We fell together ravenously, rolling around on the marble floor, laughing about what a horrible idea it is to have sex on a marble floor, and then adjourning to defile the living room furniture (though we only made it as far as the carpet). At one point we knocked a small wooden dog off a table and onto Nick's back. He paused long enough to retrieve it, and then tenderly sat it down on top of my chest.

"Listen, Spot," he said. "Sometimes, when two people love each other very much..."

We burst out laughing, which turned into kissing, which meant poor Spot got the heave. It was the most in tune we'd been in weeks; such a small, perfect moment, one that I knew even then to hold close to my heart for the times when everything around us would get darker.

Once we were actually at the gallery, face-to-sultry-face with the portrait, I wondered if it had yielded the same result for Eleanor— a happy surprise, and a memory she later could carry through the coldness of grief.

"Crikey," Nick said, as he studied it. "That's...suggestive."

"It seems so unlike her," I said. "Do you think she'd care that people will see her like this?"

"I suppose if she objected, she wouldn't have told him he had free rein with it," Nick said. "She's got a keen eye. She must have known it was *that* good."

It was. Eleanor's face was young and vulnerable and seductive, and this was the first time I'd seen her captured as a real woman and not a supercilious figurehead. It was hard to reconcile it with either the imperious woman I knew or the shy, almost fretful girl of her sister's photographs, with the weight of a nation beginning to press on her shoulders. I also couldn't imagine how that girl had grown into the kind of passionate adult who'd give something this intimate. The part of Eleanor that had set this mood must have wanted it on the record that she'd existed this way at all.

"You forget that people lived entire lifetimes before you existed," Nick mused. "It must have been hard for her when he died. They hadn't been married very long."

"Long enough for three whole babies," Freddie said, bounding into the hallway.

"Thanks for finally joining us," Nick said.

"I'm not late. I'm ninety seconds early," he huffed. "In any case, blame Father. We were having lunch, just to catch up, and it went long." Freddie straightened proudly. "He's sending me to Portsmouth later this month for a thing with the Navy."

Nick looked confused. "I thought I was going."

"Father felt it only fair, since I'm the one still *in* the Navy."

"Certainly," Nick said. "I'm extremely busy anyway. Did Father mention that he's giving me the patronage of the Imperial War Museums?"

"No," Freddie said evenly. "We've been too busy discussing how I'm taking over the British Society for Early Childhood Development."

"That's a big one," Nick said pleasantly. "Bex and I are being given Pediatric Blindness. Maybe we can collaborate on something."

"Maybe," Freddie said. "I'm going to be rather occupied with Children's Anemia but perhaps we can work Blindness in."

"That'd be fantastic, assuming our Lyme Disease schedule allows," Nick said.

"Anything for the children," Freddie responded.

"You're both being ridiculous," I said.

Freddie scrunched his face up, as if I'd asked him to do high-level calculus on the fly.

"We were just having a conversation, weren't we, Knickers?" His phone buzzed and he fished it out and brightened. "I've got to take this. One second."

As he stepped away, I turned to Nick. "Our Lyme Disease schedule?"

"It was just—"

"Do *not* say it was just a conversation, because we both know that's bullshit."

His cheeks reddened, and he cast a furtive glance at Freddie's back. "I've been working myself ragged trying to do right by my place in this family, and still there was a headline a few days back that said Freddie has been the real champion this year," he said softly.

"So? You're always telling me that stuff is meaningless."

"Well, I saw it and thought, *Right, then, I'll piss off again if that's how you want it*," Nick said. "I cannot believe he's come out of a scandal *he* caused looking so fucking golden." He again looked over at his brother, who was plugging one ear while carrying on a conversation. "I used to want our old relationship back. But right now, what I want more than that is to make the public see what it's got in me." He looked up at me, eyes blazing. "And sometimes, I want Freddie to shove it."

I told you so, Eleanor's voice said in my head.

Before I could respond, a tall man with dramatic eyebrows scuttled into the hallway. "We're ready to start," he said. "Is everyone prepared?"

Freddie hurriedly ended his phone call. "All set," he said.

"Do you need to practice with the tiny curtain, Your Highness?" the man asked Freddie. "My notes here say that you're to pull the cord."

"I've gotten very adept at these, thanks," Freddie said.

"I've been looking forward to this," Nick said. "The painting is really beautiful."

"I started a terrific biography of this artist," Freddie added.

"I finished that biography last night," Nick noted.

"Yeah, well I *wrote* that biography, so I win," I said.

Nick and Freddie turned to me, startled, as if they'd already forgotten I was there, whereas Eyebrows knotted his and appeared to be considering correcting me on that point. "Shall we perhaps get started?" he asked instead.

I smiled wide. "Yes, we are definitely done here," I said. "Lead the way."

⁂

"He did *what*?" Lacey stopped rummaging inside her suitcase, her mouth falling open.

"I couldn't believe it, either," I said, flopping down on her bed. "The dude specifically said Freddie was opening the curtain, but when the time came, Nick charged on over and pulled." I buried my face in my hands. "Petty Curtain Shenanigans is a band name, not a lifestyle."

Lacey chortled, her laugh echoing through Guest Room Number Four—the one with the best Wi-Fi signal, but also the ugliest bedspread. "That is some passive-aggressive shit right there from Nick," she said. "It's almost aggressive-aggressive. Did Freddie freak out?"

"He just acted like it was always in the plan, and then backstage he said he had a date and left," I said. "Nick swore it was a brain fart, but I don't believe it."

Lacey curled up on the bed and propped her head up in her hand. "A brain fart seems very unlike him, but so are petty curtain shenanigans," she said. "Have you talked to him about it?"

I rolled onto my back and stared up at the ceiling, which featured an incongruous fresco that would have looked more at home in an Italian villa. "He told me that sometimes he wants Freddie to, and this is a direct quote, *shove it*."

Lacey made the universal *yikes* face.

"I know," I said. "And he's so laser focused on getting back into everybody's good graces that he's hardly ever home."

Lacey started to braid a chunk of my hair, the way she often did when we were sitting around sharing confidences like this. She was back from Kenya for a visit pinned to our birthday, and although I'd done a sterling job convincing myself the long distance had been no big deal, I had nearly cried with relief when she climbed out of the Range Rover.

"It's really good to see you," I said. My voice sounded shaky. "Sometimes I feel disloyal dragging Cilla or Bea into all this, because they were Nick's friends first. And obviously I can't go to Freddie."

"Yes, you've been down that road before," Lacey said. "You need healthy boundaries there."

"We're always going to be close," I said defensively. "We can't pretend for the rest of our lives that we're only mild acquaintances."

Lacey lifted her hands as if to surrender. "I'm just saying, you and Nick know better than anyone that sometimes space is what you need to move on."

"Nick and I took some space and it backfired," I reminded her.

"You and Nick ran off and pretended to be different people. It's not the same thing," Lacey said.

"Since when are you all wise and measured?"

"Since *I* took some space to move on," she said. She visibly bit back a dreamy smile, and I peered so intently at her that a flush ran up her face.

"Aha," I said, whacking her arm. "The esteemed Dr. Oliver Omundi, I presume? When did that officially happen?"

"A while ago. I didn't say anything because I got funny about jinxing it, which is how I knew it was real," she said happily. "He's the smartest, kindest person. I like him so much that it's terrifying, because my internship is ending soon, but I'm also calm? Like I trust what we have already." She absentmindedly began braiding my hair. "I never felt like that with Freddie. I wish I could go back and tell myself that wasn't real love. It would've saved a lot of aggravation."

"Have Dr. Omundi apply his brains to time travel," I said. "It's the least you could do, considering."

Lacey pinched me, and I shrieked. "Serves you right," she said.

"Oh no, what's Bex done now?" Nick said, sticking his head in the room.

We turned to face him. He had just come back from a senior citizens fitness event, and he looked sweaty in his charity-branded polo shirt. It was surprisingly appealing.

"The usual," Lacey said. "Incurable smart-assery."

"Tell me all about it," he said, stretching out across the foot of the bed. Within seconds a deafening snore emanated from his face.

"That has to be a speed record," Lacey said quietly. "No wonder you guys haven't talked much."

"I told you."

"All this to benefit a man they call Prince Dick," Lacey marveled.

"I can't figure it out," I said. "It's like watching a knight joust for a damsel he doesn't actually like."

I had been hoping a night at home with our friends would help put things back to normal. Nick and Freddie had continued throwing themselves into their duties as if they had something to prove—to Richard, to themselves, to each other—but lately Nick had been edging ahead in this MVP race nobody seemed to care about but them. I only saw him when he was rolling out of bed at 5:00 a.m. to shower, put on a blue suit, kiss me, and leave, and then again when he got back from the far end of wherever at 11:00 p.m. to take off his blue suit, shower, kiss me, and pass out.

Lacey poked Nick's arm with her toe. He didn't move. "Should we let him sleep?"

"Might as well," I said as the doorbell rang, a harsh, tolling noise that reminded me of BBC shows set in wartime. "If he's that tired, he'll face-plant into Gaz's cake, and *that* will end in tears."

Gaz had failed the auditions for the latest season of *Ready, Set, Bake*, and while he was devastated, he was not daunted. When I opened the front door, he and Cilla were red-faced and holding a board between them on which sat a birthday cake befitting a wedding.

"He's bent on getting on this bloody show," Cilla grumbled.

"Five...different...tiers," Gaz panted as they shuffled carefully into the living room and slowly, painstakingly, slid it onto the coffee table. He breathed out hard as Cilla grabbed her back.

"I am now off the clock, Garamond," she declared.

Gaz nodded, frowning intently at his creation. "Hello, Lacey, you look marvelous, happy birthday, does this cake seem uneven to you?"

"If you could give us ten minutes before you start yammering on about your cakes, that would be ideal," Cilla said, hugging Lacey herself.

"I said she looked marvelous, which she does," Gaz protested.

Lady Bollocks swept into the room. Gemma Sands was close behind her looking unusually chic for an adult who was dressed like a schoolgirl.

"You left the door wide open, Rebecca. You cannot run this place like a barn," Bea said, dropping her handbag on the sofa. She eye-balled the cake with skepticism. "Did someone get married without telling me?"

"Hello to you, too," I said.

"You're too tan, Lacey," Bea added. "Hasn't anyone taught you about sun damage?"

"Yes, but she's been working her bum off. Best impulse hire I've ever made," said Gemma. "You should hear Olly talk about her. I'd assume he was in love, if he weren't gay as a balloon."

Cilla, who had grabbed a *Tatler* with Nick's friend Annabelle Farthing on the cover—the headline: THIRTY TASTIEST TOFFS UNDER 30—dropped it back on the table and crossed her arms with interest.

Lacey fumbled the bottle of gin she was opening. "He's what? He never...I don't think—"

"Gotcha," Gemma said, grinning. "I knew something was going on there. Happy birthday, you two. Ooooh, is that Annabelle's *Tatler*? I re-member when she and Nick got caught trying to take a bath together. It was very scandalous for the primary school set. Where is he, anyway?"

"Napping," I said. "He'll wander down eventually."

Bea made one of her usual noises of disapproval, then took off her winter-white wool coat and held it out into the air expectantly. "I waited an absolute eternity in the foyer for my hostess to fetch this," she said.

"It was at most two minutes, darling," Gemma said.

"Two, ten, thirty, it's all the same in the art of etiquette," Bea said. "I've told you a thousand times, Rebecca, if you insist on not having a live-in staff, then you're meant to be collecting people's coats and hats at the door."

"No one wears hats anymore," I grumbled, but I took her coat anyway. Bea was very good at being Bea. No one ever really told her no. I begrudgingly headed to the coat closet and ran smack into Freddie.

"I see Bea's put you to work," he said, shrugging off his dark blue wool overcoat and handing it to me. "And at your own birthday party. Shocking."

"Are your arms broken? Hang it up yourself."

"Sassy as ever, Killer," he said, but he reclaimed his coat and took Bea's in the bargain.

"Someone's got to keep you in line," I said. "How are you?"

"Better than Knickers, I assume," he said. "He's been busy."

"You know how these things go," I hedged.

"Yes, ebb and flow, and all that," Freddie said, not making eye contact with me. "I'm in a bit of an ebb at the moment. Never been broken up with this much in my life."

"Was this the...physicist?"

"No. *She* dumped me because she said she was getting back together with her ex-boyfriend. This one was a research scientist for a cancer lab," he said. "Really interesting stuff. I brought her a sandwich at her flat while she was collating some data, and asked a few questions, and she kicked me out for being 'too distracting.'" He made the air quotes with a frown. "I thought it was a sexy compliment, but then she ended it because she didn't think our lifestyles would mesh. She didn't even give my lifestyle a chance."

"You at least should've gotten points for the sandwich."

Freddie's gesture said, *I know, right?*

"Chin up," I said. "It's a cliché, but the right person will turn up eventually. You'll find your place."

We paused next to each other in the doorway that led into the living room. Someone had lit a fire in the hearth. Gaz was using a level to check the tiers of the cake for evenness and taking notes in a Moleskine notebook. Across the room, the four ladies were huddled around Lacey's phone.

"Is this your boyfriend?" Cilla asked. "Well done."

"I heard that," Gaz bellowed from across the room.

"He's *objectively handsome*," Cilla called back at him. Gaz huffed in the general direction of the cake.

"Watch out, you'll blow it over," Freddie called out.

"I'm not the Big Bad Wolf," Gaz said.

"It looks precarious," Freddie insisted. "You need to work on your structural integrity."

Gaz told Freddie in very strong terms what he could do with his structural integrity, and Freddie turned to me and yanked on my ponytail. "Still glad this is *your* place, considering this unseemly lot?"

"Damn right," I said. We exchanged uncomplicated smiles, and impulsively I wrapped my arm around his chest and hugged him. "It feels like home when you're all here."

Freddie rested his chin on the top of my head. "It does, rather, doesn't it?"

"Indeed," said a voice, and we swiveled around to see Nick, a red mark on half of his face and his hair sticking up on that side.

"Welcome, Sleeping Beauty," Freddie observed, his arm around my shoulder.

"I hope I'm not crashing the party," Nick said. The way he was appraising us made me uneasy.

"Don't be silly," I said, breaking away as casually as I could. "You passed out so hard that we decided to let you get in a catnap." I took his hand. "Do you guys want a cocktail? Lacey made some G&Ts."

Freddie grinned at me. "Just the ticket," he said, sauntering over to the bar cart. I turned to Nick and put my arm around his waist.

"I feel like I haven't seen you in the daylight in about a week," I said.

"Yes, well, 'work-life balance' hasn't been on my to-do list," he said, stretching and yawning hard enough that my arm fell back to my body.

"Oi, Nick," Gaz's voice said from behind a tower of dessert. "I saw on Twitter that you lost to an old lady today."

"Ah, yes, the infamous Lillian Chang of Shoreditch," Nick said, walking into the room and settling into a large armchair by the fireplace. "I got thrashed in a footrace by an eighty-one-year-old. It was fun, though. So much better than having to plant another tree."

"The worst," Freddie said. "I planted three trees last month."

"I planted seven," Nick said.

Cilla got up and poured herself another drink. "They've really put you to work lately."

"And rightly," Bea said, gesturing around the room. "One has to earn the spoils."

"Okay, you've got me beat on trees," Freddie said. He set his drink on the end table and steepled his hands in concentration. "How many tiny sets of curtains did you open? I did two."

Nick made a thoughtful face. "Four," he said. "But the last one had medium-size curtains so it should count for two."

"I never get to open *any*," I said.

"You're not really in the mix the way Nick and I are," Freddie said.

"There's a mix?" Lacey asked.

Bea looked at her as if she'd asked whether teabags were edible. Lacey made an exaggerated *okay, then* face and went back to cutting the rind off her Brie.

"I also cut three cakes," Nick said.

Freddie winced. "All I had was the one from the one hundred and twenty-fifth anniversary of the Gloucestershire County Cricket Club. Point to you."

"Again," Nick said.

"Guest books signed?" Freddie asked.

"Enough. We get it," I said.

"Are we counting books of condolence?" Nick asked.

"No," Freddie said. "Unless you need to, of course."

"I don't," Nick said. "I was just clarifying terms."

"You lot are mad," Gemma chuckled.

Cilla and Gaz exchanged a look, and then he popped up and rubbed his hands together. "I think I smell those Cornish pasties I put in the oven!" he chirped. "Nick, do you want a squizz at my pastry work?"

"I'm at thirteen," Nick said.

"*Thirteen* guest books?" Freddie said, genuinely shocked.

"Am I to take it that I win this one, too?" Nick asked. "Do *you* need to count books of condolence?"

"Congratulations. You're both heroes. Now knock it off," I snapped.

"This is a stupid conversation anyway," Freddie grumbled, flopping back onto the sofa.

"It's little wonder I've chosen to make my life with a woman," Bea said. "*We* don't need to measure anything and then overcompensate."

She swept out of the room. Then we heard her stop and curse as she briefly forgot which way the kitchen was. Our laughter broke the tension.

"I apologize," Nick said to the rest of us. "We should not have made you sit through that when Gaz's pastry work is in the offing."

"No harm done, but let's move on in there and give him the rave reviews he so desperately desires," Cilla said as we all scooped up our cocktails.

Freddie sidled up to me. "I'm sorry, too, Bex," he said. "We got carried away."

"Thanks, Fred, but I've got this," Nick said, and slung an arm around my shoulders.

"Aye, aye, captain." Freddie saluted sarcastically before heading toward dinner.

"Don't make the damn apology a competition, too," I hissed at Nick, pushing his arm off. "I am over you two trying to outdo each other like we're in some kind of stupid Royal Usefulness Pageant or something."

"But I look so dashing in a sash," Nick teased.

"No. Don't you do that twinkly thing," I said. "Go. I'll be there in a second."

Lacey and I watched him walk off, and then she shook her head slowly.

"They're never going to work this out themselves, are they?" I asked. It was a rhetorical question. "Eleanor was right. It is going to come down to me."

In truth, I'd trusted that once I got the boys talking again, their natural pull—those years of being each other's constant—would take over and do the rest. But I'd been fooling myself. We were deep in some insidious psychological muck. It was unfair to make me be the one to start digging us out of it when they were fully capable of picking up a shovel, but I'd underestimated how stubborn two grown men could be.

Lacey walked over and entwined her arm with mine. "Happy birthday, Bex," she said. "For once, I'm glad I'm not in your shoes."

CHAPTER ELEVEN

Nick apologized profusely once the party wound down and we were curled up in the floral fiasco that was our master bedroom. He said all the expected things—he was deranged from lack of sleep, he loved me, he had not meant to sideline my birthday—and I knew he meant them, but none of it got to the heart of why I was upset. Simply put, I was embarrassed, both by him and for him. He and Freddie had sounded like the worst, most shallow versions of themselves—which I told him, sharply, and he agreed, before giving me my birthday present: a case of Cubs-branded wine and two shatterproof glasses for drinking it on our terrace. It seemed bitchy to keep yelling at him after that.

But as Nick fell more deeply into work, I fretted that he'd sidestepped my point instead of absorbing it. He accepted assignments like he was on a mission to out-king the regent himself, and when Richard responded by putting Freddie out on the trail in kind, it redoubled Nick's desire to keep his nose to the royal grindstone. My hat was off to Prince Dick: He knew how to keep both his sons at a boil that suited his PR needs. If this was a snapshot of how Richard would run things when he really was king, the whole line would die out of exhaustion. It made me doubly antsy because of how far Nick and Freddie and I were drifting away from each other; it wasn't so much two and one anymore, as Freddie had once described our former trio to me, but more like one and one and one—three points of a triangle with so much empty space in between.

Instead of cracking skulls to get everyone in sync again, I decided to take a warmer, fuzzier tack. I hadn't celebrated a proper Thanksgiving in England since the year Nick and I first hooked up, when I'd gone to meet him at Windsor Castle and he'd ended a private tour—and accordingly, the platonic portion of our relationship—with a feast he'd arranged based on my family specialties. Maybe a flashback to that would remind Nick of a time when things were simpler and better. So I laid enough of a sob story on Marj that she felt either sorry for me or sick of me, and pulled strings to make sure Nick had Thanksgiving off. I then called my mom for cooking advice.

"Remember to take out the plastic bag of giblets," she'd said, once she stopped laughing at the idea of me throwing a dinner party for which I actually cooked. "On our first Thanksgiving together, your father forgot, and the entire apartment smelled so foul that we went to the Holiday Inn for a week."

Lacey ended up staying in London after our birthday. Ollie had decided to return to his position at Cambridge, and had asked her to move in with him when they both finished in Kenya. The prospective social buffer of their presence seemed to make it easier for Freddie to accept our invitation, though he declined to bring the chemist he'd been courting.

"Not everyone can knock off work on a Thursday for a boozy early dinner, Killer," he teased.

Lacey took over the job of making our beloved Chex Mix, and Olly was bringing something from his father's bakery. We'd invited the Omundis to join us, but they politely declined. A photo of Lacey and Olly at the theater had led to a minor resurgence in public curiosity about Lacey, and I didn't blame Olly's parents for wanting to steer clear—though I was encouraged, and pleasantly surprised, that Lacey herself also seemed disinclined to stoke the flames.

"I kind of forgot anyone here might give a shit," she'd said, but not with the awe she'd have used even a year ago.

I liked Olly instantly. He was muscular but compact—not much taller than me or Lacey, but with rock-solid biceps, from what his short-sleeve collared shirt displayed. His aura was of an endearing low-level nervousness; the way his eyebrows arched over his thick-framed black glasses gave his face the impression of constant hopeful anticipation, as if he simply cared very much about everything going well for the people in his life, and wanted to be the first to smile when it did.

"...not at all unlike elephant herds, actually, because the matriarch really sets the tone for the herd and they're very reliant on her," Olly was now saying to Nick, squeezing his left thumb with his right hand in a way that I would come to realize was his calming tic. "The whole elephants-never-forget expression comes largely from the females, and they are very hardy."

"Gran is nothing if not tough," Nick agreed.

"Oh God, and now I've called the Queen an elephant," Olly fretted.

"I've done worse," I said.

"I took it as a compliment," Nick assured him. "Come sit and catch me up on the Sands preserve—it's been eons since I've been."

"Is this the famous Olly?" called out Freddie, sauntering in from the foyer. "Delighted to meet you, sir."

"Who let you in?" I said, giving his cheek a light peck.

"You did," he said, tugging on my ponytail. "Lock your doors, Killer."

He gave Lacey a warm hug and shook Olly's hand, then very formally thanked Nick for inviting him before wandering over to the bar cart.

"How's your chemist?" I asked in a low voice, following him.

"No idea," was his reply. "She broke up with me fifteen minutes before our lunch date today."

I squeezed his arm. I heard Nick cough, but when I looked up at him, his eyes were on Olly.

Lacey and Olly, in fact, made for a great social lubricant. The common ground of the Sands preserve gave way to casual, amusing anecdotes, like the time five-year-old Olly burst into tears at the London Zoo because he'd thought all the animals were under arrest, or Nick's subsequent embarrassment that he technically owned one of the elephants there (a birthday gift), or the admission that we all lived for watching *Cotswolds Coroner* and that Freddie had screamed when the bell ringer had been butter-churned to death. By the time we were rubbing our full bellies, I was feeling misty and proud. Finally, a plan of mine had worked.

"That was shockingly not terrible, Killer," Freddie teased, nibbling on one last piece of turkey. "I might even survive the night."

"Wow," I said. "I don't think I've gotten higher praise than that for anything I've ever cooked."

"I have to admit, I had some concerns coming over here tonight," Olly said. "Lacey once microwaved a Pot Noodle without the water in it."

"Mom and Dad loved cooking," I said. "So we kind of…let them do it."

"That was doing them a favor," Lacey said.

I retrieved two Tiffany-blue paper boxes from the old rolltop in the corner, which was working as a de facto sideboard. The most amazing smell of apple and sugar and cinnamon wafted out of one of them, and the other held a stunning array of macarons artfully arranged in ROYGBIV order.

"Speaking of favors," I said, clearing some space on the table and placing the boxes on it. "Please thank your father, Olly. These are gorgeous."

Nick peeked at the lid of the box. "Macaron and Cheese," he read. "I suspect I'm going to like your parents." He bit into a white one crusted in pink salt crystals. "White truffle," he announced. "Don't tell Gaz but these are the best thing I've ever eaten."

Olly smiled. "My father says they were the hardest thing to perfect," he said. "His parents wanted him to run their hotel in Lagos, but then he went to France and fell in love with pastry cream, and that was that."

"Please do not let me have more than two of these, or else my official portrait is going to end up with a giant zit in it," I said.

"Isn't the whole point of a portrait that you can gloss over certain bits?" Freddie asked. "Although for some reason Edwin's *still* makes him look like a walrus."

"I can't wait until you're hanging in a museum," Lacey said to me.

"Imagine having generations of people visiting you on their vacations, buying postcards of your face."

"They already do," Freddie said. "Go to any souvenir stand. I walked past one the other day and someone had stuck a wad of gum on Bex's nose."

"For some reason those postcards don't feel as over-the-top to me as a commissioned portrait," I said. "But I guess it's part of the job."

I hadn't noticed that Nick was noodling with his phone until he plonked it on the table with a plasticky thud. "Yes, right, the portrait. How *is* that going? Any better?"

Richard, himself an artist, had handpicked for my portrait a British painter who'd spent most of his life memorializing wildlife in South Africa; they'd met once on a royal tour of the country and had a fulfilling discussion about pencils. At our first meeting, the guy circled me for fifteen minutes before saying, "Hmm." He then snapped photographs from a variety of angles and sketched frantically. Three of these sessions had come and gone. Number four was scheduled for Tuesday.

"He seems uninspired by my face," I said.

"Then he's clearly a fool," Freddie said chivalrously.

"Father seems keen," Nick said. "He showed me loads of the man's work yesterday."

"He did?" Freddie asked. "I thought he was swamped this week."

"He was," Nick said. "With me."

"Okay, well, we just ate a Thanksgiving meal, so let's do some traditional giving of thanks," Lacey jumped in, and I tried to send her a psychic message of my own gratitude for changing the subject. "I'll start. I'm thankful that the turkey wasn't raw."

"I'm thankful for my metabolism," Freddie said, popping another macaron into his mouth.

"I'm thankful Gran is still with us," Nick said.

"Boo! Too earnest," Freddie said around the cookie. "I'm thankful Father hasn't called about work."

"Lucky you. He's texted me at least four times," Nick said, glancing down at his phone.

Freddie absorbed this. "No rest for the wicked," he said airily.

"My turn," I said. "I'm thankful we are starting these damn renovations. Goodbye, floral bedrooms."

"I'm thankful dating colleagues isn't frowned upon at my work," Olly said.

"I'm thankful I got the chance to go to Kenya," Lacey said. "It's changed me for the better. Who knows what would've happened if I hadn't had to get away from—ahh, um."

"Yes, I'm a bit less thankful for that, if you'll forgive me," Nick said.

There was a terrible pause.

"I'm thankful for uncomfortable silences," I joked.

No one laughed.

"Well, no family holiday is, um, uncomplicated, but I'm thankful we're here together," I finished lamely.

"Indeed," Nick said into his tumbler of scotch. "Family is *so* important."

"Isn't it?" Freddie said smoothly. "I'm personally thankful you came back from when you pissed off to parts unknown. Made my life a lot easier."

"And that is absolutely exactly why we do everything we do," Nick said. "To make your life easier." He set down his glass. "Perhaps that's why Father has been leaning on me so much lately. He must be thankful for me."

"Or perhaps you're making up for all those lost weeks," Freddie said. "There were so very many of them."

"And why was that, do you think?" Nick asked, fixing him with a stare. Next to him, Olly was chewing on his thumbnail. "Remind me."

"We should be going," Lacey said. "We've got to head back to Cambridge before the food coma sets in."

Freddie made a move to get up. "No," I said resolutely. "You are staying here."

I started to follow Olly and Lacey across the room. "Go back in there, B," Lacey said. "There's your opening."

"I know, but..." I stopped in the foyer. "I need to apologize. This is not how I wanted tonight to go."

Olly adjusted his glasses. "Do you know how elephants pick their matriarch?" he asked. "Simplistically, it's because she displays courage in crisis and can navigate the terrain and the social politics." He smiled sympathetically. "If you're half as tough as Lacey is, then you've got this, and they're lucky to have you."

"Olly," Lacey said lovingly. "Only you would find an elephant analogy here."

He grinned sweetly. "Beats an 'elephant in the room' pun."

I watched the door click behind them, then took a bracing breath before walking back into the living room. Nick and Freddie were, like boxers on a break, in opposite corners staring at different objets d'art from Georgina's collection. One of them was a nude that did absolutely nothing to make this less uncomfortable.

"I kept wanting to make you two talk out whatever this is, and then convincing myself that things were improving, or that it wasn't the right time," I said. "But I was deluding myself on both counts, so here we are. You two are sniping at each other constantly, and it's got to stop. So. How do we stop it?"

Nick tapped on his forearm and stared out the window. Freddie fixated on an enamel box with a rooster on it.

"Really?" I said. "Neither of you has anything to contribute?"

"We're being scolded, Knickers," Freddie said, aiming for lightness.

"Yeah, and I resent having to do it," I said. "But you've been acting like children. If you guys aren't motivated enough to fix this yourselves, then eventually nobody is going to bother helping. Including me. And then it might be too late."

"Fix what, exactly?" Nick said tersely. "We're brothers. We get under each other's skin all the time."

"Yes, Knickers was very cranky about my smoking habit," Freddie said. "And your sister. And a lot of other things."

"Name one of them that wasn't earned," Nick shot back.

"See?" I snapped. "This is exactly what I'm talking about."

"What do you want me to say, Bex?" Freddie asked, throwing up his hands. "You left, I stepped up, Father began to respect me, and Nick couldn't stand not being the golden boy anymore. And now here we are. How's that?"

Nick turned and glared at him. "If he respects you so much, then why am I getting the plum assignments again?" he countered.

"There! You proved my point," Freddie said. "But that's hardly the only way to show respect. When was the last time you saw Father for anything that wasn't work related?"

"When was the last time either one of you cared about seeing him for anything, period?" I asked. "Am I the only person who remembers that neither of you even *likes* Richard?"

"No," Nick agreed. "But I'm very much enjoying making him regret treating me like I was worthless when we came back from Scotland."

Freddie crossed his arms. "Did you ever think perhaps you deserved that?"

"No," said Nick very carefully. "As a matter of fact, I did not."

"You checked out," Freddie said. "And while you were gone, I did my duty, and yours as well, and I don't deserve to be shoved back to the side just because you've decided to take an interest again."

"We're talking about what *you* deserve?" Nick gaped. "All summer you acted like we had betrayed you by leaving town. You and Richard chummed around and made me feel like shit. For trying to protect myself. For trying to protect my *marriage*."

"I didn't mean to make you feel like shit," Freddie protested. "*I* felt like shit. Everything fell on me. What was I supposed to do? Have you any idea how hard it was even to get up some of those mornings, knowing what was coming? I was the sleazy brother who had to smile through the sneering crowds for weeks. You lived it for one day."

"You think I only felt that for one day?"

"I think you took the easy way out, and I didn't, and you're giving me no credit for it."

"Gosh, so sorry," Nick said sarcastically. "I didn't realize you wanted credit for muddling through a firestorm *you* created. Well, congratulations! You finally suffered the consequences of your actions! Are you happy now? Is that what you wanted to hear?"

Freddie's face went red. "You don't have any idea what I want."

"I guess that depends," Nick said. "Is what you want still my wife?"

All the blood drained from Freddie's face. I may have blacked out briefly; neither of the boys seemed to notice.

"I get that we shouldn't have left you high and dry," Nick said tightly. "But you took something intangible from me, Freddie, and now you have the gall to act like I stabbed you through the heart when you fucking well slashed me through mine."

His voice cracked at the end, and with it, so did part of me.

"And that's it," Freddie whispered. His face crumbled, and he looked smaller, and so sad. "That's it right there. You're never going to be able to forgive me. Not really."

Nick covered his face with his hands, then let out a harsh laugh. "I mean, *should* I?" he said. "Everyone acts like I ought to. That night...I tried so hard. But when the adrenaline wore off and it all set in..." He wiped at his eyes. "You made a pass at Bex. You *begged her to leave me.* Why am I supposed to be the bigger man?"

"You're not," Freddie said. "But you're my big brother. You're the best of us. I believed you when you reached out to me that night, and then you left, and I was on an island. I had no one. I did what I could in order not to go mad."

"And I've been slowly going mad instead," Nick said. "I wanted to put this away. But I can't. I can't not wonder what you're feeling when you hug Bex, or whether you're flirting when you try to make her laugh. And don't tell me I'm overreacting, because I missed it the first time and it's nearly ruined me."

Nick didn't seem to know whether to be scared or relieved that he'd released the words he'd kept under his tongue for the last eight months. He wrapped his arms around his torso, as if to hold all the rest of his feelings inside. I was frozen, my hands cupped over my mouth, unsure whether to intervene or let Nick bleed this poison.

"And there's nothing for it, then," Freddie said raggedly. It should have been a question, but, heartbreakingly, was not.

Nick sank into the sofa. He was silent for a long moment. "I don't think I can tell you what you want to hear," he finally said, so quietly that I could barely hear him.

Freddie appeared to deflate. He nodded very, very slowly, started to move toward Nick, then caught himself and clenched his fists. Instead, he strode for the door.

"Freddie," I said urgently. "You can't leave. We can't..."

But I didn't know where to go from there.

Freddie paused in front of me and shrugged so helplessly. "We tried," he said.

A world of love and loss and loneliness passed in the look we shared.

"I'm not giving up on this," I insisted. "You can't, either. We can fix this, Freddie."

He broke the bond with a facetious bow. "The art of the exit, Killer," he said. "You have to know when to make one."

He cast one last agonized look at Nick. And then he was gone.

I turned to Nick, still on the couch, huddled up as if trying to hide within himself. When I crossed to him and put a hand on his shoulder, he twitched and jerked away, as if by instinct.

"Happy Thanksgiving," he muttered.

"I knew you hadn't dealt with this," I said. "That *we* hadn't, you and me together. But I was too chickenshit to push it." I took a deep breath. "In case this wasn't just about Freddie."

"I only want to feel this way about Freddie. I only want to blame him." Nick met my gaze with deepest sorrow. "But the thing is, I will never know how you looked at him or how you kissed him. And it eats at me," he said. "Was it the same way you look at me or kiss me? Or, if not, is that worse? It's agony, Bex, and it's infected me. I cannot stop thinking about it."

I'd wanted this conversation. I'd tried to have this conversation, and tonight, I'd even pushed for it. But it was brutal to hear him put to voice everything I'd been afraid of hearing, and to know that it was every bit as bad as I had feared. Probably worse.

"I'm scared I can't ever be your safe place again, because I'm part of the problem," I whispered.

"All that playacting this summer was my safe place." Nick swallowed hard. "Margot hadn't been anywhere near Steve's brother. It made it easier to push the rest of it away. But then we came home and we were right back in the thick of it. Seeing him around you..." He stared at the floor.

"We need help," I said. "I don't think we can cope with this alone."

"No. I'm not ready for that," Nick said, leaping up and pacing toward the fireplace. "This just happened."

"It happened eight months ago."

"That's not how it feels," he said.

"I get that, I promise, but we have to *go* somewhere from here. Tonight has to mean something," I pleaded. "We can't keep on this way."

"Yes, but I'm the one who has to suck it up and look past the most hurt in order to move forward." Nick pressed the heels of his hands into his forehead. "I know I've been an ass to Freddie. Because I can control that, and I can come out on top. But everything else..." He spread his hands wide, then let them fall with a thwack to his sides.

"But at least we know where we stand," I argued.

"That's just it. I have no idea where we stand." He flexed his fingers and fidgeted. "I feel like I can't breathe in here."

I closed my eyes to gather my thoughts, and when I opened them, he was already at the double doors.

"Nick, wait," I called after him. He stopped in the foyer. My stomach felt like it was trying to climb out of my mouth as I caught up to him.

"You said you forgave Freddie the night of our St. James's wedding because you felt like you had to," I said, taking his hand and holding it to my pounding heart. "Did you...is that also why you married me? Because it was easier than the alternative?"

He was quivering. I rubbed his hand as if trying to hold him together myself.

"I love you," he said. "That was the one truth I knew for certain. So I thought, *Just get married, make it real, and then we'll deal with what comes.*" He stepped away from me and my hand fell. "But what if that's why *you* chose *me*?"

"It's not," I said, a tear slipping down my cheek. "I chose you for you. I chose you when Freddie asked me to run away with him, and I chose you every day after that. I choose you now."

"I tried to push past this, I did, but as soon as we came back here the doubt crept in." I could barely hear him. "Even looking at you right now makes it hurt all over again. I just...I can't. I need time. I need..."

Whatever it was, I never heard it, because his words were lost in the slamming of the front door. For what felt like an eternity, I watched, waited, willed it to open again. But it didn't. And standing there, surrounded by the byzantine rooms of Apartment 1A, I stared down at the gold *G* on the floor of my foyer and felt nothing so much as alone in another person's life—not only Georgina's, but also my own.

ACT TWO

I beseech you now with all my heart definitely to let
me know your whole mind as to the love between us.
                                    —King Henry VIII

CHAPTER ONE

Come on, Duchess, hold still, or else I'll stab you in the ear, and it might not be an accident."

"I'm trying!" I said to Kira, my hair and makeup person and the only American in my orbit who wasn't related to me. "I wish you would go back to calling me Bex. Or Rebecca. Or even Hey You."

Kira cocked a brow at me, and reached for a bobby pin.

"Half the reason I do it is because of that face you make," she teased. "Besides, if things keep going the way they are, your title is very much in flux." Her face turned solemn. "Is there any change?"

I looked down at my nails, freshly manicured, cheerful in an incongruous way. "No."

Just as it said on the novelty T-shirt Freddie once gave her for Christmas, Eleanor had proved to be One Tough Old Bird. We'd arrived on the doorstep of the state visit with no signs of life beyond the beeping of her monitors, but she was still with us, and no news was just that: no news. The country was getting anxious, and so was the family—but, as usual with The Firm, we were expected to shove down those sentiments and put on a show of family unity tomorrow for the Dutch.

Over the last few weeks, I'd gotten really good at burying my feelings.

A familiar voice slithered to me from across the hall. We'd turned a first-floor bathroom into my glam room, because at some point Georgina had installed a giant makeup mirror circled in lightbulbs—

it was like living backstage in an old Broadway theater—and from where I sat, I could see the cracked door of Nick's nearby study. He had apparently turned on *Get Up, Great Britain!* The guest was Clive.

"But that's why this state visit is so important," he was saying. "It's our first glimpse of Richard as our figurehead. Given Her Majesty's health, we should watch closely, because this could become our new normal at any moment." He then ruined the somber mood by winking at the camera. "It's tense at the palace. You can take it from me."

"Yeah, well you can take something from me, too, and it's gonna hurt," Kira muttered. "Are you ready to try on this tiara, or are you too distracted by the loser on TV?"

I blew out a deliberately childish sigh, which made us both laugh.

"Sorry," I said. "I hate that the sound of his voice still bothers me."

I also hated when that voice told the truth, and once again, Clive was at least a bit right. Marta's already bowed frame had become more stooped. Freddie was drawn and snappish, and Richard and Nick had to juggle their own agita with accepting that their promotions within The Firm might be permanent. It all would've been much easier to handle if Freddie and Nick hadn't gone off like hand grenades.

Nick had asked for time when he left Apartment 1A, so I gave it to him, with a dose of supernatural restraint. He'd stayed out all night, and even though I was itching to know what he'd done and where he'd done it, when he returned I acted like his disappearance was the most normal thing in the world. He'd found me curled up in bed reading Georgina's first edition of *Little Women*, a tan leather volume so old that it only contained what the world now thinks of as the first half of the book. Amy March was behaving like a real brat when I heard his muffled steps on the thick hall carpet. He walked in still wearing the previous night's sweater.

"Good book?" he asked.

"A classic," I said.

We locked eyes.

"Busy day today?" I asked.

"Mostly a research day," he said.

He blinked. I blinked. He smiled. I returned it.

"I'd better shower," he said.

I scowled at his back as he closed the bathroom door. "Enjoy."

I hadn't asked him anything else. *I need time* didn't mean *Please quiz me about exactly how I spent that time*, or *Pressure me to announce whether, with respect to forever or the next five minutes, I need yet more time*. Nick hadn't come home with a new face tattoo or anything, so I resolved to let him process the blowup however he needed, at least until the damn state dinner was over. Making a good showing for the Dutch meant a lot to both of us, and the War of the Waleses had already done enough to imperil that. I did not press Nick for details, nor push him about his emotional state, nor do anything that might make this train careen any further off the rails; instead, I'd pasted on a smile and white-knuckled my way through, promising myself it would be temporary. We just had to pass the Dutch test.

It had been a long two weeks to get to this point. I was climbing the walls.

Kira clapped once, loudly. "You are somewhere else today," she said. "Can we do this? Does he want to see?" She raised her voice in the direction of his office. "Nick, we're frosting the doughnut."

"No, no, he has too much on his plate," I said hastily. "I'm good. Tiara me."

My hair had been swept into a complicated chignon, with a small foam circle pinned to the back of my head to prevent the tiara from pressing into my skull and giving me a headache. Having thusly primed me, Kira placed the Lover's Knot tiara on my head. It had sat there only once before, briefly, the day Eleanor let me choose my wedding head-piece, and I was reminded why Nick's mother hadn't liked it: The damn thing weighed a ton, and was almost too impressive for me to bear. For all Richard's talk of symbolism, I knew he also was keenly aware that the Dutch possessed the best jewels of all the European royals, and—short of raiding the vault at the Tower—this was the fanciest in his coffers. He wanted to show off.

I shook my head back and forth gently. The pearls hanging from the twenty-five diamond arches clanked in their settings.

"Yikes," I said. "I'm not going to be able to sneak up on anyone wearing this thing."

Kira took a step back and appraised me. "Maybe not, but you look great. I am extremely good at my job."

"You are," I said, nodding.

"Try not to do that," she said. "You'll dislodge the doughnut."

I winced. "And sprain my neck."

As Kira fiddled with a few pins near my left ear, I stared at myself with an almost anthropological remove. For my new family, sticking on an iconic crown for a couple of hours was as usual as trying to wear in a new pair of shoes. But in that split second when the Lover's Knot settled onto my head, for real this time and not simply as a wedding-day audition, I'd turned into someone foreign to myself. They were my eyes looking out from my own face, but what they saw was a person from a tabloid, too distant to touch. With a husband who'd been nearby the whole time but chose to stay across the hall, out of sight.

Kira's hand hovered over my head. "Are we good here? The cops will not think it's cute if I'm late bringing this back."

"We're good," I said. "I just…don't look like me, do I?"

Kira put her hands on my shoulders.

"I hate to break it to you," she said. "But I think this *is* what you look like now."

To distract myself from the tense build-up to Dutch Day, I'd picked up Georgina's journals again, relishing the peek into the life of a person I'd never known—and a side of Eleanor I'd never seen. At first, I'd simply read and reread the first one, turning its old pages slowly, savoring a diverting look inside the mind of a little girl with a lot of opinions. But then I found two more slim volumes buried in a different cupboard in Sex Den (I had given up correcting Nick on the name). The morning of our royal guests' arrival, after a night of anxiety dreams that had festered and flourished every hour, the Bex Brigade got me spit-shined and ready fifteen minutes early, and I gratefully spent that time perched carefully on an ottoman devouring the next pages.

Happy birthday to me! We spent it in Durham again. Daddy pretends we come here for the fresh air, but I know it's because London still frightens him and he thinks the countryside is safer. Once, years ago, we stayed here for ages, and lots of London was ruined when we got home and Ellie and I cried so much that Daddy sent us right back for another month. Henry said that was the Blitz. He's very clever, so I believe him. He tells us things the grown-ups don't want us to know.

Mummy thinks the Vanes are a bit common. Henry's great-great-grandfather was nearly prime minister and his grandfather very nearly was an MP and his father was very very nearly Head Boy at Eton when Daddy went there and now works near Parliament. After a bit too much wine I heard Mummy say into her napkin, "Such a lot of nothing." But Daddy is happy here. He and the Duke puff out their chests and tell boring stories about the old days, like Daddy is just a normal person. But they tease Henry something awful about not going to Eton or playing sport. He plays croquet with us, but I suppose that isn't as noble to old men. He doesn't play with us as much now that he's nearly a grown-up, too, but we had a bit of fun tonight after dinner. There was a cracking rainstorm and Ellie couldn't sleep, and I never want to go to bed, so we crept into the library to watch through the window, and Henry was there like he always is with his nose in a big book and looking serious.

I told him to cheer up and he said, "You know why you're here, don't you? It means your parents are afraid London is about to get hit again." He said he feels useless not being able to help, because he's too young and his eyesight is terrible. Then he fretted about if Hitler took over the world. (Mummy says that won't happen. I'm a bit scared, but I don't want to look like a baby so I pretend I'm not.) Then Ellie sat down next to Henry and hugged his arm and said, "Granny told me I will be Queen someday, and I need to learn to stand tall in a storm. But I don't know how to do that."

I don't like being sad, so I said, "Stop moping, ninnies. There's nothing we can do from here." I decided the best way to cheer everyone up was to have a mud fight. Ellie said it was too dark and we'd get in trouble and it wouldn't be safe, but I told her nothing bad could happen if Henry was with us. And then HE said, "You're quite right, Georgie," which are words that I do not hear often enough, and then he turned to El and he was so lovely with her. He said, "Why don't we go stand tall in a storm right now, as we are, and show it we're not afraid. Of anything," and he pulled her up and she gave him such a smile and then I realized: ELLIE HAS A CRUSH ON HENRY, which is RIDICULOUS because he is positively ancient. (Although I had a crush on Laurence Olivier last year so I suppose this is rather like that.) Henry took us out through the kitchen, and we jumped in the puddles, and laughed, and got VERY dirty and wet until Mummy called us back inside, and we were in EXTREME TROU-BLE. "I expected better," Mummy said to Henry, and he ran off as fast as he could because you do not argue with Mummy. She said to Ellie, "I don't know what you're playing at. You're third in line for the throne. Do you know what that means?" And Ellie stood up very tall and said, "I am Princess Eleanor and I am showing the storm I'm not afraid." Mummy spanked us both anyway.

Nick poked his head into our sitting room. "You've beaten me for once," he said.

I waved the diary. "I've just met your grandfather."

"Give him my regards," Nick said. "Come on, our chariot awaits."

I set the diary on the end table with a shiver. All this royal family pageantry triggered flashbacks to the last time I'd engaged in it, and been deluged with jeers. At least then I'd had Nick's hand to hold. This time I was on my own. Nick hadn't completely shut me out, but time and space had done nothing to make it easier for him to look at me through the fog of everything we'd dredged up, and every time he did, I saw the struggle.

Queen Lucretia, at least, did prove to be a gas. When Nick and I arrived at Horse Guards for the official welcome, she enveloped him and patted him on the back of the head like he was a baby (at over six feet in heels, she was one of the few women who could do that). She then grasped my shoulders and gave me a warm shake.

"It is wonderful to see you," she said, her accent a mix of twenty years in the Netherlands, a childhood in Argentina, and college in Boston. "We had a glorious time at your wedding, until the actual wedding." She tilted down and touched our foreheads together. "Fret not, my darling. Things happen. Hendrik's brother's wife tried to leave him at the altar, and the police brought her back to the palace. Now they're having twins." She winked. "*Everything* is possible with love!"

She then reached inside a cluster of large, suit-clad, Secret Service–looking men and retrieved a wan strawberry blonde in dreary beige. "This is my daughter Daphne Estrella, my North Star, my joy."

Daphne glanced at me, tight-lipped, looking like the polar opposite of all those things. She was two inches shorter and a few years older than me, but her fingers tugged at each other in the manner of a twelve-year-old.

"Hello," she said.

And that was it. Shepherding Princess Daphne to the palace had sounded like an easy, low-pressure gig, but apparently Lax had used up their combined word budget. Daphne didn't give off an unfriendly vibe, but neither did she speak as we climbed into the carriage, apparently preferring to stare out the window curling and uncurling her fingers in her lap. This had not been on my syllabus. I'd memorized the schedule for the two-day visit, and skimmed tomes about history, art, architecture, geography, and language provided by Richard because (I assume) he was afraid all I knew was that Amsterdam is a place people go to party, and that I would ask Daphne if she'd brought any weed. (I didn't tell Richard that page fifty-seven of *Conversational Dutch: From Vermeer to Eternity* featured the phrase "Which way to the red-light district?") I should have dipped into a few psychology texts instead.

"How was your trip over?" I asked as she fidgeted.

Daphne made a stammering sound, her eyes fixed on something unknowable. We hadn't even begun the procession to Buckingham Palace.

"It's a shame it's such a short ride," I said, though it was shaping up to feel like a lifetime. "It's a beautiful day. You'll get a good view of Trafalgar as we make the turn, at least."

Daphne nodded, looking as numb as the bench seat had made my butt.

"This is as close as I like to get to Trafalgar," I chattered on. "There are way too many pigeons there that are way too interested in people. And yet I know no people who are interested in them. You'd think they'd take the hint."

More nodding. Maybe I needed to throw off propriety and go for cheap humor. Nothing could be worse than prattling about birds.

"I don't know about you, but I'm pretty nervous about this state dinner," I tried. "It's my first one. I'm wearing a tiara tonight that I can barely balance on my head. You know there's a bookmaker somewhere laying odds that I'll fall on my face, because they all hate me."

Aha. A mild twitch of the lip.

"I have such great memories of this carriage route, too," I pressed on. "The last time I did it, about a hundred thousand people were calling me a slut." I took a beat. "I'm really going to miss that."

A giggle escaped, and Daphne covered her mouth with both hands.

"Care to do the honors?" I teased. "It'd make this so nostalgic for me."

Now she let out a burst of laughter. "I'm sorry, I know it's not funny," she said.

"It is. Now," I said. "Or at least, making a joke out of it is the only way I'm going to get through this without sweaty palms." I stretched them out between us. "Whoops, too late."

Daphne clutched at her chest in a sweet, old-timey way. "I'm so glad I'm not the only one this happens to," she said. "I thought you were very brave that day. I would faint if that happened to me. I'm not very good at this."

"No one has ever called me good at this," I said. The carriage jerked to life. "And I wasn't brave at all. We got by on a combination of shock and having no other choice. Inside I was a mess."

Daphne exhaled tremulously. "This is the first time I've left the Netherlands since..."

She didn't say it, but she didn't have to. Daphne had been seventeen when she was kidnapped by a group of political radicals who wanted to replace the monarchy with an atheist oligarchy. She was lucky that they had been very bad at kidnapping and were caught before a full day elapsed.

"It's been fifteen years, but it still feels fresh, somehow?" she confessed. "At first I stayed close to home because I felt safer, but the longer that went on, the bigger a deal it became whenever I did go out, and *that* made me anxious as well. I couldn't face your wedding, but Mother convinced me this would be a lower-profile way to test the waters."

"I'm glad she did," I said, pointing out the window. "Otherwise, you'd have missed getting to trot past this cute local bistro called McDonald's."

Daphne laughed lightly. "I hope it works. I do not want to be stuck in The Hague forever," she said. "My mother is the most outgoing person in all of Europe, I think. It's hard to live up to that even for a normal person. I know she frets about how I've become, and I am terribly worried that I disappoint her, so I agreed to try. But I've been so nervous." She shot me a grateful look. "Less so now."

"We're in this together," I said. "And don't stress. Between your guys and all our PPOs, we're in good hands here. You and I are gonna nail this."

I held out my fist, and she paused for a second before bumping it, awkwardly, as if it were the first time she'd done that.

"We are going to be friends, I hope," she said.

"Too late. We already are," I said. "The last time I made a new friend was in college. I'm glad to have you."

The rest of the morning was a well-choreographed blur. Daphne and I were near the end of the procession, so photographs were already underway when we arrived. Richard, in a gray suit with a dapper tie and pocket square, stood with Hax on one side—as fair as Richard was dark, and a head shorter—and Nick and Freddie on the other in their usual dueling blues. Nick had a stripe in his tie that coordinated with my deep berry coatdress and shoes, painstakingly crafted by the team at Alexander McQueen. We certainly looked the part, if nothing else.

"How did it go?" I whispered when I caught up to him.

"Quite well," he said. "The king told Richard I was very well informed during the inspection." His lips twitched. "Freddie didn't get a word in, for once."

"It's not a contest," I said through a smile.

"Doesn't mean I can't enjoy it," was his response.

Daphne, aware as she was that her home country's papers would make a huge deal out of her traveling for this, stayed admirably steady. But I could already see how her mother would be an impossible act to follow, both as a human and as a queen. Her dress was the color of sunshine; her hat, like nothing so much as a feathered pineapple. The photos of her carriage ride with Nick and Freddie were practically dental porn, so wide and open were their mouths from laughing together. She loved the exhibit of memorabilia from the UK and the Netherlands' long relationship. She sympathized expertly with the prime minister, a bucktoothed septuagenarian named Doris Tuesday, on a matter that had bedeviled the House of Commons recently. And she gushed over the official gift from Richard: a framed photograph of Eleanor meeting a seven-year-old Hax in Holland sometime in the mid '60s, in which he wore an ear-to-ear grin and Eleanor wore a hat that looked like a sea urchin. When Lax learned the photo had been Nick's idea, she had taken his face in her hands and announced he was doing great credit to Eleanor. And she did all of this with vibrant sincerity, altogether projecting a wildly different vibe than the more proper and restrained Eleanor would have.

Well, Britain and the Netherlands are wildly different countries, I imagined Eleanor saying with a haughty sniff.

The dinner was to take place in the same Buckingham Palace ballroom where Nick had his twenty-fifth birthday celebration. Back then I had to pretend I didn't love him, as we were dating in secret, but at least got to do so in a dress that I'd liked. This time, I was publicly his lawful wife, but we were barely speaking in private, and my outfit would live in infamy.

"This…is…" Donna's voice had shot up two octaves as she yanked my ball gown out of the dress bag. "A bubblegum nightmare."

The dress was a pink fabric, shot through with subtle gold swirls, like a brocade you'd use to upholster an expensive chair in a child's nursery. I poked at the leg-of-mutton sleeves, hoping they would deflate. They did not. It was like Molly Ringwald's dress at the end of *Pretty in Pink*, crossed with Nick's mother's wedding gown, with a dash of a hot-air balloon.

"Is it too late to call Harrods?" I asked.

"You can't wear off-the-rack to a *state dinner*!" Donna collapsed into a silk-upholstered chair in the back bedroom that we'd turned into my dressing area. "They told me they were on it. They told me they had a fresh concept. It's Alexander bloody McQueen and they've never steered me wrong before so I trusted them. Did someone over there have a stroke?" She put her forehead in her hands. "Am *I* having a stroke?"

"I mean, it's…directional?" I offered. "Isn't that the word *Vogue* is always using?"

Donna pulled the same face she'd made the time we tried to see if I could carry off culottes.

"*The American't* is always squawking that I'm too boring. Besides, the press pool won't be there," I reminded her. "There's only a live feed of the procession into dinner. The internet might not even get a screen grab of the whole gown."

I now regretted my can-do attitude. The skintight middle section exploded in a cumbersome poufball that began at my knee and smothered the only thing I actually liked—my gold sparkly shoes. I could barely walk.

"That's…wow," Nick managed, when I came downstairs.

"Don't ask," I said, sidestepping down until I landed in the foyer. "Mostly because I don't have any answers. I am going to need anti-chafing salve for my thighs."

"Ooh, la la," he said. "Are you ready for this?"

"As much as I'll ever be," I said. "Circumstances are not ideal."

I imbued that with as much double meaning as I could. Nick simply futzed with his cuffs and stared straight ahead.

"If I've learnt anything this year, it's that they rarely are," he said.

Our car pulled up outside, and PPO Popeye tapped on the horn. *Stand tall*, I told myself.

That was challenging with the Lover's Knot on my head. But my head-ache was nothing compared to what Queen Lucretia had to be feeling in her skyscraper of a piece. Composed of what looked like a thousand diamonds and nearly that many sapphires, her tiara was so shiny that I could barely look directly at it—and she confided in me during the cocktail hour in Buckingham Palace's rectangular pink-walled picture gallery that she had another one that she felt was too flamboyant to be worn while Eleanor was not well. That someone could consider the tiara on her head a restrained option would have been a hilarious fiction from anyone but Lax, who clearly had spent hours debating how to show her esteem to Richard while also paying her respects to Eleanor.

"My heart is breaking," she had said, dabbing at her eyes with the black tulle cape she'd worn over her evening gown. "I would trade all my jewels for her health."

Hax rubbed her back and cooed something in Dutch, and Lax blushed and planted such a kiss on his cheek that you could almost see the mark from her lipstick in the official photos.

"What did he say?" I asked Daphne.

"You probably can imagine." She sighed. "They're very devoted. Another way they're hard to live up to."

In my periphery, I saw Nick begin to walk our way, and I waved him over as Freddie materialized at Daphne's side. Nick quickly switched course and headed straight for Richard instead, and I was left pretend-ing I'd simply needed to adjust the Lover's Knot, which now sat on my head like a ten-ton lie.

"Hello, Daphne. You're looking radiant." Freddie beamed. "I didn't get to speak to you properly earlier. I reckon I was, what, sixteen the last time we saw each other?"

"At Grandfather's funeral, yes," she said, her usual nervous smile sliding onto her face. "I'm glad we're here under at least mildly better circumstances."

"All grown up now, though," Freddie said.

"We were just admiring Hax and Lax," I said.

"Yes, I rather think they should get a room," he teased. "Fortunately, we have a few extra."

"They embody *gezellig*," Daphne said. At our puzzlement, she added, "That's Dutch for...well, there is no direct translation. It's a feeling, kind of? They set a very high bar."

Freddie glanced over at Richard and Nick while Daphne fiddled with her diamond tennis bracelet. Richard met his eyes, and then placed his hand on Nick's shoulder and appeared to compliment him to one of the six old, rich men circling them. Freddie straightened and turned to Daphne.

"A high bar is not such a bad thing," he said. "I recently discovered that holding myself to a better standard can be rewarding."

"Ah, does that mean love is in the air?" Daphne asked.

"Well, I'm still working on the payoff," he admitted. "What about you?"

"Not even a whiff," Daphne said. "I have one or two friends who've tried to set me up, but they don't seem to understand that being single isn't a personality trait. People need something in common beyond an open space beside them in bed." She gave him a knowing look. "And, of course, as you understand, it's also challenging because I cannot date just any old person."

"Why not?" Freddie swiped a glass of Champagne from the tray of a passing waiter and handed it to Daphne. "Nick did."

"Cheers," I said, grabbing my own.

"It's a compliment," Freddie said. "Nick marrying any old person should have kicked open the door for the rest of us to do what we like. You two are pioneers."

I wondered briefly if I should be at Nick's side instead of yukking it up with Freddie and Daphne, but Nick had not glanced my way since embedding himself near Doris Tuesday. I resented needing to chase my own husband, and took a longer slurp of my bubbly than was strictly polite.

"My fear is, any old person might not want to date *me*," Daphne was saying. "The last one told me that he loved me but he didn't love the circus that was royal life. Then he literally joined the circus." She gave us a doleful look. "I *may* have given it a very bad review on Yelp." She paused. "That's Dutch for Yelp."

Freddie laughed. His eyes met his father's again, and this time, the nod of approval was in Freddie's direction. Daphne didn't miss it.

"Oh no," she said. "Am I your assignment tonight?"

Freddie looked down at her as if seeing her for the first time. I read guilt on his face, but I knew him well; to Daphne, I suspect his expression seemed like embarrassment on behalf of his father.

"Not one bloody bit," he said. "Prince Dick can't make me be anywhere I don't want to be." He bowed and offered Daphne the crook of his arm. "Now let's go drink too much wine and really give him something to look at." His gaze came back to me. "Good luck up there, Killer. Chew with your mouth closed."

My breath caught as we processed into the ballroom. The heavy gold candelabra and vases, the latter exploding with roses, had been buffed to a perfect shine, while the tablecloths were so starched that you could use them to cut butter. The golden cutlery and cut-glass crystal sparkled under the chandeliers, as did the ostentatious harp being plucked in the corner by a woman with aggressively long hair. The room even smelled good, in an untraceable way where you wondered if perhaps royalty came with a pleasant bespoke odor. It was impossible not to feel the weight of the room's history, to think of the people who had sat in these gilt chairs, the choices they had made and the mistakes and victories they had discussed over these same gold-trimmed porcelain bread plates and crystal saltcellars. One room frozen in time as the world changed around it.

You are part of something much bigger now, I recalled Eleanor saying to me. *You married a man and you married a country.*

But for all the priceless place settings and tiaras and immaculate linens, the state dinner was like any other formal event: a whole lot of blah blah blah, beginning with some light mingling as everyone drifted toward their eventual places—except for Marta, who bypassed the chitchat and went straight to her seat. She wore her signature scroll tiara as a choker, a mint-green silk dress, and the most exquisitely displeased expression.

"I'm too old for this," she muttered. "I've made it a hundred years on this earth, and if I die of boredom tonight, Dickie, I'm bloody well going to haunt you forever." Then she'd turned to me. "You look like candy floss."

Across the room I spied Edwin and Lady Elizabeth, nuzzling while chatting to a balding man I recognized as the famed theater producer behind the gymnastics musical *Perfect Ten*. Freddie was introducing Daphne to Bea's mother, Lady Pansy Larchmont-Kent-Smythe, once Emma's best friend and a person I'd never seen smile (admittedly on-brand for that family). I tried to make contact with Nick, or pass him by so we could at least brush pinkies the way we often did when we wanted to say a silent hello at public events, but he either was flanked by Dutch dignitaries or just never turned my way. I felt profoundly alone.

"And then you swipe right if they're sexy, and left if they're a tosser," I heard a voice say, and turned to see Agatha huddled over her cell phone with a silver-haired dowager type in a gray lacy dress and five strands of pearls, and her trussed-up daughter, everything too snug and too short for no apparent reason.

"This one's handsome," Agatha said, peering at her screen. "*And* an international financier."

The woman swiped left for her. "No one calls themselves that unless they plan to rob you."

"What about him? He's a lord," Agatha tried. "He likes horses, and to 'Netflix and chill.' Sounds fun?"

"It means he wants a fuck," said her daughter plainly. At her mother's strangled noise, she jerked her head up, then looked right at me and gasped.

"It's *you*," she trilled. "I've been dying to meet you. I've so much to ask! How do you like being British? Is it terribly dull compared to America? We get so much rain. Is that thing heavy?" She lowered her voice to what could best be described as a mini-scream, and went on: "Ooh, and did you really get a leg over 'em both? *I* would."

Agatha frowned at her phone. "This man is using a photo of Roger Moore," she said, swiping left with gusto. "I cannot be fooled."

"And whatever are you wearing?" the girl railroaded on as interested heads started to cotton to our conversation. "That dress is *fascinating*."

Something about her profound directness struck me as incredibly funny. I bit my lip to keep from laughing.

"It's McQueen," I managed, grateful that the final question had been one I could answer. "You'll be seeing these everywhere come spring. Lovely to meet you."

Finally, Richard took his place in the center of the top of the horseshoe-shaped table. I'd read about people preening like peacocks, but had never seen it in person until I watched him relish being the absolute center of ceremonial attention, moving with the body language of someone who had just whipped off his mask. At the opposite end of the head table from me, Nick—under his father's watchful eye—appeared to be doing a better job negotiating conversation between Lax and Prime Minister Tuesday than I was with my seatmates, Hax and his ambassador, who were speaking over my head in Dutch as if I were invisible.

At the appointed time, we stood for "God Save the Queen," underscoring once more the purgatory of Eleanor's absent non-absence. And then Richard silenced the room.

"It is bittersweet to be addressing you tonight," he said. "My mother has been the rock of the Commonwealth for decades. May we have a moment of silence to pray for her health."

After a beat, Richard continued. "Filling the Queen's shoes is an inconceivable task, but it is a responsibility the Duke of Clarence and I take very seriously," he said. Nick nodded gravely. Freddie stared down at his napkin.

"We are grateful to our friends from the Netherlands for joining us as planned, paying tribute to my mother while affirming that our path ahead here remains steady no matter which of us is called to walk it," he said. "And there is much to celebrate, from the bonds of friendship and family, to our own blessings, to my mother's life, and to her legacy. I will carry it proudly, as will Nicholas and his wife, and their heirs after them. I could not be more delighted that they'll be expanding their young family."

I heard a record scratch in my head. Richard was speaking theoretically—and totally out of his ass—but the entire room looked straight at me as if expecting me to stand up and give birth right there. I had no idea what to do. If I made the *no freaking way this is too soon are you shitting me you rotten git* face I was pulling inside my head, the *Daily Mail* would yell, BEX TO BABIES: BUZZ OFF! But if I went with an enigmatic smile, it would look like a confirmation. Marrying the heir had been my signature on a contract to pop out the next one, but as wrung-out newlyweds living in a museum of curios, Nick and I hadn't been ready even before the fight. There was less than zero chance of a baby now that he could barely look at me—which was not something I wanted to draw attention to, and yet suddenly it felt like twin spotlights had been trained on us, as the whole room looked to see how we reacted.

Stand tall, I imagined Eleanor saying in my head.

I grabbed my Champagne, lifted it generously in Richard's direction, and took a long, pointed gulp.

Once the dinner wound down, we could dispense with some formalities and socialize more freely, so I got back into Nick's orbit at the first opportunity and tried to back him into a quiet corner.

"What the hell was that?" I hissed.

"Something I didn't see coming," he said, then fished his phone out of his pocket and tapped on it a few times. "Kind of like this."

He handed it to me. On the screen was a photo of me, as Margot, eating my illicit burger. I swiped and saw two more, one of me ambling toward the palace with a doofy smile on my face, and another grainier one of me taking that selfie that I'd sent to Lacey in front of the Kensington Palace gift shop.

I cleared my throat. "I meant to tell you."

"I thought I was done getting Bex Bombs from Clive, but evidently not," he said.

"*Clive* sent these?" I asked. "How did he . . . is he stalking me?"

Nick shrugged. "They could have come from a source," he said. "He didn't include any exposition."

"I took a dumb risk," I said, forcing myself not to bite any of my nails.

"I don't think he can do anything with them," Nick said. "They don't look like you, and he's got no proof. I think he's just taunting me. Maybe he knows about Scotland." He stared down at them again. "Or perhaps he had a keen sense you hadn't told me."

"Finally, I get the two brothers together," I heard Daphne say, and turned to see her approaching with Freddie glued to her side. "You two have done yeoman's work tonight dividing and conquering the room."

"All part of the job," Nick said.

"Oi, Bex, congratulations on the baby," said Freddie, with a smile at us so convincing even I almost forgot it was an act. "You don't look pregnant, but perhaps you're carrying it all in your sleeves."

"Cute," I said. "But it's not polite to comment on a woman's sleeves."

"A thousand apologies, madam," Freddie said. "What's Knickers so glum about?" Freddie pulled a jovial face and went around to peer over Nick's shoulder. "Ah, hello, Margot." He looked up at me. "I thought you said no one recognized you."

Nick's hand fell to his side. "When did she say that?"

"Right after she fell through the wall in the billiard room." Freddie looked sideways at me. "Or did you . . . not tell him that part."

"She didn't tell me any part," Nick said.

A look of comprehension passed across Daphne's face. "Freddie, is that older man trying to smuggle out a fork?" she asked, grabbing his hand. "We'd better investigate."

"Smooth," I said to their retreating backs.

"But not wrong," Nick said. "That's Annabelle's husband. He's got the stickiest fingers in England. Gran was always watching him."

"Nick."

I reached for his hand. He avoided my touch. "Aha, and there's Annabelle. I didn't see her come in."

"Nick, listen to me," I said. "I'd been punchy and bored, and you were so busy that I was embarrassed to say, 'Hey, honey, have fun at work, can I please take a PPO and go get a Big Mac?'"

"I'm not your keeper, Bex," he said. "Please don't treat me that way. You don't need my permission."

I let out a frustrated breath. "I'm pretty sure I do. We don't get to be spontaneous anymore without a little subterfuge. I bumped into Freddie by accident when I was sneaking back in, and he kept the secret to be nice."

"And why did you keep it?" he asked.

"So it's not what I did that bothers you," I translated. "It's that Freddie knew it first."

Nick's jaw tensed.

"And that is why I didn't tell you," I said. "After Thanksgiving, under those circumstances, I knew it would blow up even though it was really nothing."

"Somehow, at every turn, there is something between you two that I don't know," he said softly. "That's not trivial to me."

"This is nothing like that, Nick. This was fast food and an accident."

"Keeping secrets always makes the truth look like a smokescreen," he said.

He started to walk away and then turned back and was about to say something else when Richard called for him to come discuss the next day's Parliament visit with Hax and Lax and Doris Tuesday, who appeared to have accordion-pleated her linen napkin and forgotten to put it down. Her unease was obvious, and I wondered if my own was, as well.

Transparency is a sign of weakness, I imagined Eleanor saying, and in fact, she probably had said it once. To my astonishment, I missed her. The Queen didn't like me, and I couldn't rightly say I liked her, either. But I had a very specific value to her, and since I'd stopped being called to her quarters to be lectured or stared at or instructed, I hadn't felt that value anywhere else. Certainly not with her son, who had not only declined to employ me but had restricted Eleanor's visitors to only immediate family—which, he made clear, meant only blood relatives. But if this next phase of my life was about trying to find my place in all this, I was going to follow my internal compass wherever it pointed—and tonight, Dick be damned, it pointed to the Queen. Knowing my part of the night was over, I stole away up to her rooms.

When my father died, I'd said goodbye to his body, empty of his essence—Earl Porter in flesh but not in full. I was never a religious person, although I hoped the afterlife existed; all those artists and warriors and thinkers and lovers seemed awfully wasted if their only point was to kiss the earth once and leave. Seeing Dad in front of me without his fundamental Earlness had made me a believer in the soul, if nothing else. So I was heartened to walk into Eleanor's darkened chambers and, after all this time, still not be struck by any absence of self. Her cheeks were pale, her skin was slack. The eyebrows she so frequently lofted in my direction lay chillingly still, as did she. But she wasn't gone. There was a presence here. I realized then that as long as this was true, I'd be here, too.

The nurse gave me a stern *just one minute* expression.

"Thank you," I said quietly, compelled to treat Eleanor's bed with reverence, like a church. I sat down next to her, and unbidden, tears came, a flood that made a mascara-sodden mess of the hanky Donna had tucked in my bra.

"I fucked up, Eleanor," I wept. "They're broken. We're all broken. We need you. You've got to get well and scare us all straight again, because I have no clue what to do or how to do it."

I took her hand, papery and cool, and caught myself for a second before deciding to follow my instinct and lean over to kiss her forehead. A tear fell on her skin, and as I wiped it off, I leaned closer.

"Stand tall in the storm," I whispered right into her ear. "I will if you will."

CHAPTER TWO

Right, you've picked the photo of the screaming baby," said the game show host. "Listen up. What percentage of our studio audience said it wants the Duchess of Clarence to sprog up in the new year?"

I groaned and tipped my head back in my chair.

"Sweetie, Eleanor doesn't want to hear such rude noises," admonished my mother from the screen of my iPad, propped up against a vase on the end table next to my wing chair in Eleanor's sickroom.

"Maybe I'm doing it on purpose, to annoy her back to consciousness," I said, glancing over at my New Year's Eve date. Eleanor's heart rate monitor beeped peacefully in response.

True to my vow at the state dinner, I had spent a lot of time at the Queen's bedside. I'd argued with Richard that Eleanor's prior invitations to her chambers meant she would consider me immediate family (and got surprise backup from Marta, who gave him a signature crack on the leg with her cane and gruffly said, "Get with the times, boy"). Sometimes I would sit there and say nothing while Marta, stationed across from me, pecked at various phone apps. Sometimes I ranted about the Cubs—we'd bombed out of the playoffs to the Mets, and I had a lot of feelings that only a comatose body wanted to hear—and sometimes I sketched. Dr. Google told me that reading to a patient in Eleanor's state could be beneficial; two or three times I brought over Georgina's notebooks and read her entries from the months when Henry Vane had taken over as their tutor. He'd provided a welcome and wise shoulder for the teenage Eleanor, on whom Queen Victoria II had started coming down hard in terms of etiquette and comportment, in anticipation of the line of succession swerving in her direction. Most often, though, I read the newspapers to her aloud, in case on some unconscious plane she missed her daily habit of plowing through them and would decide to wake up and do it herself.

"Can a succubus even get pregnant?" one of the comics on the show said, then laughed uproariously at himself.

"What are you *watching*?" Mom asked.

I squinted at the TV. "Some comedy game show about news polls, or something?" I said. "I'm betting hardly any of them want me to reproduce."

"Wrong! A full 84 percent of our studio audience wants a bouncing baby Bex around Buckingham this coming year," the host crowed.

"Fantastic," I said, draining the last of my drink. "At least my uterus is popular."

Richard's big mouth had the effect he surely desired: It took the low-level bump-watch I was already under, simply by virtue of being a famous married person, and shoved it into hyperdrive. *Us* reported my mother had been spied browsing the baby aisle at Target (she had been, for a friend's granddaughter). Clive opined that Nick should make sure any child of my body was actually his, and Xandra Deane wrote that I was forcing Nick into fatherhood so he didn't desert my faithless carcass (a paraphrase, but barely). Everyone else started analyzing my weight: whether I'd lost too much, or looked puffy, was too thin to get pregnant or less toned than what they considered my normal. Somehow, all those opinions existed at once. The womb-watch was officially on, and since I couldn't wander out into the street and invite people to Instagram me demolishing a pile of soft cheeses, I had to shut up and deal.

"But whose baby will it be?" one contestant asked. She pointed at Nick's photo. "Won't be his. Not after she bonked his brother."

"You can't spell *Lyons* without *lie*," said the comic, to great acclaim.

"You absolutely can. That is the only way to spell it," I said to the TV. "That joke literally only works out loud."

"Darling, switch to CNN or something," Mom said, patiently brushing crimson polish onto her pointer fingernail and then holding it up to inspect her work. "It's midnight somewhere."

"It is about to be midnight in my Champagne glass." I grabbed the bottle I'd brought and slowly turned the cork and held the bottle still. Or was I supposed to hold the cork and turn the bottle? One of them stopped the cork from—

Thunk. The cork shot out of the bottle and bounced off the monitor next to Eleanor's bed before settling on the floor. The machine beeped an admonishment at me. Marta, asleep in a chair on the other side of Eleanor, woke with a start.

"What in the bloody hell," she said.

"Sorry," I said guiltily.

"Is that Marta? Are you having a nice night, Your Majesty?" Mom called out.

"Yes, it *was* a fright, and no, it wasn't particularly nice," Marta said hotly. She waved her cane toward Eleanor's TV, which had been placed at the foot of her bed so that she and the nurses could entertain themselves. "Graham Norton, please," she said. "He's cheeky."

"I texted Nick to tell him to have fun tonight, and he sent back clinking Champagne glasses and then googly eyes and the flexing arm." I frowned, toying with the stem of my glass. "Does that mean anything or do we think he butt-emoji'd me?"

"You are asking the wrong person," Mom said.

"It means he's planning to drink his weight in bubbly," Marta said at the same time. I hadn't realized she was listening. She hadn't even turned toward me when she spoke.

"I don't know how we got to a place where I have to speak fluent emoji," I grumbled.

"You were right to make him and Freddie talk it out," Mom said. "None of those feelings were going to disappear on their own."

"I guess so," I said. "Not that it did any good. And now I feel like I went through an emotional wood chipper."

"I should've flown over."

"No, this is not how you want to ring in 2016," I said. "I'm just wallowing."

"Amen," Marta said, still looking at the TV. "Oh, that Mark Wahlburger is hunky."

Mom leaned in. "Did she say Mark Wahlberg looks funky?" she asked.

"He certainly does *not* look chunky," Marta replied, offended.

"Can you guys both stay all night?" I asked. "This is better than any party."

Well, other than the party Nick was at, which was apparently a soiree for the ages. Annabelle Farthing had told *Country Life* magazine that she was renowned for her New Year's Eve bashes when they lived in Dubai and that she was looking forward to "taking the posh set by storm." I was looking forward to Annabelle Farthing contracting norovirus and sending all her guests home. Not that Nick would necessarily choose to come back to ours.

"Why aren't you celebrating with Cilla?" Mom wondered.

"She and Gaz got roped into attending her cousin's silent retreat in Yorkshire."

I must have looked sad, because Mom suddenly tsked at herself. "You are only pretending not to need me. I am your mother. I ought to have seen that."

"I'm *fine*," I said.

But I wasn't. I'd insisted to everyone that a low-key New Year's Eve at the Queen's bedside was just what I needed. I'd ignored Cilla's entreaties to join her in the countryside, and muted Bea's phone calls; aside from one deranged moment in which I considered popping on Margot's hair and escaping to the tropics, my sole plan was to numb myself until 2015 was in the rearview mirror. In that sense, I'd been telling the truth: The Queen's chambers were exactly what I wanted. I could crawl deep into my bottle without being forced into fake-cheerful conversation, and yet I also didn't feel alone.

"Mom, please go have fun and we'll talk tomorrow, okay?" I said. "Marta and I are going to have a great time watching..." I checked the TV listing on the bedside table. "Bryan Adams's hit parade."

"I am going to hang up, but only because I have a bridge game at Hardware Pete's house," Mom said. "I think he and his wife are trying to set me up with Contractor John from John's Contractors and I am not interested, but I'll never turn down a chance to eat Pete's onion dip."

"Happy New Year, Mom. I love you."

"I love you, too," she said. She leaned up to the mic. "HAPPY NEW YEAR, MARTA."

Marta looked startled. "I'm not *deaf*," she spat.

After the state dinner, Nick had kept slipping away. Anytime I nudged the conversation in the direction of his feelings, he deflected, changed the subject, or didn't respond to me at all. More often, I caught him simply staring out the window, which I knew from past experience meant he was adrift in whatever choppy inner seas he was hiding from me. And I got the distinct impression he was circumventing going to sleep until I was already conked out, or sneaking up to bed early so he'd be snoring by the time I noticed. Sometimes I'd wake up in the night to find him wrapped around me the way he used to, and I'd breathe deeply, inhaling him, enjoying it until he stirred enough to catch himself and roll away. Other times, he didn't come up to bed at all. It wasn't healthy, and I'm sure he knew it, but he seemed to believe avoidance would keep the cracks from getting any deeper.

No such luck.

New Mentality was a subsidized in-patient facility in Dalston that served at-risk teens struggling with anxiety and depression. The organization had been making a strong play for a patronage ever since Nick had told the nation the truth about his mother's own condition a few years back, and the brothers had made mental and emotional health one of their primary causes. Freddie and Nick and I were coming by to admire New Mentality's athletic field, and then sit down for some casual roundtable discussions with the kids and staff. It was the sort of relaxed engagement both men could do in their sleep. But it was also the first time the three of us had been in close quarters since the fight and that fleeting, awkward moment at the state dinner. We were on what the palace called a "private visit," which meant there were no journalists or photographers there, and this was a blessing because even an unpaid intern on their first day would've realized something serious was up. Freddie and Nick were impassive at best, stony at worst.

I hoped they would loosen up once we got into it with the kids. We all sat on the floor of their lounge, a cozy, carpeted space done up in warm tones, which the residents had been encouraged to wallpaper with handwritten inspirational quotes, photos, and even in-jokes. Nick surprised me by breaking the ice with a short recollection of his mother, and one by one, the kids took turns discussing their unique struggles. One girl described her depression as bleaching the color out of the world; another kid said he felt like he was living inside a permanent, chilly fog. Others talked plainly about feeling anxious from the moment their eyes opened in the morning to the second they closed at night. An older teenage boy recounted lying awake obsessing about his fears, which grew and multiplied and took on lives of their own, until he felt like his brain was running on a treadmill where an unseen force kept relentlessly upping the pace.

And Nick cried.

Actual dripping tears.

Freddie shot me an alarmed glance over the top of Nick's head. Nick's public face rarely slipped, but this time it fell all the way off into his lap.

"My goodness," he managed.

The kids seemed unfazed. "People cry in here all the time," one of them said, and passed him a box of Kleenex. "You should've seen Martina the other day."

"I'm allowed to be upset," snapped a girl whose nametag ID'd her as the Martina in question. "My sister has never tried to understand me and she has some bloody nerve coming to visit *and* hitting on Jamison."

A good-looking kid I took to be Jamison winked at me. Nick simply dabbed at his eyes.

"I'm sorry," he said. "I wish my mum could meet you all. She would be very proud of you, and as inspired as I am by your strength."

It was an effective—and honest—save, but it inevitably leaked to the media that the future king had lost his composure. Much of the media and most royal watchers were sympathetic, but the *Mirror* theorized that Freddie and I had broken him, and Xandra Deane sounded the alarm that this was a breach of British tradition: A stiff upper lip does you no good if your lower one trembles, she wrote. Clive offered, You can take it from me: The Prince Regent will be furious at Namby-Pamby Nicholas, the Duke of Drip, which was incredibly hacky (as usual), but got great play on Twitter.

But Richard didn't flog Nick for any of it. I don't know if he felt too guilty to push once he heard the Emma line, or if he'd noticed that his sons no longer had any relationship to speak of and thought twice about compounding the situation. Maybe both. Regardless, Richard was still, at heart, an ass, so instead of making sure Nick was taking care of his own mental health, he tripled Nick's workload, as if to prove that this crying jag was cause specific and the heir was otherwise in robust spirits.

I'd been wondering how the hell we were all going to get through Christmas together at Sandringham, but then Richard straight-up canceled it, citing Eleanor's health. This freed up everyone to do whatever they'd always wanted to but never could, including spending the day in a place with central heating. Edwin and Elizabeth planned a proper morning of presents with their kids; Agatha invited my mother on a posh singles trip to Mallorca that sounded mortifying, but which Mom agreed to do because she had just read Shonda Rhimes's book *Year of Yes*; and I don't know what Richard had in store, but I assume it involved going to an orphanage and cutting the power. Freddie disappeared completely; Bea hinted he'd gone skiing with a tech executive he'd met. And I spent my feelings on holiday decorations.

One of the great benefits of living in a mansion is that if you really commit to decking the hell out of your copious halls, you have less time to concentrate on the fact that your husband is avoiding you. I procured and trimmed a giant, twinkling tree in the living room, and an even bigger one in the foyer. I hung stockings by several chimneys, with care. I bought whimsical holiday-themed throw pillows and swapped out our candles for winter-scented ones. We had nutcrackers and Santas and even a Grinch or two scattered all over the communal areas, every window had a wreath, and everything that I could hang a garland from was begarlanded. It screamed, "Our first married Christmas will be extremely fucking festive, *Nicholas*," in a way that I myself wanted to but knew I should not.

It didn't work. Christmas morning was gloomy and distant and very much *not* extremely fucking festive. It felt like my decorations were mocking me for being foolish enough to think I could paper over our problems with expensive holiday cheer. Nick gave me a treadmill I could wheel out to the upstairs terrace, because he knew I missed running outside—which was thoughtful but unromantic—and then almost broke down again when he burned the hell out of breakfast.

"They're just toaster waffles, Nick," I said, but it came out more irritably than I intended.

He rubbed his face. "I know. But it's just been…"

"A long year," I finished.

"Yeah," he said.

"For me, too," I said. "I guess I hoped we could put it behind us today, of all days, but apparently not."

He poked at his ruined waffle. "I want to."

"Honestly, it doesn't seem like you're trying that hard."

"Pardon me if this apocalypse was a bit too complicated to pencil into a timetable," he crabbed.

"Nick, I love you," I said. "But let's get real. It's Christmas and this house feels like a mausoleum. If you're not going to talk to me about it, or you're not going to talk to me, period, then what the hell are we even doing here?" I shoved away my plate. "Maybe I should go to Iowa. Or you should go to Cornwall. When was the last time you spent Christmas Day with your mom?"

Nick blinked. "You're kicking me out?"

"No!" I said, exasperated. "I'm making a suggestion. Any suggestion at all. This isn't going great, in case you hadn't noticed."

Nick pulled on his hair. "What kind of man leaves his wife on their first married Christmas?"

"Someone whose wife told him to," I said. "Look, things suck here right now. And I know you're always pulled in two directions on holidays, so let this be one time you're not. Consider it a Christmas gift."

"But what are you going to do?"

I shrugged. "What have I been doing for the last few weeks, besides decorating? It'll be like that, but without you snoring on your office couch."

He looked sad. "I would really love to see her."

"I'm not stopping you," I said. "Get out of here, already. Go."

He did.

"What's the time?" yawned Marta.

I glanced at my watch. "Eleven forty-five," I said. "Not long now."

I had to give Marta credit. The only New Year's Eve on which my dad stayed awake past midnight, we'd forced the issue with a 10:45 p.m. dinner reservation, but Marta, well into her eleventh decade, had been remarkable. She'd noodled around on her phone, given a lot of feedback to the various guests on Graham Norton (she did *not* care for the cut of Will Ferrell's jib), and even hummed along to the Bryan Adams concert that would bookend the fireworks over London. All while avoiding asking me anything overtly personal.

"Why the hell is your husband at a party without you?" she asked. "You're too young to be spending New Year's Eve watching telly with an old woman."

I guess it was only a matter of time.

"He's..." I searched for a lie. "He needed to stay down in Cornwall for scheduling reasons."

"So he's avoiding you," Marta said. "I don't miss a trick."

Nick had made a beeline for his mother's serene seaside home, and then...stayed there. The week between Christmas and New Year's was traditionally quiet for the royals, but Nick must have asked Richard to keep him busy, because two engagements in that neck of the woods suddenly found their way onto his diary. He communicated this only in the most basic of texts, giving me a hearty dose of what it must have been like for everyone else during our summer of hiding; I felt disregarded and terrible, and retroactively ashamed of myself.

Now, on New Year's Eve, he'd used geography as an excuse to keep hiding. He'd attended vespers at the abbey in Bath, then "decided to make an appearance" at Annabelle Farthing's bash.

Off south again to Portsmouth in the morning, he'd texted me. Makes sense to use one of her guest rooms and stay off the roads.

It didn't escape my notice that he hadn't invited me to join him. Neither had Annabelle. Worse than that, though, was that it wouldn't have been *that* impractical, or taken much effort, for Nick to come home. He just must not have wanted to. Not enough. When I told him to go, I hadn't realized I needed to worry about whether he'd come back.

Marta poked at me with her cane. "I assume it's to do with Frederick," she said. She tapped her temple. "You all think I don't see things because I'm old, but I could tell. It's not my first foxtrot, you know."

"How did you deal with it?" I asked. "With Eleanor and Georgina, I mean."

She looked at me sharply. "Eh?"

"The journals I found," I said. "In their girlhood, she and Eleanor come off like Nick and Freddie, a bit. They were clearly very close. But it obviously didn't stay that way. What happened?"

Marta's expression grew distant. I had forgotten to consider whether it was too painful to discuss her daughters this way, given that she'd long outlived one, and might yet survive the other. But then she spoke.

"It wasn't easy when we realized Eleanor was going to be queen," she said. "Heavy is the head, and all that. Georgina is little more than a footnote now, and I wonder..." She closed her eyes. "Some wounds are too deep to heal."

We sat in silence, which I thought was both of us processing this until I realized she'd fallen back asleep a few minutes shy of midnight. I wondered what alternate reality Marta had been thinking about; I'd been busy resisting quizzing her about the other thing I'd found, something better than a journal. My quest to see if Georgina owned the second part of *Little Women* had hit the jackpot in more ways than one: Tucked inside the pages, right near where Jo finds out that Laurie went and married that unrepentant book burner Amy, was a letter:

My darling,

That you should ever read those words, and see my soul in them, sends a tingle down my spine. It would take the courage of this entire nation for me to even give this to you, but I cannot live with all these words pent up inside of me, bursting to escape, wrapping you in their cursive arms, each dot in every ellipsis substituting for the kisses I long to give you... and then... and then... everything. Ellie says I'm silly, flighty, a terrible flirt. Perhaps I am. But my heart beats, too, just as hers does. Or will you agree? Will I send you this and then be told I'm only seventeen, that I don't know my own mind, that I can't know my own feelings, that I must sit still and behave?

I don't believe you could ever be so cruel. I may not be serious, but you have always taken me seriously. Did you feel what I felt when we bumped hands? Did your skin cry for mine with every touch? It must have. Mine could not burn so hotly without there being a spark in return. I am passion and I am fire, and all of it is yours, if you'd come find me.

Unless... and remember what those dots represent, my darling... unless I don't send this at all. Unless I fold it up and tuck it to my heart and keep you there instead, the only way I can guarantee that I can hold you close to me forever. What do I do? What would you do, my love, my only, my life, my

There was no final page, an agonizing analog version of your DVR cutting off the last three minutes of your show. I had yelped when I realized that was all I was going to get; I'd opened up nearly every book in the library and shaken them to see if the rest of the letter had been tucked away somewhere, and had no luck. (Instead, I found a receipt proving that shortly before her death, Georgina had spent two hundred pounds at Pizza Express.) I'd been so tempted to ask Marta about it, but the letter thrummed with forbidden ardor, and mentioning it to Georgina's mother—even sixty years later—felt like violating a confidence. So tonight, I held the letter metaphorically to me, as I'd held it physically to my heart on that Christmas night, and repeated her words like they were my own mantra. *I am passion and I am fire, and all of it is yours, if you'd come find me.*

Who knows when I actually dozed off, but my Champagne bottle had suffered a serious depletion, producing a vivid dream that Nick was shaking me awake while wearing a tiara.

"Bex," he said to me. "Come on, let's get home to bed."

I peeled open my dry eyes. My mascara, which I'd applied in a misplaced fit of holiday spirit, had turned to glue. Nick was standing before me, his shirt askew, a New Year's crown atop his head. He smelled like a brewery.

"You're here," I said, grabbing at him as if trying to make absolutely sure he wasn't an illusion. "You're alive. Are you drunk?" I blinked. "*I'm* drunk."

"Popeye drove me back," he said sloppily. "Happy New Year."

He bent down to kiss me, and I moved my face. "No. We don't get to kiss. I'm mad at you," I said.

"What do you mean?" He frowned.

"I am going to tell you," I slurred, holding up some shaky fingers. "First, when I told you to go to your mother's, I didn't mean that you shouldn't come home. Third, you've been gone a week, and you barely texted me. And second"—I waved another finger in his face—"you went to a New Year's Eve party and left me at home to spend it with your grandmother. Who is in a coma, Nick. A *coma*."

"I am a prat," he agreed.

"Thank you." I crossed my arms. He leaned toward me. "Nope, I'm still annoyed."

"The party was awful," Nick said, "and I realized it was a mistake and all I wanted was to come home to you. Does that help?"

"Yes," I said. "It does."

He knelt by my chair and laid his head in my lap. "I am so sorry I stayed away," he said. "And I'm sorrier that even when I was here, I wasn't *really* here at all."

"You had a lot on your mind," I said, unable to resist stroking his hair.

"Bex, am I a...runner-awayer?" he asked. "That cannot be the right word. I wish I hadn't drunk that last ale." He sat up to look at me. "We ran away to Scotland. I ran away to Cornwall. I don't want to be a person who keeps running away from things. But I got spooked. Everything those kids said about their feelings that day at New Mentality are things that *I* feel, too, sometimes. I couldn't stop thinking about how they couldn't stop thinking about whatever *they* were anxious about, and then I couldn't stop thinking about how maybe everything I was going through meant that I was headed toward...wherever my Mum is, and *then* I couldn't stop thinking that if it happened to me, too, then maybe..." He gulped. "Maybe you chose wrong."

"Oh, love," I said, scooting down to the floor with him. "A lot of people are depressed or have anxiety and it doesn't go to that place. All those kids were doing so much better! That was the whole point of that visit. They were getting help, and it was working."

"Exactly." Nick looked serious. "After I spent a few days with Mum, I thought, *No. This won't be me.* She didn't have a choice. But maybe I still do," he said. "I don't have the answers, but we are the problem like Maria that I want to solve, and I don't know how I thought I was supposed to do it alone."

"You know I can't resist you when you quote *The Sound of Music.*"

He sat back on his heels and nearly tipped over. "I miss you. I love you," he said, steadying himself. "You're the one thing in my life that I want to choose again and again. We do better together." He smiled broadly. "And on that tip, I've had a brilliant idea, Rebecca."

"Do tell, Nicholas," I said, plucking a very sticky eyelash out of my lower lid. "Is my mascara amazing right now?"

"It is all under your eyes. You look like Batman," he said. "And you might remember from our first Halloween how sexy I find Batman."

"You were Batman. I was Darth Vader," I said.

"Yes, and if you recall, I was very sexy," he said. "But listen. Mum and Father went on a tour of someplace or other right about a year after they got married. I can't remember where. It would be a better story if I could. But regardless. We should do that. Let's get out of here and find our Bex and Nick bubble again."

"But you just said you didn't want to be a runner-awayer," I pointed out.

"Aha! This is not running away!" His sense of triumph nearly knocked him over. "We've never tried a bubble where we're *also* being the Duke and Duchess of Clarence. This bubble wouldn't be running away from something. We'd be running *to* something." He clapped his hands. "It's the best of both worlds. A fresh start, doing work together that isn't about deflecting headlines. So we're on the job, but we can be in a bubble at the same time." He looked at me hopefully. "It's worth a shot, yes?"

"It's worth every shot," I said. "But we need to talk about Freddie. Part of the problem is that we didn't talk about him last time."

Nick looked contemplative. "Let's do that part when we're more sober." He clambered to his feet and hauled me up gracelessly. "I solemnly swear we will not do anything rash, nor leave anything unsaid. Not again. Do we get to kiss yet?"

I took his face in my hands with a wicked grin. When we came up for air, he teased, "I hope this doesn't scandalize Gran."

"All due respect to Her Maj, I don't really care."

He swept me into another kiss that was interrupted only when Marta shouted out Daniel Craig's name in her sleep. Nick extracted himself from our embrace to tuck a blanket up around her body, then turned to Eleanor and touched her hand.

"Happy New Year, Gran," he said.

Eleanor's eyes flew open and locked on mine.

CHAPTER THREE

History will likely tell it that when Eleanor came back to us, order was restored—that she woke up surrounded by her family, that her indomitable spirit had won the day, that she was undiminished and regal from the jump, that we all held hands around her bedside and offered thanks to the God that returned her to us, and that her first words were... well, anything other than what they actually were. What really happened: She awoke and started murmuring, Nick screamed and slammed his hand down on the alarm button on her nightstand, and then he called Richard while the palace medical staff elbowed us aside to buzz around her. All the while, Eleanor's gaze flicked blearily around the room, as if clocking her surroundings and deeming them wanting.

"Mother?" Richard gasped when he arrived, white as a sheet and wearing an immaculate pin-striped suit even though it was 3:52 a.m. He leaned low over her and placed a hand on her head. "Can it be true?"

That's when Queen Eleanor uttered her first words in months: "Fuck off."

*

We'd been warned about the consequences of Eleanor's four-month medical odyssey. Her team was stunned that she had returned to us at all, given how low the odds were, and it warned us that she would likely be physically and/or mentally different than the woman we once knew.

That she'd been able to get her mouth around the words *fuck off* was something of a miracle, though her voice was thick with lack of use. None of us had taken her "fuck off" instructions personally, or even seriously, but we would soon learn it was a harbinger of a saltier Queen Eleanor experience.

"Good morning, Your Majesty," I said on my first visit after she awoke, clutching a bouquet of hothouse roses I'd commandeered from the Queen's own greenhouse. "You look great!"

"Don't lie to me," Eleanor grumped. "I look old."

It was jarring to see the toll the last few months had taken. Lying there, her facial muscles inert, Eleanor had looked nearly untouched by time. Now that she was up again, her skin showed the dry, dull impact of being eighty-one years old and ailing. Her hair, usually sleek, was wild and split from overgrowth. Her mouth drooped ever so slightly at one corner, probably a permanent side effect of the stroke. Nick had told me that during his visit, she occasionally had to pause to find a word or struggled to enunciate, and I could already tell her voice hadn't strengthened yet. Her right arm would need physical therapy. These were all small trade-offs for her life, but I could tell from the way her left hand fussed at her hair and her face that she didn't care for them one bit.

"It's only been a few weeks. You're not supposed to look like nothing happened," I said. "I'm just happy to come in here and see you sitting up and glaring at me again."

"Glaring is my only solace," she sighed melodramatically. "They won't even let Fabio in to trim my ends. I'm falling apart."

Marta barely looked up from her iPhone. "By all means keep wailing about it," she said, then turned her phone toward us. "Your friend Clive went on *Sunrise* and said that if Eleanor really is fully recovered, he'll eat his hat."

"He's not my friend," I said.

"He is a reprobate of the highest order," Eleanor said. She picked up the phone on her nightstand. "Murray," she said. "Send Clive Fitzwilliam the largest hat you can find. Make sure it looks poisonous."

"I don't know if poking the bear is the best idea..." I began.

Eleanor appeared to focus very hard on spitting out the words. "Nonsense," she said. "I'm the bear. *He* poked *me*." She pointed toward my usual chair. "Sit. What did I miss?"

"Do you mean, like…globally?" I asked.

"Boring," she said. "I meant gossip."

"Uh," I said gracefully. Eleanor had once suggested that gossip was the devil's breath. "The Dutch seemed to have a blast at the—"

"Yawn," Eleanor said. "Everyone who comes up here wants to talk about"—and here, she made irritated air quotes with her left hand—"'the monarchy' and 'appearances' and 'my medical situation.' It's dull as a dirge. I assumed our resident American would be the most willing to indulge in a little…what's the phrase you use? Shit-talking?"

"Uhhhhhhh," I responded again. I hadn't been prepared for this level of feistiness. "Let's see. Lacey—"

"I don't care," Eleanor said. "Next."

Apparently some things hadn't changed. "How about this? Freddie's been seeing a marine biologist."

"That won't last," Eleanor said. "But I suppose I should be relieved he behaved himself while I was gone."

"*Gone.* Stop acting like you were on vacation, dear," Marta said.

I cleared my throat. "Anyway," I said. "Lady Elizabeth almost named the baby Eldrick, which she thought would be a nice tribute to you, but Agatha talked her into Peter."

"Remind me to give Agatha a little bauble for that."

"Richard tried having a goatee for about a week," I said. Eleanor made a disgusted face. "Agatha talked him out of that, too. No one saw it."

Eleanor tapped her chin. "Perhaps a medium-size bauble."

"But Nigel has been wearing a lot of high-fashion sweatpants and *everyone* has seen those."

"Foul," Eleanor said. "Back to the small bauble."

I turned to Marta for confirmation. "And I heard Edwin finally played a four-letter word in Scrabble?"

"Yes, but the word was *word*," Marta said. "Also, Rebecca has done very little of note, Nicholas cried in public, and they've still not let Idris

Elba be James Bond. If they don't pony up soon, what will have been the point of my living this long?"

"Nicholas cried?" Eleanor looked astounded. "In front of people?"

"He'd had a rough week," I hedged.

After our reconciliation, Nick and I were taking it slowly, almost as if we were courting again. We stayed up late eating takeout and watching terrible TV—Nick was heavily invested in *Love Island*—and snuck over to Lacey and Olly's flat for a game night. Family business was on a mild pause after Eleanor's surprise reawakening while everyone figured out what it meant and what it did or didn't change, so we could afford to hole up and compensate for some of the time together we'd missed. We'd also enlisted Marj to find Nick a therapist, and a day later she got him in with a highly recommended hotshot named Dr. Heath Keplington, so chosen because Marj thought Nick had great female influences in his life but needed to meet a man who knew how to communicate, and also—she admitted this—because he had the name of a soap star and the looks (and locks) of a young Hugh Grant. Nick now mentioned Dr. Kep about six hundred times an hour, so it seemed to be a match made in psychological heaven.

Accordingly, Nick had kept his promise to discuss Freddie with me once we weren't addled with New Year's liquor and lust. He'd even brought it up himself, a few nights later, when the two of us were drinking hot chocolate out on the terrace. Snow was in the forecast, and you could smell it; the clouds felt heavy and exciting and full of possibility. We bundled up and sat outside on old plastic beach loungers and turned our faces to the sky, waiting for the flakes to fall, enjoying the romance of the warm drink and the chill on our cheeks.

"This is so relaxing," Nick said happily. "I missed this feeling."

"Relaxed looks good on you," I said, bopping the pom-pom on top of his Cubs knit cap, which tragically he had never been able to wear in public.

"Mum would have loved this," he said. "It snowed an enormous amount once when we were kids, and we stayed out until well past dark trying to build a snowman. We'd forgotten clothes for him so Freddie went in and grabbed whatever he could find." He smiled. "Father's Coldstream Guards hat smelled like a wet dog for a while. Mum had to hide it while it dried out." Nick's grin faded. "I wonder if Freddie remembers that."

I said nothing.

"Thank you for not asking," Nick said. "I know you want to hear that I'm ready to forgive and forget, but I'm not there yet." He tipped his face up to the sky. "We had such a good thing, the two of us, and then the *three* of us, and then he buggered it. Leaving everything else aside, it was so careless and thoughtless and stupid of him to risk all that."

"But also, you *can't* leave everything else aside."

Nick shook his head. "Dr. Kep thinks this has all changed who Freddie is to me, and that I have to mourn the old him before we can be anything new."

"Dr. Kep is probably right," I said to Nick. "And I know it bothers you that Freddie and I still hang out, but—"

"Did you ever consider it?" Nick blurted out.

"Consider what?"

Nick busied himself with retying one corner of the cushion to the chair's metal frame. "Choosing him," he said. "I know, I know, you didn't, but you've never told me how hard you had to think about it."

I looked at him for a second. "We said honesty, so okay, here goes," I said. "Yes. I did consider it. You have to understand, it wasn't about Freddie to me. It was more of me weighing, one last time, whether I thought the life that comes with you is one that I could live."

"It wasn't because any part of you loves him?" Nick sounded nervous.

"I didn't say that. A part of me does love him," I said. "All of me loves him, actually. He's Freddie. I stopped getting to make new friends when you and I got serious. He filled that void for me." I took Nick's hand. "He's not the brother I was willing to face the wrath of the world with, and he's not the one I will write love letters about, which I'll leave in Sex Den for some future generation to find. But in my own way, even if it's not the way he wanted, I love him."

"Dr. Kep thanks you in advance for the billable hours," Nick cracked, but he wasn't smiling.

"I'm not saying that to hurt you. But I am done dancing around how I feel." I turned on my side to face him. "I miss my friend. I want to be able to see him without you thinking it means anything."

Nick closed his eyes. "This is going to be hard."

"It is," I agreed. "But if we both back away, and then you realize you're ready for him again, he might be too far gone for either of us."

"You're keeping my foot in the door, as it were," he said.

"However you want to look at it."

Nick stroked my cheek with his gloves. His fingers caught a strand of my hair, which became electrified with static.

"We always do have sparks," he said teasingly.

A remote control landed hard in my lap. I emerged from my reverie to see Eleanor looking impatiently at me.

"Find something on TV that isn't awful," she said. "Richard made me watch a highlight reel of things I'd missed in Parliament. Can you imagine the torture?"

"I mean, you did tell him to fuck off," I said.

"*Language*, Rebecca," Eleanor said, horrified.

I clapped my hand over my mouth.

"Ah. I see your sense of humor fucked off with him," she said.

I burst out laughing. "I don't even know what to say right now. I'm so off-kilter."

"I'm getting a little revenge for those things you did while I was in my semi-coma," she said.

"Do you remember any of that?"

"I was vaguely aware of people coming and going, and I heard snippets of words here and there, but it was very dreamlike, and surreal," she said. "I do recall you stomping around talking about your sports team, but then your hair caught on fire, which I assume I hallucinated." She frowned. "It was a strange state to be in, and now, I can't feel that passage of time anymore. It's as if I just blinked."

"We felt every day of it," I said. "Richard did you proud, but the public missed you."

"Did he enjoy having my job?"

Richard's face the night of the state dinner flashed into my mind. He was glowing, glad-handing dignitaries, deeply pleased with himself. "He wasn't happy about the *reason* for his regency," I hedged.

"He came in here with a whole list of accomplishments, to suggest that perhaps he should remain in the position while I am rehabbing," she said, her nostrils flaring. "He's probably right but I sent him packing anyway. He was very cross." And then she winked at me, not without some effort. I started flipping through the channels to avoid reacting.

"Stop there," Eleanor said, when I landed on *Entertainment Tonight*. "I have a bad feeling about Brad and Angelina. Although they did send me beautiful flowers." She waved at a tremendous bouquet of out-of-season peonies. "Now. There's something we need to discuss."

"Oh yes, about that," I said. "Nick and Freddie are—"

"Rebecca, if you don't have that under some semblance of control by now, please keep me in divine ignorance of your failure," Eleanor said. "This is important. This is about me." She put her hands to her chest. "I have cheated death."

Next to her, Marta grunted.

"*Cheated death*," Eleanor repeated, "and now I'd like to have more of a life. I intend to have fun."

We looked at each other. The longer she said nothing, the more certain I was that being Eleanor's official purveyor of post-near-death fun was about to become my full-time job.

"Well?" Eleanor prodded. "Where do we start?"

Everything that popped into my mind was inappropriate for an ailing octogenarian—beer pong, bungee jumping, skinny-dipping in the Buckingham Palace pool (though I tucked that one away for me and Nick).

"Have you ever been to McDonald's?" I heard myself ask instead.

Marta made a *not bloody likely* noise, and Eleanor said, "Something inside the palace, for now. Something reckless but simple. Perhaps I shall order a crumpet *untoasted*."

"Careful, don't sprain anything," I said.

She balled up the sheets in her left hand. "I don't hear any better ideas from you."

"How about…a margarita?" I asked. "Have you ever had one of those? Are you even allowed to right now?"

"I have not, and I do as I please," Eleanor said. She tapped her chin. "I should also like to buy clothing on the internet. Things I don't need, seasonally inappropriate, and very unlikely to fit properly. Mummy, I expect you're writing this down."

Another noise from Marta. I translated it correctly and took out my phone and opened up a new note.

"And you can show me a baseball match," Eleanor continued. "You natter on about it so much, I should see what the fuss is about."

"It's the off-season right now," I said. "But I can teach you how the game works, so that once they start up again, you'll be ready to go."

"Good. That will entertain me during the interminable physical therapy for *this*," Eleanor said, casting a disdainful look at her arm.

"If you don't mind my asking," I said, "why me? I always felt like…more of a thorn in your side."

"Too right," Marta said.

"Because other than my mother, you're the only member of this family who has ever cursed regularly in my presence, which means you are capable of speaking to me like a human," Eleanor said.

I gazed at her in wonderment. Her hair was a mess. She wore no lipstick, nor a giant fancy brooch chosen for maximum intimidation. She had a pillow mark on her cheek from her earlier nap. Before my eyes, she had begun morphing from Her Majesty the Queen, my most terrifying opponent, into…my grandmother-in-law.

"Well, then, it's a good thing I didn't fuck off," I said.

I left the palace upbeat. It was as if Georgina—at least, the way I liked to imagine her—had gotten bored in the Great Beyond and resurrected herself through Eleanor. I was still giggling when I arrived at Marj's office at Clarence House, to Nick's bemusement.

"Your grandmother," I said, dropping into a chair, "apparently wants to have fun."

He was nonplussed. "What does fun *mean* to her exactly?" he asked. "Are we talking medieval torture, or Parcheesi, or..."

"She wants me to teach her baseball," I said.

"To play?" he sputtered. "She can't even use her right hand."

"No, goofus. To watch." I sat up straight and wriggled my shoulders proudly. "I, Rebecca, Duchess of Clarence, and daughter of Earl Porter of the Iowa Porters, am going to turn the Queen into a Cubs fan."

Nick grinned. "God save us all."

"That is indeed the dream," said Marj, sweeping in behind us and dropping a binder onto her desk. She sat down behind it and folded her hands together. "You are aware, of course, that Nicholas broached the topic of going on tour. Congratulations. The Prince of Wales and the Queen agree that it is time for our newlyweds to engage in a little diplomacy."

She opened the binder to the title page, which read *A Selective North American Adventure*. "You'll go in July, which gives us about five months to plan. You'll start in Canada, and then pop over the border to Rebecca's homeland. Strengthening the special relationship, and so forth. It'll mean a lot of work, but we've procured help."

She waved at someone in the hallway—I hadn't even noticed that the door was open—and suddenly, standing beside Marj was Lady Bollocks.

"Bea?" I said, startled. "Are you, like, an expert on Canada, or something?"

"I did live there for five years," Bea said.

"You did?"

"No," Bea said. "But the fact that you didn't know for certain is telling."

"Everything is a quiz with this one," I said to Marj, hooking my thumb at Bea as if we were some kind of vaudeville act.

"Beatrix was essential in our efforts to prepare you to join this family," Marj said, "and so I thought she'd be ideal in this capacity. Which brings me to another announcement."

At this, she closed the binder and looked at Nick with a lifetime of tenderness. "This tour shall be my swan song," she said. "I'm retiring this summer."

"What?" Nick sat bolt upright. "Marjie, no. How can we live without you?"

"My dear." She beamed. "It's been my honor to watch you grow from a sweet little boy into a fine young man, and a privilege to help you along that path." She rested her hands in her lap. "But I'm tired. And I'm old. And I have a husband whom I don't see nearly as much as I'd like. I plan to work in tandem with my replacement on this operation, and then hand over the reins."

"Marj..." Nick shook his head. "I can't believe it. You've been brilliant. I hope you know you're irreplaceable."

"I certainly hope not," Bea said.

With growing alarm, I noticed a satisfied smile lurking at the edges of Bea's mouth.

"Beatrix is the easiest hire I've made," Marj said. "She's trusted. She's loyal. She's already worked with Rebecca, and she knows the two of you very well but isn't afraid to crack the whip, as it were."

"With Bea that will probably be literal," I muttered.

"And there's her impressive resume, and all the crisis management work she's done with major global organizations," Marj said.

"She *has*?" Nick said.

Bea crossed her arms and looked stonily at me. "You really do think that I hang about doing dressage all day." She and Marj traded an amused glance. "You're about to get rudely awakened."

"If she can handle the Red Cross, she can handle you two," Marj said. She put on her glasses. "Beatrix and I have already hashed out the logistics for the next several months of planning."

"Logistics about the logistics," I quipped.

"We'll run point together until you leave, and then I'll merely consult while Beatrix is in charge," Marj said. "Once you're home from what I'm certain will be a smashing success, I shall step away completely, and you'll be all hers."

"In other words, don't muck this up, or else we will not have a pleasant beginning." Bea leaned over and placed her hands on the desk.

With her slicked-back hair and black pantsuit, she looked like a panther poised to spring upon its prey. "Is that clear?"

Nick and I raised our eyebrows at each other. As a friend, Bea's loyalty was peerless and fierce. But almost any directive from Eleanor promised to be a vacation compared with being under the professional, official thumb of Lady Beatrix Larchmont-Kent-Smythe.

CHAPTER FOUR

"That is appalling." Eleanor sat back in her armchair in disgust. Her pewter topknot bobbled. "Does that man need an eye exam? That pitch clearly painted the corner."

I bit back a smile. "Are you having fun yet?" I asked.

"There's an awful lot of spitting and adjusting oneself," she said.

"I did warn you," I said.

"Yes, well, you were also correct that a proper game is very diverting," Eleanor allowed. "I particularly like the players who pull their socks up over their trousers. It's jaunty."

True to her word, Eleanor had spent the last ten weeks having me explain the rules of baseball. Our lessons had started off rocky; I hadn't realized how weird baseball is until I had to dive into the nitty-gritty with a person who felt the need to interrogate absolutely everything.

"Are you telling me," Eleanor had said irritably, "that you pitch *the* ball, but you can also pitch *a* ball, and they mean different things?"

"Yes," I said. "You'll get used to it."

"It's nonsensical," Eleanor said. "They need to call it something else. A *fault*, like tennis. Or a *miss*."

"Okay, but a missed swing is already a miss," I said.

"A ball is already a ball," she fired back. "Ludicrous."

Eleanor also felt that the "safe" signal looked like it should mean "strike," and deeply disapproved of the concept of a checked swing

("No wonder men these days don't understand commitment," she sniffed). But she was a scrupulous pupil, so much so that I exhausted myself cuing up illustrative ESPN highlights to answer her questions, and nearly went hoarse the day we discussed the designated-hitter rule. A few times, I had to call in sick, just so I could plow through the piles of trip-related homework Bea had assigned. My dedication was paying off, though: Eleanor was easily more fluent in the sport than Nick.

Marta had scoffed at all this, going so far as to loudly fake snore while I tried to explain what a balk is. But now, as we watched the Cubs' opening game on the DVR, she sat in her usual corner tweeting GIFs of Jake Arrieta at the Los Angeles Angels Twitter account and hurling opinions like fastballs at the TV.

"You may suck it, young man!" she crowed at Mike Trout, who looked aggrieved after striking out.

So maybe I wasn't the best influence. But it was mutually satisfying: Eleanor got to cross items off her Death-Cheating Fun List, and I got my own Cubs fan club inside the walls of Buckingham Palace. It tickled me knowing that the swirl of tourists and taxi drivers clogging the Mall imagined something far more refined happening inside.

"I don't know what Trout was thinking swinging at that," Eleanor said, licking some salt off the rim of her margarita before taking a sip. That, at least, had been an easy item to check off, and it had been a huge hit—save for one hiccup when an errant Applebee's commercial led to her demanding a mangorita, and the kitchen couldn't hunt down decent fruit.

I patted myself on the back theatrically. "All this and it's only opening day. You'll be a salty, heartbroken veteran in no time. I am a brilliant teacher."

"No, I am a brilliant student," Eleanor boasted. "Always was."

"Yes, I've read all about it," I told her. "Although Georgina seemed to think you were mostly applying yourself because you had the hots for Henry Vane."

Eleanor shot me a stern look. "I did not have *the hots* for anyone. I was a child."

"You know what I mean," I said. "Lots of little girls get crushes. I had a huge one on Derek Jeter."

"What's a Derek Jeter?" Marta asked.

"I can assure you that our feelings developed appropriately," Eleanor said. She tried to flex her right hand. It fought her. "Georgina got to finish her schooling in France, but I was made to stay in the country I was meant to rule. Henry was the only friend I had left. He always treated me like an equal, whether I was a little girl or the future queen. That dynamic has been rare in my life."

"And that's how you fell in love?" I asked. "Nick and I were friends first, too."

"Naturally I was drawn to him," she said. "Henry was shy, you know. Meeting people was difficult for him also. And then when his father died and he became the Duke of Cleveland, his mother expected him to try to carry on their political legacy, but he was never aggressive enough to make a success of that sort of life."

"Their political legacy had been crap for generations by then, anyway," Marta said.

"He ended up with a much bigger legacy," I said. "He must have loved you very much to step into this spotlight if he was so shy."

Eleanor had a faraway expression on her face. "He would have done anything for me. He was very protective."

"I'm sorry I didn't get to meet him," I said. "Or Georgina. I live in her house, and I've read so many stories about her but I still feel like I don't have the whole picture of who she was."

Eleanor sucked on the inside of her cheek and glanced over at her mother, who was dozing off.

"My sister was everyone's favorite," she said. "Pretty and funny and lively. Everything that makes life easy for a person. But because of that, she thought everything *else* should come easily to her, too, and it made her impetuous and selfish. She had a wild imagination and a skewed perception of the world. Don't put too much stock in those journals of hers."

Marta's head had dropped forward. She let out a snore.

"I did find part of a love letter recently," I confessed.

"Georgina had many suitors," Eleanor said. "That Elvis Presley bit is, regrettably, absolutely accurate. She once served Agatha the worst sandwich because of that man."

"I *wish* this had been to him," I said, "but she wrote it way earlier than that. There was no name on it. She must not have ever sent it? The whole thing sounded forbidden."

Eleanor glanced at the snoozing Marta, then looked back at the Cubs. "There was one young man," she said. "The son of one of Father's equerries. He'd become a veterinarian. Mummy and Daddy told Georgina in no uncertain terms that he was beneath her, and sent the lot of them away. She was heartbroken."

"That's awful."

"They thought it would pass, and she'd settle down, but she was always stubborn, so terribly stubborn. She shut most of us out, and spent her life chasing pleasure with an increasingly vapid series of handsome idiots," Eleanor said. "You've seen the pictures. Frankly, it always made me worry about Frederick, even before that cataclysm with you. He and Georgina have many things in common, and falling for the wrong person is one of them."

"His tastes have elevated since me," I said. "He's dating an expert in nuclear disarmament."

"And the marine biologist?"

"Ehhhh..." I hedged.

Eleanor made a noise indicating that this was no surprise.

"Personally, I have found being romantically unencumbered to be freeing," she said. "Frederick should try being alone for longer than fifteen minutes. It's unrealistic to expect to find peace in the arms of someone else if you can't find it within yourself." She glanced over at me and raised a brow. "Yes, I'm quite wise. Don't look so surprised."

"I'm not surprised. I just think you should tell him that," I said.

"What makes you think I haven't?" Eleanor said. "Now, call down to the kitchen for some Champagne. Our Cubs have won their opening game."

"This is the building where Congress works."

"The Capitol," Nick said. "With an *O*."

"First president?"

Nick scoffed. "George Washington. Everyone knows that."

"I didn't make these notecards. Take it up with Bea," I said, setting that one aside on the messy "correct" pile that was spilling across the desk in our Apartment 1A royal tour war room. "My turn."

Whenever it felt like my entire life was in flux—the shifting sands of my relationship with Eleanor, whatever was going on with Freddie and Nick, the ever-changing expectations of the public, even the wallpaper in my bathrooms—it was reassuring to have one thing I could count on: Lady Bollocks assuming I was a dumbass. Seemingly every day Nick and I took deliveries of neatly collated tour binders titled and annotated in her persnickety penmanship. The first ones focused on each city we were visiting, then expanded into the organizations we'd be touring, dossiers on local dignitaries, dress-code suggestions for specific situations—the one for the Calgary Stampede was called *Western Wear (Respectful)*—and even one that listed the political opinions I was to avoid while on American soil during an election year (in short: all of them). Cilla had texted me one day that she'd walked in on Bea and Marj chortling over an office supply catalog, and I was happy that Marj was handing the reins over to someone who shared her organizational élan and who was, in many senses, the devil I at least knew. But that didn't mean I enjoyed Bea's ensuing weekly quizzes, which required cram sessions.

"What is the name of Winnipeg's Canadian Football League team?" Nick asked.

"We're not even going to Winnipeg!" I protested. "I'm sorry, but there is no way Bea knew Canada *had* a football league until two months ago."

"If I've learned anything, it's that we've no idea what Bea knows and when she knew it," Nick said. "I need your answer."

I leaned back in my chair, an old, overstuffed chintz number. "The Winnipeg…Wombats?"

"That is not even a sincere guess," Nick said. "It's the Blue Bombers.

Famous Canadian Kiefer Sutherland is going to be so disappointed in you."

"Is he from Winnipeg?"

"No idea," Nick said. "His binder hasn't arrived."

As intense as Bea was, it was fun for me and Nick to be united against a common enemy who wasn't also a close member of his family. We knew her whipcracking was ultimately for our benefit, and so as the months wore on and the spring rains ceded to early summer sun that we were too trapped indoors to revel in, we kept ourselves sane by keeping a running tally of who was scoring higher on her tests and who managed to get more words in edgewise during her lectures. It made us feel closer to have an in-joke to grin about while Bea monologued about what would happen if we forgot that Toronto is not Canada's capital city. And it helped deflect the weight of what was, essentially, an international audition for the Commonwealth. Instead of faking jollity with Freddie, acting as Eleanor's personal fun ambassador, or being forced to clean Marta's iPhone screen, we finally had an assignment that was all about us being us.

"Are you excited, at least?" Lacey asked. "Because the *Daily Mail* said you're so work-shy that you made Richard give you the rest of the year off. Hand me that level, please."

I dug through the tool kit on the floor of her front entryway until I found the neon-green level. Lacey had invited me to the cozy shoebox of a flat she now shared with Olly, ostensibly to catch up in person, but mostly to help with a variety of small tasks. "I'm trying to keep you grounded," she'd teased. "Also, Olly takes two hours to decide which screwdriver to try. He's fired."

"I don't know if excited is the right word," I said to her now. "*Motivated* might be better. I want people to see what I'm worth. And Bea seems skeptical that I can pull this off without violating the Diplomatic Code, which I know she made up, but I still want to prove her wrong. How many nails do you need?"

"Two," she said, marking spots on the wall with a pencil. "Bea doesn't think you're that incompetent. She's just being Bea. Don't let her rub off on you."

I handed over the nails. "I am looking forward to having something concrete to do, since I am so disappointing otherwise."

Lacey clenched a nail in her teeth and shot me a frown over her shoulder. The *Mail* had recently written a story suggesting that I was abdicating my royal responsibilities by not producing an heir.

"The *Mail* is full of it," she said, pounding the other nail into the wall. "Having babies is not your only purpose in life."

"It kind of is, though," I said. "Producing the next monarch is the only part of my job description anyone can agree on. Even three old ladies at Crocheting for Cancer asked Nick when we're going to get on with it already."

"That's so rude," Lacey said, punctuating this with one final strike of the hammer. "It's none of anyone's business."

"Again, though, it kind of is," I said. "If I don't go into labor soon, they'll probably call for my head."

"You never even wanted kids that much, did you?" she asked. "I used to assume you'd be my kids' hippie aunt, like the one in the Ramona Quimby books, who is all cool and carefree and gives the best presents."

"I never really thought about it," I said. "I assumed I had my whole life to figure it out. And now here I am, married barely a year, still not sure what I'm doing, and being told I'm late getting pregnant."

"Don't let their retrograde shit get you down. You'll get around to it when it's right for you," Lacey said. "Until then, everyone else can mind their knitting. Or their crocheting. Whatever. Does this look straight to you?" She stood back to admire her handiwork. The framed black-and-white photo was of her and Olly laughing with two elephants in the distant background.

"It looks beautiful," I said. "What's next?"

"The kitchen," she said. "Olly is still using a bunch of old stuff he got from his parents. We need to clear out."

"Aha, there, I can help you," I said, following her into the petite, bright blue space. "It's the one skill set I've honed."

Lacey reached into a cupboard and pulled out a saucepan that was chipped and peeling on the inside. "How can a person eat anything that was cooked in here?" she marveled. "It's probably giving us lead poisoning or something. It's definitely not good for—" She stopped speaking suddenly and pursed her lips.

"Uh, no, try again," I said. "What did you just decide not to tell me? This is the same expression you had on your face the day you told me you lost your virginity, so it must be big."

"Okay, well..." Lacey wrung her hands. "If you're behind schedule on the babies, then I'm unexpectedly way ahead."

"*Lacey*," I gasped. "This is huge news!"

She clapped both her hands over her mouth, as if she could shove the words back inside. "We just found out. It's early, so we're keeping it to ourselves, but I can't not tell *you*," she said through her fingers.

"Congratulations!" I threw my arms around her. "I mean, I assume you're excited. Are you excited? I guess I should have asked you that first. Lacey! I cannot believe you let me blather on about my own stupid uterus this entire time!"

Lacey hugged me back. "I still can't believe it's real," she said into my hair. "I don't remember being lackadaisical about birth control, but here we are, so...I think it's fate." She pulled away and smiled, and it was brighter than the room's paint job. "It'll set back my graduate work for a bit, but I have my whole life to hit that target. I'm really, really happy about it, Bex," she said. "It feels really, really right."

"Then I'm really, really thrilled," I said. "I am going to be amazing at coming over and giving the baby very loud gifts and then leaving."

"Yeah, well, that street goes both ways," Lacey said, but she was grinning. "You have a contract to fulfill, remember? Don't give me all your rude ideas."

I leaned against the counter and dropped my head on her shoulder. "I'm so happy for you, Lace."

"Good," Lacey said. "Because I need a favor."

"Anything."

"Can you help me plan a wedding?" she asked.

I grinned at her. "Because mine went so well?"

"Nowhere to go but up," she said.

How's the prep going, Killer?

Two days before we were due to leave for Canada, I was standing on a wooden box in my dressing room amid a ring of mirrors as Donna ran a final check on the weights keeping my skirts in place so that I didn't scandalize North America with a glimpse of my cellulite. She had been working relentlessly on looks for all fifty-two engagements in our diaries—plus emergency alternates in the event that I accidentally sat on a piece of chocolate and melted it to my butt, or something similarly horrific—and she was so stressed that she'd taken up smoking just for an excuse to go outside.

It had been twenty-nine hours since I got a text from anyone but Bea, so when I saw that my phone had a message from Freddie and not, say, a stern reminder about a pedicure, I was so pleased that I actually yelped.

Donna panicked. "What happened? Did I stab you? Are you bleeding? Are you *bleeding* on a Greta Constantine that took me nine weeks to get?!?"

"No!" I assured her. "No, I'm sorry. Everything is fine. I just got a text. It doesn't have anything to do with the tour."

"That must be nice," Donna said under her breath as she stabbed another straight pin into my hem.

True to my name, I am slowly killing Donna, I wrote back to Freddie.

Sounds like she needs a break. Up for an adventure before we lose you to the Frozen North?

"Hmm," I said to my phone.

"Now what?" Donna asked around the three pins she had clenched in her teeth. "You're frowning."

Come on, Margot, live a little.

"You know what, I think we should give ourselves the rest of today," I said to Donna. "We can't burn you out before we leave. My skirts will be fine."

Donna leaned back on her heels and grinned. "Bless you," she said. "Kira and I need you tomorrow to do a final run-through of your hats, and at this rate I'll be a hunchback by then."

"You guys have been working so hard," I said, wriggling out of the dress and handing it to her. "Thank you."

Donna took it from me almost tenderly and carried it back to its hanger. "It's actually exciting," she admitted. "I've never been to the States. Did you know that Kira went to Columbia? She wants to take me on a nostalgia tour if we have time."

"I'll make sure that you have time," I promised. "I wish I could come."

Meet you at your place in 5? I typed to Freddie.

I'll come to you.

As Donna carefully zipped my dress back into its wardrobe bag, I bounded up to the bedroom to fetch my Margot wig and got back down to the foyer right as the bell rang. When I opened the door, I saw a man in a full, bushy beard, oversize aviator sunglasses, and a flat cap pulled down over a stringy blond wig I recognized from a long-ago Oscars party where Freddie came dressed as Gwyneth Paltrow.

"You look like a pervert, Fred," I said.

"Some would argue that I am one," Freddie said. "Is Nick around?"

"He probably wishes he was," I said. "Richard called him over to Clarence House to review game tape of the opening of Parliament."

We had, of course, already watched the whole thing live. Marj and Bea had interrupted a meeting to flip on the TV, and we fell mute at the surreal sight of Richard processing into the House of Lords to give the traditional government-penned Queen's Speech on behalf of his still-recuperating mother. It was one of the monarch's most visible ceremonial roles, a performance for the whole country, much bigger and more formal and official than any state visit.

"I don't mind telling you, I wasn't sure I'd live to see anyone else do this," Marj had said, fiddling absently with a cardigan button.

Richard was merely a stand-in, a prop, and he knew it. But he'd held his head high under the weight of the crown—at Eleanor's insistence, he'd worn the custom ceremonial one from his Prince of Wales investiture rather than the iconic one belonging to the monarch—and he'd both stood and sat ramrod straight, as he'd been taught. *I'm ready*, his bearing said. *For someday.*

"King Richard," Bea mused. "Even when Eleanor was unconscious, it didn't feel this real."

"Crikey," was all Nick had offered, the color draining from his face.

As Freddie stood on our doorstep, a curious expression playing around the corners of his disguise, I told him, "He didn't admit it, exactly, but I think the whole thing freaked Nick out. It made his future feel awfully close."

Freddie looked sympathetic. "Father practiced his whole life for that moment. I think he forgets not everyone was looking so forward to it," he said, and there wasn't a trace of malice in it. "But Knickers is going to have his turn someday, whether he likes it or not, and he's got to be every bit as ready."

I shivered. "Enough of that. Shall we?"

"Yes indeed," Freddie said. "I hope you're wearing sensible shoes."

"Freddie," I said patiently as I followed him into the gravel courtyard, "if the time ever comes that I'm not wearing sensible shoes off duty, please hurl me into the Thames."

Freddie guided me out of the courtyard, and onto the private road that led out of the protected palace walls. We strolled around the far wing of the compound, past an array of charming potting sheds, a tennis court, and cottages that housed offices and occasionally low-level relatives visiting from out of town.

"Where are you even taking me?" I asked. "Don't we look like security threats, lurking around in these wigs?"

"Patience, Killer," Freddie said over his shoulder. "Besides, your PPOs are well acquainted with your disguise. They'll just think I'm some creepy weirdo you've picked up off the street."

"As is my habit," I said.

"Exactly. And anyway, we're here."

"Here" was a long, narrow garden shoved between the outbuildings and the ivy-covered brick wall that separated us from the public Kensington Gardens. There, in the middle of the wall, was an unassuming white-painted wooden door.

"I used your little trick the other day—and my God, that was risky," he said. "I scared the hell out of two people on the cleaning staff when I burst into that janitorial closet. I had to tell them we'd run out of toilet cleaner."

"It's an imperfect system," I agreed.

"So I did a little exploring," he said. "Look."

He pushed open the door a foot, and I stuck my head through the crack to see the vast green lawns and dusty footpath of Kensington Gardens spread before me. Nearby, a Labrador retriever looked askance, but his owner, chatting away on her cell phone, didn't even notice my head poking out of a hedge.

"I feel like I'm wearing an invisibility cloak that slipped," I whispered. "What if someone sees me randomly emerging from this bush?"

"Act casual," Freddie hissed.

I slithered out the door and into the gardens, and Freddie followed.

"Found it, Margot!" he shouted, pulling a golf ball out of the hedge, tossing it in the air, and catching it with a satisfied flick of the wrist.

"Where would we be golfing near here?" I asked. "We don't even have clubs!"

"We were playing catch," he said.

"With *golf balls*?"

"Just go with it," he said. "No one cared. Mission accomplished."

We strolled down the wide dirt path that ran parallel to the palace, silent together under the sunshine. It was a scorcher of a summer day—the kind where half of England wonders how much it would cost to install central air—and the gardens were packed with people exercising, walking their dogs, or sitting on rented lawn chairs around the Serpentine leafing through magazines and chatting. I couldn't even see the end of the line at the ice cream cart.

"You need an alias," I told Freddie. "I'm Margot, and Nick is Steve. But who's this guy?" I waved at Freddie's disreputable-looking costume.

"Oh, I know who he is," Freddie said. "I used an alias at Eton, but then we all sort of stopped because I decided I didn't care if people knew what I got up to. My fake name is Niles. I was into *Frasier* as a child."

"Really?"

Freddie shrugged as we cut through the grass, moving into a part of the park that was more secluded, all high, leafy trees and bucolic niches broken up here and there by petite obelisks dedicated to dead British explorers—a surprise burst of history in the midst of your perambulations.

"I was always interested in shows about brothers, I guess," Freddie said. "It felt familiar. They got along swimmingly, they liked the same things, but one of them was slightly more uptight than the other. And they had a cranky father, although he always reminded me more of Great-Granny."

"*And* there's a sassy foreigner who eventually marries one of them," I said.

"It's practically a documentary." He shot me a rueful grin. "I liked to tease Nick about being the Niles of our family. I used the alias because it made him laugh."

He kicked aimlessly at a small rock on the pathway.

"He's not ready yet, Fred," I said. "But he'll get there. I think."

Nick had kept his twice-a-week appointments with Dr. Kep, and it felt like the fog was lifting as far as he and I were concerned. Dr. Kep had been strict about us going on dates—or "dates," because we couldn't just pop out to the pub for some fish and chips—and had put us on a sex fast.

"Physical intimacy is a crutch. Intellectual intimacy is true connection," Nick had repeated to me. (*Intellectual Intimacy* was also the name of Dr. Kep's latest bestseller.)

"In other words, we shouldn't screw ourselves right back to where we were," I said.

"Such a tawdry summary," Nick said. "Kep will be sorry that isn't his subtitle."

But that progress was divorced from whatever therapy Nick was doing about Freddie. The brothers had settled into being absent from each other's lives except as coworkers, and I was committed to keeping my foot in that door until one of them came over and kicked it open himself. But I had no idea how long it was going to take.

"In retrospect, it was incredibly naïve to think there wasn't going to be any fallout with him," Freddie sighed. "Nick's just always been so...reasonable. It was easy to convince myself that his even keel knew no bounds." He scratched at his costume beard. "How is he? How are you two doing?"

"We're good," I said. "We were in a strange place. But I don't think he'd mind me telling you that he's been seeing a therapist. It's helped a lot. Have you thought about doing that, too?"

"Technically I *have* seen a therapist," he said with a wink. "More than one. But let's talk about you. Are you ready for the trip?"

"The prep has been insane, but yes," I said. I wrapped my arms around my torso. "I can't believe I get to go home. I realized yesterday that it's the first time I'll have been in the States since my dad died."

Freddie looked surprised, then elbowed me affectionately. "We're going to need ice cream for this."

Ten minutes later, he returned with two vanilla cones that had Cadbury Flakes poking out the top.

"A Double-99," he said, handing one to me. We sat down under a leafy tree and leaned against the bark. "English summertime classic."

"That line looked way longer than you took."

"I gave my money to a woman near the front and said these were for two sobbing children. So please look sad, and young." He licked some off his finger. "Now. Back on topic." He affected a rich baritone. "*I'm listening.*"

I snorted with laughter. "Thanks, Dr. Crane. Longtime listener, first-time caller," I said. "It's not a big deal. I think about Dad all the time, no matter where I am."

"I know you do," he said. "That's not what stood out. It's the way you talked about America. You called it home."

"No, I didn't."

"You absolutely did," he said, and took a sloppy bite of vanilla soft-serve.

"Huh." I frowned at the toes of my sneakers, stretched out in front of me. "I wonder how often I do that."

"You never talk about missing America," Freddie said. "You never really talk about America at all."

I pulled out a Flake and nibbled the end. I'd lived in the UK since I graduated from college, and although I thought about my parents often, I didn't dwell too much on home (there was that word again) in my day-to-day life. There were things I missed about my country of origin—measuring things in inches and pounds and Fahrenheit, being able to watch baseball live—but I lived in a palace with a person I loved very much. Still, my heart had leapt a little bit to see the United States on the itinerary, even though we weren't going anywhere near Iowa.

"It's not that I don't feel at home here." I chewed on the Flake as some chocolate pieces crumbled onto my shirt. "But I guess I didn't choose England so much as I chose Nick. And it was a package deal. It always felt like my home here was the person, and not the place."

"It probably doesn't help that everyone here thinks of you as 'the American,'" Freddie said.

"I'm not legally an American anymore. I certainly don't feel British. I'm..." The Flake was melting in my hand, so I popped the rest into my mouth while I searched for the words. "Kind of nothing. And people have expectations of me here that are not necessarily the expectations I imagined for myself, but I still have to live up to them, and...I don't know. It's hard to find myself in that sometimes."

Freddie looked up at the canopy of leaves over our heads. "I understand how that feels, a bit," he said.

I blew out my breath. "Wow, this really did turn into a therapy session."

"My hourly rates are very reasonable, if you want to keep talking it out," Freddie said, elegantly slurping the drips from the bottom of his diminishing cone. "But if you haven't been in America for a while, it also means you haven't left us for a while. Maybe you'll miss bits about England in the same way."

"Or I'll get over there and decide all those Americans are irritating and start complaining about why there aren't proper scones," I said. "I'll keep you posted."

"Right. About that," he said, rubbing at his left knee. "It looks like I won't be here."

Flake number two chose that moment to faint gracefully out of my pooling ice cream and into my lap.

"Crap," I said, picking it up and brushing at the stain. "I already used up my napkin." I blotted at the puddle of ice cream on my cargo shorts. "Whatever. No one cares how Margot looks in public. What are you talking about? Where are you going? Can I not just call you?"

Freddie was staring off to the right at an obelisk that sat atop three stone steps, with the word SPEKE carved into the base. "See that?" he said, pointing. "That right there is an expensive homage to futility. The good Mr. Speke believed he'd discovered the source of the Nile, but the day before a public debate with his archrival about it, he died mysteriously by his own gun."

"Whoa," I said. "I smell foul play."

"The thing is, Speke turned out to be correct. Everyone celebrated this amazing thing he'd done, solving a geographic riddle. But he was long gone. Isn't that sad?" he asked. "Plugging away at life, bit by bit, and then dying before you find out whether you did anything of consequence."

I blinked. "Am I going to like where this is going?"

"Probably not." Freddie took a deep breath. "I'm joining the Special Boat Service," he said. "It's an elite tactical wing of the Royal Navy. I'd like to serve properly again before I settle down and get the hook like Nick did."

"You're right," I said. "I don't like this. It sounds dangerous."

"It's intense," he said. "They do a lot of hostage rescue, and anti-terrorism work. I'm not allowed to tell you where we're going, and it might change, but historically they've been sent to the Middle East and Libya."

"Freddie, oh my God." I felt like I'd been punched in the stomach. "How can Eleanor and Richard let you do that? How can the Navy allow this? Are you even trained for that? You could be killed." My voice had gotten very shrill.

"I'm a prince, Bex," he said. "If I'm in the mood for a spot of counter-terrorism, I can show up and say so."

"That is the most ridiculous—"

"I'm teasing," he said. "I've been in training for months. Why do you think we've seen so little of each other?"

"Um, because texting makes people lazy?" I said.

Freddie shook his head, though he did smile. "I put this in motion at the end of last year," he said. "The selection process was brutal. I had to swim five hundred meters in full combat dress and then do an endurance march with a twenty-five-kilo weight." He shuddered. "Don't even get me started on the interrogation training. I squeezed about twenty-four weeks of work into half the time. But everyone at the Royal Navy has been superb. No one has called me a dilettante to my face, although I'm sure they all think I'm a spoiled brat with something to prove. And I probably am." He glanced over at the Speke monument again. "I couldn't keep going to engagements and making small talk and cutting ribbons anymore. I need to *do something*, Bex. My whole life, I've skated by on charm and goodwill and money, and it hasn't added up to anything real."

Across the park, two spaniels were wrestling over a rubber bone. The faint squeaks of the toy and their delighted yaps were the only soundtrack to his monologue.

"Is this because of Nick?" I asked. "Are you running away now, too?"

"No. And yes," Freddie said, looking down at his hands. "I don't know. Obviously, I'm unhappy that we've fallen out. But I'm losing myself here, and I don't know how to find my way back without making a big change." Freddie plucked a strand of grass forcefully. "I got broken up with again yesterday. Another one bites the dust, eh? She didn't see the point because she knew she'd never want to end up with me, not for real. No one throws over a career in bloody global nuclear disarmament to spend the rest of her life opening tiny curtains. She wasn't wrong. None of these women were wrong. *You* weren't wrong. I don't bring anything to the table but a title."

"And a lot of really explicit online fan fiction," I said. Freddie didn't smile. "I'm sorry. I was trying to cheer you up. You know I think you bring more than enough to the table for anyone, but this seems extreme. What did Richard say?"

"It was his idea, in part," Freddie said. "I actually went to him for advice."

"Damn, you *were* desperate."

"I told you he's not all bad," Freddie insisted. "We really did develop something last year, whether you and Nick believe it or not. He understood me. He's always had such a clear path, and I haven't, and that's always been my problem. I need something important to focus on that will help shape me into more than the Ginger Gigolo." Freddie cracked his knuckles. "He suggested I get myself on one of the ships, but that didn't feel like enough. So I floated this as an alternative."

"I can't believe he went for it," I said.

"He didn't, at first." Freddie tapped his hand against his thigh. "I had to level with him. It was...specific. I apologize if any of that violates anything you consider your privacy, but..." He swallowed hard. "We got through last year with me doing a minimum of opening up, and that needed to change."

"No, of course," I said. "I'm just always surprised when Richard forgets he's supposed to be an ogre. And I wish the answer wasn't putting your life in danger."

"I'll be all right," he said. "Father pulled some strings to get me into the selection program, but I earned my qualification, so I'm ready. It's not like they're going to let me take the lead on anything that requires finesse. And we both know that they have loads of protocols in place to yank me if things go really pear-shaped." He leaned his head back. "Mostly what I need, I think, is to figure out how to grow up. I've been spending this entire year dating proper adults but I was still the same old me."

"Please don't change too much," I said, nudging his calf with my foot. "A lot of us like you, just as you are. How long are you supposed to be gone?"

Freddie shrugged. "Father thinks I'll be able to swing it for a couple of months. Everyone's going to be distracted by your North American adventure, and then we can vamp until someone realizes I haven't popped out to kiss a baby in a while," he said. "The plan is for no one to know I'm gone until I'm back. And maybe then...maybe it will have been long enough for him. For both of us."

We smiled at each other, a little sadly, as a light breeze ruffled the leaves above us. I reached out and took his hand, and we sat there in the peaceful quiet of the park until dusk fell.

CHAPTER FIVE

That was...was...." Nick reared back his head and unleashed a loud sneeze. "Outstanding," he finished.

"Gesundheit," I said, taking a running leap and flopping onto the bed in our cabin. "Damn, your horse allergies won't quit."

"It's worth it," Nick said. He sniffled. "Who knew I was so good at picking winners in barrel racing?"

He collapsed next to me and crawled over to press a kiss against my clavicle. "We should have done this sooner," he said. "No one told me how hot you'd look in a cowboy hat."

"Yeah, I finally understand the upside of a long overseas tour," I told him.

He sat up to face me. "The thrill of international travel?" he asked. "Meeting world leaders? Getting to sample all the local delicacies?"

"Hotel sex," I said. "It's the *best*."

Nick laughed. "And without even a single binder to guide us."

As promised on its shirts, Canada *was* for lovers. After each jam-packed day of meet-and-greets and charity engagements and touristy excursions, I expected to collapse with exhaustion until it was time to get up and do it again. But instead, it was invigorating, and every night we fell on each other like one of us had just been released from prison. The third day of the tour, I woke up with a hickey. (It was, thankfully, on an area of my body no one else would see.) The sex fast was definitely over, and we were making up for lost time.

Nick and I were pulling off the public-facing aspects, too. We began in Ottawa, where we were greeted by the prime minister, some rowdy well-wishers, and a bouquet of roses that photographed beautifully against my white dress. We swept through the capital city in two days before moving on to Prince Edward Island, Newfoundland, and Quebec. We met homeless teens going through job-training programs, visited sick children in shiny new hospital wards and brave adults tackling the mental health issues that had become Nick's priority, learned to make poutine, and raced dragon boats in Anne of Green Gables country, where even my predictable "Lady of Shalott" joke went over a treat. At every stop the crowds were large and welcoming, save for a few anti-monarchy demonstrators and one environmental group protesting that we flew private—a problem I understood, but couldn't solve, given how often I was expected to change my clothes in transit. Lady Bollocks was on a high: The onslaught of photos from the week (me celebrating my victory on the low seas, Nick sieving gravy, both of us having earnest conversations with adorable tots) were so winning that even that cranky old stooge Xandra Deane had to admit we were killing it. Finally, Nick and I were doing something right.

We'd arrived in Calgary early that morning and spent an entertaining day at its Stampede, world renowned for its rodeo but also for the raucous party at its fairgrounds (scientists once tracked an uptick in both STDs and pregnancies after it ended). A photo of me and Nick feeding each other funnel cake while wearing cowboy hats was currently trending on Twitter. Everyone loved it. Almost.

Do feel free to leave the hat in Canada, Eleanor had texted me from her new iPhone. She'd followed it up with a link to one @KingIdrisElba—avatar still an egg—who'd tweeted that we looked like rodeo clowns.

No way. I'm bringing it home for Richard, I replied.

Good. It can keep him warm after I get my crown back.

Eleanor had been making good strides in her recovery, but her gait remained halting and her right side didn't routinely obey her commands. Richard insisted she shouldn't return to her duties yet, and to her profound irritation the doctors agreed, so all the Queen could do was sit and stew. Eleanor was getting a taste of the waiting Richard had done for a lifetime, and she didn't care for it one bit. It was hard to tell if this was The New Eleanor, who'd shed her filter, or a natural clash between two people who had, in their own ways, each been bred to rule.

After the Stampede, Nick and I had been flown by copter up to Jasper, a town in the Rockies with a beautiful resort where Eleanor and Henry had stayed back in the early '60s, shortly before he died. The mountains wore their snowy caps proudly even in midsummer, and the greenery was lush, hugging the perfectly clear blue lake around which the Jasper Park Lodge was built. We'd been placed in the same charming log-and-stone cabin Eleanor and Henry had taken—a quaint, freestanding building on the edge of the property, overlooking the lake and the vast expanse of natural wonders surrounding it.

"I wish we could go for a ramble," Nick said, gesturing out the window. "Get lost in the woods."

"Or eaten by bears." I walked over to the chilled bottle of local Chardonnay that was waiting for us, next to a plate of cookies. I poured a glass. "One of the magazines they left in the bathroom has a story about a sassy local bear who keeps playing with the lobby's sliding doors."

"We could sneak out, you know," Nick mused, sliding off the bed and stepping out onto the balcony.

"And give Popeye a heart attack?" I said as I joined him. It was cool and still outside, the lights of the far-off lodge reflecting onto the lake, and the stars above us as bright and bountiful as I'd ever seen.

"Our PPOs are asleep—"

"Popeye never sleeps."

"So we could pop out into the wilderness—"

"*Is* there actual wilderness at a five-star resort?"

"And get up to no good." His fingers crept under the waistband of my jeans.

"You're bold in Canada," I told him, running my hands up his chest to lock them behind his neck.

"It's all this fresh air," he explained.

"But you're also forgetting that we can get up to a lot of no good right here, without worrying about wild animals."

"Besides each other," he teased, lowering his lips to mine. Neither of us said anything else for a long time.

We weren't the only ones who felt the touring life agreed with us. BuzzFeed wrote an entire listicle called "Here's Forty-Five Photos of Nick and Bex Eye-Banging All Over Canada," while *People*'s website went with the more delicate euphemism "The Look of Love." When the tour moved west to Vancouver, even British Columbia's lieutenant governor noted with a wink that we seemed "awfully inspired" by the Great White North. You can see my blush in the photos. Nick had been right: Taking the Duke and Duchess of Clarence Show on the road was a fresh start for our marriage *and* our jobs.

Our last stop in Canada was at Whistler, which included a trip on the famed gondola that stretches more than two miles between the resort's peaks. Nick and I had been allowed to ride totally alone in one of the twenty-five-person glass-enclosed pods, gliding a mile high above a perfect canopy of evergreens sparkling in the sun. Below to the left, I saw a bear edging toward a river that snaked down the slope.

"Eleven minutes of heaven," I said. "This is incredible. A private gondola, this view to ourselves. We are the luckiest people."

Nick intertwined our fingers. "I have never felt luckier," he said. Then he scooted so we were touching and nipped at my ear. "On many levels."

"We shouldn't miss a second of this view," I teased. "What if there's a quiz?"

"Seen one tree, you've seen them all," he said. "But I've never fooled around with my wife while dangling from a pod over the earth, and I don't mind telling you, the danger is very alluring."

I pretended to pat myself down. "Where *is* that schedule? I didn't see a visit to the Mile-High Club on it."

"Tell me, madam, are they letting anyone else ride this in either direction while we're here?"

"I don't believe they are, sir," I said. "Besides, it sure would be hard to tell what we're doing in here, if we're in the right place."

"So we can investigate the blind spots." His hand drifted. "For eleven minutes."

"I dare you," I purred.

Nick whistled, low and under his breath. "You're on."

Lacey and I had graduated from Cornell in upstate New York, so I'd done Manhattan more than a few times. We would take the long train ride into the city for a weekend spent whipsawing from the Guggenheim to Saks Fifth Avenue to nosebleed seats at Madison Square Garden, to a French bistro she knew Jennifer Aniston frequented, to a subterranean bar whose only sign was made of lightbulbs that spelled out BAR. I took us on the subway and wanted to walk for blocks; Lacey preferred cabs, especially at night, when people would turn their lights on and leave their windows open and we could peek into their apartments and their lives—their dinner parties, their built-in bookshelves, their dying balcony plants, packaged as thirty-second soap operas during the crawl up Tenth Avenue. As the skyline rose up now in front of me and Nick, I felt like I was reuniting with an old friend.

"It's so *lumpy*," was Nick's poetic take.

"That is not a word I have ever heard used about New York," I said.

"I just mean, everything along the way is pretty low and flat, and then, boom, all that height. It's like when you shave your legs and miss an entire knee."

He tickled mine and I swatted his hand away. I looked out at the city, all tall boxes and stone and steel, peppered with cranes and scaffolding, a city created so much by modernity as opposed to one carved by history that technology simply caught up to without asking permission. So much of our relationship had been Nick opening doors for me—sometimes of literal castles—but this was Bex Porter's turf. I had a past here, and I was excited to introduce it to my present.

Nick had cast aside Bea's seminal achievement in underestimating our intelligence—a binder called *Washington, DC, Is Not a State*—and was glued to the car window like a little kid. "A hot dog cart!" he narrated. "Oh, I think I read about that restaurant. Ooh, look, yellow taxis. Can we get bagels?"

"I am definitely not leaving without a bagel," I assured him.

My phone buzzed. So did Nick's. Simultaneously, we glanced down at them and made matching strangled sounds.

SHE'S A ROYAL BEXHIBITIONIST!

Bon appetit! The global media may be made to masticate its recent worshipful words about the Duke and Duchess of Clarence's Canadian cavorting, because it appears our lady is a tramp. Photos exclusive to *The Sun* reveal a half-naked Reckless Rebecca flashing her goods in the Whistler gondola, risking the reputation of the entire monarchy for one tacky tryst. You can take it from me: This not-so-clandestine cock-up shames not only the country but the Commonwealth. The Queen and her regent Richard will be roiling with rage . . .

Clive's column ran next to four photos shot from a long-range lens. It looked like someone had gone rogue and flown an illegal drone that we hadn't noticed; its distance from us meant the photos weren't in superb focus, but you could see my bare breasts. My skin felt hot from shame. Nick and I had not actually rounded the bases up there, but he had bet the inner daredevil of my youth that I couldn't take off my shirt and get it properly back on again before we hit the other support pole. The resultant snap was me taunting my husband in a funny, flirtatious moment we had thought was our own.

"Those bastards," Nick seethed.

The faces of the people who had now seen my nipples—poorly

censored in print, or in their entirety online—flashed before my eyes. Agatha. Richard. The Queen. Freddie, depending on where he was and whether he had Wi-Fi. Everyone who was currently renovating our flat. Gaz. *Gaz.* He would die of embarrassment before I did. My breath quickened, and I rolled down the window to inhale some of New York's complex July air. It didn't help.

"I am going to sue *The Sun* into obsolescence," Nick added, almost to the rhythm of his pulsing forehead vein. "And I'm going to fly back to London and murder Clive. I should have murdered him last year when I had the chance."

"I am an idiot," I said, turning to him. "We were there for work."

"We'd given them their shots," Nick said. "We wanted one goddamn moment of privacy together." All of a sudden, the anger seemed to drain out of him, replaced with regret. "And I goaded you. If this is anyone's fault, it's mine."

My phone lit up. Bea. I declined the call. It immediately lit up again, and we did the dance two more times. My stomach was churning. I wasn't ready to hear my failures cataloged by Lady Bollocks.

A text popped up: ANSWER THE PHONE, REBECCA.

"It's all over the internet," Nick said, scrolling through his phone. "But only *The Sun* used the photos. They must have paid a fortune. Or Clive has this jackal on retainer." He dropped the phone and rubbed his face. "Those disgusting pricks."

My phone blazed again. I closed my eyes and swiped to answer. I couldn't hide from Bea forever. "I assume you're going to have me executed?"

"Not this time, but I believe this is, in your parlance, strike two," said a voice that definitely didn't belong to Bea.

"Dammit," I blurted. "Sorry. Hi, Your Majesty. I am *so* sorry."

"I presume this means you've seen the latest drivel produced by Mr. Fitzwilliam," Eleanor said.

"Yes," I said. "You can take it from me. Unfortunately."

"And so you know how unacceptable it is."

"I do, but—"

"And you can envision my reaction to it."

"I can, and—"

"And you are enormously sorry for the impropriety and reckless exhibitionism."

"I am, but I can explain—"

"Enough. Take this from *me*, Rebecca," the Queen said. "While I relish your squirming, this may not be the disaster you imagine."

Nick gestured at me to hand him the phone. I swatted at him.

"Neither is it a *delight*," she stressed. "But your Clive overplayed his hand. If you read his piece without the visual aids, it sounds as if you and Nicholas stripped down and fornicated in front of the press pack. But anyone who sees the pictures can tell that the two of you…"

"Thought we were alone," I finished for her. "Which we did."

Nick nodded vigorously at me.

"Yes," Eleanor said. I could hear the rustling of papers through the phone, and I pictured her at the desk in her private quarters, my breasts in front of her, and wanted to die all over again. "It was a clear, studied violation. Many people have come down on your side." She paused. "Yes, Mummy, I'll tell her. Mummy wants you to know that *actual* Idris Elba retweeted a criticism of Clive. Xandra Deane called him a calculating reprobate. Clive, not Mr. Elba."

I couldn't help giggling. Next to me, Nick watched in astonishment.

"Stop laughing, Rebecca," Eleanor snapped. "This isn't amusing. It was certainly invasive, but that doesn't mean your judgment wasn't poor. No one is impressed that you were bonking on the job, I can assure you." A smile crept into her voice. "Although they *are* impressed you are bonking at all. I would not have endorsed this as a way to close the book on the rumors about your tiresome love triangle, but it may have worked."

"Wow," I said. "That is unexpected."

"It is indeed." The smile disappeared from her voice as quickly as it had come. "And this will be the final unexpected moment from the two of you. Finish the remainder of this tour impeccably. No excuses. No mistakes."

"Roger that," I said. "You won't need to call again."

"I will if the Cubs don't snap this absurd losing streak. It's embarrassing to me," Eleanor sniffed. "Good luck. Do tell the mayor that the Mets ruined my week."

"I would, but he's just seen me half-naked."

"Pish, everyone knows what breasts look like. Yours aren't remarkable," Eleanor said, and then she hung up on me.

We pulled up alongside the towering white cupcake of a building that was the Plaza Hotel. The mayor, tall as a skyscraper himself and about as blocky, awaited us on the curb near a discreet entrance on the side street between the hotel and Bergdorf's, and seeing him, I was suddenly seized by nerves. We'd gotten lucky that the sleazy photographer in Whistler had incited pity, but one more misstep and we'd burn through the goodwill we'd earned by being charming at the beginning of the tour. I didn't want an expensive disaster on my hands, nor the blame for it laid at my feet.

The mayor, as befitting a professional, gave no indication he'd seen the photos—though it seemed as if he tried extra valiantly to block us from the paparazzi who'd gathered on the curb, as if he, too, was worried one of them might be the same jerk who'd cashed in on my body. Nick and I performed our standard song and dance of seeming surprised and delighted by the attention of the public, and we'd almost gotten to the door when someone at the back of the crush of spectators called out in a loud Brooklyn accent: "Don't let the bastards get you down!"

Our smiles in those pictures are extremely genuine.

We rode up the private elevator to the fashion designer Tommy Hilfiger's two-story penthouse atop the hotel, where he was hosting a welcome reception for us with, per our *New York City Day One: Coming to America* binder, "local luminaries, top businesspeople, and select influencers." The penthouse was an enormous salute to Italian marble, with a deck overlooking the green expanse of Central Park, and a turret room hand-painted as a tribute to Eloise that felt like it was trying too hard. The mayor led us into a dramatic living room with black glossy lacquer walls and leopard-print marble columns, where everyone tried to pretend they didn't jump ten feet when the doors opened. Some of the faces were strange to me, but many, I knew: our host, petite and preppy; the famous actor who owned half of Tribeca; the singer who hated Kanye, next to the other singer whose husband toured with Kanye; the bobbed British editrix of *Vogue*, whose handshake was warmer than I would have anticipated. Next to her stood a dark-haired young actress starring in an upcoming adaptation of *Tess of the d'Urbervilles* and her costar/boyfriend, both of whom seemed nice but also stoned.

The actress was the only one who broke protocol, pushing my outstretched hand away to envelop me in a warm hug. Behind her, I saw the *Vogue* editor blanch.

"You are a kindred spirit," the actress said to me as the rest of the party struck up its own nervous chatter. "I saw that photo online, and I was like, *Yeah, mama.* I love the feeling of sun on my breasts."

"You are like *literal* bosom buddies," her costar/boyfriend chimed in.

"Don't let the paparazzi stop you from finding your light. It's so *healing*, right?" the actress said as cater-waiters descended on the room with trays of miniature American foods and chilled Miller High Life in crystal Champagne flutes. I looked at one with longing as the actress continued. "Sometimes I go outside naked and do a handstand. Every flower needs sun. Every garden needs nutrients. It's like I can *feel* the earth impregnating me with its power." She released me. "Also, your tits looked bomb. I didn't know British people had boobs like that."

"Literally no one did," her boyfriend said, pulling his phone out of his pocket and tapping away at it. "Babe, I'm hungry, let's chase some passed apps."

She squeezed my hand. "In case you get a chance," she added, "my people are trying to option *The Bexicon* and if you could put in a good word for me, that would be amazing. I will totally do you justice."

With a wave, she and her boyfriend were off. Nick was across the room in conversation with the singer who hated Kanye, which I hoped was *about* Kanye so that I could get some dirt later. I surveyed the room from beside a potted plant taller than I was and watched everyone pretend they weren't looking at me. Even the staff seemed to have been told to treat me like wallpaper; food whizzed past me without anyone offering me a miniature grilled cheese. Over by the crudités, I spied two women pretending to take a photo of themselves that was, I was sure, framed to fit me "accidentally" in the background. The *Vogue* editor swept past them and snatched the offending iPhone out of the blonde's hand with one smooth movement on her way over to me. It was such an Eleanor move that I caught myself chuckling.

"I made it clear that there were to be no unauthorized photos at this party," she said tartly. "If she thinks she'll be at Fashion Week again anytime soon, she'll discover she is very much mistaken. Good luck with your little blog now, *Monica*."

She exhaled hard and then smoothed her not-at-all-ruffled bangs. "How sweet," she said, lightly touching my flag pin, which I'd affixed to my floral dress. It had been Nick's idea. "How are you finding New York?"

"So far, hugely different than when I was a college student," I said. "If you smashed together all the places my sister and I stayed in, they'd still be smaller than our suite here."

"Undoubtedly," the editor said. "You, in particular, cannot go home again. But at least now you have heated floors. I'm terribly sorry, but you'll have to excuse me. I need to tell Tommy that under no circumstances is he to bring back the cargo short. I shall circulate diverting people your way. Please give my best to Richard. We dated for three weeks in the very early eighties. He had fine calves."

She left me with this disturbing mental image as she swept off to save us from the tyranny of many-pocketed shorts. But she did not fail me: I was approached by a variety of people over the next hour and a half, each of whom chatted at me for fifteen minutes until someone new drifted in to change the subject. I got the impression that I was being handled, while the real muckety-mucks circled to Nick. But plenty of the guests wanted something from me, too: Tommy showed me a trench coat and floated the idea of naming it after me, if I wore it first; the actor gave me business cards for three restaurants he owned in Tribeca and told me they had open tables that night; the very blond, very tan wife of the mayor boasted that she'd designed all the tablescapes at this event, despite the fact that there were no tables present. Amid the barrage, I caught my gaze drifting out the window and down to the bustling New York sidewalks. I had walked those streets while most of these folks lived in the clouds.

And even now, I was not, as a person, interesting to them; I was, as a duchess, interesting to their Instagrams, or their pocketbooks. It had been silly to think that the New York I would be showing Nick would be the New York I had experienced. We would not sprint to catch the subway, or duck into the Met to look at Madame X, or spend all day wandering the park, or even go sit up on the new High Line and people-watch. My days of making those kinds of memories were over.

We'd better get our damn bagels.

My boobs made the front page of the next day's *New York Post*, alongside a photo of us arriving at the Plaza and some inside shots by the official event photographer. The headline: BEX MAKES THE BREAST OF IT.

At least the writer had complimented my composure, which was a welcome boost heading into a busy day. Nick had a solo trip to Washington, DC, where his brief morning meeting with the president to discuss mental health initiatives was our justification for detouring to the States in the first place. Originally, Marj had made this a day off for me, but two weeks before we left, Bea suggested that I do some unaccompanied duchessing to individualize me a bit, and Marj had agreed.

My first event of the day was touring the 9/11 Memorial, which I very much wanted to see, and was also the absolute last place I wanted to stumble. The mayor's wife met me downtown accompanied by a petite, earthy woman who had lost her spouse in the tragedy and had devoted the past fifteen years to fighting Congress to get benefits for the families of victims and first responders.

"I don't know if my husband would approve of me doing this with you," she said, before cracking an enormous grin and adding, "He really hated the Cubs."

The memorial itself was serene and moving, especially the reflecting pools in the footprint of the fallen towers with the names of the victims etched in bronze panels around them. I ran my hands over her husband's name, wishing that I didn't have to do it in front of a press pack. They made me feel like I was giving a performance, even though what I felt was sincere.

"You must miss him," I said to the widow as they snapped away.

"Every day," she said. "I wish we'd had more time together. But when you love someone, it's always too soon to lose them."

"I admire your courage so much," I said as we headed inside to the museum.

"I don't know if it's courage. I'm just a doer," she said. "'You'll always feel better once you get off your butt' is my motto. If you can't change your own circumstances, then change someone else's."

The rest of the day was a whirlwind of meetings with philanthropic organizations, a facility I had found myself that was like New Mentality—I'd been proud of that discovery—and a museum Bea dug up that wanted to start its own version of Paint Britain, the charity I'd started before Nick and I got engaged. She'd told them I could discuss my experience as a cofounder, which made me look knowledgeable and further gave me a chance to do some watercolors with kids, something that Bea knew played to my strengths. It was 6:00 p.m. by the time I made it to my final appearance of the day, at the Empire State Building. I smiled to myself, remembering the time Lacey and I had overdrawn our account and she'd tried to sweet-talk the operator into letting us up to the top for free by telling him that she was supposed to meet someone up there who might be the love of her life.

"I've seen those movies, kid," he said. "All of 'em. Isn't a day someone doesn't try that line on me."

Lacey had begun to protest, then gave up. "You caught me," she said. "That was lame. We're just two idiots who screwed up our budget."

"One idiot who screwed up our budget," I corrected her, "and one idiot who assumed the other idiot was not, in fact, an idiot."

He'd unhooked the rope for us. "Lucky for you, I'm retiring tomorrow," he said. "Say hi to Tom Hanks for me."

This time, after posing for a few photos and making engaged faces at the building's new exhibit about its construction, I walked onto a waiting elevator, which dumped me out on the viewing deck, empty and secured for me. My protection officers were downstairs (watching me on CCTV in case something crazy happened, like a sudden hurricane or a visit from Spider-Man). There was no docent to talk me through the sights, no members of the public for me to meet, nobody's hand to shake and no one to smile for—and, hopefully, no long lens trained on my face, or any other parts of my body. I was totally alone, for the first time in two weeks. I relished the feeling of smallness that came from beholding a seemingly boundless city spread out beneath me. In the scheme of things, who even cared if my boobs were in the paper? The people we'd visited on this trip did important work every day of their lives—not because the *Daily Mail* would approve, or because it would bring good PR to their extended family, but because it was their calling to help. It was about time I treated my job like that, too.

"Cracking view," said a voice, and then Nick's hands were wrapped around my waist. "Definitely beats the White House Rose Garden."

I turned sideways and gave him a peck. "I wish I'd seen that," I said. "I've never been to DC."

"I didn't get this kind of view of it, sadly," Nick said, dropping a coin into one of the viewfinders. "But it's dwarfed by New York. Why isn't this your capital?"

"I'd tell you, but I don't want to spoil *Hamilton*," I told him. We had box seats as our final hurrah in New York before heading for Heathrow.

"It does seem to be, as they say, a hell of a town," Nick said. "I wish we could stay longer."

"I wish we could, too." I sighed. "It was a rude awakening, realizing I couldn't show you my New York. No one is going to let us sneak into some grungy dive bar and monopolize the jukebox until we get kicked out for playing too much Wham!"

Nick turned away from the viewfinder to peer at me. "That cannot be a true story," Nick said. "There is no such thing as too much Wham!"

"Tell that to the darts league that complained," I said.

"You two clearly had fun here," he said, abandoning his viewfinder completely and coming to stand hip to hip with me. "You sound like you miss those days."

"In some ways," I said. "Doesn't everyone miss a time in their life when things were simpler?"

"I'm not sure there *was* that time in my life," he said. "I don't mean to sound self-pitying. It's just interesting, to hear you talk about a feeling that I won't ever experience. It's like people who don't eat bacon, but want to know why we're all mad for it. How do you describe what bacon tastes like?" He twined his fingers in mine. "I suppose I want to make sure you're not having any regrets about our life."

"That's the thing," I said. "I miss some stuff about those days, but this trip has given me a dose of perspective. I always thought of doing public appearances as a trade-off for getting to be with the person I love. But it's wrong to be that passive about it. When we get back to London, I want to have a real voice in this. Will you back me up?"

He leaned in and kissed me firmly. "Yes," he said. "Wholeheartedly. But do you mind waiting a day to plan our attack? We've got a surprise stop on the way home."

"*Hamilton* isn't a surprise," I said.

Nick grinned broadly. "I'm not talking about *Hamilton*," he said. "Although I *did* decide not to throw away our shot."

✐

"Fine. You were right," Nick said the next day. "I don't understand it, but I cannot deny it. Your watery beer tastes perfect when it's cold and in a plastic cup on a hot day."

"I told you," I said. "Next time I say that it's Miller Time, don't make fun of me."

Nick touched the brim of his cap, as if to salute. "Yes, ma'am."

"Also, just FYI, I'm not sure you've ever looked sexier to me than you do right now."

Nick winked, then gulped some beer and focused on the action from our nosebleed seats along the third base line. I pulled down my own careworn hat—Nick had packed it without me knowing—and looked out at what Earl Porter always referred to as our vacation home: Wrigley Field, where my beloved Cubs were taking on the Texas Rangers. When

Nick told me yesterday in New York that he'd gotten tickets, I'd gone mute for a full minute.

"This better not be a joke," I finally said.

"Bex. I would never joke about the Cubs," Nick said.

"We're going to an actual baseball game. In actual Wrigley Field. In actual seats."

"I paid for the tickets, so if we don't have actual seats, I'll be cross," he said. "That is, if you..."

He trailed off. Or maybe I stopped hearing him. My father and I had been planning to catch another Cubs game together, but instead he'd died on the way to one by himself. The ache of that loss pressed on my chest. I breathed slowly.

Nick put his hands on my shoulders. "Nothing's been done that can't be undone," he said softly. "If this is too hard for you, say so, and it's off." He tipped my chin up toward him. "This was your special thing with Earl, and I don't want to intrude on that. But I don't know how feasible it'll be to do this again, and I want to know this one massive part of you that I've never experienced. And of your father." He swallowed hard. "I miss him, too."

Crack. My eyes clicked back into focus. Anthony Rizzo belted a beautiful ball deep into center field, and I stood up to cheer as he rounded first and made it safely to second.

"And a man on third, and no outs," I gloated, sitting back down. "We are about to bust this game wide open." I covered my mouth with my hand and whispered, "Suck it, Rangers."

Nick laughed. "Afraid of a lip-reading expert?"

"Yes, obviously," I said. "I don't want to start an international feud with Texas."

In the end, we hadn't told the press pack; we'd simply let everyone return home—our arrival in England wasn't covered anyway—and then gone the other direction. We knew they'd be unhappy if they heard, but it was worth the risk. Nick wanted this to be as mundane an experience as possible for us both. No royal treatment, no throwing out the first pitch, no tour of the locker rooms, no customized "Clarence" jersey handed to us by Kyle Hendricks before he took the mound. The point of this detour was to blend in, one last time, and if anyone got photos, more power to the industrious person who sold them. So the PPOs had made a security plan with the Chicago PD designed for maximum discretion, and we dressed down in sneakers and hats, my hair tucked up into mine, both of us wearing sunglasses that hid a good portion of our faces. Nick's were hideous wraparounds that were distant cousins of ski goggles, and they were so aggressively ugly that I worried they'd attract attention, but so far no one in Chicago cared. We were just two yahoos sitting in the upper deck drinking light beer and shoveling Cracker Jack into their mouths.

"This is an insanely pleasant way to spend an afternoon," Nick said. "Cricket needs more organ music."

"Wow," I said. "Between this and your scandalous preference for coffee, I'm beginning to think you were born in the wrong country."

"No kidding," Nick said, licking the last drop of mustard off his thumb and tucking his third hot dog wrapper under the seat. "Maybe I should defect."

The game had moved along at a brisk pace; aside from one run batted in by the Cubs, there had been no action until the bottom of the sixth. The seats around us weren't totally filled, though I knew PPOs Stout, Twiggy, Popeye, and Furrow were fanned out in the adjacent sections. I'd caught Furrow standing up and yelling something that, by the reactions of the Cubs fans around him, had been very entertaining and not at all flattering to the ump.

My phone buzzed in my pocket.

Finally headed into the thick of it. Last Wi-Fi I'll have for a while. Where are you?

Freddie had been assigned to a Special Boat Service unit that was on furlough in Europe, giving him time to acclimate in a low-pressure environment before seeing any action. His dispatches were infrequent, but funny, often about something absurd he'd done in Frankfurt with his terrible Niles wig while trying to stay hidden—or, once, a selfie of him with Daphne, whom he'd visited during a holiday weekend. It was a relief to see him with a friendly, familiar face, as if she extended our reach across the globe and could therefore help us collectively will him back safely.

I snapped a photo of Wrigley and pressed send. One last hurrah before we head back home.

His response was immediate. Excuse me, did you refer to London as 'back home'?

I paused. I checked. I had.

Another message: Your line here is, 'Yes, Freddie, you told me so, you are brilliant and wise.'

I sent back the middle-finger emoji. Then: Good luck out there. Hope the helmet fits over your massive ego.

I pocketed my phone and leaned back, breathing in the smell of peanut shells and hot dog remnants and beer, so much beer, as I gazed out across the jewel of a field. If New York had felt far removed from my memories of it, Wrigley Field, with its clock over the league scoreboard and its iconic ivy-covered walls, was still as familiar to me as my own hands. The irony was that I knew I was here to say goodbye. Freddie had been right. Something in my perspective had shifted, something necessary. I had a job and a life in England, and while the States would always be dear to me, London was my home.

Another crack. Addison Russell hit a perfect single up the middle. He drove in two runs; by the time the inning ended, the Cubs had a 6–0 lead. I leapt out of my seat and screamed, pumping my fists, then threw myself delightedly at Nick, folding my arms around him.

"What a first game," I crowed.

As I went to kiss him, our hat brims knocked together, and a gust of wind blew mine clean off my head. My hair tumbled out, and I pushed up my sunglasses to keep it out of my face as I searched around for my lucky cap.

"Here you go," said a teen girl from one row up, who'd caught it on the stairs. I turned to thank her, and saw her eyes widen.

"Has anyone ever told you..." she said, then she looked past my shoulder and her mouth dropped open even wider. "You ARE her. You're THEM."

Oops.

Nick and I met eyes. He shrugged. Then he took off his cap and waved.

I turned back to the girl. "Thanks," I said. "I guess I need a better disguise next time."

"Can I get a photo?" she stammered.

"Officially, I'm not allowed," I said regretfully. "But I also can't control what you do when I'm not standing next to you, so...." I shrugged theatrically, and we exchanged smiles. I made a point of staring at the field from a favorable angle for her—with any luck, she'd sell the photo for college money—before trundling back to my seat.

"What now?" I asked helplessly.

Nick put an arm around me. "Now we watch your Cubs win and worry about the rest later," he said.

The low murmur in our section swept around the stadium. Twitter knew by the third pitch of the seventh inning. A roving TV camera had crept toward us by the time the Cubs got the second out. When the chords of "Take Me Out to the Ball Game" sounded during the stretch, I shot Nick a panicked look.

"Dad always said it was against our religion not to sing," I hissed.

Nick stood and held out his hand. "Then by all means don't piss off the powers that be."

Our whole section was staring at me, and I finally stood and gave them all a look like, *How can I resist?* The Jumbotron stuck with me for the entire final verse, and by the time I counted out *one, two, three strikes you're out*, I was laughing too hard to sing the last line audibly. The crowd whooped and I took a sweeping bow. Nick hugged me to his side.

"So much for doing this the regular way," I said.

"It's still bloody fun," Nick said. "Oooh, look, now we're on some kind of kissing camera."

I glanced up, and sure enough, they'd slapped the Kiss Cam graphic on our faces as a chant rose up through the stadium. I pretended to think about it, and then planted one right on Nick's lips. When I pulled away, he shook his head in mock disapproval and then dipped me just as he had on the Buckingham Palace balcony. The cheers were deafening.

"Hell of a way to end this trip," Nick said. "And I don't mind saying that I feel extremely smug about it."

I laced my arm through his and squeezed it. "You should," I said. "You win. Future king of the Commonwealth, current king of the Grand Romantic Gesture."

"What a blunder. I've gone too big," he teased. "How can I possibly top this?"

"By getting me one more hot dog," I said. "And then by taking me home."

CHAPTER SIX

BEX AND NICK (FINALLY) PLAY BALL

But Was It Enough? asks XANDRA DEANE.

Palace sources say Queen Eleanor herself blessed the Duke and Duchess of Clarence's surprise stop at Wrigley Field, but those same insiders confirm there are factions inside The Firm who are unhappy about it.

The Duchess strung together two triumphant days in New York City after the release of invasive topless photos. Critics of the royal couple warn that allowing the sum of the tour's parts to negate the scandal might be shortsighted.

"Yes, the drone was illegal, but they were not on private property," an insider points out. "Their immaturity is a concern, and shouldn't be rewarded."

The Queen reportedly accepted the explanation that the Duke and Duchess—who otherwise made no public errors—believed they were safely alone, and encouraged them to make the Chicago detour that even detractors admit got solid reviews. Comments on royal social media pages praised the pair for demanding no special favors, and one analyst suggested it was a stroke of genius to frame them as regular people who, ergo, make regular mistakes.

"The more relatable and human they look, the more people think, 'Well, we've all done silly, risky things in our lives,'" said the source. "Whoever is pulling the strings over there knows what they're doing."

"I think this is the first good review I've ever gotten from Xandra Deane," I said, folding the *Mail* in half and setting it down next to the toast rack on our antique dining table. "Although, really, it's a good review of you, Puppetmaster Nick."

"I swear to you, I didn't think about anything when I bought those tickets except that it would make us both happy," he said. "But Xandra may have nailed the reason it did not give Bea an aneurysm."

"I just thought she was too busy back here to fight you," I said.

"Bea," said Nick, "is never too busy to fight anything."

But Bea's hands *had* been full in our absence. Several crews had swarmed Apartment 1A and done large-scale renovations—putting in new floors, pulling down wallpaper, putting *up* wallpaper, and doing wiring and plumbing upgrades, most of which had been her suggestion in the first place. Marj, as her last act, shuffled the decks at a few of the royal households and cherry-picked some experienced staff for us, including—to Bea's massive relief—a fiftyish butler named Greevey whose presence meant I would no longer open my own front door, at least during the week.

I had insisted we keep a few major relics from Georgina's life. My new office used her heavy oak desk as its centerpiece. We'd snagged a beautiful dark wood bedframe for our master, and of course we'd made it clear that no one was to touch the wardrobe that was the access point to our Narnia sex den, on pain of death. I'd also put my foot down and insisted we keep the *G* monogram in the entryway, as a tribute. But everything else was spruced up and reorganized and minimized to a few key pieces that stood out instead of getting buried underneath seventy-five weird trinkets. I missed 1A's flea-market uniqueness, but it was undeniably better this way. A fresh start, for our fresh start.

But we had a Conclave in an hour, and I was nervous to face Richard. He had been incommunicado since we returned to London, and in the absence of compliments on our performance, I was concerned he was waiting to lay out a scolding in person. Which would complicate Nick's and my own plan for the meeting, for which we arrived early and immaculately pressed, carrying a repurposed tour binder—*Saskatchewan: Just In Case*—full of press clippings and printouts and notes.

"*Duchess of Clarence: Conclave, July 2016*," Nick read as I dropped it onto Richard's conference table. "Bea is going to have notes on that title."

"Welcome back, darlings! A gondola. Who knew you two had the *nerve*!" Lady Elizabeth trilled, sailing into the room gaily, smelling like jasmine. If Bea's every movement was like a dire weather forecast—thunderous, storming—then Lady Elizabeth's felt more like a yacht gliding off the Saint-Tropez shore.

Nick and I exchanged glances. "That bit was perhaps not our finest hour," he said.

"It could've happened to any of us," Elizabeth said, dumping her Chanel bag onto the ground and heading straight for the gleaming chrome coffeepot on a carved side table. "Do you know how many times Eddybear and I might have been caught out? One of our children was conceived at the Windsor Horse Show. I feel pregnant again even *thinking* about that day."

"Heaven save us all," Agatha grumbled from behind her copy of *Horse and Rider*. Nick's old friend Annabelle Farthing was on the cover of this magazine, too, in jodhpurs and hanging on to the reins of a beautiful chestnut Thoroughbred. "The ones you already have are terrors. One of your lot took a wee in the drapes at Clarence House."

"Reminds me a bit of your ex-husband," Nick said lightly. "How is Julian? Still awful?"

"I assume so, the pig," Agatha said.

Richard entered, and we all scraped back our chairs and stood. "Be seated," he said. "First, an update on Her Majesty's health…"

He droned on in a manner devoted to rationalizing his continued role as regent. Then we worked through his upcoming month of engagements, then Nick's, Agatha's, and Edwin's, and lastly mine. (It was clear that, to Richard, putting me at the end constituted a sick burn.) I stifled a yawn and glanced at Freddie's usual chair, which sat eerily empty.

"...and then after that, we're attending a gala premiere of a new play based on the quiz show *Countdown*," Elizabeth finished. "It's going to be marvelous. Ken Branagh is doing all the roles, even the maths lady."

"Stirring," Richard said drily. "Finally, Rebecca's diary. Given some of the hullabaloo from the tour, I'm sure everyone will agree that we've seen enough of her for the time being."

"Much of the press was positive, Dickie," Agatha pointed out, although it looked like it pained her to say it. "Mummy was pleased. She is still the boss, you know."

"The *Times* said they were refreshingly relatable," Elizabeth piped up.

"And *The Sun* said they seemed dreadfully common," Richard retorted.

"*The Sun* is a rag, and you know it," Agatha snapped. She glared over at me. "They did a perfectly reasonable job."

This was officially the nicest thing Agatha had ever said about me, and it gave me a boost.

"Actually, I've been working on something about that," I piped up, and hoped no one could hear my voice shaking. I flicked open my binder.

"Oh no, not another binder person," Elizabeth murmured.

"I want to keep supporting Nick and Freddie in their work as much as possible," I said. "But I also don't want to be seen as a tagalong. I think I should show the public that I can stand on my own, and that I'm taking this job very seriously, and to that end I've taken the liberty of compiling some potential patronages I'd like to investigate."

I pushed the binder across the table to Richard.

"We also think we need to bring some of this under a proper new Clarence Foundation umbrella," Nick said. "We ought to be more involved in shaping our own ventures, hand-selecting organizations and projects that have a specific meaning to us. Obviously this doesn't preclude you sending us on other outings," he added hastily, "but we think it will help shape a larger cohesive purpose for us as a team."

Agatha's lips had puckered into an O of astonishment. Richard laid a hand on the binder as if trying to read it through osmosis.

"How very clever of you both," he said, and I couldn't tell if he meant it. "Thank you for the additional reading. I shall do it at my own convenience and get back to you."

Agatha, who had clearly assumed he'd tell us to get stuffed, jerked her head between us and her brother like a ticked-off chicken.

"I assume that concludes your portion of this agenda, Rebecca," Richard added.

"Actually, there is one more thing," I said. "My sister is getting married, so Nick and I will need to be on hand for that. Probably in November. I wanted you to have advance notice. She's also expecting a baby."

"Goody, I love babies!" Elizabeth chirped. "Hearing that makes me broody."

"Indeed," Richard said. "Perhaps, Rebecca, this is one instance in which you should use your sister as inspiration. Certainly, no duty of yours is more important than delivering this family its next heir."

Nick opened his mouth to say something, but Richard was quicker.

"Moving along," he said. "I've been briefed on Frederick's whereabouts. He was in Afghanistan by last reports, and safe, but I won't hear more until the mission he's undertaken is over, or unless he's forcibly evacuated."

"I still cannot believe you let him go," Agatha scolded.

"He's been expertly trained. And it's very difficult to say no when your child is motivated to do good in the world," Richard said, although I noticed that his lips had gone white. "I suppose you've never run up against that situation with Nigel."

"Nonsense," Elizabeth said, leaning across the table to pat Agatha's hand supportively. "I'm sure his campaign to legalize ecstasy is going to revolutionize the club scene. *And* create jobs."

Agatha frowned hard at the table. "The situation is just very frightening," she admitted. "I'm worried about him, and I don't like it at all."

Nick handed her the handkerchief he always carried. "Neither do I," he said. "But Freddie made a choice, and I trust that he and Father knew what they were doing."

No one but me could see how hard his other hand was gripping the seat of his chair.

In a burst of traditionalism, Lacey and Olly had decided to get married before the baby was born. Once Lacey's twelve-week scan confirmed that everything was progressing well, Mom flew over for an extended stay, moving into a lovely bright three-room suite on the first floor of Apartment 1A that Nick and I had set aside for her specifically. It was a relief to have her within reach as we braced ourselves for the fearsome Bridezilla we'd always assumed Lacey would become.

"So," Lacey told us as she kicked back in a chevron wing chair in Mom's den and undid the top button of her jeans. "I'm not sure if you're going to like what I have in mind for this."

"I do think it might be a bit too chilly in November to do it on a yacht," Mom said.

Lacey rolled her eyes. "I haven't wanted to get married on a yacht since I was fifteen. I'm not asking Good Charlotte to play the reception anymore, either."

"I don't even know what that means," Mom said.

"Anyway, there are all these specific rules about where you can have a wedding in England if it's not in a church," Lacey continued. "But neither of us is religious, so a church definitely isn't happening no matter what. Sorry, Mom."

"That's all right, sweetie," Mom said. "It's your wedding, after all."

"And I technically had two church weddings, so it all evens out," I piped up from my perch on the window seat. Outside in the courtyard, Nick was getting out of his car, elegant in a dark blue suit. It was delightful to realize that seeing him from afar still made my heart skip.

"We're leaning toward a really basic civil ceremony at the registry office, and then a small party afterward," Lacey said. "And that's it. No fuss."

"Say what now?" I said, turning away from ogling my husband. "I'm sorry, is this the same person who made a wedding guest list that had four hundred and fifty names on it when she was nine?"

"You went as a bride for Halloween three years in a row," Mom said.

Lacey covered her face with her hands. "People change!" she said. "Bex always said that if she ever got married, she'd be barefoot in cut-offs in someone's backyard, and that didn't happen, either. All I want is to hug the people I love. And to not serve lamb because the smell of it makes me want to puke right now."

"I don't know," I said, tapping my lip with my pointer finger. "You're also wearing Birkenstocks today, which you have always hated, so it is possible that you have lost your mind."

"You clearly have," Lacey shot back. "Mascara *and* eyeliner? When you're off the clock?"

"It makes my eyes look bigger!" I protested.

We both started giggling. On some level, it did feel as if we'd pulled a fraternal-twin Freaky Friday without anyone else noticing.

"It's going to be perfect, Lace," I said. "Small and simple sounds beautiful."

"Exactly. Besides, it's the marriage that matters," Mom said. "My wedding was a nice day, but my marriage was a great life. That's all I've ever wanted for you girls."

Eleanor was substantially more confuzzled.

"She's getting married . . . in a *room*?" she asked, wrinkling her nose.

"I mean, technically a church is also a room," I said.

"It's so *ordinary*." Eleanor turned the word over in her mouth less like an insult than a marvel. "I've never been to a wedding like that. Won't it look like some sort of business conference? Is there even an aisle? She might as well get married in Heathrow." She tilted her head. "I should offer my presence. To make it festive."

I laughed, and Eleanor looked offended.

"Did you seriously just say that?" I asked. "You can't stand my sister."

Eleanor leaned back against the cushions of the mint-green sofa in her sitting room and glared at me. "You don't need to like a person to attend their wedding," she said. "And this has at long last made her interesting to me."

"You never did give Lacey any credit," I said.

"When exactly did she earn any?"

"The last few years were as weird for her as they were for any of us," I said to her doubtful face. "I think we're all finally growing up, or at least growing out of it. People change."

"No, they don't," Eleanor said. "They simply change costumes. Underneath, they're who they always were."

"You're using a blender in your sitting room to make exotic margaritas," I argued. "That's change."

"That's a post-coma reawakening," Eleanor pointed out. "Besides, you of all people should know about costumes."

She handed me her phone, but I already knew what it would show: a blurry, blown-up photo of me and Freddie as Niles and Margot, the day we had ice cream in the park. It went viral after some random person spotted us in the background of her vacation photos and decided we looked familiar. (@KingIdrisElba had responded to her that Freddie was dressed like he "lives in a van down by the river.") It was the first real test of the new world order in which Nick had to accept that Freddie and I had our own separate friendship, and other than a brief comment about our recklessness, he'd taken it like a champ (or at least bitten back anything else that was on his mind). But social media, as always, had its suspicions, and as I scrolled through them I ended up clicking over to the Instagram account of a guy called Duchess Dreadful, who'd used it as evidence that Freddie and I were still having a torrid affair. E! News disagreed, putting it side by side with another one of me and Freddie and pointing out all the ways it couldn't be us; a user called GOOPSux had written, "OMG it's not Freddie, it's Homeless Beachy Gwyneth Paltrow." Gwynnie herself had responded, "#goals."

"For the most part, people seem to think it's absurd that you two would stroll out wearing daft wigs in what is essentially the front yard," Eleanor said. "And they are not wrong. You look as if you're trolling the park to buy cocaine."

"We were not," I said. "If it's even us, which obviously it isn't."

"Of course not," she said. "Certainly, no one in this family ever needed to procure illicit drugs from strangers, *outdoors*." She cackled at the expression on my face. "You should see yourself. You look positively scandalized." Her face went distant. "I did smoke grass once on Mustique in 1968. I ate an entire block of cheddar."

"What?" I squeaked.

"This was very risky of you two," she continued, snapping back to attention, "but it almost worked. I should give it a go."

"What?" I squeaked.

"I could take the tunnels out," she mused. "Although I suppose the tunnels might have caved in by now. God knows how many lovers of Georgina's might be buried down there."

"What?" I squeaked.

"Perhaps I *will* come to your sister's wedding," she concluded. "I'd like to see what a truly ordinary party looks like." She frowned at me. "Do not say *what*. Your conversational skills are subpar today."

"You hit me with a lot right there," I said. "Where is all this coming from?"

She smoothed her hair. "If you must know, I'm bored. Richard still has my job. The doctors won't let me ride. The stables are very far away and I haven't made it all the way there without getting winded," she said. "I have too much time to think, cooped up in here, being forced to lift those weights over and over again. Exercise is tedious, Rebecca. And the baseball! All we do is win, win, win. It's not even hard."

"A century of Cubs fans just felt a tremor in the force," I said, knocking on the wood end table next to me. "Seriously, it's so typical that the year I get you to watch is a year where they're not ripping our hearts out with their bare hands." I paused. "Yet."

"I need something to look forward to other than this guttural post-season heartbreak you keep promising me," she said. "In the olden days, you know, queens *put* people in prison. They didn't *live* in one."

"Going to a wedding reception in some random Cambridge pub is probably strictly against doctors' orders," I pointed out. "Isn't your blood pressure still unstable?"

"Perhaps what's making it unstable is being queen without being *the* queen," she retorted. "It's unacceptable."

"Have you talked to Richard about it?" I asked. "He's king without being *the* king, which doesn't sound all that great, either."

She shot me a look of disbelief. "What's not to love? All of the power, and nobody died. He's buzzing from all the papers applauding his scrupulous devotion to duty," she said. "The only one on my side is Xandra Deane, bless her."

Xandra, bless her twice, had turned the fire hose of her indignation onto Richard, calling him Prince Peacock and snarling that her "palace sources" suggested he was shoving Eleanor out of the spotlight to satisfy his ego. God save the Queen, so she may in turn save us from a king who puts position over patriotism, had been the kicker in her most recent column. Richard had been furious. Eleanor had ordered four more copies.

But I couldn't imagine this going on much longer without Eleanor showing her face. Vanity had carried her this far—Eleanor, from a long line of rulers whose queens were proudly hardier than its kings, cared too much for that legacy to appear in public any less than her best. That was clearly wearing off, though. The clock on Richard's regency was approaching midnight, and the question wasn't whether Eleanor would turn him back into a pumpkin but *when*.

We were notified about ten days after our Conclave that "Trafalgar still stands," which was the code phrase for "Freddie is still safely in possession of all his body parts." I received a quick text from him saying that he was learning firsthand that it was wise to shampoo a beard, and then came another long stretch of silence before we heard he was in Syria. It was wearing heavily on Nick. He tapped his foot or his fingers nervously every time Richard offered an update, and had started combing the morning papers for international news with a renewed vigor, as if half expecting his brother to pop up in one of them.

"What was he thinking," Nick muttered one day over a piece about unrest in Jalalabad. "Agatha was right. You can't cram all that training into one month."

"He seemed ready, Nick," I said.

"And how do you know that? Did he demonstrate it for you?" Nick snapped, and then looked surprised at himself. "Sorry. I don't know where that came from. You didn't ship him off."

"Freddie wanted to go," I said. "I think this is his Scotland."

"Scotland didn't involve live ammunition." He shoved back his chair so firmly when he stood that it nearly tipped backward. I let him leave. We had drawn our boundaries, and this territory belonged to Dr. Kep.

It was helpful, emotionally, that the Palace arranged for Freddie to be extracted for two separate weekends of foreign appearances, to keep anyone from wondering where he was. First, he went to Belgium to represent the family at the hundredth anniversary of a World War I battle—the photos of which Nick examined closely before concluding his brother looked haggard—and then later to the Netherlands to open an exhibit of seventeenth- and eighteenth-century British portrait artists who'd been influenced by Van Dyck. Daphne, in the know and considered a safe accomplice, had joined him in Utrecht for the opening.

Freddie seems well, but subdued, Daphne had written. I think he has found the operations to be more brutal than he imagined and I don't press him to talk. He seems relieved by the silence.

That didn't sound like a "well" Freddie to me, and I'd texted back and said so. Her reply: I suppose I know him differently than you do, of course.

Between worrying about Freddie, beginning to sketch out a Clarence royal foundation with Nick, placating Eleanor's restlessness, and helping Lacey choose passed apps for her reception, I, at long last, had an extremely full plate. I have never been as grateful for baseball as when the postseason started and Eleanor could apply herself to the rigors of a multi-game series. Her Majesty actually changed her sleep schedule so she could be awake to cheer on the Cubs when they played, and hex the Red Sox, the Dodgers, and the Indians when they didn't—basically, any team that wasn't us that she thought looked good.

And improbably, impossibly, we did look good. Really good. We were the National League's top seed. We took out the Giants. Booted the Dodgers. Made it into the World Series, and we hadn't yet wet the bed. It sucked that Dad hadn't lived long enough to experience this run, but it was also possible that the stress of it would have killed him if he had. Mom couldn't watch; without my father's booming asides, baseball was noise to her that woke up painful echoes. Lacey had enthusiastically accepted my updates, but preferred to gestate in Cambridge while I trudged over to Buckingham Palace at weird hours and then eventually maintained a guest room there for game nights and the subsequent mornings.

"I can't believe I have to move in with my grandmother if I want to see you," Nick said after we won game two. "Is this what people mean when they say they're sports widows?"

"Yes," I said. "And no offense, but I hope it becomes an annual problem."

We promptly lost the next two games, both of which ended with me curled in the fetal position on the floor.

"I cannot believe you brought this idiotic team into my life," Eleanor said, throwing the remote across her sitting room. "Wasting all that winning in August when they knew perfectly well they'd need it now. I'm finished. Forever."

"Right," I said. "Same time tomorrow night?"

"Be punctual," she said. "I don't want to miss your anthem. Everyone sings it so badly."

I wasn't, and we didn't, and the guy from Staind did absolutely mangle the "The Star-Spangled Banner." We won, and Queen Eleanor pointed at the sky in triumph while I, the Duchess of Clarence, screamed into a throw pillow that had probably once been leaned on by Queen Victoria herself. Either of them. When we took game six in Cleveland, I had to stack two cushions in front of my face during my yelling to avoid triggering a PPO panic.

Game seven. On the road. For all of it.

Richard sent Nick to Wales for something I did not have room in my brain to remember, so Lacey came in from Cambridge because she couldn't stand the idea of me going through this without moral support. I rolled out of my nap room at 1 a.m. and threw on my hat and my Kris Bryant jersey to meet her at the porte cochere.

"Listen up, kid," I said, talking into her belly button. "You're going to hear a lot of words today from Auntie Bex, and you need to ignore all of them except for 'GO, CUBS.'"

"This should be highly educational," Lacey said. "The worst Olly ever says is 'Oh, rats.' He is the most adorable square." She looked up at the foyer with a rueful smile. "This is better than the last time I was here."

"It could hardly be worse," I reminded her.

"You're tempting fate."

"Ladies." Althorpe, Eleanor's long-suffering Palace butler, appeared. "Change of plans. Follow me."

Lacey gave a comical little sigh, and we followed Althorpe past the famous palace staircase and through a gilded glass-paned door. A narrow, rickety set of steps extended down, covered in thick green carpet that smelled faintly of chlorine.

"Are we going to the pool?" Lacey asked, confused. "Ooh, wait, is there a bowling alley in here? I always wondered."

"I don't think the Brits are into bowling that isn't done on lawns," I said.

The staircase expelled us into a low-ceilinged basement hallway, the walls dotted with portraits that had been hung fairly carelessly and painted with even less rigor. One of them was of Queen Anne, but seemingly by way of Picasso; next to her hung a rendition of Marta in which her head was three sizes too small. There was also a portrait of Richard on horseback that looked like it was meant for the front of a romance novel.

"It's a wall of shame," I breathed. "These are horrific."

"I hope you're never down here," Lacey said.

"I hope I *am*," I countered. "That way only about three people will ever see my portrait."

Althorpe threw open a set of heavy double doors to reveal the spacious in-house movie theater, furnished with about twenty high-end leather couches and captains' seats that had their own tables for snacks. Lacey and I were agog. The Cubs—my Cubs—were about to play for their lives on the wall of Buckingham Palace.

"An immense moment demands an immense screen," came Eleanor's voice.

When she rose with some effort from her seat, I blinked. It looked familiar. But it couldn't be.

"Eleanor," I said, dropping all formality. "Is that…?"

"A Coucherator," she said. "Nicholas spoke to your mother and had one flown in. There is a treat in it for you."

She opened the refrigerated compartment of my dad's life's work, so roundly mocked by the British press and Eleanor alike. Inside was a perfectly chilled case of Miller Lite. It was only then that I noticed a side table stuffed with Cracker Jack, Doritos, Pop-Tarts, and hot dog condiments.

"Althorpe will deliver the tube meat momentarily," Eleanor said.

What the hell, I thought, and threw my arms around my grandmother-in-law's satin-clad shoulders.

"Yes, you're welcome," she said, patting my back with a stiff palm. "It was mostly Nicholas's idea. He spoils you."

"Enough blathering," said Marta, sitting up from one of the couches. "I am ancient and I could die at any minute and I do not want the last thing I see to be you two blubbering." She peered at Lacey. "Something is different about you," she said. "Did you cut your hair?"

Lacey looked down at her prominent bump and then shrugged. "Yes," she said. "I actually did do that."

"She's right. Enough talking. Beer me." I plunged my hand into the cooler of the couch-fridge, sitting there like my dad's proxy, and pulled out a can and cracked it open, licking off the foam that spurted from the top.

"Disgusting," Eleanor said.

"If we win, you have to drink one. While wearing a Cubs hat."

"I accept, simply because if you've taught me anything, it's that we are going to lose this game in agonizing fashion," Eleanor replied, claiming her side of the Coucherator with an irritated expression.

Then she wriggled a little. "This is not uncomfortable. I might keep it."

The game was a seesaw. Our 3–0 lead became 5–1 and then 6–3, and then suddenly in the bottom of the eighth an exhausted and overused Aroldis Chapman gave up the tying run.

"Whyyyyy," I moaned, sliding into a heap on the floor. This was it. It was over. In my entire lifetime of rooting for the Cubs, they finally decided to push it as far as possible before breaking my heart. Game seven. Kill me.

"My stomach hurts," Lacey said. "From the Cracker Jack," she added when I sat up quickly and squawked. "Sorry. I didn't mean to freak you out."

"And I'm sorry I dragged you over here to witness my emotional ruin," I said. "You're getting married in a week. You need to be sleeping."

"I *was* sleeping during about four of those innings," she said. "You just didn't notice. I think Eleanor was ranting about Jon Lester's pitch count."

"She's the best student I've ever had," I said. "It kills me that I can't take you to Wrigley someday."

"Says who?" Eleanor said.

"Your doctors, probably," I said. "Also, I can't imagine anyone letting you get away with asking an ump if he's as blind as a bat, or just doesn't know what a swinging wooden one looks like."

"Her trash talk needs work, Bex," Lacey said.

"That's a season two project."

"That's enough from both of you," Eleanor said, but I could see the corner of a smirk.

The Cubs blew a chance to break the tie in the ninth, and right before the tenth inning began, a freak cloudburst sent them into the locker rooms.

"Ohhhhhhh," I moaned. "Extra innings. In game seven. In a rain delay." I clutched at myself. "I can't do this. It's torture. My skin is going to crawl off and move to Tahiti and leave me here in a pulpy pile of innards."

"Vivid," Marta said, yawning.

"I must say, this has been a gripping program," Eleanor said.

Lacey popped a cube of cheese into her mouth. "I wonder what they're doing in the locker room."

"Banging their chests and talking about destiny," I suggested around the thumbnail I was biting to the quick. It was the only nail I had left. "Maybe one of you should kill me now and get it over with."

"Toughen up," Marta commanded. "They're coming back. You're going to miss it."

But instead, I witnessed a miracle. We scraped together two runs after an intentional walk. ("Hit him with a pitch if you want to give him a base," Marta grumbled. "Much more fun.") My spleen nearly exploded when we got the first two outs of the bottom of the tenth. My appendix considered bursting when the Indians stole a base, then drove in a run. But unbelievably, improbably, the hitter at the plate who could have been the winning run for the Indians—the one whose RBI took game three from us—grounded out. One hundred and eight years of futility were wiped off the board with a textbook toss to first base. We won. We…won?

"WE WON!" I screamed, hurling my Cracker Jack in the air and clinging to Eleanor as I jumped up and down. "OH MY GOD WE WON. DAD. WE WON!"

"GO ON, MY SONS!" Eleanor yelled. Her primary point of sporting references was still horse racing. "Brilliant. WHAT heart. WHAT a RESULT."

"Watch your blood pressure," Marta said.

"Hang my blood pressure, Mummy," Eleanor retorted. "We are the WORLD CHAMPIONS."

Lacey laughed and wrapped her arms around my neck. "Your Majesty," she said. "Only you would manage to adopt baseball's lovable losers the exact year they become legends."

"It's no accident," Eleanor said. "I know another legend when I see one."

I ran around the room waving my hands in the air and yelling like a maniac, before returning to present Eleanor with her ceremonial beer.

"A promise is a promise," I said, my adrenaline still pumping.

Eleanor stared at it with a wrinkled nose, then popped open the can and took a deep swig. "Dreadful," she said. Then she reached over and shoveled a handful of my Cracker Jack into her mouth. "And this is like scraping out the inside of a candy bar," she said. Then she grinned. A popcorn kernel was stuck in one of her incisors. "How marvelous."

She tugged on the pristine Cubs hat I'd brought her from my US trip, which I documented for Nick. My head was awhirl with elation and sadness; I felt full and empty at once. My dad should have been here. But in his stead, we'd adopted Eleanor, and to a lesser degree Marta, and having them as surrogate Porters moved me more than I expected. Eleanor clutched my arm and gazed adoringly at Ben Zobrist's postgame interview, that pesky Cracker Jack still wedged between her teeth, the beer resolutely refusing to wash it away. Part of her long silver hair had tumbled free of its bun; she evoked a witch who'd overslept. And she was, without a doubt, having capital-*F* Fun.

"Rebecca," Eleanor said to me, cupping my face in her hands and then patting one of my cheeks with something approaching affection. "My dear, if I ever read about this in one of those Andrew Morton travesties, I shall strip you of your title."

CHAPTER SEVEN

Given England's propensity for wetness even in the mildest of months, Lacey and I had made several jokes about her getting married in the cold November rain. ("Should we have candles?" I'd asked. "It'd be hard to hold them," she replied, and our mother looked completely confused.) But England kindly overlooked the easy Guns N' Roses reference, and instead served Lacey a jewel of a wedding week. The sapphire sky bore no sign of the wintry gloom that we knew lurked around the corner, and the air was crisp like an apple, with a welcome bite.

My sister had demanded nothing challenging of me. The council registry office's room needed only a flower arrangement or two, which Olly's sister had gotten from a friend's shop. The pub for the reception did have to be closed and cleared by my PPOs, but people booked it for parties all the time, so no locals would be suspicious. I helped with the cake tasting at Gaz's; he'd done twelve different samples with pots of flavored buttercreams so that they could mix and match, and I got nauseated after trying all of them, but that was hardly a trial. I was to be an official witness, but I got to wear whatever I pleased. The bride stumbled on the perfect dress by accident while passing a vintage shop in Cambridge, and had even been unfazed by the minor media excitement that ensued when someone recognized her shuffling up the high street in her new hometown and reported to Clive that she was knocked up.

> Looks like the wrong Porter sister is pregnant. Take it from me: The Palace is in a lather about Lacey; the more the unwed Porter pops, the more prurient the public prying will be into this impropriety—and the more obvious it is that the Duchess herself is heirless.

"This Clive has the morality of a pigeon," Olly said the next time he saw me.

"*Are* pigeons notably immoral?" I asked. "Honest question."

Olly thought about it. "They shit on everything and they won't go away," he said. "I vote yes."

And so, all that was left for me to do was show up. Easy. But the night before the ceremony, Lacey called in a tizzy, saying that she and Olly had wanted one more personal touch and she was having trouble making it happen: They hoped to scatter as many elephant trinkets around the party venue as possible, as an aesthetic nod to what brought them together.

"The ones I bought online just got here, and at least half of them are broken," she moaned. "And there's nothing in the local shops that isn't hideous. I can be a chill bride and still get pissed about wanting better elephants, right?"

"I'm on it," I said. "Leave this to me."

Finally, Georgina being a hoarder was paying off. I'd seen elephants all over the living room before her whimsical detritus was cleared out, so I trundled down into the cavernous storage room of Apartment 1A to dig through some boxes. I found a beautiful one made of jade—I couldn't think why we'd spurned it; it would fit nicely in the front hall, although perhaps that line of thinking is exactly how people become hoarders. I set it aside, along with a small white porcelain elephant, and a few others carved of wood. When I lifted out the last one, I heard a clattering and dug around in the bottom of the box. My hand closed around something cold and round, and when I pulled it out, a long chain came with it. A necklace.

I turned it over in my palm. The charm was in the shape of a portly camel, fitting neatly inside my cupped hand, with a small hinge along the bottom and a pin-size latch at the top. I ran my thumbnail under the latch, and half the camel flipped open; a small silver key and a knot of paper tumbled out.

My heart leapt. Slowly, carefully, I undid every painstaking fold, until a scrap lay in front of me that was barely legible around all the creases. I flicked on my phone flashlight and leaned over it.

very heart. I understand the obstacles. Ellie will see only the betrayal. We may lose her, but we will gain life. For I die when I can't feel your presence. I suffocate when I don't breathe your air. I love you. I am yours. Always. Be brave.

Forever,
Georgina

"Holy shit, I found it!" I crowed aloud to the crumbling, crumpled piece of paper. Then I squinted at it and realized something was scribbled on the other side. She'd addressed it with a crooked heart, and *H. V.* written inside.

"H. V.," I murmured. "H. V. Who are you?"

I tucked the page in the back pocket of my jeans, taking care not to rip it, and then heaved the box back where I'd found it, atop a chaise longue that had an old rusted French weathervane standing next to it with an *O* where the *W* would have been. I turned to figure out how to carry the elephant trinkets upstairs when suddenly I sat down hard on the couch.

A vane. Vane. Henry. Nick's grandfather. Eleanor's husband.

H. V. was Henry Vane. It had to be.

I raced up the basement stairs, leaving my pile of elephants for later as I speed-walked through the house to get to my bedroom and up to Narnia. It was serene as ever up there, but my brain felt like it was on fire. Did he reject her? Did she demand the note back, hurt and enraged? Or did she never send it, and hold her secret to herself for her whole life? Did this break her?

Nothing up there had a keyhole that would fit the silver one she'd hidden with the letter's end. I unzipped the throw pillow case in which I'd stashed the original pages, pulled them out, and added the last— only one, but somehow it made the whole thing infinitely heavier in my hand. I heard Nick enter the bedroom below me and came within a second of calling out to him. But my voice died in my throat. The doomed love of a sibling's partner. A spurned spare whose relationship with her sister never recovered. This all felt uncomfortably familiar. Was Georgina's future the same one that awaited Freddie? If I told Nick, would he feel like destiny foretold that he'd never forgive Freddie, and needlessly self-fulfill a prophecy?

I prayed he wouldn't notice the armoire door ajar. The letter burned hot in my palm. But then Nick's footsteps receded and I let out the breath I'd been holding. I wasn't about to let Lyons family skeletons intrude on another Porter wedding day, so I folded the whole thing up with the key inside it and zipped them back into the pillow. The secret had kept for half a century. It could keep again. For now.

Nick and I drove into Cambridge the morning of the wedding. My loyalty as far as ancient university towns went obviously lay with Oxford, but its rival was nonetheless powerfully charming. If Oxford felt like living history, then Cambridge and its picturesque river dotted with punters was a living postcard, and especially on my sister's wedding day, I would be delusional not to see them as gems of equal beauty. We could arm-wrestle for ultimate bragging rights later.

The service at the registry office would be families only, and then we'd head over to the pub for a small party. The Eagle was an ancient, boxy spot on a nondescript street off King's Parade, famously where Watson and Crick barged in to announce their discovery of DNA, and it had won Lacey's heart because the ceiling of the otherwise generic back bar was covered in graffiti, courtesy of British and American World War II pilots who'd burned their names and squadron numbers into it with lighters and candles. (She liked the nod to the alliance of her and Olly's birthplaces.) My haul of elephants waited for us on the tables there. Everything was ready.

"Do you think she's going to come?" Lacey asked as Kira wrapped her hair into a loose chignon.

"No," said Mom.

"Yes," said my aunt Kitty, who was nose deep in *Tatler* across the room.

"No," I said. "She was being extreme. I cannot imagine she's going to want to burn her energy on this. No offense."

"Trust me, none taken," Lacey said. "I do not need to have hostess anxiety about the freaking Queen."

"It would be amusing, though, if she went to Bex's wedding because she had to and Lacey's by choice," Aunt Kitty said.

"Katherine, enough," my mom tsked.

"No, she's right," I said. "Eleanor definitely would have called in sick to the Abbey if we'd given her the option. Of course, if we knew then what we know now, Nick and I would have, too."

"Not me," said Kitty, smoothing her brown waves. "Semi-King Richard is a fine hunk of man in person. I'm just sorry he's not at this one."

"Ew," I said.

"He's not even divorced!" Mom said.

"I've got three under my belt," Kitty said. "Perhaps I could offer my counsel."

Mom tsked again, but she was laughing. Kira wove a few final pearl pins into Lacey's hair and then stepped back to admire her work.

"Beautiful," she said. "This updo turned out so much better than one I did for the *Made in Chelsea* wedding episode. Of course, I had to buttress that one in case someone threw a drink at it."

Lacey was radiant in a vintage, short-sleeve, bias-cut cream gown. I had loaned her one of Georgina's extravagant fur-trimmed capes, and when Lacey swung it over her shoulders and gazed in the mirror,

Georgina's face as I'd seen it in photographs flickered over my sister's. Lacey's was the picture of a glamorous courthouse wedding, the kind I imagined Georgina herself might've had if she'd been born with romantic free rein—or at least found requited love. That letter had been jockeying for my mind's attention all morning. I'd decided ten times to tell Nick about it, and then eleven times not to, in part because I wanted to read it again and make sure it really said what I thought it said, and implied what it seemed to imply. Try as I might—and I did, the whole way to Cambridge in the car— I couldn't think of anything else *H. V.* could have stood for in that context.

Lacey hung back in her readying room while I checked that everything and everyone was in place for the ceremony. We'd met the Omundis twice in the run-up to the wedding, and they were mercifully unperturbed by any of the notoriety surrounding me, or Nick, or even my sister. Olly's parents were as compact as he was, and shared his vibe of being so grounded as to be rooted to the earth. His sister Natasha, who Lacey told me was the pioneer behind some groundbreaking new surgical laser, was almost intimidatingly accomplished and had gone on a long rant to Nick about the latest spate of *Times* Cryptics. Her wife, Karmen, had rolled her eyes at me and whispered, "Total gibberish, right?"

There was a huge flower arrangement sitting on one of the windowsills at the far end of the registry council's ceremony room that was new since I'd stuck my head in earlier.

"Love from Niles Kensington," I read off the card that was peeking out from between the dahlias and roses, and smiled at the sight of Freddie's pseudonym.

"Who's Niles Kensington?" asked Natasha.

"A...distant cousin," I lied.

I could see from Natasha's face that she had a follow-up question about this, but the officiant stepped into his spot behind the flower-bedecked wooden podium in the front of the room, and we all had to take our seats. Olly walked to his spot while frantically trying to defog his glasses; he finally gave up and tucked them into his pocket.

"Please make sure I say my vows to the correct indistinct blob," he said.

When Lacey entered on my mom's arm, and I saw the love and awe on Olly's face, I instinctively squeezed Nick's hand. Lacey had struggled when I met Nick, the only other person who'd ever been as important to me as my twin, and now it was my turn to watch her embrace a life partner who wasn't me. For a long time, we'd assumed there wasn't room around us for other people. Now, as she and Olly recited their vows to each other, there was only calm. You don't stop doing a puzzle when you find two pieces that fit; you build around them, and the whole jigsaw hangs together better. When the ceremony ended, we collectively swarmed the happy couple, and I hugged Olly a little extra tightly.

"Are you *crying*?" Lacey asked Nick.

He grinned. "I'm a sucker for a good love story, Lace," he said.

"Aren't we all," said a familiar voice, and everyone turned to see Queen Eleanor herself in a lime-green dress, slowly making her way toward my sister.

"Gran," Nick sputtered. "When did you...?"

"I waited until after you'd begun," she said. "Naturally, I didn't want to make a fuss."

Olly covered his shock by hurrying over to offer Eleanor his arm, bowing awkwardly as he did so.

"You seem like a practical person," she told him. "That is a most welcome change for this family." She turned to me. "Close your mouth, Rebecca, you look like a trout. I told you I wanted to see a civilian wedding. It was very efficient. Far better without the priest up there doing all of that boring speechifying. Perhaps I'll engage in a little Church of England reform."

My mom shot me a look that said, *Manners, Rebecca*.

"Uh, everyone, this is..." I stammered.

"They know," Eleanor said. "Please, no formalities. We're all family today."

"I need to call Father," Nick said, mostly to himself, groping his pockets. "Where did I leave my bloody mobile?"

"Thank you for the support, Your... ma'am," Lacey managed after we introduced Olly's family, and they excused themselves from what had to be a surreal moment and made for the exit to gossip in peace about this development.

"You can thank me by giving my driver the address of the reception," Eleanor said, "as Rebecca chose not to pass that along. I should like to buy those nice people a tequila on the rocks. Do you suppose they have that at the pub?"

"I clearly need to speak to your protection officers," Nick said, hurrying over to a suit-clad man near the door.

"This is a bad idea," I said to Eleanor, waving a stunned Lacey and Olly ahead of us. "Your doctors are going to kill you."

"I'd like to see them try." Eleanor tilted her chin high. "I suspect I am invincible."

*

By the time we arrived at The Eagle, the pub was humming with a collection of Olly's friends, some mutual pals he and Lacey had made in town, and several of his coworkers. Gaz, Cilla, Bea, and Gemma were clustered around the entrance discussing the latest episode of *Cotswolds Coroner*—in which a man was killed by a Peloton bike— and, as requested by Nick, mobilized as soon as they saw us to try to block the view of Eleanor's entrance as much as possible. It was an impossible task, in part because Eleanor kept nudging them ever so slightly out of her way. The party quieted somewhat while the crowd parted and performed a series of wobbly curtsys and head bobs.

"No, no, do not stand on ceremony tonight," Eleanor announced. "The bride is very special to me and I simply want to toast her. Consider the bar open."

Everyone cheered, and a chorus of "God Save the Queen" broke out.

"The bar already was open," Mom said.

Gaz and Nick had secured a corner booth, but Eleanor marched right past them and chose a table with a clear view of the entire party. Lacey hurried over with a large water.

"I assigned Hazel at the bar to your needs," she said nervously. "Just wave at her. I hope you like, um, passed apps."

"I loathe everything about them," Eleanor said, settling into her seat. "Unwashed hands grabbing things off communal plates makes me queasy. Rebecca will fetch me an array."

"And one drink," I said. "Maximum. This is not safe."

"Between your officers and mine, this pub is the safest place in England. You're welcome." She placed her purse on the table. "Will you all stop acting as if I am a china figurine? I'm here now, and I mean to enjoy myself. The reception is where the real amusement happens, and the Queen is so rarely invited to this part." She glared at me. "Sometimes the Queen even has to cancel them."

"Don't act like you were the person who had to call the caterers," I said.

"It was very taxing all around," Eleanor said serenely.

Nick's gaze bounced between us as if he were watching a tennis match. It occurred to me that this was this first time he'd ever seen me and Eleanor interact during the Death-Cheating Fun List era. He looked a little surprised.

"Fine," I said. "I'll go get your refreshments. If you're sitting here doing nothing, it will make people nervous."

"Nonsense. Being at a wedding with the Queen is a coup," she said, folding her hands neatly atop the table. "Tequila on the rocks, light on the rocks, please. Put it on Niles Kensington's tab."

"How do you know about Niles Kensington?"

"Underestimating me is always a mistake," she said.

Nick slid onto the bench at her left, still shaking his head, and I walked over to where my friends stood at the bar and placed the Queen's order.

"You owe me five quid, Beatrix," Cilla said.

"More fool you," Bea said, pulling a crisp note from her clutch. "I'd have taken that bet at five million."

"Is she in her right mind?" Gemma asked, chewing aimlessly on the plastic stirrer that was meant to go in her vodka tonic. "No offense."

We all watched as Gaz crossed the pub's polished wooden floors toward Nick and Eleanor's table, overcommitted to his courtly bow, and knocked a glass of water onto the floor.

"Yes, that seems right," Bea said.

"Ohhhh, I feel sick," I said. "I'd better deliver Her Majesty's drink in case she gets any wild ideas about coming to the bar herself."

"I genuinely don't think you can rig an exercise bike to electrocute someone," Nick was saying when I carried over the tumbler of Cuervo and a sampler of snacks.

Eleanor patted the spot on the bench next to her. "Good, now Nicholas can clock out," she said. "He's ruining *Cotswolds Coroner* for me. Go put some Rod Stewart on the jukebox." She held a bacon-wrapped date up to her face to examine it better. "And I can already tell we'll need more of these."

"*Rod Stewart*," Nick muttered as he walked off.

The open bar had served its intended purpose. Olly's DJ friend was turning up the music while another pushed some tables against the wall to make a dance floor. Olly bowed before my sister and led her out for an impromptu spin as the DJ grinned, and pushed a button on his MacBook. In the absence of an official first-dance song, his friend had chosen Carly Rae Jepsen's masterpiece "Call Me Maybe." Eleanor tapped her foot to the beat and smiled at Olly spinning Lacey around with a light air of being worried he'd jostle the baby.

"It's awfully nice to see young people in love," Eleanor said. "I barely remember what that was like."

"But you did find it," I said. "You were one of the lucky ones."

"Yes, well." The music switched to a slow song, and Lacey buried her face in Olly's neck. "I never got to see Georgina this way," Eleanor added. "I often wonder if things would have been different if she'd only accepted what she couldn't have, instead of . . . well."

I felt a nervous slosh in my gut. This was my opening. But I shouldn't. I couldn't. Could I? The words bubbled up, and before I could catch them, I blurted, "Was that Henry?"

Eleanor slowly turned to look at me, holding my gaze. She held herself still, and said nothing. She barely seemed to breathe.

"I found the last page of her love letter," I stammered, queasier by the second. "Addressed to an H. V. Henry Vane. Right? I've been trying to think of what else it could be, or how to tell you, but the way you said that just now…it is him, isn't it? It's true."

"Hmm. The truth." Eleanor tapped her glass with her middle fingernail. "The truth is that Georgina never could help herself. Damn the torpedoes. That was her modus operandi."

Out of the corner of my eye, I saw Lacey coming toward me with two Champagne flutes, and shook my head subtly. She turned on her heel as if she had forgotten something, and neatly deposited the drinks in front of our mother, who was chatting with Olly's father.

"It wasn't an insult, you know, when I called this wedding ordinary. There hasn't been anything ordinary about my life since the day my grandmother called me in and told me my uncle couldn't have children. *You cannot make the same mistakes as everyone else. You're special now.*" She chuckled roughly. "It is a brutal thing, knowing that what makes you special to your family is your birth order. Georgina especially didn't care for it, because it meant I was more and she was less, and that was unacceptable to her."

Eleanor took a deep swig of her drink. "I'm sure you remember the story I told you about Georgina, falling in love with an unsuitable young man," she said. "That story was not, in fact, about Georgina."

"Oh," I breathed.

"It was foolishness. I should have known better. If I'd kept to my place, and kept him to his, Robert wouldn't have been mine, but…" Her gaze drifted out the front windows and onto the darkening street. Whatever she was seeing, it wasn't the people out there. "At least he might have been alive," she finished. "He died shortly thereafter, in a car accident. Henry was very kind to me then, at a time when kindness was in short supply. We would sit outside for hours. Sometimes, he would read to me. Sometimes we said nothing at all. But mostly, he made sure I wasn't alone, and eventually I felt like I couldn't ever be hurt again with him by my side. I needed him." Her face hardened. "Then Georgina decided she did, too, and it ruined everything. As it may for you."

I reached out and covered her hand with my own, and for a second, she let me.

"Heartbreak doesn't heal without scar tissue. If it happens enough, you harden. To everything," she said, signaling Hazel and pointing to her empty glass. "I don't want that for those boys."

"I think they're both tougher than Georgina was," I said. "Look at how Freddie—"

"I'm not talking about Georgina." Eleanor sat back against the wall, eyes unusually bright. "What you couldn't read in that letter, Rebecca, is that it worked. She made Henry love her back. And I had to live with it. I'm not only the Nicholas in this story. I'm also the Frederick."

I didn't know what to say. My stomach churned. "I'm so sorry, Eleanor."

She blocked her mouth with her hand as if she were rubbing her cheek. "I have trusted you," she said, "with my greatest pain. I trust again that you will lay it to rest now, where it belongs, along with Henry and Georgina themselves. Nobody but you and my mother knows, and it will stay that way."

"I can't keep this from Nick," I told her. "It's not possible."

"It is, and it's easy," Eleanor said. "You simply don't mention it. This is not your secret to tell. What good will it do for him to know how history has repeated itself?"

I hated promising to lie to my husband, even if it was only a lie of omission. But I didn't know how to push back, and I decided that I could figure out whether to keep that promise later.

"All right," I said. "You win."

"Enough," Eleanor said. "I came here to enjoy myself. I am the Queen. I don't sulk in corners."

She rose, and made her way toward the crowd—to what end, I did not know, because I still felt woozy and sick from our conversation in a way that was becoming increasingly urgent. Trusting that Nick had a handle on things, I scurried as casually as I could to the bathroom, and barely made it in the stall before depositing fragments of appetizers and my entire glass of Champagne into the toilet bowl. I sat back on my heels and breathed deeply, glad to be done with that.

Wait, no, I wasn't done with that.

"Bex?" I heard Lacey say. She pushed open the stall door, then wheeled around and locked the bathroom itself. "Oh no, sweetie," she said, coming to brush my hair off my face.

"I'm okay," I told her. "I've been tired lately, and—"

Ugh. I still wasn't done.

"Blargh," I said as I got up to rinse out my mouth. "I hope it's not the passed apps. Eleanor went to town on those." I frowned. "I should check on her."

Lacey folded her arms and followed me out of the bathroom and back down the pub's narrow hallway toward her wedding reception. "It's not food poisoning," she hissed. "I recognize that look on your face. Because I saw it on mine about six months ago."

I stopped in my tracks. "You're hilarious," I said.

Lacey raised a brow. "Weren't you just telling me how tired you've been?"

"My sleep schedule is off because of the World Series!"

"And your boobs look bigger."

"This is a fantastic bra," I said.

To my relief, Eleanor was not doubled over in the corner revisiting everything she'd consumed that evening. Instead, Gaz was expertly guiding her in an offbeat waltz to Sir Rod's "Forever Young." She whispered something to him and he kissed her hand with a flourish before twirling her carefully. For a woman who'd been on at least partial bed rest for God knows how long, she seemed impossibly spry.

I, however, speed-walked back to the bathroom, and felt Lacey's hands holding back my hair as I vomited. Again.

When I was done, hopefully for real this time, I leaned back against the wall and inhaled sharply. Big mistake. Like all pub bathrooms, this one smelled of bleach and urinal cakes.

I thought back to the last few months. I guess I *had* been less aggro about taking my Pill at exactly the same hour every morning. I'd gotten confused when we were on tour about adapting it to the time zones, and never got back on track. But they weren't that sensitive, were they? Besides, I'd had my...

Wait. I counted, and then I looked at my twin sister, whose smug smile met my frozen wide eyes.

Then I grabbed the bowl one more time.

ACT THREE

Men and kings must be judged in the testing moments of their lives.

—Winston Churchill

CHAPTER ONE

Niles Kensington might have missed the wedding, but he made it back for the funeral.

Three weeks after Lacey got married, I woke up in the middle of the night, and Nick wasn't in bed. This wasn't, on its own, surprising; he'd always been a bad sleeper. But even through a bleary half-open eye I could tell he wasn't in the corner reading or up in Sex Den with a crossword, and I didn't hear a telltale clanking from the kitchenette down the hall. The alarm clock next to the bed cheerfully hit 2:48 a.m. My standard instinct was to leave Nick to his insomnia, but under the circumstances, it seemed prudent to check.

I tiptoed downstairs. I could hear the low sound of the TV emanating from Nick's study.

"For those of you up late with us tonight, we'll be back after the break with live updates from outside Buckingham Palace," a woman was saying as I poked my head inside the room. "I'm Keldah Ansari and you're watching BBC News."

A somber version of the usual theme song started clonking as a graphic flashed onscreen: *GREAT BRITAIN IN MOURNING.*

"What updates could they possibly have?" I wondered, leaning against the doorjamb. "It's the middle of the night."

Nick, sprawled on the brown leather sofa in his sweatpants with a bowl of Hula Hoops resting on his chest, twitched at the sound of my voice.

"Sorry," I said, flopping down next to him. "I didn't mean to startle you."

"I thought you were asleep," Nick said. He moved his knitting to make more space for me. "Everything okay?"

"I'm fine," I said. "Mom keeps telling me that I won't sleep through the night for the next eighteen years, anyway."

As soon as Nick and I had gotten home from Cambridge, I made a beeline for our upstairs linen closet. It contained a trove of items Bea didn't want us to be seen purchasing: pregnancy tests, condoms, lube, anti-diarrheal meds, super-plus tampons ("Anything above regular is gossip fodder," she'd said very seriously), and, for some reason, dental floss, as if the nation would be scandalized to learn that royals have to fend off gingivitis.

It's too soon. We're not ready. The thoughts flew through my head on repeat, like the Times Square news crawls except at warp speed. *I cannot be pregnant. It's too soon. We're not ready.*

I'd snuck into Half Bath #3, the one with the little brass tiger faucet knobs, and ripped open the pregnancy test with shaking hands. I'd never held one before. The closest I'd ever gotten was in high school, when Lacey made me buy her one at Walgreens during what would turn out to be a baseless panic. I let out an involuntary laugh as I tipped it into my palm and it landed like a feather in my hand. Such an innocuous plastic wand; how light a trifle for such a heavy situation. I'd known this moment would come for me eventually, and I'd imagined it being amid either a fit of hopeful anticipation, or tearful panic. Instead I'd felt numb. And still a little nauseated. It should have been statistically unlikely that both Lacey and I would get pregnant accidentally within the space of a year. We couldn't each be that fertile and that forgetful at the same time.

But we were. I was. *Pregnant*, the wand screamed at me. Maybe the proverbial twin connection, the one that meant Lacey and I often didn't need to finish our sentences or craved the same junk food at the same time, also extended to our wombs. Except Lacey had been thrilled by her unexpected pregnancy, and the primary emotion I was experiencing was terror. *It's too soon. We're not ready.*

When I slunk out of the bathroom and dove under the covers, I mumbled the news to Nick through the duvet like a ten-year-old confessing to her mother that she stole money from her wallet and blew it all at 7-Eleven. It had only taken a few seconds for Nick to slide down under the covers with me. I hadn't been sure he'd even understood, but there are only so many ways you can interpret, "So, it looks like I'm pregnant," even delivered through a duvet.

We'd stared into each other's eyes. In his, I'd seen both wonder and a little confusion about whatever he was seeing in mine.

"Gosh," he'd finally breathed into the humid little bed-cave we made. "This is a huge surprise."

"No kidding," I'd moaned.

"But a nice one," he'd replied. "Isn't it? We're going to be parents. A little you or a little me running around here smashing Auntie Georgina's souvenir eggs." He stroked my cheek. "I think it's lovely news. But if you don't feel that way..."

I could see the balloon of his enthusiasm leaking air, and I turned my face into the mattress. "Dammit," I said. "I ruined a big life moment."

"You've ruined nothing," Nick said softly. "It was not your responsibility to make it a certain way."

"Yeah, but I always imagined us deciding to try, having a lot of fun doing it, and then finding out it worked and you picking me up and twirling me around. And instead I acted ambivalent, and made you feel sad about something you really want," I said. "And what am I even stressing about? We're married and we love each other, and we'll have plenty of help and we have plenty of money. So."

Nick frowned. "Those are all fine reasons to have a child, if you want to," he said. "But I only want that if we both do."

"I have to want that, don't I?" I asked, my mouth still half in the mattress. "It's been made very clear to me that having a baby is one of my primary responsibilities. I don't get to not be ready. Whatever is in here, he or she is the heir to the throne. There isn't room for me to have complicated feelings about it, because my jurisdiction has pretty much ended."

The words had tumbled out of me almost faster than they'd come to mind. Nick took a breath, then winced, and peeled off the comforter. We took greedy gulps of the colder, fresher air.

"I hate that you feel that way," Nick said. "It's your body, and it's our baby. No one is in this but you and me. This room is the jurisdiction."

I tilted my head. "Theoretically," I said. "But you can't ignore the fact that if we don't have a baby, this whole thing falls apart."

"Bollocks. Gran's aunt and uncle didn't have babies, and that's worked out all right," Nick pointed out.

"That wasn't because they didn't want them," I reminded him. "It's not even that I don't want one! Eventually. It's just..." I rolled onto my back. "The obsession about when we're having a baby is already intense. But we've only been married a year and a half, and for a lot of that time, you and I were not okay. You, specifically, were *really* not okay." I gulped. "Maybe it's not even pregnancy itself that's freaking me out. It's us. I don't want to break us if we're too fragile for this right now."

Nick took my hand, but didn't look at me.

"I am never going to try to talk you into something you don't want to do," he said. "But we are so much better than we were even six months ago. We'll get ready. We'll do the work. That's why it takes so long for babies to percolate in there. They give you months to prepare."

"I get what you're saying. I do." I let out a frustrated grunt. "I just wish this had happened when we decided it was the perfect time."

"The perfect time doesn't exist," Nick said. "For anything. It was never the right time to kiss you, for example, but once I started, I couldn't believe we'd waited. Maybe this will be like that."

"You're so composed," I said, turning onto my side to look at him. "You are going to be a great father. Why is that so sexy?"

Nick grinned. "How do you think people end up with multiple children?" he asked. "Personally, I can't wait to see you snuggling our baby. Whenever it happens. I just hope it gets your nose."

I half laughed, burying my face in my hands. "Our baby. We're going to have a *baby*."

His answering smile almost split his face in two. "Do you want to get out of bed so I can pick you up and twirl you around?" he asked.

"Maybe," I said. "Wait, no. I haven't even been to the doctor yet. What if it's a false alarm? We can't deploy the twirl casually."

"Mad as ever," Nick said. He wriggled closer, and kissed me. "I love you," he said. "Congratulations. I think we'll be aces at this, I truly do."

"I believe you," I had said. "So please don't take this the wrong way. But I think I need to throw up again."

Now, Nick shook the bowl of Hula Hoops under my nose.

"How's the nausea?" he asked. "Is the peanut hungry?"

"I believe it's the size of a cherry at this point," I said. "Or is it a raspberry? Anyway. Our little piece of fruit and I are always hungry."

I poked the fingers of my right hand one by one through the little potato rings and then slid one into my mouth with my teeth. It crunched satisfyingly.

"These would taste great with peanut butter," I said. "Am I already turning into one of those pregnant women with crazy cravings? Stop me if I ask for pickles in my ice cream."

"Whatever my little raspberry wants," Nick said.

We grinned at each other and clinked Hula Hoops before each biting them off our middle fingers. I was still barely pregnant; when we'd gone to the doctor, he told us I was probably six weeks along, handed me some prenatal vitamins, and ordered me to check back in a month or so. With each day that passed, every time I bumped my boobs and they hurt, every time I scrambled to the bathroom to barf in the middle of the night, this pregnancy had started to feel more real, and I was relaxing into the idea that this was the universe hard at work. And it was delicious for me and Nick to have a secret, one private thing that belonged only to us, as we went about our otherwise very public business.

Keldah Ansari came back on the news over a shot of Buckingham Palace, where a crowd of mourners was sobbing and placing wreaths next to framed photos, or lighting tiny glass-potted candles.

"She would have hated this," Nick said.

"Unreservedly," I said. "That almost makes it better."

"She was the crabbiest person I've ever known," Nick said, and his voice was thick. "She once gave me a welt the size of a plum from whacking my shin with that cane."

If death could not take Eleanor, then apparently it settled for the next queen over. Marta died as she had lived: in the middle of a late-night Twitter fight. Her last communication to the world had been a GIF of Jennifer Lawrence sarcastically giving a thumbs-up, sent to @DuchClarH8r, who had been complaining I didn't deserve to wear Emma's ring because I was a crusty social-climbing hag.

I was touched. Royal historians had no idea what texture they were missing.

Marta had made it a generous 104 years, so although her passing was somber news, I couldn't say it was an actively *tragic* development; enjoying a century of robust health and then dying in your own bed is the best-case scenario for any of us. She had lived through two world wars, the moon landing, the Berlin Wall coming down, and the invention of television and the internet and her beloved mobile phone. She had been the final empress of India, a muse for Dior in her middle age, and had hosted Gandhi, Churchill, and Kennedy at her dinner table (albeit not at the same time). Marta's life lent itself beautifully to hours of televised retrospectives—not least because when you're that old, everyone has oodles of time to prepare for your exit. Every time I turned on the TV in the eight days since her death, I found a program called some variation of *A Nation Pays Its Respects*, or *Farewell to Great Britain's Great-Grandmother*. Or, as Nick was watching now, round-the-clock news coverage, even without news to report. Marta would have had no patience for how cloying most of it was, but she would have been delighted to see Idris Elba tweet that he felt "gutted."

"The body of Queen Marta the Queen Mother will lie in state through tomorrow, with Britons and tourists alike lining up for a chance to walk past and say bon voyage to the late queen," Keldah said, over a shot of a sobbing woman standing in line at Westminster Hall. "For more on what to expect in the next few days, we go to our special correspondent, Clive Fitzwilliam of *The Sun*. Welcome, Clive."

"Piss off, Clive," Nick muttered.

"Thank you, Keldah. I'm delighted to be here," Clive said, and then his face arranged itself in a sad expression. "And gutted that it's under such mournful circumstances."

"You take Idris Elba's feelings right out of your mouth," I told the TV.

"The crowds in Westminster have far outpaced the wedding of the Duke and Duchess of Clarence, though, of course—you can take it from me—the Queen Mother is substantially more beloved," Clive said. "The hope is that all well-wishers can get through before the funeral. A few lucky ones will catch the family members taking up the rotating guard posts near the casket, so there's that to look forward to."

"*Look forward to*," Nick repeated. "Yes, there's so much to enjoy about a wake, you simpering twerp."

I studied Clive's face as he yammered on about everything from the logistics of the funeral procession, to the dignitaries who were expected to attend, to our innermost feelings. His slick handsomeness had tapered into something hawkish, and his dark hair had what looked like bottle-gray strands at the temples, giving him an air of gravitas and expertise that he didn't deserve. I hoped he'd had a miserable time trying to keep up with his royal column now that he'd lost his best sources— us—and people were accordingly starting to side-eye the accuracy of his scoops, but this was a massive all-hands-on-desks news moment, as it were, and he clearly intended to maximize it.

"...and we expect to see the Prince of Wales, his sons, and Prince Edwin standing guard over the casket together," Clive said. "But the real headline is the public reappearance of Queen Eleanor. A nation waits with bated breath for its broadly beloved..."

Nick muted the television aggressively.

"Aren't you curious to see what *b* word he was going to use for her?" I teased. "Boss lady?"

"Bloodline begetter?"

"Big cheese?"

"I dare him," Nick said, picking up his phone in what I knew he imagined was a casual way. The only new item on his lock screen— a selfie we'd taken on the edge of a cliff in Scotland—was a news alert about the weekend's Premier League games being rescheduled out of respect.

"Are they back yet?" I asked softly.

He turned over his phone and dropped it on the couch. "No idea."

When Marta died, Freddie had immediately been recalled from Wherever—sincerely, we didn't know—and Richard had gone to fetch him himself from his preferred private airfield. It was a kind gesture from someone who rarely deployed them, and it made us both anxious that he knew something we didn't, which my inner armchair psychologist suspected was why Nick's insomnia had him up at all hours watching the same newsreel footage of his great-grandmother repackaged by different channels. Right now, the news was showing Marta and her husband, Richard, returning from a royal tour of Australia that had gone on for eight entire weeks. I'd never seen him in motion before; he was tall and fluid, almost graceful, and smiling. He didn't at all look like a person who would drown in an ill-advised boat outing. Eleanor and Georgina were greeting them as they disembarked from the plane, looking very young and yet also vaguely old, thanks to their '50s hair-dos. Eleanor was willowy and refined, on the cusp of leaving her teen years behind, and Georgina at sixteen was already a bombshell. Their arms were intertwined, and they didn't even unravel themselves when they curtsied to their parents.

"It's weird to see this, knowing what we know now," Nick said. "I'm glad you told me, and it is juicy, but it's quite sad to watch them and wonder how long they had before..."

He trailed off, and looked at his phone screen one more time. Nothing.

The Freddie who walked through the doors of the ornate private vestibule outside Westminster Hall was not the same Freddie who had left us. He was thinner, and tired, with the air of someone who'd been lugging something very heavy and hadn't registered yet that he'd put it down. His new beard looked freshly trimmed, like the well-considered choice of an adult man and not something he grew out of laziness in the field. He looked older. Almost gaunt. At the sight of him, I let out a breath that I felt like I'd been holding for six months. Nick simply stiffened. It was then I noticed Freddie's right arm was in a sling over his military uniform.

"It's nothing," he said as he came in the door, holding up his left hand. "Don't freak out."

"I'm not," I lied.

"You are," he replied. "Broken arm, is all. Rough outing a couple of days ago."

"Rough is one way to put it," Richard said, coming into the vestibule behind Freddie in full military regalia. "Two other men died."

My hands flew to my mouth. Freddie gave me an awkward one-armed hug.

"Lots to be grateful for," he said. "I saw the least of it."

"Holy..." Nick caught himself, and took his brother's free left hand in an unconventional handshake. "No one told us about any of this."

"That's because, technically, it's classified," Bea cut in, appearing behind Richard with a clack of her heels and shooting his back a look that could only be described as treasonous.

"But *you* knew?" Nick asked.

Bea straightened her collar. "I work for Freddie as much as I work for you," she said. "Who do you think was in charge of making sure this stayed under wraps? I don't mind saying that it was challenging."

Freddie leaned over and punched her companionably on the arm. "You get full marks, Beatrix," he said. "A job very well done."

"I would have appreciated being more in the loop," Nick said.

"It's done now, Nicholas," Richard said, although not unkindly.

"It is that," Freddie said. His voice was hollow.

"So does that mean you're back?" I asked. "For good?"

Freddie shrugged his elbow in my direction and said nothing.

"We were running on borrowed time with the press, anyway," Bea said, glancing down at her vintage Cartier watch. "Speaking of which, you were supposed to be in there taking your spots three minutes ago. Where *is* Edwin?" She scuttled across the very small room and started tearing through her luxe leather tote bag for her phone. "If he's forgotten, we'll shortly be planning *his* funeral."

Part of the ritual of Marta's body lying in state was that four people—members of the military, generally—took turns in a seventy-two-hour round-the-clock watch over her body, one at each corner of her flag-draped coffin, which was topped with both flowers and her iconic crown. One shift was always taken by the men of the royal family in their respective military uniforms, and Nick, Freddie, Edwin, and Richard were up that afternoon.

"Service in here is wretched," Richard said. "Come outside with me while I call him, Beatrix, I need to discuss what Frederick will be telling the guests."

He stalked out, Bea trailing behind him, navy-blue Smythson leather notebook in hand, leaving me and Nick alone with Freddie for the first time since everything fell apart on Thanksgiving. Nick shoved his hands into his trouser pockets and rocked back on his heels.

"How was your flight?" he finally asked.

"We barely made it out. The weather was terrible," Freddie said. "I came straight from the airport and changed in a bathroom I never knew was here. Of course, why would I? No one's died lately." He closed his eyes, and his face seemed to crumble with the effort to open them again. "No one here, anyway."

I could see an ache settle on Nick's face. His arms tensed, as if he wanted to hug his brother but was uncertain whether it would be welcome. So his hands remained at his sides.

"We're awfully glad you're back," he said. "I hope it was...or rather...that you found what you were looking for."

Freddie's face was unreadable. Nick and I exchanged glances as the heavy wooden door banged open and a storm-faced Richard and Bea came back inside, followed by a chastened-looking Edwin, who was trying to straighten a medal that looked like he'd made it himself. Edwin's Naval career had not been illustrious, nor entirely voluntary, and it had been a tragedy for no one when it was cut short due to crippling nausea.

"I couldn't find my hat," he fretted. "Elizabeth has a head cold and so I told her she could sleep in, but I realized she was the last person to wear it, when we were—"

"Enough," Richard said, his upper lip curling. "The RAF has already gone over its allotted fifteen minutes. Mother's watching this, Edwin. There's a *livestream*. Stand up straight."

Edwin's lip trembled. "Stand. The last word I played against Granny," he moaned.

"That's good!" I said. "Five letters!"

"Technically it was *and*, but close enough," he said, wiping his streaming ducts.

After a flurry of last-minute adjustments, the men walked through to stand their somber watch. Bea pulled an iPad out of her tote—like Mary Poppins's carpetbag, it contained an infinite supply of useful items—and pulled up the livestream, propping the tablet up on a table against a religious-looking object that was probably now being lightly defiled. Nick and Freddie had taken the positions at the foot of Marta's casket, while Richard and Edwin (still fiddling with his jacket) stood at the head. The public kept shuffling through the vast candlelit room up to the coffin, seemingly oblivious to the four taciturn princes fifteen feet away, save for one young woman who afforded Freddie a sly grin. The Freddie of yore might have twinkled at her a little, but this one was stony and listless.

"Does he seem okay to you?" I fretted.

"He'll feel like himself after a night in his own bed," Bea said. "And Daphne gets here tomorrow. She'll help get him sorted."

"Will she?"

Bea cocked her head and studied my face. "Does that bother you?"

"Not at all," I said. "I just didn't know she was doing so much heavy lifting."

Bea made a note in her book. "A true friend's work is never done, and Freddie needs as many of those as he can get right now," she said. "You look tired. Do you need a chair?"

"No." In truth I was dying to sit down—my four-inch Sarah Flint heels were killing me, and my black sheath was pinchier than it used to be—but I wasn't about to admit it to Bea.

"I don't want you to be uncomfortable," Bea said.

"Since when?"

"Since the entire world is going to be watching you at this funeral tomorrow, and we can't have you walking like your feet hurt," she said. "What other reason could there be?"

I tried to hold a neutral facial expression. I had wrapped the pregnancy test in paper towels before shoving it in a sausage-roll box and disposing of it in a dumpster behind one of the staff buildings, like a dead gerbil I was trying to hide from a child. Bea didn't seem like someone who'd root through people's trash, but then again, Bea had also once counseled me that other people would. She had a way of making me feel exposed, and she was doing it again now. I turned away from her inquiring eyes, and we watched the rest of the fifteen-minute shift in silence.

CHAPTER TWO

Royal funerals make royal weddings look like Vegas elopements. There are days upon days of somber events, almost all of them involving cannons and bells, weeping distant relatives and mopey dignitaries, and men and women marching in full regimental garb. And every single moment of this one was being broadcast, from Marta's body making its way from Buckingham Palace to the Palace of Westminster; to the three days it lay in state there; to its journey into Westminster Abbey for her actual service, and then out again, this time to Windsor Castle for her burial next to King Richard and Georgina. Her coffin was escorted along this very long and winding path to eternal rest by different contingents of men in her life, ranging from Richard to Marta's personal chauffeur and her long-retired social secretary, who was himself so old that I was worried he wasn't going to live through the walk.

My first official participation was the morning of the funeral, as the royal family followed the casket and the accompanying pipe band on foot—excepting Eleanor, who would arrive by car—from Westminster Hall into the church. Agatha held Richard's arm; Edwin had a tot on each side and walked behind with Elizabeth, who carried the baby, which obligingly spit up on her lapel as she shook hands with the archbishop.

"Ugh. Could you be a dear and turn that into wine, too?" She'd winked, waving her hand in a magic-making gesture toward the archbishop, to his barely suppressed horror.

When Clive later wrote that "anyone who's anything anywhere" came, he wasn't exaggerating. This guest list made our wedding look like we'd rounded up a bunch of randoms at the Tube. It was all I could do to keep my head down and look solemn, as in my periphery alone I spied three American First Ladies, four British prime ministers in addition to the beleaguered Doris Tuesday, at least half of the England national football team, the president and First Lady of France, the prime minister of Canada, Angelina and Brad sitting on opposite sides of the room, and the heads of every single royal family in Europe—including the former king of Belgium, who was in the middle of a paternity scandal and had been hiding out in Mallorca. I wished fleetingly that I'd gotten the Cubs to pay their respects.

Despite my valiant effort not to rubberneck, the truth was that I could have gawked all day if I wanted to, because for once no one was looking at me. *Everyone*—from Brad Pitt to the Prince of Monaco and his young Olympian wife—was waiting to see Eleanor. And she knew it.

I firmly believed she'd also known no pub in England, not even one with PPOs in it, could contain guests' urges to snap iPhone photos. A few grainy pictures of her appearance at Lacey's reception had leaked to the press, in which the Queen looked hale and hearty enough to back her truculent son into a corner: step out of the regent role and announce her full recovery, or stir up suspicion among royal watchers.

"What an unfortunate situation, but of course we must do as the optics demand," Eleanor had said airily the day the photos ran. "Pity a lady can't simply wish a loved one well in peace."

I'd nearly choked on my sandwich, and not just at the notion that Lacey was her loved one. Eleanor could play innocent all she wanted, but I'd go to my grave swearing this was a carefully crafted checkmate.

Initially, I'd been hugely annoyed that Eleanor manipulated my sister's wedding day for her own gain, but the emotional wallop of Marta's death knocked all that away. I'd grown fond of her during the past two years, but that was nothing compared to what I worried Eleanor might be feeling. Due to the early deaths of both their husbands, and later Georgina, they'd been each other's touchstones for a lifetime. Eleanor was now the only one left in her family who remembered what she was like before she was a queen. I hoped the loss wouldn't have an adverse effect on her own vigor, but when I went to see her, she was every bit as feistily frank with me as she'd been since she woke up.

"You are the only person I can say this to," she'd said. "But while of course I'm very upset about Mummy, I am pleased that my debut will be a splash. If you're making a comeback, *make a comeback*."

"I'm sure Marta would agree," I said.

"I doubt that," Eleanor said. She massaged some lotion into her right hand. "For every ear-bending I got from Victoria II about duty and etiquette and the requirement that I have no fun, there were three from Mummy. It was like the current battering you against a rock. After a while you simply go limp."

"I can't imagine you going limp against anyone," I said.

She laughed harshly. "Where do you think I learnt that?"

"Marta always came across as more of a...harmless curmudgeon to me." I shrugged. "Maybe all the losses in her life eventually changed her, mellowed her a little."

"I told you, people don't change," Eleanor replied curtly. "However..."

She stood up and walked over to the elegant Danish credenza set against the far wall of her sitting room. She rummaged in the top drawer for a bit and emerged with a velvet box.

"I thought you might like to have this," she said, coming over and setting it in my hand. "We haven't dealt fully with Mummy's will yet, but I think she'd agree you could use a little luck."

I opened the box to find a small emerald-and-diamond brooch in the shape of a four-leaf clover. "Eleanor, it's gorgeous. I couldn't possibly take it."

"Nonsense. It matches your ring," Eleanor said. "Besides, you brought a great deal of amusement to my mother's life over the last few years."

"That's a diplomatic way to put it."

Eleanor smiled. "You may remember that I am a master of diplomacy, Rebecca," she said. "Wear it to the service. We'll leak to the press that it was bequeathed to you, which will give you a boost with the public. That is a gift, too."

"Thank you. I'm touched. Really," I said, lifting the brooch out of its box. It glimmered in the light. "It turns out I am becoming a jewelry person after all."

"Of course you are," Eleanor said. "The only people who think they aren't are the ones who've never worn really good jewels."

We both turned and looked at the chair Marta had favored, all those days and nights by her daughter's bedside. Her iPhone charger was still plugged into the wall.

"It has been quite a year," Eleanor said, sounding resigned. "Perhaps the building will burn down next."

Back in Westminster Abbey, I glanced down at the brooch, which I'd pinned to my lapel. I had awoken with my stomach in knots, and I was comforted by the sight of the gems twinkling back at me in the dim December light that wafted through the church windows. Freddie, Nick, and I took our seats in the second row, with me directly behind where Eleanor would end up, and right in front of King Hendrik-Alexander and Queen Lucretia and Daphne, the last of whom leaned forward to squeeze Freddie's shoulder when we took our seats.

Custom held that Eleanor was meant to lead the family procession into the church, but she'd made an edit. Instead, she was the last to enter, walking up the aisle alone, ensuring that all 4,400 eyes in the church—and the millions watching the service from home—would be on her.

It was a masterful performance. Eleanor's stride was appropriately slow, yet assured. Only those in the know would recognize her slightly clenched fists as a sign she was stilling herself, trying to ensure no one spotted the disproportionate weakness that remained in her right side. Her back was ramrod straight, her face under her black hat relaxed but serious. I couldn't imagine the effort it took—the sheer amount of careful self-control. The curtsies and bows from the rest of the guests rolled from the back of the church to the front, following her like a slow-motion version of the wave. It must have looked spectacular from the overhead cameras.

Unexpectedly, Eleanor stopped right in front of me, putting a hand to her chest in a show of emotion and then dabbing at her eyes. I looked up to see her staring at me very hard, and saw in the tilt of her head a suggestion that I should stand and take her arm. Nick nudged me with his leg and I shot up out of my seat, feeling the heat of Richard's glare on my face as I—the interloper, and not him—walked her the rest of the way to Marta's casket.

Behind us, someone sneezed. The ensuing echo gave me a little cover.

"Are you okay?" I murmured, trying not to move my lips.

"Tired," was all she said through a motionless mouth.

I said nothing more. While Eleanor's grief was real, I realized it also gave her a convenient excuse to have a steady arm escorting her the rest of the way. And so I led her to Marta, where she placed her posy next to her mother's crown and leaned toward the coffin.

"I'll never forget," she whispered. And then, so subtly that I almost missed it: "But I'll never forgive, either."

When she turned to me a second later, it was gone, her face the picture of dignified sadness once more. I took her back to her seat to commence the final farewell, but didn't hear a word of the service over my own racing thoughts.

"It's lovely to see you, but I'm sorry it's under these sad circumstances," Daphne said to me and Nick later, during the post-funeral reception. We were in the Blue Drawing Room at Buckingham Palace, and I was perched on the world's most uncomfortable silk settee and thinking about whether or not I needed to throw up. My constant need to barf had tapered, but I hadn't felt right since Eleanor's salty final salute to her mother—something I wasn't entirely sure she knew I'd overheard.

"We're happy you were able to make it," Nick said.

"Of course," Daphne said. "Marta was my father's godmother, you know. We spent a lot of time looking at old photos of them last night.

I'm relieved that we've seen some new advances in hat trends since he was born." She waved across the room at Freddie. "I hope he got some sleep last night. He's had it very hard."

"So we heard," I said.

"When I die, stuff me into a bottle and shoot me into space," Freddie said, sidling up to us and bowing to Daphne with a wry smile.

"Please don't even joke about that," she said.

"I don't mean *now*," he said. "By the time I kick it, Bex and Nick will have had three hundred babies and no one will care about me anymore. Put me in a Coke can and recycle me and go about your day. Don't even invite anyone. Although, I've got to say that Great-Gran's turnout is fantastic."

He turned to survey the room, and then winced, as if he'd pulled something in his hurt arm. Daphne gave him a reproachful look.

"It's nothing," he insisted.

Daphne looked at me, exasperated. "He always says this."

"Well, he's home now, so we can all keep tabs on him," I said.

"And accordingly, you can stop talking about me as if I'm not standing right here," Freddie said.

"Sorry," I said. "Oh, we also rented out your place as an Airbnb, just so you know. I guess we have to evict them now."

"I'm really going to miss that income," Nick said. "Bex and I were spending it all at the track, and I don't know what we're going to do."

Freddie laughed, but he didn't return the conversational volley.

"Nick, I think your father's trying to get your attention," Daphne said, gesturing over Nick's shoulder, where Richard was, in fact, fixing him with a stern expression, accompanied by a head flick toward the handsome old man next to him.

"Ugh. That's Lord Tarlington," Nick said, straightening his tie. "He's got some initiative about vegan British sausages that Father natters on about. I don't know why we're doing this today."

"Why not?" Freddie asked. "Look at Gran. She's talking shop right now, I guarantee it."

He nodded toward Eleanor, who was perched on an armchair under the lamp that had the most flattering light, and chatting to Doris

Tuesday with a pitying look on her face. There was a line of people twenty deep waiting to speak to her.

"Your father is waving at us now," Daphne narrated. "He looks agitated."

"Right. Well, excuse me," Nick said. He gave Daphne a polite double-kiss farewell, and then pecked my cheek. "Freddie, we didn't really get a chance to speak earlier, so. We should catch up over a meal. Whenever you're free."

Freddie's face registered surprise, then shifted back to neutral. "Certainly," he said.

In short order, Freddie and Daphne and I got sucked into the mingling crowd and separated. I cruised around the room trying to avoid getting drawn into any long conversations, and looking for something to eat or drink that might settle my stomach. But none of the food seemed appetizing, and after about ten minutes, my back hurt and my head felt spinny. I wanted to take off my heels and go home. But I wasn't even sure we were allowed to go home before Eleanor did, and I definitely wasn't interrupting Nick's immersion into Lord Tarlington's sausage empire. Instead, I exited the room as elegantly as I could, and kicked off my heels as soon as I found an empty hallway, digging my toes gratefully into the plush carpeting. I padded down the hallway, pumps swinging from my fingers, eyeballing the gilded detailing until I ended up in front of a door down at the end that I'd never opened before. It led to a fairly unremarkable drawing room—well, unremarkable for Buckingham Palace; there was still an oil painting of King Albert riding a white horse hanging over the marble fireplace—with a set of French doors opening up onto a Juliet balcony that overlooked the gardens. I pulled the doors open and stepped out into the crisp December air.

"Fancy meeting you here," came Freddie's voice.

I whipped my head around to see him leaning against the wall. "Jeez, you scared me." I shivered. "Aren't you cold?"

"It feels good," he said. "Too stuffy in there. Take this." He shrugged off the jacket of his military uniform, which had been draped over his own shoulders, and offered it to me.

"Thank you. I'm sure this is against regulations, but I won't report you," I said. "I was getting woozy in there. Being outside is helping."

"Great minds." He rubbed his hands together and let out a puff of breath, which dissipated in a cloud in front of us. "You must have been working on Knickers pretty hard, to get him to invite me to dinner."

"Nope," I said. "That was all him."

"I didn't see that coming," he said, scratching at his beard. "I'd started to make my peace with the thought that we'd keep drifting away from each other."

"You can't mean that," I said, leaning on the concrete balcony railing. I felt a little queasy.

Freddie shrugged. "Prepare for the worst."

"Isn't the phrase 'Prepare for the worst and expect the best'?" I asked. "You left out the optimistic part."

"The last six months have made me into more of a pragmatist."

I regarded his profile, so handsome, so sad. "Was it awful out there?"

"The accident was awful," Freddie said. "But it was not the only thing I saw that I will never forget." He looked out into the bare, leafless garden. "I had a lot of time to think out there. My problems that felt so big are nothing. I will always have a warm, soft place to land. Not everyone has that. We're pretty bloody lucky."

He flapped up his hurt arm like a broken wing. "It makes me want to yell at everyone to please stop acting like I'm some kind of hero because of *this*. I cannot tell you how untrue that is."

"I suspect you're selling yourself short," I told him.

"Selling myself is the only thing on the agenda at the moment," he said. "We promised the press an interview, in exchange for their cooperation in keeping my deployment hidden. Time to pay the piper. Got to make it all about me again."

His face was miserable. I leaned in to give him a sideways hug. He squeezed me back, briefly.

"I'm so tired of myself," he said. "It's good to talk to you again. Did I miss anything interesting?"

I wanted to tell him about the baby, but it felt disloyal to do it without Nick. "Same old," I improvised. "Trying to figure out this whole duchess business. It went well on tour, but now we have to apply that to real life."

"Yes, Your Royal Highness, I saw how well it went on tour," Freddie teased. "People are going to be scandalized if that keeps on."

I whacked him on his good arm. "You know what I mean."

"I do, I just couldn't resist. How's that easy and minor task going?" Freddie asked as a nearby bird took off from a barren branch with a loud flutter.

"It's been a breeze," I started.

Pain hit my abdomen. The edges of my vision went blurry.

"Are you all right?" Freddie asked.

A sharper pain shot through me, and I hunched over, blindly reaching for something to steady me. My hand closed on the railing. "*Shit. Oh, shit. Shit, shit, shit.*"

Freddie looked alarmed.

"What is it?" he asked. "What's wrong? What hurts?"

I moaned. My head was throbbing. A warm, sticky wetness spread on the inside of my thighs. My other hand went straight to my abdomen.

"Freddie," I said as another pulse of pain hit me. My knees buckled. Freddie gracefully caught my weight with his free arm and drew me toward him for stability. He pecked the top of my head.

"I've got you," he said.

There was a gentle throat clearing behind us.

"I'm sorry to interrupt," Daphne said, her face creased with concern. "Should I get someone?"

I peered up at her through my tangle of hair, and I thought I saw a hint of appraisal in her face. And then I found that I couldn't make any words come out of my mouth.

"Yes," Freddie said tightly. "Find Nick. Now."

CHAPTER THREE

Just like that, we were a family of two again.

Everything that came next was a blur, a montage set to my own ragged breathing. The only possible positive about having a medical emergency at Buckingham Palace is that its staff is peerless in the art of making you believe you're alone, only to appear at your elbow in the moment you realize you need them. Before Daphne could even return with Nick, I was scooped into a guest room, helped into a crisp medical gown, and laid in a towel-lined bed while someone paged the Queen's gynecologist. In half an hour, Nick by my side looking green and worried, we got confirmation of what I already knew. My pregnancy was over as unexpectedly as it had begun.

"I wish I could say that's all she wrote, my dear," the doctor said, with the practiced softness of a man who's spent his life delivering this news as often as delivering babies. "But there is some tissue we should remove. We can perform a dilation and curettage in the palace surgical theater, unless of course you'd prefer the medicinal option, which involves taking a pill and then waiting…"

As he talked, I simply stared, watching his mouth move, hearing him, believing his words, but hardly comprehending them. My pregnancy had happened in the first place because a hundred infinitesimal things happened to go exactly right. How cruel that all that magic could be undone in one split second.

I realized the doctor had stopped speaking and was now looking expectantly at me. His eyes went to Nick, as if to ask whether the decision was being abdicated to my husband. Nick put a comforting hand over mine. "Are you up for this? Do you want to decide, or do you need a minute?"

I squeezed my eyes shut and put my hands over my abdomen. I had just slipped into a rhythm of seeing this as a stroke of biological luck rather than a shock. That little spark of life had made its way into my heart, and now it was gone—and yet not, because part of it still clung to me, and I wanted to reciprocate. Even for an extra second. *I'm sorry,* I thought as deeply into my body as I could, as if it were listening. *I'm sorry it took so long to want you. I'm sorry I couldn't tell you we were happy.*

"Your Royal Highness?" the doctor asked, possibly of either one of us. "Shall we prepare the surgical room?"

I curled in a ball in the bed, one hand in Nick's, the other still on my belly. I imagined that I was protecting it one last time, this little piece of us that we'd never have again. It had known when to join us. Maybe it had known when to go, too.

"Prep the room," I heard myself say. "We have to say goodbye."

I'm sorry, I'm so sorry.

Our second married Christmas wasn't much merrier than the first, although at least Nick and I spent it together. After the miscarriage, I'd been released to the care of my husband back at Kensington Palace and granted permission from Eleanor to skip Sandringham. But as soon as I was back on my feet, the steady stream of well-meaning visitors had begun. Mom flew over to dote on me, reminding me that Lacey and I had only arrived after a few miscarriages of her own. Lacey had come over once, and the pain of seeing her healthy pregnant belly was so intense that I made up a bout of nausea and then confessed to my mom that I couldn't deal. (Mom ended up telling her a white lie about Greevey having the flu.) Gaz brought me treats and let me in on the secret that he'd made the finals of casting once again for *Ready, Set, Bake*. Cilla entertained me with stories of the emails her relatives were sending behind each others' backs about the planning for their upcoming family reunion—disagreements ranging from which cheese wheel was the most festive, to whether Cousin Victor had set fire to Aunt Cheryl's shed—and our staff hovered over me whenever no one else could. My primary function had become reassuring the loving, worried faces around me that I was going to be all right, and it was making both me and Nick edgy.

So when Annabelle Farthing sent a few "You Still Haven't RSVP'd" nudges about her New Year's bash—a Paperless Post that Nick had been ignoring after it was so fraught the year before—I suggested we give it a try. Last year, I couldn't stand the idea of being around unbridled revelers, but this year, I was counting on a room full of strangers to provide emotional relief from the suffocating, well-meaning, head-tilted sympathy I was getting from the people who actually loved me. I wasn't exactly party-ready. But I needed a jolt, and besides, it was just one night.

I gasped when her property appeared over the tree line. I'd imagined a pleasant rambler of a house, but Merysfield Park was a proper stately home—an ostentatious three-story Elizabethan crafted from honey-colored stone and crowned with a thrilling jumble of Dutch gables, Gothic pinnacles, and a preponderance of orderly rectangular windows peering solemnly at us, set on a hundred acres and newly open to the public to pay for its upkeep. Tonight, the path to the house was lit with what had to be three hundred candles set inside hurricane jars, and the trees lining the gravel driveway were hung with fairy lights.

"Impressive, eh?" Nick said as we inched ever closer to the drop-off. "They filmed that new *Pride and Prejudice* here."

It smelled like pine inside the high-ceilinged foyer, where half of Annabelle's staff was taking coats and hats in full livery. In the corner, near the two fully decorated Christmas trees—the source of the smell— two men in Elizabethan gear were playing the lute. Her golden retriever was wearing a bowler hat.

"Nicky!" Annabelle cooed, sidling up to us in a snug red velvet halter sheath, her expansive blond locks falling loose and feathered around her shoulders like a vintage Farrah Fawcett poster. Reflexively I ran a hand down my own body, over the stomach that was soft and kneadable from hormones and a long deferral of gym time. I hated that I cared, and also that I hadn't thought to care until now. I'd spent months before my wedding being reminded that my appearance was part of my job, and therefore fodder for dissection, but I'd had a weird relationship to my body in the last few weeks—as if I'd been afraid to do anything with it, lest I provoke it into betraying me again.

"Happy New Year, Annie," Nick said, kissing both her cheeks politely.

"And it's *so* brilliant to see you, Bex," Annabelle said, turning to me. "We missed you last year. I had to work overtime to keep a smile on this one's face." She nudged Nick affectionately.

"Your house is...beyond," I said, staring up at the Gothic arches in the hall ceiling, some forty feet above my head. It was rare that Nick and I found ourselves in a house that was more awe inspiring than his grandmother's. "It must have been hard to leave it for Dubai."

"Honestly, the upkeep is a grind," she said conspiratorially, as if she dusted the gargoyle carvings herself. "And terribly expensive. But I've had so much fun curating it since we've returned. We've added costumed Tudor docents, and calligraphy workshops, and the National Portrait Gallery is sponsoring an Elizabeth of Bohemia exhibit in our Long Gallery right now that is splendid, if you want to peek. And having the film, of course, was tremendous. I've also remanicured the lawns so we can charge admission to the public." She put her hand to her heart. "We're so fortunate," she added. "It's imperative to give back. Anyway, please go have fun! There's croquet on the back lawn, and an actual game of whist in the parlor. Isn't it marvelous?"

With a peck on Nick's cheek and a squeeze of my hand, she floated off to see her other guests, as a gloved waiter deposited some kind of signature cocktail in my hand. It smelled like warm spiced cider, but had been generously augmented with rum. If I had to be unhappy, at least I could be unhappy with a drink in my hand.

Nick turned to me and raised his brows. "I don't know if I've fully prepared you for this lot," he said. "You're going to want to drink that fairly quickly."

We pushed through a crush of formally dressed partygoers into a wood-paneled library, complete with a roaring fire and floor-to-ceiling bookshelves. Almost immediately, a nearby cluster of pasty men in suits stopped arguing and parted to receive Nick as if they'd been waiting for him to complete the picture all night.

"And, right on cue," Nick said under his breath, before extending a hand to one of them. "Baxter, hello."

"We've got to stop meeting like this, eh, old boy?" said Baxter, clubbing Nick's back with a meaty hand. He seemed like he'd started his New Year's drinking early and was too blotto to pretend to care about me. "We were talking about Doris Tuesday's latest," he said. "Mixing up Manchester United and Manchester City? *Ghastly*. Seems like Tuesday's got a case of the Mondays."

The three other men guffawed as if they'd never heard anything funnier, and I watched as Aggressive Pleasantness settled over Nick's features like a fog rolling in over the ocean.

"When it's your turn, do us a favor and tell the PM to get stuffed from time to time, okay, old bean?" Baxter said. "And if you could put in a good word and get us all antique country piles of our own..." As he waved his arm drunkenly toward what looked like a priceless tapestry hung near the massive carved fireplace, his glass knocked into Nick's and splashed rum cocktail all over Nick's white shirt.

"Bloody hell," Baxter said.

"Accidents happen," Nick said. "I'll go mop up and get a replacement at the bar."

He reached for my hand, but Baxter surged past and took him by the elbow. "Allow me, chappie. I'm empty anyway," he said, shoving both of them through the crowds. Nick shot an apologetic look back at me before he and Baxter got swallowed up in a fresh surge of partyers.

Awkwardly, I turned back to the group, and found that the other three men had vanished while my back was turned, off to search for other mediocre white men at whom to make self-congratulatory noises. I saw no one I knew or even recognized. There was a cluster of women by the door, so I drifted in that direction, but one of them spied me coming and tensed up and said something in a low voice to her cohorts, so I walked right past and back into the entryway as if that was where I was heading all along.

But I felt foolish standing flat-footed and alone as new arrivals greeted old friends, flowing around me as if I were a rock in a riverbed, to be skirted at all costs. I pulled my phone out of my bag and punched in a message to Cilla.

Is it too late to come to Yorkshire?

She sent back a photo of Gaz huddled underneath three blankets, wearing a thick turtleneck sweater. Bloody heat's gone out. Think we can all get to Lisbon by midnight?

I resolved to press on; Nick would surely find me, if I didn't stumble upon him first. But Merysfield Park's rooms flowed into each other higgledy-piggledy, and were dimly lit, and I swiftly regretted my decision. Even children know that the emergency protocol when you get separated is to stay exactly where you last saw each other, and it was becoming apparent that I was in a social emergency that had me feeling every bit as small as when I was six and lost in Kmart. I strode through room after room with faux purpose, as if I were on my way to see friends in the very next one, rather than trying to outrun the judgments floating past me.

"...of course Nick's ditched her already. No surprise there..."

"Maybe he just wanted her off the sofa..."

"...so dumpy. Is she pregnant?"

That one stung. People talking about me as if I weren't in the room wasn't unusual in and of itself, but I hadn't expected to be confronted with it at a private social event with the supposedly tight-knit posh set, and certainly not with such vitriol. Annabelle had never been anything but friendly to me, but her set of aristocrats clearly viewed me as a fast-moving train they couldn't believe hadn't crashed yet.

"...shocked he brought her at all, thought this was his freebie..."

"...seemed pretty open last year, wonder what's changed..."

I didn't know what that was about, but I didn't love it.

I surfed the tide of guests who seemed to all be gossiping about me until, eventually, I ended up in a room with no fewer than four sets of doors thrown open to the chilly December air. Tall wire baskets of fur throws stood near each exit with a sign that read FAUX YOUR PERSONAL USE, as if to make clear, in a room with four stuffed buck heads on the wall, that no animals had been harmed in the warming of anyone's bodies. I took one and wrapped myself in it, feeling like a proper Tudor, and found a little lovers' bench framed by what in spring would be beautiful rosebushes. The longer I sat there alone, the sadder I felt. This time last year, Nick had been *here* instead of with me? And I'd been with Marta, the thought of whom gave me a twinge of grief all over again. Getting drunk to Bryan Adams sounded like bliss right now.

"Oh, thank God," Nick said, appearing to my right, bundled in his own throw and looking ridiculous. "I did three laps looking for you and then got waylaid by Penelope Eight-Names wanting to talk about my grief over 'our' relative's passing." He pulled his tie loose around his neck. "She's so many cousins removed that she never even *met* Great-Gran."

"I wish I'd managed to bump into her," I said. "She would have at least talked to me."

Nick tightened his fur around himself and sat down. "I feel like Henry the Eighth in this thing."

"I guess that makes me Catherine of Aragon," I said. "At least I get to keep my head."

He sighed. "This is not any less awful than it was last year." He paused, then nudged me. "Perhaps mildly less."

"It's not the most fun I've ever had," I admitted. "Everyone here seems concerned that you're missing out on a 'freebie' tonight."

Nick was quiet.

"Care to explain?"

He rubbed his eyes. "I should not have let you talk me into accepting this invitation."

"Hang on, I didn't push you into anything," I said, holding up a warning hand. "It was late, we had no other plans, we needed to get out, and more importantly, I didn't know there was anything that I didn't know. A mistake you should correct right now."

Nick set his jaw. "Annabelle made a pass at me last year," he confessed. "And it's my fault." He fidgeted. "I may have led her on."

"*May* have."

He shifted. "Probably did. Definitely did."

My heart sank. "Cool," I said numbly. "That's just... that's fucking great. I can't wait to hear all about it."

He tugged at his hair. "I hate reliving this," he said. "I've been reliving it all night."

"Well, this is the first time I've heard anything about it, so I'm afraid you're going to have to power through," I said curtly.

Nick had the good grace to look ashamed. "Right. Well, you'd kicked me out..."

"I did not kick you out, and I certainly wasn't under the impression that we were on some kind of marital break," I interrupted.

He held up his hands. "The point is, I was unraveling," he said. "That quarrel dug up all my paranoia about every inside joke or every lunch or every conversation you and Freddie ever had, and whether it meant something deeper. I was scared that you'd married me because you felt you had to." He clenched his fists, as if grabbing at the words. "So, yes. I came here without you on purpose. Out of selfishness. Annabelle wanted so badly for me to come. I knew she was flirting, but it made me feel chosen, somehow. Like I was someone's top pick. When she was so delighted to see me, I couldn't help myself. I flirted back."

"That was a dick move," I said.

Nick shuddered. "The shabbiest. All because my stupid ego wanted a bit of revenge. And then I drank too much. For liquid courage at first, I suppose, but then out of guilt because the flirting felt wrong, and cheap, and awful. Somehow my better sense prevailed the drunker I got," he said. "So I decided to leave. I went up to my room to get my things, and Annabelle followed me and asked if I was absolutely sure." He fidgeted. "I said yes. I gave her a hug goodbye, and she, er, tried again. I ran. Almost literally."

"How exactly did she try?" I asked. "I think I have a right to know."

A flush ran up Nick's face. "She made me a very explicit offer."

I stared up at the sky. The stars twinkled robustly. "Nick," I said. "Do me a favor. The next time someone tries to bang you, please tell me about it."

"I should have. I convinced myself that because I said no, and very much meant it, there was no need for me to rock the boat," he said.

"Well, as a philosopher once told me, keeping secrets always makes the truth look like a smokescreen," I said sarcastically. "Did I get that right?"

"I suppose I deserved that."

"Yep."

He searched my face. "Are you angry?"

"You bet," I said. "This is messed up. Partly because I am mad at you, and I should be mad at you, but I also feel like I can't be because of this tit-for-tat logic you just laid on me. Like you're saying I brought this on myself."

"That wasn't my intention," he argued. "But I can't pretend it wasn't a product of everything that's happened since I found out Freddie tried to sleep with you and *you* didn't tell *me* about it."

"You are going to win every argument we have for the rest of our lives, based on that." I stubbornly crossed my arms. "I can't be doing penance for that forever."

"You're not. This was a year ago," he argued. "Things were very different then."

"Why are we even here?" I snapped. "We could be freezing our asses off in Yorkshire with Gaz and Cilla. We could have gone to the Maldives, or Paris, or stayed home in our pajamas. Why did you let me talk you into attending a party full of people who think you slept with the hostess last year? How could you parade me in front of these people without telling me any of this?"

Nick paused. "You seemed keen, like you needed a party, and I wanted to help lift your spirits," he said. "But a useful side effect was proving to Annabelle that I meant what I said, and that you and I are solid. I assumed any grapevine would have already snuffed itself out. These people all look the other way for each other as easily as breathing."

"I should have gotten a vote, Nick," I said. "I'm not just a prop. Regardless of what other people might think."

"I am an idiot," Nick said, taking my hand and rubbing my ring. "May I be honest?"

"I thought you already were."

Nick ignored that. "I let myself get swept up in how well we'd been doing all year, and the baby news made me so *happy*. We were happy. I didn't want that to end. And then..." His lips trembled. "I've felt so gloomy. I don't know how to pull out of it, and I knew laying this on top of it wouldn't help either of us."

He looked so glum, his face mirroring the way I had felt inside since the miscarriage. My heart cracked. I propped up my elbow on the back of the bench and rested my chin on my arm.

"You have to stop sparing my feelings, okay?" I said gently. "About the baby, about whatever else is going on in your head, about the Annabelles of the world. I'm sure there will be more of them." I took a deep breath and looked up at the sky. "I was scared when I got pregnant that we weren't strong enough. But we have to stop treating our marriage like it's something that could break."

"I just don't like fighting with you," he said.

"Too bad, because we're definitely going to fight about *something* over the next fifty years," I said.

A smile played around the corner of Nick's mouth. "Not possible. I'm perfect, you see."

"Except when you floss in front of the television."

"At least I don't leave all my shoes on the ground by the door."

"I can't walk that far in half of them! If you love me, you'll let me put a shoe rack in the coat closet."

Nick did a pitch-perfect imitation of Bea. "No, Rebecca. You're not a farmer."

We giggled, the tension mostly broken.

"This part is always so easy with us," I said. "We have to get better at the rest."

My head fell on his shoulder, and we watched as everyone in the rowdy croquet game in the distance turned to scurry inside for the countdown.

"Happy New Year, Bex," he said. "I hope we get this one right."

"Me too," I whispered as a cheer went up inside the house.

CHAPTER FOUR

With every day that passed, the ache of our miscarriage throbbed a bit less. Ultimately, along with time, what really helped bring me back to myself was art. It was restorative to concentrate on creating with my eyes and hands; to take blankness and craft it into something better, and believe that my body would be able to do it again, too. And because art requires a singular focus, an almost meditative kind of attention, I didn't think about anything other than the leaf or the cloud or the blade of grass that I was trying to re-create. I had to be in the moment, and my brain could push everything else to its edges.

The view from our bedroom terrace had a gloomy beauty this time of year, and I'd taken to starting my day out there in a puffer coat, sketching for as long as my schedule let me. Today, the dense cloud cover had brought the park's wintry grays into the starkest relief, so I'd made an enormous travel mug of coffee and was elbow-deep in its shadows when an urgent rapping came on the glass door. I turned to see an anxious Greevey.

"Ma'am, you have a guest," he said, querulous and urgent.

"Who is it? Tell them I'll be down in a minute," I said, glancing down at my charcoal-smudged hands.

"I tried to keep her in the reception room," he said through clenched teeth, just as I heard a familiar imperious voice behind him: "This isn't nearly as hideous as it used to be."

I forgot myself and covered my mouth with my hands. "El...er, Your Majesty?" I called out, wincing privately at Greevey.

"Hurry up, Rebecca, I haven't got all day," was her reply.

Greevey apologized in mime, and I gave him as reassuring a thumbs-up as I could; he disappeared as I glanced fruitlessly around for the hand towel I'd apparently forgotten to bring outside. I improvised with a piece of paper, and caught my reflection in the glass of the door. I'd rubbed charcoal on my cheek by accident, and my hair was a disaster. Well, I'd seen Eleanor at her most vulnerable. She could handle a little mess.

I stepped off the terrace and into my bedroom, where I found the Queen rocking a fuchsia suit—as if this were a public appearance and not simply a social call—running a finger along the dresser. She lifted it and held it close to her eyes.

"Passable," she said, brushing off her hands. "My goodness, Rebecca, you look like a chimney sweep. And do you usually let the butler up into your chambers?" Eleanor drew her eyebrows together, then smacked a throw pillow in our plush corner chair before settling down in it. "He seems a bit gormless," she added. "Ran out of here like I'd threatened his life."

"With all due respect, I am pretty sure the sight of you scared the shit out of him," I said, perching across from her in front of the bedroom fireplace on the large, tufted ottoman that we used as a coffee table. "Why didn't you call ahead? I would at least have taken a shower."

Eleanor shrugged. "It was a whim. I am a deeply whimsical person." She cleared her throat. "I assume you're recovered from...the unpleasantness," she said, but her tone was gentle.

"Almost back to normal," I said. "Thank you for visiting me at the palace. I was really touched."

"Nonsense." Eleanor waved her hand at me, as if to flick aside the gratitude. "You were on my way."

Eleanor had come down while I was in recovery, sat by my bed for about ten seconds, and then stood up and said, "How tedious. I don't know how you managed it with me." I had assumed this was a Valium dream until Nick told me that she had seemed worried.

"It may not have been a big deal to you, but you were the first face I saw that didn't give me bad news, so I appreciated it," I told her now.

Eleanor allowed a small smile to cross her lips before glancing around with renewed interest. "If I remember correctly, this was all mustard yellow and orange," she said.

I shook my head. "Florals. Lots of them. None of them matched."

"She must have redecorated since I was last in here," Eleanor said. "I suppose it was, oh, 1972."

"That long?"

Eleanor folded her hands in her lap. Her right one still didn't want to close all the way. "I see you kept that ridiculous monogram in the main entry."

"I couldn't bring myself to change it," I said. "It felt like we'd be erasing her from existence. I don't know what it was like here in 1972, but in 2015, it was crammed fuller than a museum. It probably could have *been* a museum."

"Georgina always collected things," Eleanor said. "Mementos. People."

"But in the end, this was all she had, and we had to get rid of so much of it," I said. "It felt like there should be a piece of her still here."

Eleanor's gaze went out the window. I wondered if she was imagining what might have been if the sisters had stayed close. If Georgina hadn't made a play for her sister's husband. If they'd let their differences die when Henry did.

"Do you still have those journals?" she asked suddenly.

"Of course. Do you want to see them?"

Eleanor raised an eyebrow. I walked over to my dresser and opened up the drawer where they all lived. I glanced briefly at the doors to Sex Den. The letter and the mystery key had lived up there safely since I'd hidden them, but I couldn't very well reveal it to her by bounding through the armoire to fetch them. I itched to ask her about the key, but this house had to have two hundred locks; the odds of anyone knowing what went where were as minute and slim as the key itself. Better to keep it to myself for now. All of it.

"The letter isn't in here. I put that in the safe," I said, figuring it was an acceptable white lie. "But I have all these." I took out the weathered leather journals and brought them back to the Queen, resting them on the gold-painted table to her right. Eleanor picked one up, flipping through it idly, her hands stopping to trace Georgina's penmanship—exuberant and round. She riffled the pages with her thumb, stopping at random and beginning to read out loud:

Ellie turned twelve today. It was sad really. Grandmummy was an absolute beast. We hardly see her except when she's angry about something, and today it was Ellie. All through dinner Grandmummy kept saying things like, "Well, it's clear the throne has to pass to this one," and, "Since we've no other options for succession . . ." and poor Auntie Inge got so upset that she pretended she had a headache so she could leave. I don't blame her. It's not her fault she couldn't have babies! And it only got worse. After dinner, Grandmummy cleared everyone out except Ellie, but of course I peeked through the door and saw Grandmummy telling Ellie she didn't hold her fork well, didn't sit properly, didn't listen prettily enough, didn't chew gracefully. (!!) Ellie stared at the floor. "Don't be weak, on top of it all," Grandmummy said. "We must toughen you up." And then she made Ellie put a book on her head and walk back and forth across the room for thirty whole minutes, and Ellie didn't say a word, she just quietly did it over and over. Mummy wouldn't do a thing to stop it. I was so cross. El was sobbing in bed later, her neck was so sore. I climbed in and started to rub it for her and she said, "I'm going to fail at this," and I told her that she won't because she's the strongest person I know. I've never seen anyone stand there and endure Grandmummy so well. I'd have thrown a tea service at the old bat! Ellie might be the toughest one of all of us. She can do anything. In fact, I

Eleanor stopped and closed the book with a thump. Her left pointer finger tapped the top of her right hand. She said nothing.

"This must be hard for you," I offered.

"Frederick's interview is today," she said, instead. "With the BBC."

"I know," I said. "He sequestered himself to get ready for it."

"You should be there. Both of you," Eleanor said.

"Is it open to us?"

"My grandmother would have said a true sign of character is when you can weather something completely alone." She shook her head, standing up and trying to stretch her right side without appearing ungainly. "I've done that. He'll be by himself in front of that camera, but he'll remember who stood in that room because they were paid to, and who came because they wanted to be there for him."

"Is this what brought you all the way over here?" I asked.

Eleanor clucked with irritation. "Most people would be thrilled that the Queen showed an interest in their personal health," she said. "And now I've done it. My time is valuable. I shall see myself out. Good day, Rebecca."

The thick clunk of her heels grew quieter as she descended the stairs. I glanced back at her chair. The journal had fallen onto the floor, as if its work here, too, was done.

Freddie's interview was set for that afternoon at Clarence House. One camera, one interviewer, a small handful of questions, and the transaction would be complete: safety and silence in exchange for a scoop. The major British media outlets would all get the footage first, and everyone else would have to chase them.

We were already due at Clarence House for a more formal explication of Marta's will, so Nick and I sneaking in to support Freddie would be fairly simple. I scooped my hair into a bun, curled a couple of tendrils in the front so it looked less severe, and picked jeans and a blazer—professional, but comfortable, a mix of off duty and on that suited the day's strange agenda.

Calling our meeting spot at Richard's residence a "conference room" was an undue compliment to all the hideous ones I'd seen at various workplaces over the years. Its massive mahogany table was surrounded by priceless, mismatched antique chairs with silk-covered seats. The famous unfinished portrait of Queen Eleanor had been rotated out and replaced with a landscape that looked as if it had been stitched together from the work of several different artists with a variety of skill sets. The colors were beautiful, and parts were supremely accomplished; others, more childlike, but not without perspective. It was a fascinating piece.

"Paint Britain," came Richard's voice behind me, and I turned to see him staring up at it as well. "I made it with several of the children."

"It's really special," I said sincerely. "Almost a shame to keep it hidden."

"I like it here," he said.

Richard's gaze was still fixed on the painting, so I took the second to stare at him. It was such a challenge to burrow inside his façade. He'd been, in turns, unpleasant and manipulative and cruel; the same man who'd embraced Paint Britain, an organization I'd helped cofound, had also removed me from it when he'd decided I was a liability.

"I'm glad Paint Britain is in the hands of a patron who cares about it," I said, and meant it. "I miss it. And I'd really like to be involved again whenever you think it would be appropriate."

Richard looked at me then. The one thing we had in common was a love of art, so I knew he was aware how much it hurt me to be elbowed aside. He also knew what it was costing me to ask a favor of a man who viewed them as debts to be paid.

"That can be arranged," he said, and I was so surprised that I beamed at him.

"Let's get this done, Dickie, I haven't got all day," Agatha said as she stomped in and dropped her tote on the table. "I'm going to a workshop about the female orgasm at three."

"Bravo! You found the flyer I left you," Elizabeth said, sweeping in with Edwin in tow.

Richard turned green and excused himself to, presumably, go call and yell at the tardy solicitor. Edwin stared mournfully at his phone.

"Scrabble decided she'd been idle too long and conceded our last game to me," he said mournfully. "She'll be idle forever now. I hate it."

"It is really weird going to visit Eleanor and having her not there," I said. "She was in one of those chairs pretty much every day."

Agatha dabbed at her eyes. "They were very close," she said.

I heard Eleanor's hiss in my head, clear as a bell. *I'll never forget. But I'll never forgive, either.*

"They did seem devoted to each other," I said casually. "But they're both such strong personalities. I'm sure they had some epic arguments in their time."

"Eleanor doesn't argue," Elizabeth said as she poured the first of five Splendas into her tea. "She simply says things, and lets you decide whether you want to be wrong or not."

"I walked in on a real cracker of a fight once," Edwin said. He absently fiddled with his gold cufflinks. "I had gone in to look for my blankie and they were shouting at each other."

Agatha swiveled her head around. "When was this?"

He flushed. "Gosh, clearly ages ago. Something about Auntie Georgina being terribly vain, perhaps?" He furrowed his brow. "And something about Scotland? I chucked up my breakfast all over the floor right then, so I don't remember much. But I do know it was wretched seeing them so furious. I never saw it again."

Agatha's face was frozen in a skeptical expression.

"I could've misheard," he allowed. "They were very bad sausages."

I had no choice but to file away that nugget without a follow-up, because Richard charged into the room with the apologetic solicitor, a balding gentleman with an egg-shaped head and oval glasses and a nervous habit of tenting his fingers in front of his mouth as he spoke. This had the unfortunate effect of creating a triangular megaphone, which made it hard not to react as he began his lengthy presentation by blasting us with the words "ALLOW ME TO EXTEND MY SYMPATHIES." Edwin, never one to manage his emotions adeptly, kept giggling at the solemnities; Agatha's knuckles were white as she clutched at her bag.

Marta, as the daughter of the Swedish king and the wife of an English one, had a fair bit of personal fortune and property to mete out. Dunheath Castle, her beloved private retreat, was willed to Edwin and Elizabeth, under the assumption that Eleanor's Balmoral would eventually pass to Richard. He got the ski lodge up in Jämtland, Sweden, unused by anyone but him for nearly a half century now, with the intention of it eventually going to Freddie. Nick and I were willed an estate outside of Stockholm that had housed some distant relatives until about five years ago. It was a stunning canary-and-white manor on the water with a giant terrace and regal double stone staircase in the back, descending to the impressive lawns.

"It's basically Captain von Trapp's house," I hissed to Nick, passing him the file that had been handed to me. "There's even a gazebo."

"Please make me lederhosen out of drapes," he murmured back.

An assortment of baubles was divided evenly among me and Elizabeth and Freddie, for the use of his future bride; Freddie, who wasn't present due to his forthcoming interview, had already accepted them and promised to donate them to a museum collection if they went unused, which I found a bittersweet stipulation. I'd been given, among other things, a topaz cocktail ring that I recognized as the one Marta had been wearing when we watched the Cubs win. As this was announced, Agatha's fists were balled up so hard, she could have crushed all the aforementioned pieces into a fine dust.

"And, finally, Princess Agatha is to inherit Queen Marta's sapphire suite," the lawyer finished, the words *sapphire suite* booming out so loudly they nearly reverberated.

"Oh!" Agatha gasped with pure, uncontained joy. "But of course I'd prefer she was still with us," she recovered theatrically, even as she smacked a hand on the paperwork and drew it toward herself with unseemly haste.

Richard capped off the meeting with a few lingering agenda items, and then everyone scattered—back to their day-to-day lives, their meetings and workshops, the official book closed on the life of a matriarch who'd seen more than a century. Life and death was as much a business affair in The Firm as anything else.

Nick drummed his hands on his leg nervously. "Ten minutes to go," he said. "I wonder if he's ready. Should I check on him? Maybe not. Maybe?"

"He's probably nervous enough without you staring at him," I said. "Why don't you go kill some time by irritating Barnes? I need a Diet Coke, but I'll meet you in there."

"Excellent plan," Nick said, kissing my cheek as he headed off toward Barnes's office. It gave me a frisson of joy to think about how annoyed Richard's imperious right-hand man would be to get any kind of unscheduled visit from anyone.

I heard a voice emanating from the foyer, and followed the sound in time to see the staff greeting another arrival for the day: Princess Daphne, shrugging off her plaid wool coat, with blond waves that looked recently brightened bouncing out of a matching hat.

"Bex!" she said. "You look wonderfully well."

"Thank you," I said, returning her smile. "And thank you so much for the flowers. They were the prettiest thing in the entire house."

"I wanted you to have some good cheer," she said. "I know how it feels when the walls start to close in but you're not ready to leave them. I'm just sorry I couldn't have visited myself. I had to dash back home for Christmas."

"But you're here now," I said, masking my surprise. We walked into the main drawing room, where the camera crew was finishing its setup, and sat down on a sofa that had been pushed to the side of the room under a painting of the Duke of Wellington riding into battle at Waterloo.

"Freddie is uneasy about this," Daphne said. "He needed moral support."

"You two seem to have gotten really close," I observed.

Daphne peered at me through long, darkened eyelashes. "Does that surprise you?"

I wasn't sure how to answer that, and in the end, I said so.

"Perhaps I should rephrase," she said. "Are you uncomfortable with that?"

"Of course not."

But I was, a little. I couldn't put my finger on why.

Freddie walked in at that moment, handsome in a gray suit. He looked tense.

"There's a lot going on in that head," she observed, nodding toward him. "Freddie was very worried for you that night, you know. Frightened."

"He wasn't the only one," I said.

"Frightened in the way one is when they might lose someone important to them," she pressed.

I shifted to face her. "Daphne, Freddie and I will always be important to each other."

"I think you know that I don't mean friendship," Daphne said. "And the way you reached for him..."

"I was having a miscarriage," I said, feeling defensiveness creep into my tone. "I don't know what you're insinuating, but—"

"I'm phrasing this badly," Daphne amended, waving her hands in an apologetic gesture. "It's simply that from where I stand, from where I *was* standing, I couldn't help but wonder if there will ever be room there for anyone else."

"Are *you* in love with him?" I felt like an idiot for not seeing it sooner.

"No. Maybe? I would be lying if I said I wasn't interested," Daphne said. Her face took on a dreamy expression. "So many people still see me as that sad, anxious victim. Freddie sees me as a real person. I'm starting to hope someday he might see me as a woman, too. He looks to me for advice, for companionship, but nothing else yet." She fidgeted. "But when I saw him react to you that night, I realized it's possible there is no chance for me at all."

Freddie squinted in our direction and then spotted us, the blinding lights on him having put us in comparative darkness. Relief spread over his face. He waved, and then beckoned. I stood instinctively. Daphne did, too.

We paused. Our eyes met. I nodded and sat back down as Daphne hurried toward Freddie, into the light.

Nick sidled in as they shushed the room. Daphne tucked herself unobtrusively into a far corner next to a curio cabinet full of priceless china bibelots, and I spied Richard with Bea and her ever-present note-book along the back wall. Nick and I moved over to stand next to them, a mismatched menagerie of supporters, all of us trying with varying degrees of success to act like this was no big deal. Freddie had never done a solo interview, only joint ones with Nick, and I could see on his face that he felt the weight of this.

Terry Dempsey, the BBC journalist who'd been tapped for this, greeted Freddie with a firm handshake and then tugged down the tail of his suit jacket so he could sit on it. "Saw it in a movie once," he said sheepishly. "Keeps the shoulders from rising up on me."

This was meant to break the tension, and Freddie smiled, but I could see his foot tapping anxiously against the leg of the chair.

Terry opened with a softball about Freddie's prior military career, which let him ease into the approved explanation for his decision to enter a war zone: a desire for service, a sense that he'd never reached his fullest potential in the military, and absolutely zero mention of the family feud that had made him feel so adrift in the first place.

"But surely that didn't require such a perilous posting," Terry said.

Freddie nodded. "What mattered most was that my cohorts knew I wasn't out to be a tourist within the military, ticking off a box. I wanted something where I'd be constantly required and inspired to prove my dedication. You might recall, I've not been particularly dutiful thus far in my life." Terry chuckled obligingly. "To make an impact, and put to rest any questions, I needed a place where anything less than full throttle wouldn't be acceptable."

"And what did you learn, do you think?" Terry asked. "What was the gift of this experience?"

"*Gift?*" Nick hissed incredulously. "It's not a birthday treat."

Freddie held his face impassive, but I could tell from his tapping toes that it required effort. "It is impossible to come out of the service without a sense of perspective," he said. "One can always do more with what one is given. I've gained an even greater respect for people like my grandmother, my father, and my brother, who've understood better than I the way a life of good fortune must be shaped by a proper sense of duty."

"But why the cloak-and-dagger approach?" Terry asked. "Why simply vanish?"

"Officially it was out of concern that I'd be a target, but for me, it was the threat I might pose to the other soldiers," Freddie said. "Their work thrives on secrecy. I would have shouted it from the London rooftops, but the attention could've put their lives in even greater danger."

"And it *was* dangerous," Terry said. "I'm told you saw quite a bit of action, and that it's the reason for your arm being in a sling."

Freddie gulped. On the monitors, he simply looked serious, but we could see his left hand gripping his knee. Next to me, Nick frowned.

"I can't give specifics, Terry," Freddie said.

"You were injured," he pressed. "It's very brave to risk yourself like that."

"No. Courage isn't what I did," Freddie said. His hand migrated from his knee to rub at the seat of his chair. "Courage isn't trying to find purpose in a short burst of service. It's giving your life to it, however long that life might be. I saw several of those lives cut short, and the tragedy of it will never leave me."

He was fighting to keep his voice even. Nick tensed up. "I don't like this," he said in a low voice.

Terry jumped back in: "Did you ever wonder if you'd make it home yourself?"

Freddie's fidgeting increased, to where it was visible even on the monitor. "Many of my friends didn't come home. Many more yet might not."

"You were afraid," Terry said.

"There were times..." Freddie began, and then shook his head. "What I mean to say is, you can't imagine how, particularly at night, when you hear..." His face looked in danger of crumpling altogether. He bit his lip and turned his face away, his shoulders beginning to shake.

Nick stepped forward. "That's enough," he called out, then clapped his hands authoritatively. "Thank you so much for coming out, but I'm afraid that's all we can do for you today."

I'm not sure who in the room looked the most surprised. Terry swiveled and stood, his hands on his hips. His head bounced from Nick to Bea, whom he clearly felt more comfortable confronting, because he directed his complaint to her: "With all due respect, I was told we'd have twenty minutes and it's been a fraction of that."

"We've had a scheduling change," Bea improvised, crossing the room, then taking Terry's arm and guiding him toward the room's exit on the opposite side. She waved the cameraman and the sound guy out the door after him. "You've certainly got enough at this point. We'll have your gear packed up in a flash, and naturally we'll supply you with a lengthy exclusive statement from the prince that can give a fullness to your piece..."

The door closed behind them. Across the room, I saw Daphne pull a pack of tissues from her purse and head toward Freddie. But she didn't get there first. It was Nick who reached his brother, Nick who put a hand on his shoulder, Nick who pulled a ragged Freddie to his feet and wrapped him in a hug. Freddie's head collapsed on Nick's shoulder, and he let out a wrenching sob.

My heart seized.

"Come on," I whispered, gesturing for everyone else to hit the door. "Leave them be."

Daphne cast the brothers one more look, then nodded and squeezed past me. Richard lingered at the door, watching.

"You could stay, sir," I said delicately. "You have a place there, too."

Richard thought for a moment and then looked down at me. "No. I don't think I do," he said. "This moment is for them. Let them have it."

He turned on his heel and left. My hand on the knob, I glanced back at Freddie and Nick. They hadn't moved. Freddie wept freely, coming undone in his brother's embrace; Nick stood firm and solid, rubbing his back, the bright light of the still-burning TV spotlight seeming to keep the darkness around them at bay.

CHAPTER FIVE

B ex!" Cilla called to me across the living room. "Nick is hogging the baby!"

"I am *not*," Nick whisper-yelled from the sofa, where a dark-haired infant was sleeping on his chest. "But he cries if anyone else tries to hold him. It's not my fault that I'm his favorite."

Next to him on the sofa, Lacey yawned expansively as Cilla began handing out teacups: to me, to Bea, to Olly, and to Lacey, who wrinkled her nose but accepted it.

"I wish this was wine. But my tolerance is terrible now," she said, scooching up into a seated position and blowing on the wafting Darjeeling. "Nick, feel free to keep him all week if you want. I can practice getting my drink on, and he can keep you company in the middle of the night. He's very perky at three a.m."

"Of course he is. The middle of the night is interesting," Nick cooed to the baby. "I understand you, Danny. No one understands you like Uncle Nick."

On his chest, the baby wiggled his teeny fingers in his sleep. I felt it in my gut. Watching Nick be adorable with my sister's accidental blessing was carving me up in a way that I could not control. I turned away and busied myself looking for coasters.

"I wish evolution had created babies with respect for the mother's sleep cycle," Lacey said, yawning again and falling against Olly.

"At least it invented a nine-month gestational period," said Olly. "Elephants go for almost twenty-two."

Daniel Earl Porter-Omundi had been born three weeks ago, after thirty-six hours of what Lacey called "an excruciating hellscape" of labor. It had started while Nick and I were in Hampstead revealing a plaque marking the refurbishment of John Keats's house, and the baby arrived the next day while we were giving out shamrocks to the First Battalion Irish Guards on Saint Patrick's Day. (In the photos, if you look closely, you can guess how late I was up fielding texts that said things like, "I hope Olly gets a kidney stone the size of Montana.") Our little Danny Boy was perfect, from the top of his sweet-smelling head to the bottom of the wrinkly feet that fit in my hand. Nick and I had met him at the hospital, but this was his first official outing—and one of Lacey's as well. The toll of being alert was evident on her face, even as she seemed delighted to have adult company. She'd come over in her maternity overalls and a topknot and immediately instructed Bea not to say a word. Bea had simply steered her to the couch, pushed her down gently, and put a pillow on the coffee table for her feet.

"He doesn't do much, does he?" Bea peered down at Danny. "When do they become fun?"

"Some still haven't," I said. Lacey snickered.

"Don't lean over him, you'll spill your tea," Cilla said crossly, swatting at Bea's legs with a napkin.

"I have no intention of leaning," Bea said. "I am not sufficiently interested in babies, and I am even less interested in leaning."

"Hello? Could someone please come help me carry something?" came Freddie's voice from the foyer.

"I don't understand where your staff are," Bea grumbled.

"It's a Saturday. They don't work weekends unless we're hosting a thing, which has never happened," I said, getting off the sofa.

She made a face. "You are hosting a thing. *This* is a thing."

I frowned at her. "A thing is when the prime minister of the Bahamas comes over. This is family."

Bea pulled off the trick of furrowing her brow with irritation but also looking vaguely pleased. Gemma and I exchanged grins before I headed out and found Freddie in the foyer, a giant stuffed elephant wearing a blue bow tie sitting at his feet.

"Hi," he said. "Can you help me? I did all right up the steps but my arm still hurts a bit, and God forbid I go back into a cast because I went overboard at Hamleys."

Together, we hoisted the elephant and carried it into the living room, where Olly's face lit up like a Christmas tree.

"I love it!" he said. "I mean, Danny will love it."

Freddie laughed, giving Olly a hearty handshake and pecking Lacey on the top of her head. "I really bought it for you two. How are Mum and Dad?"

"Thrilled to be out of the house," Lacey said, stabbing at a piece of salami on the charcuterie board that Nick had put together. "Also excited to eat deli meat again."

"I hope that goes double for unpasteurized cheeses," sang Gaz, bustling in with an equally pretty board of selections from the Food Hall at Harrods. Cilla stole a piece of Brie as he passed, and then, when he stopped in mock annoyance, fed him half.

"Ah, brilliant, Freddie's here!" he said, dropping the tray with a clang on the table.

"A phrase hardly ever uttered in polite society," Freddie said.

"Fortunately, that doesn't apply here," Nick said. "Other than Danny."

Lacey snorted. "Please. That kid blew out a diaper ten seconds after I changed it. He has no manners."

"Cheese, Knickers?" Freddie said casually as he carved off a piece and plonked it onto a cracker. "Since you're trapped under something heavy? The Stilton is nice and smelly, just the way you like it."

"I'd love a piece, and maybe a slab of that truffly Camembert while you're at it," Nick said, gesturing with his elbow.

"Coming right up."

Their manner was easy, but I knew they were aware of how much everyone in the room was rooting for this reconciliation to be real. Cilla and Lacey and I launched into aggressively casual-not-casual chatter about nursing bras, a subject about which two of us knew nothing, just to try to defuse their sense that they were being observed—even though of course they were.

Their rapprochement had begun after that day in Clarence House. Nick and Freddie had stayed in that room for some time, and when they'd emerged—Nick first, then Freddie five minutes later—we'd all left separately, Nick and me to our place and Freddie and Daphne back to his. I waited until we were home, and let Nick take half an hour to decompress on the couch before I even ventured into his office. He was still lying on the sofa staring at the ceiling, a small smile playing at his lips.

"How's it going?" I asked, peeking in and wiggling a can of lager I'd grabbed from the kitchen. "Want me to leave you alone a bit longer?"

"Never," he said, sitting up. "Oooh, just what the doctor ordered." He popped open the can and slurped at the eruption of foam. "I'm sure you're wondering what was said."

"Meh." I shrugged.

He grinned and took another deep sip. "Good, because the answer is, nothing."

"Bullshit," I said, flopping down next to him on the sofa.

"Not at all," he said. "That's the thing." He shook his head slowly. "You saw me hug him, and you saw him cry. We stood like that for a while, and then he sat back down to blow his nose, so I took the interviewer's chair opposite him and we...I don't know, just sort of stayed like that. I couldn't even tell you how long we sat there. And then we both somehow knew when it was time to get up and leave."

"You seriously didn't say anything?" I asked. "Freddie went that long without speaking?"

Nick nodded. "Shocking, I know," he said. "I kept thinking, *I wish I knew what to say, I should think of something to say,* and then in the middle of all that I realized I already knew what he needed." His eyes turned moist. "To know that we still have that ability to be a comfort to each other, just by being in the same room...." Nick swigged his beer and let out a happy sigh. "For the first time since we had words that Thanksgiving, I feel optimistic," he said. "The great irony being that today we didn't use words at all. Now let's get you one of these beers. I don't like day-drinking alone and I shall need at least one more."

He and Freddie started rebuilding: a billiard game here, a chat about cricket there. The next week, Freddie hitched a ride with us to a Conclave rather than go it alone, and when he agreed to do a charity polo match in part to curry favor after shorting the interview—pictures of him on horseback always rated well—Nick popped some allergy meds and joined him. Nick then invited Freddie to a session with Dr. Kep, and the three of us even snuck out one night (sans wigs, but in low-pulled hats and unremarkable clothes) for dinner at Bumpkin, a cozy South Kensington gastropub that we knew would seat us in a corner and let us be. We split a sticky toffee pudding and a bottle of red, laughed about Cousin Nigel's new girlfriend—a terrifying thirtysomething socialite by the absurd name of Prunella Packham Packham Packham—and generally kept it as light as possible.

But this was the first time Freddie had come back into our house for a purely social call. Over the last few weeks, I'd gotten the impression that, as much as things seemed to be moving in a positive direction, he'd been reluctant to revisit the scene of his and Nick's most emotional bloodletting, and I couldn't blame him. So I stacked the deck with our best friends. Gemma was perched on Bea's lap nibbling on some grapes, Lacey was curled up with her back against Olly's chest as he absently rubbed her arm, and Nick was cooing at Danny. It was bittersweet to see him so besotted.

"Look at all of you," Freddie said, reaching down to squeeze the baby's bare left foot. "Happy families. It's bloody heartwarming."

"Been a spell since we've all been in the same room, eh?" Gaz said, wrapping an arm around Cilla and surveying the room with an almost paternal pride. "It's like old times."

As he said this, Danny stirred and started to mewl.

"Right you are, mate, it is like old times," Nick said, grinning at Gaz. "Except usually it's you doing the sobbing." He clucked at Danny until he settled down, and then squinted at the table. "Is this cracker *purple*?"

"It's aubergine flavored," Gaz said. "All my crackers are based on the mighty nightshade. Those pink ones are tomatoes, those darker pink ones are chili peppers, and those pale thingies over there are potato crackers and I'm worried they're a little bland." He bit on his thumbnail. "We start filming *Ready, Set, Bake* next month, and that's the first challenge."

"You'll be awesome," I reassured him.

A flush ran up Gaz's entire face. "I do not know how you lot do it," he said. "They put the cast photos up online yesterday and I spent six hours reading things people said about my face. Some of them were lovely, but one person said he thought I looked like a bloke who would have fat fingers, and now every time I look at my fingers, I wonder how I can possibly move them when they're so fat."

"Garamond," Freddie said, placing a hand on his shoulder. "That is the first lesson: Do not ever read the comments. Someone on the *Daily Mail* website said that they could see the mites that live in my beard, and I itch every time I think about it."

"Remember the person who went on that massive tweet-storm about how a fascinator I wore was insufficiently respectful to military veterans?" I asked.

Next to me, Bea snorted. "Her suggestion was a *mantilla*. People would have thought you'd lost your mind."

"The last time I left the house, a blogger wrote an entire article about how my casual trousers are too wide," Nick added. "She used a lot of caps lock."

"They were too wide," Lacey said. "I've been telling Bex to throw those out for months."

Nick looked aggrieved. "I think they're jaunty!"

Lacey shook her head. "No. You look absurd in them." She took another sip of tea and grimaced. "I am so tired of tea. Maybe I should try some wine again, in friendly confines, and pump and dump later. We have enough milk."

At this, Danny's eyelids fluttered again, and he made a more demanding noise, as if he knew his food supply was the topic of conversation and he was getting concerned.

"I'll warm some milk now," Olly said, leaning over to take the baby.

"Nonsense, let me," Cilla said, standing up. "I'll feed him, too.

You still need a break, and Nick's gone well over his allotment of baby time."

"Yes, good idea. You should take him," I said, a little too quickly. "Nick, uh, will get all cocky about it if you don't."

"Oh, right, that's very nice," Nick said as they did the awkward dance of transferring Danny from one adult to the other. "First Lacey insults my trousers, then I lose the only person in this family who hasn't been rude about me."

"*I* haven't been rude. Yet," Freddie said, leaning in and popping two of Gaz's potato crackers into his mouth. "A bit of pepper on these, I think, Gaz."

"That's because you *also* have a pair of trousers that are too wide, and you know it," Lacey offered. "Those green ones. They're ridiculous. Burn them."

Freddie chuckled, and turned to Olly. "Once, we were at a club and she turned to me on the dance floor and screamed, 'Those are practically bell-bottoms!' "

"She was right," Bea said.

"About what?" Cilla asked, coming back in from the kitchen with the baby tucked into the crook of her arm, a bottle in his mouth, looking like an absolute pro. "Oh, please," she said, in response to my impressed face. "I nannied for ages. I could feed this baby blind drunk. Not that I would do that."

"It looks good on you," Freddie offered. "You should get one of your own."

"No, thanks!" Cilla said, cruising the room as Danny slurped, rubbing his cheek with her ring finger to keep him sucking.

"Really? I'm keen to have a baby," Gemma said, ruffling the edges of Bea's bob with her fingers. "They're so squidgy and sweet. Beatrix and I have a whole binder of sperm donors."

"You *do*?" I asked. "Wait, of course you do. Bea has a binder for everything. I just didn't think..."

"I don't know why not," Bea said. "I'm very maternal."

Nick's chortle turned into a cough, and he said, "But you've just told us you're not that interested in babies."

"In general, yes. They're very bland," Bea said. "But I would be quite interested in *my* baby, because my baby would be top-notch."

"Baked goods are my children now," Gaz said. "Well, and my legal practice, but that's substantially less delicious."

"I spent enough time with my sister's kids to know that I rather enjoy getting to give them back at the end of the day," Cilla said. "Besides, children deserve to have adults around them who spoil them irresponsibly and will bail them out of jail and take them for expensive drinks before they're legal. Gaz and I will have our work cut out for us as their groovy aunt and uncle."

"Children are also very loud," Gaz said.

"*You're* very loud," Nick pointed out.

"Yes, exactly," Gaz said, sidling up to Cilla and tickling Danny's foot.

"Mine won't be loud," Bea said. "Mine will *know*."

"We could use Gaz as a donor," Gemma said thoughtfully. "He's trustworthy, Oxford educated, funny..."

"Devastatingly handsome," he added, flexing comedically like a very small, portly Chris Hemsworth.

"Between us, we could make a glorious ginger," Gemma finished. "Garamond II. Or perhaps Arial if it's a girl."

"We are not having another font in this family," Bea said. "One Garamond is more than enough."

As the conversation drifted away from babies, Lacey decided to give in to her basest desires and pump so that she could enjoy a drink while we were all together. As Freddie started telling Olly something he'd heard from Daphne about the Netherlands' native elk population, I excused myself to the wine cellar. Not the official palace one, which contained a modest ten thousand bottles for formal company that we'd yet to put to use, but the adjunct one Nick and I had added to the basement that held our actual low-budget plonk. *The guzzlers*, we called them. When I came up the stairs, Cilla was waiting for me, tapping Danny in an attempt to get him to burp.

"I'm sorry," she said. "I was thoughtless."

"What are you talking about?"

"The baby thing," she said. "I was so cavalier about it, and you just had a miscarriage and you're watching your husband with your sister's baby..." Her face was scrunched up with concern. "I wanted to kick myself, and when you left the room I got worried."

"It's that elk story. I couldn't hear it again." I lowered my voice. "Freddie thinks it's hilarious but I'm sort of tapped out on Daphne stuff."

Cilla transferred the baby to her other shoulder and started whacking his back more vigorously. "No cause for alarm," she told me. "Sometimes you really have to smack the gas out of them. What's going on with Daphne?"

"She's in love with him, or at least hot for him," I said. "But you didn't hear it from me."

"Who hasn't been in love with Freddie, in one way or another? Even Bea's shagged him. I'm the only one that hasn't." She looked thoughtfully at the ceiling. "Maybe when we're very old," she offered. "I can see that. Gaz is dead. Freddie still has all his hair. It's one late night at the Connaught bar, and boom, I'm in the club with the rest of you."

Suddenly, she looked mortified. "Shit, sorry, I've run my mouth *again*. I know you didn't actually...My God. Do you get pregnancy brain from *holding* a baby?"

On her shoulder, Danny burped. It was a flamboyant belch, one that seemed too aggressive to come out of such a small body. "Exactly," Cilla said to him, rubbing his back.

"That was loud!" I said. "That's the Porter in him for sure."

"My grandmother always said that a hearty belch was the sign of strong character in a baby," Cilla said. "My point was, this is very predictable of Daphne. How does Freddie feel?"

I shrugged. "He talks to me less and less about that stuff."

"Probably for the best," Cilla said. "Right, I'll deliver the wine on my way to the loo, if you'll take Danny. I can't give him back to Nick. Who knew he was such a baby hog? I'll have to lock him in the basement to hold yours." She paused. "Are you okay to take him?" she asked kindly.

I put the bottles on the table and nodded. "I think so," I said. "Gotta get used to it, right?"

Cilla looked at me with sympathy, and handed over Danny, warm and smelling like slightly sour milk. She grabbed the wine with a flourish. "I'll pour you a glass," she said. "Give him a tap and make sure he's finished."

"Hello there," I said to my nephew. We stayed stock-still for a bit as I registered how it felt to hold someone that was at least a little piece of you. It both stung and felt wonderful, so I walked with him, back and forth, then around the kitchen until we ended up over at the kitchen window, which overlooked our back garden. Daffodils were pushing up, eager for a turn in the sun.

"So now you've met everyone," I said. "They're all mad as pants, as Cilla would say, but I love them."

In the other room, someone had turned on some music, and I heard uproarious laughter. I rubbed his furry head with my finger and he gurgled. The sun was going down, and I could see the makings of my reflection in the glass. Danny fit right into the nape of my neck, all cuddled up and milk-drunk, and my heart twisted with yearning. I closed my eyes, and for a second, it was my baby I was rocking. I felt hope and hollowness all at once.

"I hope you don't take this personally, but I have to give you back now. This is harder than I thought it was going to be," I whispered to Danny, who was squinting at me as if to say, *Wait, who are you again?* "Your parents are great, but I wish we could keep you. Please don't tell your mom. It makes me sound like an asshole. I shouldn't be jealous."

Danny grabbed a fistful of my hair and pulled. "The problem is, you're very cute, and I'm still sad and a little scared that what happened before will happen again and that we'll never have any luck," I said, lowering him and wresting my hair from him. "But now that I'm not mad at your uncle anymore, we're trying for real, and...it'll be fine, right?"

Danny blew a raspberry in my direction. "That's excellent feedback," I said. "Danny, you're a great listener. And the best part is, you won't remember any of this in ten minutes, much less when you're old enough to tell anyone what I said. I'll get back to you when I have something to report. Deal?"

I kissed his nose, and we rejoined the party.

CHAPTER SIX

I didn't have anything to report.

Still.

"All in good time," the doctor said when, in May, I went in for my checkup.

"Patience is a virtue," he said when, in July, I went back because my home kit—and my body—indicated I hadn't ovulated.

"Rome wasn't built in a day," he said two irregular months later, when I asked about Clomid to help shoot a few more eggs along. "If there's no bun in the oven by Christmas, we'll pop the bonnet and take a closer look at the engine. Perhaps your uterus is hostile! After all, you are American." He'd made himself chuckle with that one. "Try to relax."

The doctor was the Queen's trusted gynecologist, and the father of our old college friend Joss, who'd reportedly vanished to Morocco to find herself. He'd been very kind during my miscarriage, but in my ensuing appointments, I got the impression that he thought my concerns were an overreaction, and I didn't appreciate it. In my heart, I knew we had time, but my system was struggling to reset. Everything was irregular, including my doctor's dismissiveness of my questions as hysteria, and with every negative pregnancy test I'd started fantasizing harder about shoving one up his bulbous British nose.

"There is nothing less relaxing than a man with his hand inside your vagina telling you to relax," I griped when I met up with Nick after the last appointment.

"I'll try to bear that in mind," he replied, kissing me hello.

We were at the Imperial War Museum London for a cocktail reception Richard was throwing celebrating sixty entrepreneurs under sixty, in honor of his own milestone birthday. I quickly pasted on a smile for the benefit of a nearby klatch of middle-aged white guys who seemed interested in me in a manner I'd become accustomed to from the unbearably posh set: assessing whether I was a hot enough piece to have caused Nick so much trouble.

The Imperial War Museum lives in a hodgepodge of an early nineteenth-century building that looks like someone merged a court-house and a church, but that actually used to be a psychiatric hospital (and is, therefore, like so much of the rest of London, almost certainly haunted). The party was in the huge central atrium, modernized and brightened, with fighter planes from different eras suspended above our heads as if still in flight. Richard had a lot of faults, but bad taste wasn't one of them.

"Is it rude to ditch the party and just look at the planes?" I asked Nick, staring up at a 1940 Spitfire that had flown in the Battle of Britain.

"It's grand, isn't it?" Freddie said, striding over to us while tugging at one of his sport coat sleeves. He looked around, his eyes falling on the wreckage of a car that had been destroyed in Iraq, which had been on tour as part of an anti-war performance art piece. "It used to feel a bit more theoretical, though."

Nick touched his shoulder. "We can make an excuse and get out of here if you want to," he said.

"Food poisoning," I offered. "We all ate some bad shrimp."

Freddie smiled at us. "Let's not tempt fate into actually serving us bad shrimp," he said. "Father did offer to let me off the hook, but he was good to me when I needed it, so I said no." He looked guilty. "But I accidentally double-booked. Daphne's in for a quick shopping trip with her mum, and we were meant to have dinner."

"If anyone understands, it'd be her," Nick said.

"Thank God for that," Freddie agreed. "I don't have to explain any of the hows and whys of the family job to her. That's rare in a friend."

On the word *friend* I made an inadvertent doubtful noise around the glass of water I'd grabbed from a passing waiter, and Freddie shot me a quizzical look.

"I, uh, my underwire snapped and it stabbed me a little in the boob," I said.

"Save that one for someone who doesn't know you as well as we do," Freddie said.

Nick nudged me. "Is this about Daphne's crush on Freddie?"

"That's ridiculous," Freddie scoffed. "Daphne is like a sister. She's going to marry some disgustingly respectable Dutch landowner and I'm going to end up with..." His voice trailed off. "I don't know. To be determined. Maybe no one." He looked around the party, which had gotten crowded over the last forty-five minutes. "I can't imagine coming to these things by myself forever."

His voice sounded a strange combination of resolute and resigned.

"You're not by yourself," I said. "You're with us."

"A lifetime of being the fifth wheel," Freddie said, shoving his hands in his pockets. "Delightful. You're a couple, Gaz and Cilla are a couple, Lacey and Olly, Bea and Gemma. Even Aunt Agatha is blazing her way through Tinder." He sighed. "One of the things I liked about the Boat Service was that it was just a bunch of people on their own, coming together to figure things out as a team. I don't have a team here."

"Yes, you do," Nick said. "The three of us are a team."

"You're not a fifth wheel," I insisted simultaneously. "You're...a third wheel. Tricycles have three wheels, and if I remember correctly, they are rad."

"That's a terrible metaphor, Killer."

"Then we're a tripod," Nick said. "Without one of us, the other two would fall over."

Freddie laughed, the most genuine one he'd let out in a long time. "That means a lot," he said, patting Nick on the back companionably. "Thank you. But we've already learnt that you two are your own little team, too, and at the end of the night, I'm just one person." He looked off into the distance, at something neither Nick nor I could see. "Daphne understands *that*, too," he said. "Except, in this analogy, I think her parents are playing your role."

"There are worse comparisons," I said to Nick, who nodded.

"Hardly anyone gets that kind of love, though," Freddie continued, more to himself than to us. Then he shook his empty glass. "I'm going to give my heart to a fresh vodka soda."

Once he was out of earshot, Nick turned to me. "I know this is an odd comment," he began. "But it feels good to be discussing his romantic life again without wanting to vomit."

"You are a paragon of personal growth," I said. "Dr. Kep is worth every penny. Maybe he's the fourth wheel that turns this tricycle into a car."

Nick put his arm around me. "Stop trying to make 'tricycle' happen. Tripod was the clear metaphorical winner." When I frowned, he amended, "But I wouldn't have got there without you, so..."

"We *are* a good team," I told him. "In all our permutations, whatever they turn out to be."

Two hours later, I was standing next to a massive World War II–era tank and having my ear talked off by a man who owned a company that claimed to "disrupt Big Candy," which really meant selling less of it in fancier bags for more money. He'd regaled me for fifteen minutes about the history of Turkish delight before switching to the offensiveness of hard licorice.

"I'd sooner eat bog paper," he was saying. "Who decided to shove *that* at people? Big Candy at its most insidious."

"I love licorice," said Freddie, appearing at my side. "I've got loads of it in my pockets so I can snack on it through the night. Would you like some?" He pretended to feel for it in his suit jacket. "Which one is it in...I can *smell* it..."

Candy Bloke glared at us. "You'll have to excuse me," he said, hurrying off toward the men's room.

"Thank you for rescuing me from that person," I said to Freddie. "But please don't make me eat licorice. He was right about that."

"I don't have any, so you're safe," Freddie said. "Although I didn't think I liked it, either, until I tried some of Daphne's salty Dutch licorice. I ordered an entire case last time I was over there."

"And when was this?" I asked.

"A few weeks ago," he said. "It was a quick visit. Don't look at me like that, Killer. I merely came over to see if you're as bored as I am. Daphne texted that Lax flew home already, but she stayed and wants us all to pop by the hotel for drinks." He took out his phone and tapped at it. "Let's see. She wrote, 'My suite has the most spectacular view. Best experienced under cover of night. Tell Bex I have Aperol.'" He raised his brows and pulled an enthusiastic face.

"Ooooh," I said. "I do love a spritz."

"I'll find Knickers and meet you at the back," he said.

Daphne was installed in a three-bedroom penthouse at a newer luxury hotel right next to the Tower, tucked away on a narrow street that appeared to be undergoing construction for no reason—and that therefore was perfect for covert entrances and exits, as nobody wanted to drive on it. Her suite had three flop-worthy king beds, a full kitchen, and a wall-size TV, but the star was a wraparound terrace that jutted out over the Thames. The view was dominated by the river, the cacophony of modern buildings on its south side, and the iconic Tower Bridge, which felt close enough to touch.

"Blimey," Nick breathed.

"Impressive, isn't it?" Daphne asked, easing the cork out of a bottle of Dom. "Mother favors The Savoy, but I wanted something new. Living on the edge, as it were." The cork shot over the balcony. "Perhaps too literally."

"The downside of living in London is that you never get to stay in a hotel in London," Nick said, easing into a canvas deck chair and stretching his legs out to rest his feet on the edge of the firepit. "It's a treat."

"How long are you staying, Daphne?" I asked. "I didn't even know you were coming."

"I was meant to fly back tonight. It's such an easy day trip. But I changed it to tomorrow morning so that Freddie and I could at least have coffee and one of your sausage rolls," she said. "I was a bit nervous to be by myself, but Mother convinced me to, as she said, live a little."

Daphne blushed. "There is a security officer in the next suite, but only one. It's a start!"

"Good on both of you," Freddie said, dropping a slice of orange in my spritz and handing it to me before taking some Champagne for himself.

I took a greedy sip of my drink, and then felt my stomach lurch, so I set it down onto the lip of the firepit. I had been cutting back on alcohol, just in case. I knew that countless women found out they were knocked up after a month of carousing, and their babies turned out fine, but I felt increasing pressure to create the most perfect possible environment. *Come on in; this uterus has been eating organic.*

"Since I came over for the state dinner, Mother has invited me on all her trips here," Daphne explained. "She likes to shop in London. The attention we get at home isn't what you all receive, but she does find it easier in the UK, and she thought I might, too. She calls these our *missions*, and every time we successfully complete one, we both feel a bit more ready for me to spread my wings."

"It's been a very handy way to keep in touch," Freddie said. "Lax apparently needs a lot of scented candles."

"She says Jo Malone smells more authentic if she gets it here," Daphne agreed.

"Please drag me along on your next mission," I said. "I need to see the kind of damage Lax does to Harrods."

Daphne smiled. "They adore her, as you might imagine. She is always telling me she wants me to dress more outrageously." She looked down at her gray flannel dress, prim and long-sleeved but undoubtedly expensive. "The last time we were here, she kept sneaking leather trousers into my dressing room, even though I am so obviously not a leather trousers person."

"You don't know that," Freddie said.

"She would tell me, 'Be more open-minded. You'll surprise yourself,'" Daphne said. "Wise advice for us all, perhaps."

The autumn night air nipped at us, so Daphne lit the firepit with the push of a button, and conjured up warm chocolate chip cookies from her kitchenette. The hotel had also stocked her living room with a hoard of old board games, and we ripped through a round of Yahtzee, before moving on to Cluedo (and my accompanying rant about how Americans were correct to rename it the more sensible Clue, which both Nick and Freddie had heard multiple times, and Daphne politely tolerated). The entire experience had a cozy, quaint feel. Freddie was obviously fond of Daphne, and as the night progressed, I waited for that spark of chemistry that would make Nick and me jump to our feet with excuses to leave them alone. But even when they touched each other—a pat on the back, a teasing smack, a light hug—I saw none. It was like drinking a flat soda: You can only taste the echo of the real thing, in a way that makes you want to give up and go find it. So we stayed, and played until the wee hours, until I arrested Colonel Mustard one last time.

"Bloody cheek of him," Freddie complained. "How can it possibly be Colonel Mustard again? What is that, three times tonight?"

"It's always Colonel Mustard," I said. "That's just a fact. It's like guessing C on your multiple-choice exams."

"Wait, is that true?" Freddie asked. "I could have used that information sooner."

"Oh, please," Nick said. "You paid people to take your exams."

"Once!" Freddie protested in Daphne's direction.

"It's harder to do that when you're homeschooled," Daphne said. "My tutor would have noticed if suddenly the cook was doing my mathematics in a wig."

Freddie drained his drink. "Another round?"

"It's hideously late," Nick said, standing up and rubbing his hands on his thighs. "I've got to be up in a few hours. We should let you get to bed, Daphne."

"Nonsense. I'll have another," Daphne said.

"As you should," Freddie said. "I'm too sozzled for Stout's driving, so I'll pass out in the spare bedroom."

Daphne walked us to the door. As Nick turned away and pressed his phone to his ear to ring Stout, she gave me a hug.

"Freddie seems like he's been good for you," I said, returning the hug.

"Good for me, and good for my alcohol tolerance," she said. "Or perhaps bad for it. But it does feel as if I'm catching up on what I was too timid to try when I was younger. Staying up all night, drinking too much. Eating greasy breakfasts."

"Nick and I have a ton of experience in all those things, so call anytime," I said.

"This *was* nice, wasn't it?" she asked hopefully. "I could get used to this. It felt so... natural. Do you think..." She bit her lip and looked over her shoulder at Freddie, abject longing on her face. "Do you think he enjoyed it, too?"

I knew what she wanted me to tell her. As I looked into the happy face of this woman who'd cut herself off from the world for so long and was starting to find a way back in, I couldn't imagine dashing her dreams by telling her what I really thought—but I couldn't stomach lying to her, either.

"We all had a blast," I hedged, with sincerity.

"Daph," Freddie called out, the effects of the drink audible. "Your bubbly's going to lose its fizz."

She threw her arms around me again and then pulled away and went to him. They clinked glasses, and as he sipped, Daphne turned and raised hers at me with wide, excited eyes, in clear anticipation of something I wasn't sure she'd get. Then she took his hand and they disappeared onto the balcony, alone.

CHAPTER SEVEN

Lifting up my shirt, I stared down at my stomach, which had puffed up enough that it spilled over the waistband of my jeans.

"Hello, friend," I said, patting it. "Your day is about to get a bit worse."

Then I pinched the flesh and jabbed the needle straight into it.

I'd gotten good at giving myself this fertility drug, which was a hormone cocktail designed to help my body cook up some extra eggs. I kept it in the mini-fridge in our upstairs sitting room, and every day I'd load my dosage into the pen, screw on the slim, short needle, and shoot myself up—sometimes on its own, and sometimes mixed with another drug meant to make sure my body didn't decide to release any precious eggs ahead of schedule.

"How are you with needles?" had been the first question from my no-nonsense fertility specialist, a fortysomething woman with the thickest, glossiest black hair I'd ever seen.

"I mean, how is *anyone* with them?" I asked.

"That's fair," she had replied. "But if you're serious about this, you'll get good with them. Trust me."

I'd doubted her very much, and planned to make Nick do it. But then the nurse had demonstrated the injection for me, and it was a benign little pinprick. In two days' time I could poke myself without a flinch, and the only trick was finding a spot that hadn't already bloomed into a little bruise. Sometimes, like today, I even managed without drawing blood.

"Well done," I told my stomach, peeling the backing from a bandage and putting it on the minute puncture mark.

During the months we'd tried Clomid, it had done nothing but bloat me, to the excitement and then consternation of a public who noticed the puff and assumed it meant an announcement was forthcoming. So we jettisoned the Queen's gynecologist for Dr. Shirin Akhtar, a specialist who'd listened to me patiently and started me on an artificial-insemination cycle right around the holidays. This had meant not only smuggling fertility meds in a cooler to Sandringham, but excusing myself briefly from the Christmas Eve meal to take the timed shot that released all my pent-up eggs. Eleanor had not been pleased—you do not leave the table before the Queen, even if your bladder is about to rupture—but I wasn't about to blow the timing of this cycle for decorum, so I'd feigned a blinding migraine.

The meds had produced a decent amount of eggs. I felt their weight. I felt optimistic. All those little would-be babies floating around in there. But then thirty-six hours later, as I lay in the stirrups, Dr. Akhtar had come to me with her syringe full of Nick's genetic material, looked very kindly at me as she lifted the sheet, and said what every woman wants to hear when she's about to get a much-anticipated shot of sperm.

"Just so you know, this probably won't work," she said, pressing the plunger on the syringe. "His sample is not what we'd hoped. Time to bring out bigger guns."

Our first round of IVF, my eggs had winnowed down to only two viable embryos, neither of which took. Now we were on round two, and it was harder to hide the effects of the hormones: a zit here, more pudge there. I tried not to mind, because the side effects were all in aid of the big prize, and the robust public speculation was at least rooted in warm feelings. Well, other than those from Clive, who that morning had released an opus headlined BABY FEVER OR BABY NEVER? in which he alleged I was intentionally gaining weight to gin up speculation—and thus our popularity—but had no intention of ever having a baby because I was too vain to risk my figure long-term.

"Even the headline is annoying," I'd grumbled. "It only *looks* like it rhymes."

"Clive is nothing if not annoying," Bea agreed. "In the absence of real reporting, he's taking potshots. That's never good for one's longevity."

"I thought potshots were the bread and butter of the British press."

Bea shrugged. "The difference is that most of them have earned their stripes," she said. "Clive engineered one outstanding scoop, but now what? He has no real sources and no experience to know how to find them. Take your shots and you'll be pregnant soon enough to shut him up."

"Thanks, Dr. Bea," I said. "I hope you're right."

"I'm *always* right." Bea folded her hands. "Now. How are you otherwise? House doing okay? Married life satisfactory? Nick and Freddie still getting along?"

I blinked. "What is this? Do you have a small-talk checklist?"

"Marj kept it all business, and look where it got everyone," Bea said, somewhat callously. She clicked her tongue. "Is Freddie behaving himself, or should I prepare for another round of Daphne rumors?"

A patron at the Starbucks across from Daphne's hotel had spied Freddie leaving the morning after our game night, and snapped some covert video. It hadn't taken long for someone to figure out the famous guest he might've been visiting; the story didn't have legs yet, given the lack of concrete evidence, but Richard had nearly burst out of his pin-striped double-breasted jacket with pride.

"I must say, this was unexpected," he'd said, beaming. "I, of course, saw the potential long ago, but I had given up on it coming to fruition."

"Nothing is coming anywhere," Freddie had insisted, exasperated. "Bollocks, that sounds awful. What I meant was—"

But Richard hadn't even heard him. "A power union," he'd said. "I knew you had it in you, Frederick." And he'd clapped a fatherly hand on his son's back as Freddie gazed up at him in surprise.

Since then, the tenor of Freddie's denials about Daphne had shifted into careful non-denials, wherein he only reassured us that we shouldn't worry—without actually clarifying what, or whom, he thought we might worry *about*.

"I don't think Freddie knows what he's doing right now, but I'm a little concerned that the power of suggestion won out," I said to Bea. "And if it did, then it definitely means more to her than to him. I don't want her to get caught in the crosshairs of whatever he's exorcising right now."

"Noted," Bea said. "I'll keep a close watch, with extreme discretion, of course." She cleared her throat. "The good news is that we have plenty of work to distract you. The Clarence Foundation's patronage count is ticking up nicely, and now that the New Mentality partnership is official, I'm working on setting up events where you and Nick can visit local secondary schools to talk about the importance of...you know. Talking," she said. "Next week, there's the event with the succulent enthusiasts—don't forget, we need your hair up for that, we can't have you getting your head stuck on a cactus—and then your portrait unveiling is in six weeks."

"About time," I said. "I was beginning to think I was unpaintable."

"Nonsense," Bea said. "That first artist was just unemployable."

I had sat for that guy multiple times over the course of a year, at tedious length, with no even half-finished painting in sight. Eventually, he bailed, penning Richard a letter explaining that he simply couldn't compromise his wildlife portfolio and his "unconventional worldview" by branching into "staid human portraiture." This had annoyed Richard sufficiently that he'd tabled the whole thing until the end of his regency, when ennui bumped it back onto his to-do list. He'd made a few calls, then given up and hired the person who did Edwin's, which, yes, made him look like a walrus, but that was not entirely without realism. He'd been polite, and professional, and a tad perfunctory, keeping our sessions to a brisk thirty minutes, and I would be seeing the fruits of his labor for the first time on the wall of the hallowed halls it would grace forever.

"I'll be glad to have that over with," I said. "I'd prefer to be at the easel than on it."

"On that tip, you'll like this news," Bea said. "Richard's office has asked that you sit in for him at a Paint Britain board meeting on Tuesday—"

"Really?" I asked, elated.

"It's in the calendar," she said, smiling. "In permanent marker. I'm working on ways to get that under the foundation umbrella as well." She gave a satisfied breath. "It's so much nicer having more of this under my control."

"*Our* control," I said.

"That's what I said." She looked put out. "And speaking of control, your eyebrows are fresh out of it. Kira takes one vacation and you turn into a woolly mammoth."

By the time of the portrait unveiling, my eyebrows had at least been wrangled back into shape, but internally I was a mess from the non-stop IVF roller coaster. We were waiting for my blood test results to find out if we'd managed lucky number three, but if the royal show had gone on even while the Queen was in a coma, it definitely wasn't pausing for this.

"I hope I don't look like a walrus," I fretted to Nick as our car pulled up outside the Piccadilly Theatre, on the back side of the National Portrait Gallery. "What if walruses are his only talent?"

"You're not going to look like a walrus," Nick promised, extending a hand to help me up and out of the car. We put on our Pleasant Walking Faces as we entered the museum through its gift shop, before switching to our Pleasant Greeting Faces as we shook hands with the gallery director. My palms were sweaty. The painting was already on the wall, and the artist was currently standing next to it, providing the press scrum with solo shots and offering preapproved sound bites about how sensational and breathtaking yet also easy and normal I had been throughout the process. Nick and I were simply to walk up and greet him. And it.

"Are you thrilled and excited for this moment?" asked the gallery director, a tall, bespectacled older man with the demeanor of a British Tim Gunn.

"Absolutely," I lied. "I feel honored."

"We've given you the most wonderful placement," he said. "Right next to the Princess of Wales and the portrait of Her Majesty the Queen that you unveiled two years ago."

"That seems unfair to both my mother and the Queen," Nick said gallantly. "I'm sure they will both pale in comparison."

The scrum of photographers turned toward us, clicking and flashing, as we arrived at the mouth of the narrow corridor where the portraits of the living royals hung. When the pack parted, I came face-to-face with myself, and my amiable bearded murderer.

Because it was *hideous*.

My skin had a jaundiced pallor, my hair subtly streaked with grays that I worked hard to thwart in real life. I was not smiling, but rather smirking, as if mentally belittling whoever dared look into the face of this Medusa—an effect heighted by the jowls I'd been given, which were, yes, walrus-adjacent. And the bags underneath my (dead) eyes surpassed the luggage we'd brought on our royal tour. This portrait looked like a cursed relic composed of all my secret sins and worst thoughts, waiting for a soul to claim.

So that was great.

"What an unbelievable likeness you've created," I said, kissing the artist's furry cheeks as he looked excessively pleased with himself.

"It would be impossible to hold a candle to the real thing," the artist said, clasping my hand.

"Could you ever have imagined?" fussed British Tim Gunn anxiously.

"I . . . cannot believe it's real," I replied carefully.

Nick put a hand on my shoulder and shook the artist's with his other one. "You've done some incredible work," he said. "This painting will truly go down in history."

For five more minutes we made small talk under the gaze of my ghoulish avatar, its monstrousness infecting my inner monologue until I felt equal to it. We said our farewells, piled back into the car, and were silent all the way back to the palace.

As soon as our red-painted front door closed behind us, I grabbed at my skull. "It's a Horcrux," I shrieked.

Nick's lips twitched. "Whatever do you mean?"

"I'm Voldemort, and that thing is a dark, rotting piece of my soul. The longer we stood next to it, the meaner I was to that man inside my head," I said, kicking off my heels.

"I thought it was beautiful."

I gaped at him. "You did?"

"Yes," he insisted. "I can't believe you're telling me you didn't like it. It's marvelous."

"It's an abomination and it's going to hang there *forever*."

"He really nailed your eyes," Nick continued. "When I looked at it, it was like falling in love with you all over aga— Ow, that hurts, what is in your handbag?"

"My phone," I said, thwacking him again for good measure. "I don't want to miss Dr. Akhtar's call. You are torturing me and I can see right through it, Your Royal Highness."

Nick chortled. "Guilty," he said. "But I *do* love it. Is that wrong? It's so funny."

"Funny to you, who looks super handsome in the one where you and Freddie are in your uniforms," I said. "Less funny to me, the Troll Phantom of the Palace Bog."

Nick picked up my hand and kissed it. "Perhaps it can be 'out for cleaning' quite a bit, then."

I nodded. "Yes. Good. Let's make that happen."

"And when it is," he said, "I'll have them send it over to hang in the loo."

I whacked him again with my purse. As if in response, my bag began to vibrate. It was the clinic. My nerves made me feel as if someone had reached into my body and was holding my ribs in a vise. I held up crossed fingers to Nick as I answered.

"Hello?"

"Hi, Bex," Dr. Akhtar said. "I'm so sorry..."

I didn't have to tell Nick anything. He saw it all play out on my face as there, in the foyer, I started to cry.

It didn't improve from there. As spring rolled into summer, I started to feel like a human pincushion. Nick and I didn't even log the passage of time in months anymore; our mile markers were now shots, procedures, waiting times, and disappointments. We had pushed so hard, starting every new cycle as soon as we could once my body reset from the last, and every time, my efforts yielded double-digit eggs but not enough quality fertilized embryos to freeze for later. And none taking up residence in my womb.

"We know implantation is not impossible," Dr. Akhtar said to me during one of my checkups. "But I'm not seeing the results I'd like, and I think..." She cleared her throat. "Have you considered outside help?"

I'd blinked. "Another specialist?"

She shook her head. "Another sperm sample," she said.

"Oh," I said, taken aback. "No. I don't think so. It's not at that point yet, right? It hasn't been *that* long."

"Nicholas's numbers aren't where I'd like them to be, and sperm donation can have very successful results in—"

"No," I said firmly. "We've got this. We're a team. It'll work out."

Dr. Akhtar looked at me skeptically. The truth was that I couldn't bring myself to make Nick feel as cruddy and self-defeating about this as I already did. Not yet. It felt too early to ring that alarm, not without turning over any other stones, so I crossed my fingers and we made her prescribed lifestyle changes to improve Nick's samples. He took aspartic acid and vitamin C. He exercised more and stopped watching TV or looking at his phone after 9:00 p.m., in the hope of a fuller night's sleep. He tried zinc. Fenugreek. Vitamin D. I'd already cut out alcohol, but now we both did, and eliminated caffeine as well.

"It seems unfair that this is causing us this much stress, yet we can't have either of our favorite coping mechanisms for dealing with said stress," he'd said to me.

"Tell me about it," I said, blowing my nose and rubbing it red. "I'm not even taking anything for hay fever, in case."

The one thing that did help was Gaz, who'd become a huge fan favorite on his first season of *Ready, Set, Bake*, in part because of how hard he wept: for his successes, for his failures, for the contestants who went home. Of which, sadly, he was one, bowing out in the fifth week after—of all things—he burned the puff pastry on a game pie. (He had sequestered himself for three weeks to grieve, at which point we stormed over to his flat with a bag of groceries and forced him to cook himself out of the darkness. He redid the pie to resounding success.) There was an entire Instagram account called The Gaztronomics, devoted to photos and GIFs and fan art and fun facts people dug up about him, including that he'd once punched the now Duke of Clarence in the jaw. (Which he had, but only to keep Nick from decking a paparazzo.)

"What does it say about me that this made him go up in people's estimation?" Nick wondered.

"That you're very impressive and huge and that only a superhero could level you," Freddie replied.

"Good answer," Nick said.

"Or that they think you're a miserable git who deserved it," Freddie said. "But surely it's the first one."

Gaz had been so popular that when the baking stalwart decided to do a fan favorite season, Gaz was the first call, and he'd come prepared. The show taped each episode over one weekend in the country and then aired it a few days later, so Gaz had holed up in his office or his flat working and cooking in alternate bursts as he baked his way through each round (and successfully defended the Oxford Street branch of Boots from a slip-and-fall accusation), including a dizzying Desserts Week in which his rum-raisin cheesecake had been par excellence, his chocolate roulade had been an absolute nightmare, and his croquembouche had enough bouche to scrape him through. By the end, it was him, a young mother named Marian, and a seventy-year-old named Wayne, who Gaz told us had a much younger boyfriend who'd refused to go on camera because he thought Wayne was more sympathetic if he seemed lonely.

The tent they erected for filming moved each season, and was currently parked on Annabelle Farthing's enormous Somerset lawns, which come finale time would get their locational due and a boost of tourism. When Nick read about this coincidence in a fawning article about

Annabelle's conservation work on behalf of a rare crocus, he got what he considered a great brainwave: having Annabelle smuggle us into the finale garden party to congratulate or console Gaz in person.

"No," I said. "We are not asking that woman for anything."

"She owes me one," Nick pointed out. "And she'll make sure we're protected."

"While I would love to cash in on Annabelle's theoretical guilty conscience, this will never work," I said. "People know we're friends with Gaz. Don't you think they'll be extra watchful?"

"*We* won't be there," he said, shoving the tail end of a Gaz-made practice croissant into his mouth. "Steve and Margot will be there. Possibly with their old chum Niles Kensington."

"Niles has already been caught in public with Margot," I pointed out.

Nick scoffed. "By the time anyone in attendance even thinks to look that up, we'll be long gone."

"I could wear last summer's pants, I guess," I said grudgingly. "No one will be looking for a duchess with a visible muffin top."

"It's thematic. You're dressed as a baked good," Nick said.

"This seems highly risky," I said. "And Freddie will never say yes."

"Have you *met* Freddie?" Nick asked.

Thirty seconds later, we had Freddie on FaceTime, and he was clapping his hands with glee from what looked like the inside of his coat closet.

"Yes, absolutely yes," he said.

"Aha! I knew it," Nick said. "Bex didn't think you'd go along with it. '*Too risky.*'" He used sarcastic air quotes.

"Why in the world would I veto such a foolhardy and stupid plan?" Freddie asked. "Have you *met* me?"

"That's what I said!" Nick crowed.

"I just thought that since Freddie has been on hrmbsthvrunkjjshal-iut..." I trailed off.

Nick blinked. "Did you mutter a bunch of gibberish and hope we wouldn't notice, because you can't actually explain yourself?"

"No," I lied.

"Look, Bex, we've had a tough couple of months. A tough couple of *years*," Nick said, taking my hands. "This will be fun. Let's go be there for Gaz, for all the times he's been there for us."

I narrowed my eyes. "Are you really using infertility and all our past bullshit to guilt-trip me into saying yes to this?"

Nick shifted on his feet. "Is it working?"

I glared at him. Freddie, on the phone, started humming the *Mission: Impossible* theme, and between that and Nick's faux angelic expression, I couldn't help but laugh. "Fine," I said. "Fine! Yes, you jerks. But if we get caught out, I'm making sure Eleanor comes for your heads first."

It was cool outside the day of the finale, perfect for three people who needed to layer up without fear of sweating off any of their facial disguises. PPO Twiggy drew the short straw of carting us all out to Annabelle's second back entrance, where Annabelle had stationed one of her staff members to guide us to a parking spot and then sneak us to the party unobserved. The tent sat on a side lawn, huge and white and cheaper looking in person; the garden party was a football field away, already peopled with past contestants and the finalists' family members. No one seemed to care much about us.

"A recurring theme seems to be that nobody is as observant as I fear they are," I said to Nick.

"Or not as interested," he replied.

"I'm fine with either one," Freddie said, readjusting his Gwyneth Paltrow wig. "I swear this wasn't always so itchy. I hope Gwyneth hasn't gotten lice."

The competition was still raging inside the tent as Gaz and the other two cooked up their final confections. We could see a cluster of monitors in the distance, turned away from us, where the director and producers would be watching feeds from all the active interior cameras so as not to let their logistics distract the contestants. It made for an odd juxtaposition—bucolic country picnic on one side, and a bustling production on the other, about to collide.

"Fascinating, isn't it?" said a familiar voice, and I turned to see Annabelle, who gave Nick and Freddie very sedate handshakes and then squeezed me on the arm, her expression one of studied polite indifference.

"Bloody great publicity for the estate," Freddie said.

"And the location fees are going to pay for a new roof on the stables," Annabelle said. "Once the episode airs, we're expecting an uptick in requests for weddings, too, which will bring in enough to repair the heating in the east wing."

Nick squinted at one of the plastic sides of the tent, which were mostly opaque to us but which let in some light and scenery for the bakers. "Do I see *fire* in there?"

Freddie craned his neck. "No, that's just a light," he said. "I think."

"I'm glad you came today, Bex. That wig is amusing," Annabelle said as the boys drifted closer to the tent to determine whether anyone's chances were literally going up in smoke. "You and Nick should come out more often. We're reopening the tennis courts, and—"

"Nick told me about New Year's Eve," I said. "You can dispense with pretending that we're old chums."

Annabelle blanched.

"That was a dark spell," she said, the words tumbling out of her mouth in a rush. "I'm not proud of it. And I don't deserve your forgiveness."

"I'm glad you agree, because I wasn't offering," I said.

"But I can assure you that there is absolutely no chance I will behave like that ever again." She lowered her voice. "Artie and I are expecting a baby."

A stab of unseemly envy hit me right in the gut, so strong that it almost knocked me sideways.

"It's been such a surprise," Annabelle continued, placing her hands over her still very flat abdomen. "We weren't even trying. You know, at his age, I had assumed...anyway, he's over the moon," she said, a slow, self-satisfied smile spreading over her face. "And, of course, so am I. Everything feels so different now. I'm not the same person I was that night."

As she spoke, my envy turned a corner into jealousy. I wanted to tell her to go away. To stop making it all sound so easy. That I felt betrayed by my body, that I wanted a refund for years of birth control; that watching all the adorable happy kids playing on the lawn in front of us felt like karmic punishment for the misery I'd once brought Nick; that my butt stung from the progesterone shot. I wanted to tell her how much I resented her both for having what I didn't and for trying to have what I already did.

"How nice for you," I said instead. It came out sounding sarcastic, which I suppose it sort of was.

"Thank you. Surely I'll be congratulating you and Nick someday soon, too," she said.

Her eyes flickered down to my waistband and I pulled my coat closed. Then she pointed toward the tent, where a camera crew, the two hosts, and the two judges were filing out toward a smaller tent.

"Deliberations. We'll be close now," she said. "You should catch up with the boys. I'll ring you when it's over and it looks like traffic's clearing up enough for you three to sneak out safely. Those disguises are charming, but everyone will know it's you if they see the Range Rover."

Two camera crews materialized in the crowd as Annabelle speed-walked toward her house, and I rejoined Nick and Freddie. We drifted around the lawn, steering ourselves as far away from the cameras as we could. Fortunately, production wasn't interested in three unphotogenic weirdos, and focused mostly on the family and familiar faces in the crowd—including Cilla, who was twisting a handkerchief in her hands while trying to look calm. She'd brought her sister, her mother, and three cousins with her. We hadn't told her we were coming, but I saw her do a double take when Niles Kensington crossed her periphery, followed by a disapproving twitch of the mouth that you'd only notice if you knew her as well as I did.

Before she could scan the crowd again, the producers silenced everyone. The air was thick with tension. I saw Cilla's sister take her hand.

"And, ACTION. Go for Jilly," the director said.

"Hello!" came the plummy voice of Jilly Hall, the petite, spiky-haired comedian who cohosted the show. "It is my honor and delight to welcome you all to the finale of *Bready, Set*, oh, piss up a tree, let's go again."

"Still rolling," called the director as a giggle spread through the crowd. "Go again."

"It is my honor and blight to, oh, bloody bollocks, keep rolling…It is my honor and delight to welcome you all to the grand finale of *Ready, Set, Bake*, the show that takes thirteen home chefs and turns them into master baters OH PANTS, I'm fired. I fire myself."

The crowd cracked up, defusing the stress and tension of the moment, which in retrospect was probably her intent. Jilly then laid down one flawless take, and invited out the contestants with their final bakes. Wayne's was a reproduction of his childhood home done entirely in filled pastries. Marian had built a Christmas tree cake with removable, edible ornaments in different flavors, and Gaz's was, to our delight, a dessert reproduction of the Bodleian Library from Oxford. Each had telltale chunks missing from the judges' tastings, and the bakers all looked emotional and nervous. Gaz, in particular, seemed about to keel over, and close to tears per usual.

"And the winner is..." Jilly said as Gaz wrapped an arm around Wayne and Marian. "MARIAN!"

Marian shrieked and dropped to her knees as three kids ran up to her and threw their arms around her. Gaz burst into tears and applauded, while Wayne clapped more sedately, seeming put out—though that might have been because one of Marian's kids trod on his foot.

"The right baker won," Gaz wept in his exit interview as Nick and Freddie and I lurked as close as we could manage. "Her tree was a work of genius. And perhaps it was karma that I lost by building a library I hardly went to at Oxford, eh? I knew I should've built the pub instead."

With a laugh, the cameraman got one more shot of him hugging Cilla, and then trotted off to find Wayne, who seemed much happier now that his boyfriend had appeared.

"Jolly good job, Garamond," one Niles Kensington said, striding up confidently and offering Gaz his hand.

"Thanks, good sir," Gaz said, pumping Freddie's hand absently. "Much appreciated."

"Brilliant," I added, coming up to Freddie's right side.

Nick followed. "Rooted for you the whole way. It's a crime."

Cilla goggled at us. I sensed a lecture about to burst forth from her mouth but Gaz spoke up first.

"No, not at all, no miscarriage of justice here," he said. "I should know, I'm a lawyer in my spare time." He chuckled. "My sponge was a hair dry, and the cardamom in one of my fillings barely came through."

"I'm sure it was wonderful just the same, *Gaz*," I said, staring intently at him.

Gaz shifted under our collective gaze. "Taste it if you like—it's over there," he said. "Actually, I hope you won't think I'm rude if I excuse myself to sample the other two cakes? I'm dead curious."

Freddie blinked. "Er, yes, of course, one more handshake." He clasped Gaz's paw more firmly this time, and Gaz looked down at it, surprised.

"What a grip you've got," he said, saluting Freddie and then walking off. Cilla, fighting laughter, trotted after him while flashing me the universal *I'll call you* gesture.

"You know how all Superman does is change his outfit and put on a pair of glasses, and everyone's fooled?" Nick said, watching them go. "I thought that was unrealistic. Then I met Gaz."

Freddie and I laughed. I felt my phone buzz in my purse. Unknown number.

"There's Annabelle," I said, tapping the screen to answer. "Is the coast clear?"

"Hello, Rebecca. Are you enjoying the garden party?"

Clive. He'd found us. Somehow.

I looked around to my left and right as subtly as I could.

"Don't panic in public. It'll blow your marvelous disguise," he said.

My skin crawled, and I fought my facial muscles into submission.

"Sorry, mate, wrong number, eh," I managed in Margot's bad Aussie accent, before hanging up with a flick of my thumb, keeping the phone up to my ear as if I were still talking—as if, by some miracle, Clive magically would think the woman he was looking at wasn't me.

"It wasn't Annabelle," I rasped to Nick and Freddie. "We've got to get out of here. Now."

CHAPTER EIGHT

But what did he *want*?"

I looked down at the phone in my lap. My fingers were still wrapped around it.

"I told you, I don't know," I said to Nick. "I hung up on him. I didn't know what else to do. What if he was only guessing that we were there?"

Freddie drummed his fingers on the car door. "Yes, maybe *that* is what he wanted," he said. "To mess with us. To remind us that he's out there."

"As if we could forget," I said. "He wrote a story last week that I spend two thousand pounds a month on eyelash extensions."

"We should've changed our mobiles," Nick said. "I knew we should have. It just felt like a lot of palaver at the time." He blanched. "What if he's tracking yours? What if he's hacked us?"

"If he was doing that, we'd know already," Freddie said. "For one thing, his stories would be better."

"We still need to change them," Nick said. "You, too, Freddie. And perhaps even Daphne."

"Hang on a sec," I said, releasing my phone so I could hold up my hands. "Before we go crazy here, don't we want to know what he's up to?"

"I suppose so," Nick said.

"Then why don't we let him tell us?" I asked, swiveling so I could face them both in the Range Rover's back seat. "Clive's real nemesis is his ego, right? Bea said she thinks people are realizing he's a one-scoop wonder. I bet he's stirring the shit because he's running out of options. So maybe it's better if he can reach me. He's the villain in a movie who's going to monologue himself into trouble."

Freddie cocked his head. "You mean, if he can't resist calling you to lord something over you, he's actually giving *you* ammo."

"Maybe," I said. "He shouldn't have told us anything last time, either, but he couldn't help himself. Maybe he'll call again and do the same thing. I bet he'll call again. You watch."

I settled back into the leather seat, and a companionable, if charged, hush fell over the car. My phone sat in my lap, bouncing with the wheels on the road, a little silver time bomb waiting to go off.

My phone was never far from me after that. It was next to me on the couch, it was in Stout's pocket, it was in my purse hooked to a battery to keep it from dying. Nick started jokingly referring to it as my pet rock. Once he set a place for it at the dinner table. I jumped every time it rang, but so far, no Clive; it was usually Lacey or my mother, or Bea with some sort of persnickety complaint about something I'd done with my hands in a photograph or the way I was crossing my legs. And then, of course, sometimes it was Dr. Akhtar.

After my most recent IVF didn't take, Dr. Akhtar called me into her office. It was bright and white, all modern edges and metal utilitarian furniture, much colder than the warmth she projected to her patients. She smiled as she gestured for me to sit in the leather rolling chairs opposite her, but it was regretful.

"You know what I'm going to say, Bex," she said, taking a seat behind a gleaming silver desk, a file as thick as the Bible plonked on it in front of her. I realized with sinking sadness that it was mine. It was sobering to see all our failures—what felt so keenly like *my* failures—stacked up like that.

"I know you'd hoped all we needed to do was help with the embryos, and the rest would take care of itself," she said. "That hasn't been the case. We can certainly continue trying if that's what you want, but I don't see that changing." She tapped her manicured nails on top of the desk. "Have you given any further thought to donor sperm?"

"No. I don't even..." I couldn't finish the thought. Because I genuinely didn't know how that thought ended. "So how would that work?"

"It's entirely up to you. Some people use a sperm bank, all of which have expertly vetted and profiled samples," she said. "And others use a family member."

I flinched, imagining Edwin, fertile as all get-out, offering up some extra to me. Or...

I almost blacked out. I knew what the other option was. Dr. Akhtar remained impassive, but she had not been living under a rock during my wedding; her clinical remove was impressive, but I couldn't mimic it.

"Absolutely not," I said. "Nope. No way. No."

"Why don't you bring Nick into the discussion?" She opened her desk and took out three glossy pamphlets. The top one featured a photo of a blissful-looking family, caught in a vacation snap posing joyfully in front of, all places, Buckingham Palace. *Bank On It: A Guide to Understanding Sperm and Egg Donation*, it read. "We'll move forward however you decide. I just don't want you to feel caught on a hamster wheel with no end in sight. There are choices." She cleared her throat. "And I often advise my patients to take a break, because IVF and its ups and downs are stressful, and hard on the body. You should take a time-out."

"You're cutting me off?" I said.

"Not at all," Dr. Akhtar said. "I'm telling you to rest, and refocus on what you really want to do next." She leaned forward, the picture of sympathy. "We can also explore surrogacy, but we'd still end up needing a donor. I would not have suggested that if I didn't think it was your best shot at a successful pregnancy. Give it real thought."

My head was swimming as I walked out of her office. The suggestion that Freddie, *Freddie*, might help impregnate me was so impossible that it was borderline hilarious. I blinked blindly at the pamphlets and felt hysterical giggles bubbling up in my throat.

There was absolutely no way I could bring this up to Nick. The entire sperm donor conversation would naturally open the door to this, which meant it was all a nonstarter. We would have to find another way, even if it meant devoting my life to prayer. *It is not an option. Freddie is not an option.*

I put on my sunglasses, pushed open the heavy emergency exit whose alarm they'd disabled for me, and stepped into the empty back alley. Before I climbed into the back seat of the Range Rover that was idling at the corner, I casually dropped the brochures into a trash can, where they landed on top of a discarded Starbucks cup and a half-eaten serving of what looked like chow mein. They didn't need to come home with me.

But it was harder to leave my thoughts behind, and my conversation with Dr. Akhtar was playing on a loop in my mind all the way back to Apartment 1A. I kissed a waiting Nick hello without really seeing him, and didn't even notice my phone was vibrating inside my purse until he poked at me.

"That's your pet rock talking, isn't it?" he said.

Startled, I dropped my purse onto the carpet, and scrambled to grab it back. My fingers fumbled with the clasp, but I fished my phone out and took a steadying breath once I saw UNKNOWN NUMBER shouting at me on caller ID.

"Hello?"

"Greetings and salutations, Rebecca."

Showtime.

"I wondered when you'd call back, Clive," I said, for Nick's benefit. His forehead vein started to pulse.

"I've just come from the National Portrait Gallery," Clive said. "That painting is really something. It truly captures your essence."

"Yes, as someone not to be trifled with," I said.

"We could have had a good thing going, Bex," Clive said, in a faux wistful tone that sounded practiced. I flashed on an image of him standing in front of his bathroom mirror, running through his lines.

"You in the palace, me in the press writing fawning stories. You could have planted anything you wanted."

"And what do *you* want?" I asked. "We both know this isn't a social call, so to speak."

"It is a courtesy call," he said. "One last chance to trade me some information, to protect yourself."

"Clive, spit it out, or hang up," I said. Nick reached out and we bumped fists.

"I know you can't get pregnant," he said. "I'm sure you wouldn't want that made public. That your failures are threatening the entire path of succession."

"Thanks for the concern," I said. "But if that's all you've got, I'm afraid I'll have to go. This is much less compelling than I'd hoped."

At this, Nick nodded enthusiastically.

"Then how about this. Nicholas had an affair. *So* sorry to break it to you," he said. "But I did warn you away from him. I'm sure you wish you'd listened." He laughed coldly. "New Year's Eve is a devilish holiday to spend apart, Bex."

My stomach twisted a little. I knew this wasn't true, but I still hated hearing those words in that order, and I didn't need to hear any more.

"Thanks for calling, Clive," I said. "But unfortunately, your career isn't of interest to me. Best of luck in the future."

I hung up and turned to face Nick, who was practically climbing out of his skin, standing behind the sofa.

"He knows about the infertility," I said, tossing the phone onto the coffee table, where it landed with a clatter. "I don't know how. Maybe..." I briefly flashed on the brochures I'd thrown away in Dr. Akhtar's back alley trash can. "Maybe he's been following me. Or maybe he's bluffing, and got lucky." I faced him. "But he also knows about Annabelle, or at least he thinks he does. And I'm pretty sure he's going to run it."

Nick covered his face with his hands. "That fucking party. Those bloody people are lying through their teeth."

"Right, but the thing is, they don't think it's a lie," I reminded him. At this, Nick uncovered his face, and I saw that it was pale. "Someone must have decided to talk. Apparently Clive *has* been working hard to massage some actual sources. I'd be proud of his work ethic if I didn't hate his guts so much."

"God, Bex. I am so sorry," Nick said.

"So it seems likely that now the whole world is about to think *you* cheated on *me*," I said. "I guess you got more of a tit-for-tat than you bargained for."

Nick rubbed at his face again. "I can't tell if you're trying to be funny, or you're furious, or..."

"All of the above," I said. "It's almost poetic. Same reporter and all."

"Damn it to hell." He scowled. "What do we do now?"

"I think we have to do what we didn't do last time."

"Murder him?" Nick offered, and I laughed in spite of myself.

"Tempting," I said. "But what I meant was, I think we need to call in the authorities instead of trying to fix this ourselves."

"The police?" he asked, confused.

"In a manner of speaking."

He blanched. "Last time it would've been Marj," he said. "So this time you must mean..."

But the esteemed Lady Bollocks had already gone home for the evening, which is why Nick and I ended up briefing her on this latest disaster in the Mayfair apartment she shared with Gemma, and which I had somehow never been inside.

"I prefer to keep my professional life and my personal life separate," Bea said, when I pointed this out.

"But we were friends before you started working with us," I pointed out. "And I'd never been here then, either."

"I didn't like you then," she said, leading us from the marble-floored entryway into their drawing room, where Gemma was sprawled on a sofa covered in zebra-print silk, and fuchsia and emerald throw pillows. The drapes were in a fabric that evoked lush plant life; the whole room felt like a mini-jungle right there in the middle of London, expensively styled and as bold as Bea's own taste always seemed conservative.

"This place is gorgeous," I said, in spite of myself.

"It was in *Architectural Digest* last month," Gemma said. "Bea designed it herself."

"When did you have time to do that?" Nick asked.

Bea pushed up the sleeves on her black cashmere sweater. "I am a monument to efficiency," she said. "Stop blathering and get to the issue at hand. Gemma and I have dinner reservations at nine."

At this, Gemma sat up and set her book on a brass occasional table shaped like a woman's face and sat forward, her chin in her hands. "The Laird of Trembleton's brawny loins can wait," she said.

Bea listened patiently at first, but when we got to the more sordid details, she snapped a pencil she'd been holding and gripped the pieces like shivs until we finished.

"Is it written on a stone tablet somewhere that whosoever accepts this job has to deal with Clive Fitzwilliam unearthing a sex scandal?" she snapped. "Apparently this and blackmail are Clive's only skills. I could kill him. I'm not best pleased with Annabelle, either, for that matter," she added. "Nor, frankly, with you, Nick."

He looked chastened.

"I need you to be scrupulously honest right now," she added. "No sparing anyone's feelings. I will not ask again, and I do not want to look foolish. *Is* this true? Were you unfaithful?"

"No," Nick averred. "I was not."

Then she turned on me.

"I asked you," she said, "whether everything was all right on the marital front."

"And I told you the truth," I said.

"You didn't answer at all, come to think of it," Bea mused.

"This stupidity of mine was ages ago. It's lunacy that he's bringing it up now," Nick said.

"Lunacy is you thinking people weren't watching your every move the second you showed up alone," Bea said.

"There, we are in agreement," I said.

"But everyone at that party knows better than this," Gemma mused, more to herself than to us. "At least two-thirds of them are sleeping with someone other than their spouse. They know the rules. Gossip if you must, but you don't talk to the papers, especially Clive, even if you *were* shagging Annabelle."

"Which I was *not*," Nick interjected. Bea waved her hand as if this were immaterial.

"She's right. Even if you were, someone violated the code," Bea agreed. "Appalling. What is Great Britain coming to?"

"Right," Nick said, rolling his eyes at me. "But, like it or not, we're here now. You helped us through the last one, as our friend, but this time we're coming to you as our, er, boss."

Bea seemed mollified by this statement of her authority. She paced around the drawing room for a moment, stopping in front of the tiled fireplace to reposition a frame of her and Gemma on what appeared to be a catamaran.

"Leave it to me," she said.

"What?" I asked. Nick and I exchanged glances.

"Leave it. To me," Bea responded.

"Shouldn't you . . . tell us what you're going to do?" Nick asked.

"Do you trust me?" Bea asked, crossing her arms over her chest.

"Yes," Nick said, looking over at me.

"I guess so," I said. She turned to glare at me. "I mean, yes," I hastily corrected myself.

"Then there is no need for you to know anything else." She clapped her hands together. "I hate to be rude, but we've those dinner reservations, and as you can tell, I need to sort my hair before I'm seen in public."

Bea's crisp dark bob looked exactly the way it always looked: perfect.

"Bea," I said as she escorted us to her black-painted front door. "I know we say it a lot, but you're not *actually* going to kill Clive, are you?"

"Not personally," Bea said, and closed the door in our faces.

"Nick!" I said, climbing onto the bed and shoving him. Nothing. I rolled him harder. "Nick. Nicholas. Wake up."

Nick stirred. "Pistachio housecakes," he mumbled.

"You choose *now* to be a sound sleeper?" I said, aggravated. I eased myself up so I was full on sitting atop him. Nada. I resorted to tickling him anywhere I thought would work. His lumbar region did the trick. He shot up like a cannon, sending me tumbling to the side.

"What is it?" he asked.

I slid off him and tossed *The Sun* onto the bed.

"Bea," I said. "She gave him exactly what he wanted. *That's* how she took care of it. No wonder she didn't want us to know what she was going to do."

"Clive?" Nick asked. His hair was ridiculously mussed from sleep. He rubbed his eyes. I poked at *The Sun*.

GOING DUTCH: FREDDIE HAS A ROYAL STEADY

And Clive Fitzwilliam Hears Wedding Bells

After three years of upheaval, the royal family finally has something to celebrate: a royal romance between playboy Prince Frederick, 29, and Daphne, Princess of Orange, 33, heiress to Holland's throne. You can take it exclusively from me: This clandestine coupling is more than titillating talk.

"A wedding is absolutely in the cards. They're utterly besotted. Everyone at the palace is over the moon," confides our exclusive source. "The Queen loves her. Princess Daphne is serious, well educated, and refined."

"*Besotted*," Nick said. "This is Bea, isn't it?"

"Sure sounds like her."

"*This* was her plan? Freddie's not going to like it." He hauled himself up to lean against the back of our headboard. "Nor will Daphne."

"Neither will you," I said. "Read the rest of it."

What a refreshing change of pace from our recent royal bride, Rebecca, the Duchess of Clarence, an icon of impropriety who has stirred up scandal in her wake. Per our latest report, succession itself is now threatened: Rebecca's refusal to take proper care of herself has led to suspicions by royal doctors that she is barren and unable to bear the heir that history and a hereditary monarchy demands, meaning the line will sidestep the cuckolded Clarence duke and his salacious succubus and—as it did with the Queen herself—land in Freddie's lap. How might a Dutch union complicate that?

Nick's eyes got progressively wider. "Crikey. That is rubbish," he said. "What was Bea thinking?"

I grabbed my phone and opened Twitter, after sending up a little hello to Marta, whom I imagined trawling the internet from an armchair in the Great Beyond. People were abuzz with the romantic fantasy of it all: Daphne's abduction made for a particularly juicy backstory, and so the Tragic Princess Finds Safety with Hero Prince fanfic wrote itself.

"Interesting. Check this out," I said. "Apparently on *Sunrise* this morning, they really let Clive have it for some of this."

I hit play on a clip that was going around of new substitute anchor Penelope Ten-Names—whose second husband had brought with him two more hyphens—and her cohost looking aghast as they passed around the morning papers.

"It's jolly for Freddie and all, but those comments about the duchess's fertility are beyond the pale, don't you think?" said the main anchor.

"I do," Penelope said. "Implying Rebecca is to blame for those issues, if they're even real, is disgraceful. Abhorrent. And after he ran those photos of her during the royal tour, it's clearly not reporting; it's a vendetta. He should be run out of town." She turned to the camera with a snarl. "And you can take *that* from *me*."

Nick looked impressed. "That's going to go viral."

"It already has," I said. "You're welcome, Penelope." Then I scrolled further and shot Nick an uneasy look. "The Daphne stuff is already getting messy, though."

When the story broke, someone thirty thousand feet above Europe tweeted that Daphne was at that moment sitting in first class on their commercial flight to Gatwick. The paparazzi swarm lying in wait when she exited the airport was so overpowering that she stopped dead in her tracks, turned on her heel, and fled back into the airport.

"Goddammit, Bea," Nick said, almost to himself. "You threw them under the bus for me."

"I didn't throw anyone under anything," Bea said to us later that morning in her office. "This is how the game is played."

"It's not how Marj played it," I said.

"It's how the game is played by people who know what they're doing," Bea retorted sharply. "All due respect to Marj."

"But it's not even true," Nick said. "Won't Clive be angry when he finds out? What's stopping him from releasing the story when no engagement materializes?"

Bea shrugged. "People break up all the time," she said. "He can be the first to get that scoop, too. You said you trusted me, and so I did what I thought was best, and now the world is fawning over Frederick instead of hiding in Annabelle's bushes."

"Why would they be hiding in *Annabelle's* bushes?" Freddie asked, rounding the corner into the office. "Bea, we need to talk about Daphne. It was a mob scene at Gatwick. Father had to charter her a plane back to The Hague."

"I'm so sorry," Nick said.

Freddie furrowed his brow. "It's not your fault that Clive got bored of waiting you out and turned on me." He took a beat. "Did he *not* get bored of waiting you two out? What am I missing?"

Nick reached over and kicked the door closed with his toe.

"Clive was going to publish a piece alleging that Nick and Annabelle Farthing slept together on New Year's Eve two years ago, and have continued their affair ever since," Bea told him.

"*What?*" Freddie said.

"It didn't happen," Nick said quickly.

Freddie was agape. "But there was reason for suspicion?"

Bea stood and gestured for Freddie to take her chair. "First of all," she said, "I need a bigger office."

"I'll give you an entire floor if you can convince me this was necessary," Nick snapped.

"We had to act. So I gave him a better story in exchange for his silence," Bea said. "It's what you'll recall I was in favor of doing before your wedding, too."

"That story also would've involved me, so I suppose I'm the go-to fall guy, then," Freddie said.

"And it was an idea *you* originally volunteered," Bea shot back. "Forgive me for borrowing from your playbook, Frederick, but you were so enthused about it last time. And it worked here."

Freddie ran a hand through his hair. "Using Daphne is outrageous."

"She may not like the attention, but the implication will not be unpleasant," Bea said. "I did what had to be done."

"I mean, congrats, then, I guess?" I huffed, crossing my arms over my chest.

"Finally, someone speaking sense. You're welcome," Bea said.

"You danced with the devil," Nick said, getting up as if he wanted to pace, before realizing he didn't really have room, and sitting back down. "Everything we refused to do, on principle, you did without even telling us. We look weak."

"I have news for you, Nicholas. You already did." Bea looked down at all of us for a moment. "Marj is a wonderful woman, a very kind, very smart woman. But her fatal flaw in this position was that she had watched you grow up, and it turned into a tendency to pull her punches with you. I am not going to do that. Did you hire me to do a good job, or to blow smoke?"

"You've *never* blown smoke," Freddie said.

"Exactly," Bea said. "So listen up. One tawdry love triangle was bad enough. Two is a pattern. What's the next domino? Some random tart who was at a party with you once, claiming you're the father of her child? My job is to stanch the bleeding, and to do that, you're going to have to swallow some compromises."

"And the compromise involved compromising me," Freddie said.

"Fifty-third verse, same as the first. The Ginger Gigolo takes the heat off Nick again."

"I didn't *do it*," Nick said.

"It certainly sounds like you did something," Freddie spat back.

"You've done plenty over the years," Nick shot back. "Let's not pretend otherwise."

"Enough," Bea said, and she stomped her foot for emphasis. "Yes, Freddie, you were the human shield in this instance. But this ultimately is a good story for you, even if it's false. Daphne reflects positively on you."

"It's not a positive for Daphne when she's being chased back into bloody Gatwick Airport," he argued.

"Daphne is the heir to the throne of the Netherlands, and the sooner she gets accustomed to people taking an interest in her private life, whether or not you are involved, the better," Bea said. "I didn't say she had to like it. But perhaps you have now done her that service, in addition to helping your brother and Bex avert a scandal they might not have been able to outrun."

Freddie looked down at his hands and then over at me, and then at the floor.

Bea crossed her arms tightly. "There you go. Crisis averted, with very few casualties."

"It didn't *entirely* work," I pointed out. "He still used the infertility stuff. Did you approve that?"

Bea pursed her lips. "No. I regret that I didn't bargain harder for that, for your privacy's sake," she said. "But when I saw it, I *may* have telephoned Penelope and gone on a rant about vendettas. I see she's turned that into a viral moment. That temporary anchor job is about to become permanent."

"Everyone wins, except for me and Daphne," Freddie said, standing up. The chair he was in shot backward and hit the wall.

"For the last time, it's a positive—"

"You once said you worked for me as much as you worked for them," Freddie said coldly, hooking his thumb in my direction. "But this isn't working for *me*. This was putting them first, pure and simple.

You didn't even notify me. Or Daphne. I realize I put myself in that position when we were boys, to take the pressure off my brother. But I was used that way while they hid out in Scotland, too, and I thought I'd earned a bit more respect." As he spoke, he turned and made for the door. "I need someone of my own in here who'll handle my interests with an actual eye toward me. You're fired."

He pulled open the door. "Where's Cilla's office? Never mind, I'll find it myself."

Bea dropped down into her vacated chair, stunned as I had ever seen her.

"He probably didn't...mean it?" I attempted.

"You and I both know he meant it," Bea said. This time, the smile on her face was morose. "This doesn't happen often, but that was one outcome I did not predict."

CHAPTER NINE

It seems you forgot to mention one important thing that happened while I was indisposed," Eleanor said that afternoon, pushing *The Sun* at me. Then she looked around. "I always regret it when I decide to use this room. The walls give my guests such a sickly cast."

We were having tea in the Green Drawing Room, which had just reopened after having its eponymous silk walls recovered (a once-every-thirty-years assignment). The sofas around us were also green, as was the porcelain on the mantel, whose matching tea set was on our table. I found it festive, but even with the curtains thrown back to let in the waning afternoon light, I had to admit it gave Eleanor a nauseated pallor.

I picked up the paper once more. Clive's story had included a grainy photo of Freddie and Daphne together back at the state dinner, with some purple prose about how long this romance had been brewing. It was an oddly banal shot; they weren't even looking at each other in it.

"I didn't mention it because nothing was happening back then," I said. "He likes her well enough, and he's lonely, but marriage is far-fetched."

"Loneliness breeds rashness. Look at what he did with you," Eleanor said. "We tried something like this with Georgina, you know. Thought we'd found her a lovely possibility in the old Greek line. He was *very* handsome. She refused to meet him. She locked herself in her rooms for the entire visit."

I laughed. "Georgina never comes off as rude like that in her diaries. Just strong-willed."

"Of course not," she said. "A person is always the hero in their own story, and thus an unreliable narrator. She's hardly going to put pen to paper to write about what an embarrassing ninny she'd been."

I contemplated that while I chewed. "I suppose so."

Eleanor poked at her copy of *The Sun*. "This may not be the worst idea I've ever heard, even if it is Clive Fitzwilliam's fiction," she said. "See, it says right here that I love her. Perhaps Frederick should consider it."

"Even if *he* doesn't love her?"

Eleanor put down her teacup with a clatter. "Rebecca, consider this," she said. "He tried to make a go of it with all those career women. People he believed he could love, perhaps even some he actually did. None of them wanted any part of him. Why do you think that is?"

"Chemistry?" I offered.

"Don't be obtuse. When has chemistry been Frederick's problem? Think back to your own life," she said. "Not being able to go to the market. Not being able to go to work. Not being able to throw away your rubbish without worrying people will go through it. Breaking up and having the world watch you, simply because you once dated a prince. Marrying him, and having the same." She flicked garnish off a tea sandwich with a clear-painted nail. "And now imagine that person, for Freddie, trying to coexist with you. Think of how difficult it was for Nicholas to watch you two be friends. Do you think very many women will gamble their entire lives on that?"

"Are you saying," I said slowly, "that it's my fault Freddie is still single?"

"I'm saying, perhaps all three of you would be happier if he chooses to make his life with someone who helps put more distance between you," she said. "Someone unfazed by how this life works."

"Distance between family members doesn't necessarily solve any-thing," I said. "You of all people should know that."

Eleanor put down her teacup harder than usual. "I beg your pardon?"

"Georgina," I said. "She kept away, and you two never made up, and then she died and that was that." I cocked my head. "Then again, you and Marta lived in total proximity and I heard what you said to her coffin, so maybe there is no right answer."

"Whatever you think you heard, it has most certainly been exaggerated by your active imagination," Eleanor said. "My mother was a challenging woman who was every bit as hard on me as my grandmother. What daughter wouldn't carry a few resentments after everything we lived through?"

Her cheeks were flushed. I sensed I should back down. "I suppose I'd prefer that Nick and Freddie followed yours and Marta's example than yours and Georgina's, is all," I said.

"Perhaps you should worry less about Freddie and Georgina and focus more on your own concerns." Eleanor settled deeper into her chair and nudged *The Sun* again. "It seems that you have some pressing ones."

I took a tiny egg salad sandwich off the tea tower and placed it on my plate. "Some people would say that this is none of your business."

"Tell that to Clive Fitzwilliam, who thoughtfully plastered it all over his paper," she said. "Was that another of his inventions, or is it true?"

I felt a blush run up my face. "We've been trying since the miscarriage. No luck."

Eleanor looked concerned. "That's been some time," she said sharply.

"You're telling me." At this, Eleanor raised her brows, but did not speak. "But we're seeing a very good specialist," I continued. "She'll get us sorted."

Dr. Akhtar's brochures popped into my head again. I had not brought up the issue of sperm donation with Nick at all; instead, I'd told him that Dr. Akhtar thought my body could use a little break, and we'd broken out some of the plonk.

Eleanor was staring intently at the smoked salmon. I could not read her.

"Don't worry," I told her, but my voice sounded quivery. "We'll figure it out."

Eleanor placed her hand, cool and dry, over mine. Then she patted it sharply, more monarchical than maternal. "See that you do, my dear," she said. "If I die without your having added a few heirs to the line, I shall be enormously cross."

"It's about time," Nick said as Freddie bounded down the steps to the courtyard, an overnight bag slung over his shoulder. "I'd hoped Cilla would keep you on a tighter clock."

"She is," Freddie said. "But unfortunately, her husband brought a large lunch spread over and it demanded to be consumed in full."

Freddie had indeed walked right out of Bea's office, offered a job to Cilla as his personal secretary, and gotten Richard's stamp of approval—all within the span of an hour. It seemed to put a bounce back in Freddie's step that he'd been granted even this much autonomy, and Cilla and Bea—bruised, but aware she'd brought this on herself—had spent one very long dinner at Dishoom formulating a workflow plan and generally cementing that this was not going to make either of them unhappy.

Freddie paused and felt around in his pockets for something. "Do I have my cigarettes?"

"I thought you'd quit," I said.

"No one ever really quits," he said.

"Come on," Nick said. "We're going to be late."

"Keep your knickers on, Knickers," Freddie said. "It's not like they can leave without us."

"I reckon Gran would try," Nick said as PPO Twiggy popped the back gate of the Range Rover and Freddie threw his bag on top of mine.

"Gran might leave one of us," Freddie said. "But she can't leave all of us. That's the whole point of this little trip."

Nick and Freddie and I were joining Eleanor on the Royal Train to commemorate the hundredth anniversary of the armistice that ended World War I, which had been signed on a locomotive in France. The festivities began with a splashy exit out of London in the evening, after which we'd eat and sleep on the train, and disembark in Inverness at

10:00 a.m. to coincide with the exact time the war ended. Eleanor and Freddie would then attend a brunch with veterans while Nick and I unveiled a new exhibit of military art at the cathedral. This anniversary was a big deal, historically, but Eleanor also knew that any event featuring her and the three of us was going to get a ton of media coverage, and she was apparently in the mood for some splashy positive PR.

Nick and I had been enjoying our IVF vacation. We'd relaxed, had some cocktails, drank coffee instead of green juice, recklessly skipped our vitamins, and used the Buckingham Palace hot tub for the first time. But, as good as that freedom felt, we couldn't completely brush aside the limbo we were in, like floating in a warm bath but knowing that the water will soon get cold. The idea of a train trip sounded romantic and pleasant. The British Royal Train had a posh reputation, but none of the three of us had ever seen it in person; it was expensive to run, so Eleanor was persnickety about using it. But the internet told me it had eight cars that served as rooms: one for dining, one for lounging, a kitchen, and then bedrooms (all of which came with their own en suite bathroom). It was a fancy condo on wheels, albeit one that forced its guests to sleep in twin beds whether they liked it or not.

"Boo. I never sleep well without you," I said, peering over Nick's shoulder at his laptop screen, which showed a caramel-wood-paneled sleeping car.

"It's not like we'd be getting it on with Gran on the other side of the wall," he said.

I flicked his ear. "I was talking about actually sleeping," I said, laughing. "You perv."

The train was even tinier inside than it looked on the computer—my bathroom was narrower than my wingspan—but twice as tactile. Everything that could be covered in velvet was, 85 percent of the wallpaper was flocked, and the furniture was a careworn collection of secondary antiques that had been well polished and tended but still bore the nicks and scrapes of a century of being exactly where they were. My sleeping car was a prim affair with a scratchy lacy comforter—the aura of the spare bedroom in which you'd stick the maiden aunt of whom you're particularly fond. There was a small pile of books on the table next to it. They were all about God.

We'd seen Eleanor only briefly, for the photo at the station before we boarded and pushed off. She had declined what I termed the Bid Farewell to Your Wartime Sweetheart press opportunity, for which the three of us waved out the windows and Freddie blew a theatrical kiss, preferring instead to disappear into her own quarters. We didn't cross paths with her again until dinner. It turns out it's complicated to eat a formal meal on a swiftly moving train; we had to skip the soup course because no one wanted to risk spilling bisque on Eleanor, and I had to hold on to my glass of water with my nondominant hand the entire meal.

"We should have just gotten Burger King," Freddie said as the empty teacup in front of his place rattled. "Much less perilous, and no need for the fine china."

"It is a sign of breeding if you can navigate a full supper in less than ideal circumstances," Eleanor said, and truly, somehow her crystal glass was the only one without a dribble of claret trickling down the side, as if the laws of physics didn't exist in her bubble. In contrast, the cloth around mine was a dappled mess, and when we got up to adjourn to the sitting room for digestifs, it was obvious I'd spilled more on my lap.

"Strike one," I said.

"At least," Eleanor said as Freddie took her arm.

We carefully transferred into the adjacent car, which had plush booth-style seating along one set of windows and a series of sofas built in under the others. A bar cabinet in the corner had a key swinging beguilingly from the lock. Freddie deposited Eleanor at one of the window seats, where she rested her right elbow on a table between two of them, and caught his balance before unlocking the bar and carefully beginning to pour us all some port.

"I'm sure you've all wondered why I've called you here tonight," Eleanor said as she accepted hers.

"Uh-oh," Freddie muttered. "I knew I was right to bring the cigarettes."

Eleanor chuckled. "I've always wanted to say that," she said. "Your expressions were priceless. Rebecca, you've not improved your poker face at all."

"Good to know," Freddie said, handing Nick his port. "On that note, poker, anyone?"

"Careful with these nightcaps," Eleanor said. "Being drunk on a train is a nightmare and the morning after is worse. Henry and I did a whistle-stop tour of the southern coast after Richard was born, and we both overindulged. We look nauseated in all the photos."

She crossed her ankles. "Besides, I should think too much of that would be bad for your attempts to conceive."

"Not mine," Freddie said, overly jovially.

"Any minute now with my port," I told Freddie.

"Gran," Nick said, a warning note in his voice.

"It's a perfectly reasonable topic of discussion between family members," Eleanor said lightly.

"We're taking a little break right now," I said.

"A little break," Eleanor repeated. She drummed her fingers on the red velvet arm of her chair. "Did I fail the other day to impress upon you the importance of this task?"

Freddie handed me a full glass of port and raised an eyebrow. "May I be excused?" he asked. "This is not my business."

"Sit down, Frederick," Eleanor said.

"It's nobody's business, actually," Nick said to Eleanor. "With all due respect."

"This *family* is my business," Eleanor said. "And I should have been informed earlier that we might have another Queen Ingeborg situation on our hands. No heirs, and a shift to the left for the whole line."

"It worked out for you," Freddie said.

Eleanor fixed him with a steely stare. "Would it work out for *you*?"

Freddie slowly sat down.

"We need a solution," Eleanor said. "To *this*." She waved in the general direction of my uterus. "I am aware of how many science experiments you've done, and it's rather a lot for there to be no results yet."

"It's me," Nick said, looking directly at his grandmother. "I'm doing everything I can to, er, improve what I'm offering."

"It might also be me, though," I said quickly. "It's going to be fine, Eleanor. I promise. We're...exploring it. Discussing our options."

Eleanor cradled her port glass. "Enlighten me."

"The options mostly seem to be, keep trying," Nick said.

"You're telling me your impressive specialist hasn't mentioned using a donor?"

Nick shook his head, but it was me that Eleanor's eyes were boring into, and I never could hide from her.

I cleared my throat. Nick turned to look at me with surprise. "Dr. Akhtar did mention a sperm bank," I admitted. "Once. Or twice."

"When?" Nick asked. "Were you even going to tell me?"

"I was not, because I told her no," I said tightly. "We don't need it."

"Correct," Eleanor said. "Those people are strangers."

"Some couples go well into double-digit rounds of IVF. We'll get this," I said.

"We don't know that," Nick said, looking suddenly stressed.

"Then we can adopt," I said.

"No." Eleanor's head shake was crisp. "That is a nonstarter in your situation. Next?"

"I mean..." I exchanged glances with Nick. "That's sort of it. If we can't do it together, we need someone else. That's the normal way this goes."

"But you have agreed, time and again, that normal is not the way *this* goes," she said, gesturing to the room, as if it represented the monarchy itself—which, in a sense, it did. "Do you really mean to suggest that the throne should pass to an outsider?"

"Our child wouldn't be an outsider!" I said. "He or she would be just as—"

"This is not the time for mawkish tripe," she said. "Of course there is nothing wrong with adoption, or specimen banks. But it would be against the law for that child to inherit the throne."

"It is medieval that anyone cares how we build our family," Nick spat. "It's the twenty-first century."

"The monarchy has survived since the medieval period for a reason," Eleanor said. "And your child might care. That child might care very much, if you had to sit down and explain to it that while it is special, and loved, it cannot have what your firstborn is traditionally destined to have, because it doesn't come from the right place. How different that child will feel. How very alone. Can you do that to him or her?"

Nick downed the rest of his port and went to slam down his glass, but thought better of it and walked it over to the bar. Then he paced over to the window, leaning against it as the scenery juddered past.

"So, what?" he said. "I make Bex go through another twenty rounds of IVF with my crap DNA? All for your dynastic ego?"

Eleanor tutted. "The solution is obvious," she said. "And I'll wager your Dr. Akhtar has also already brought that up with one of you, who has chosen not to share it with the class."

She stared right at me again, and my skin went cold. This was an ambush.

"Don't, Eleanor," I said. "Please don't."

"His DNA is as close as it can be," she prodded.

"Stop," I whispered. "You can't do this to them."

"He's of Lyons blood," she persisted.

"It's unconscionable."

"And the baby would carry a natural family resemblance," she finished. "We've put the affair rumors to rest, so this is rather a safe option, don't you think?"

It took a full extra second for the force of her suggestion to hit the brothers.

"Bloody hell," Freddie said, his face flushing bright red.

"I need air," Nick said, fumbling to open a window. "I might also jump out."

"I realize this is fraught," Eleanor said calmly. "But if Rebecca doesn't have a baby of Lyons lineage, then Frederick, you will be Nicholas's heir. Is that your desire?"

Freddie's head was cradled in his hands. He said nothing.

"Indeed," Eleanor said, waving her empty port glass. Nobody moved to refill it, until Nick finally snatched it out of her hand.

"You sound like a madwoman," he said, ripping out the cork and refilling her glass with haste. "This cannot happen."

"It would be a beautiful favor to ensure the happiness of his family," Eleanor said, "and also the smooth continuation of the Lyons Dynasty."

"Oh, is that all?" Nick said.

"I was honest with you, Eleanor," I said. "I trusted you when I admitted that we were having trouble. I could've easily used some random sperm and told you Nick got me pregnant."

"Now I wish you had," Nick said.

Eleanor pushed herself out of her chair and pointed a finger into my face. "Do not joke about the family I've fought for," she hissed. "You do not know what it means to have this weight on your shoulders. To carry the past, the present, and the future, all at once." She straightened. "It is an elegant solution, and no one but the four of us would be the wiser. Stop pouting about what's been done, all of you, and think about what you can yet do."

Freddie stared at the ground. "This is really why we're all here, isn't it?" he said tartly. "You wanted us in a confined space to boss us around. To force my hand. Nothing ever does change, does it?" He blew out his cheeks. "I am the pawn you use to protect the king, and the queen, and to hell with it if I'm caught in the crossfire."

"Now you're being dramatic," Eleanor said.

"I'm called the spare for a reason," he said emptily. "The extra piece in case the machine breaks down. Not a person. A part." He stood. "And I've had enough of it."

He faced his grandmother and the two of them squared off, stock-still, in a charged stalemate. Eventually, Eleanor dusted her hands together as if this were sorted.

"I'm going to bed," she announced. "I trust you three to do the right thing."

The three of us, however, said nothing. Not right away. Freddie slumped back down into his corner of the couch, while I pressed myself further and further into the arm on the opposite side, as if the mere allusion to our past had somehow sexualized the sofa cushion between us. Nick turned and looked at us, back and forth, one after the other, for an interminable time before grabbing the port to fill his own empty glass. The train hit a bump as he went to pour it.

"The hell with it," he said, swigging straight from the bottle and then holding it out to Freddie.

"Going to need something stronger than that, mate," Freddie managed.

"We're not doing it," Nick said.

"But we can't unring that bell," Freddie said.

"Typical Gran," Nick fumed. "In one swoop she—"

"We're going to figure it out, Freddie," I interrupted, anxious not to follow Nick's train of thought. "This is an absurd suggestion."

Freddie got up then, and grabbed a bottle of scotch. He took a sip and winced as it went down his throat. Then he ran a hand through his hair and faced us.

"Is it, though?" he asked. "Is it really?"

"*What?*" Nick asked. His mouth hung agape. "No. We can't...*no*, Freddie. Surely you see it. We can't...we've just gotten each other back, and..."

Freddie tilted his head for another drink, then stared down the bottle neck. "You *should* have a baby," he said. "You deserve to have a baby, and now I can do something concrete to make up for the worst mistake of my life." He chuckled bitterly. "It's poetic, actually. Isn't it? That the best way, the final way, I can apologize for trying to sleep with your wife is by getting her pregnant?"

Nick froze, and the movement of the train buffeted him to the right. He caught himself on the back of a chair.

"Freddie, stop it," I said. "It's not funny."

"That's true. It isn't," Freddie said. "It is elegant. It's practical. It's foolproof. Gran is right. Let me do this. Think about it, Knickers. We used to talk about being better fathers than ours was to us. You can have that chance, and I can make up for nearly ruining your family by helping give you one."

Nick shook his head. "We have put that behind us. There is no karmic debt to pay," he said. "It is over. Let it stay over."

"Bex, please make him see," Freddie said, turning to me.

"Stop it," Nick burst out. "You can't turn on your special Freddie-Bex bond to try to get me to roll over on this one. This is impossible. *That* is why this is impossible. What about you? What if this stirs up…"

"It won't," Freddie said.

"Of course it will!" Nick exploded. "How can it not?" He was borderline frantic. "You act like this is so easy, but Bex was the one thing you wanted enough to throw your life away, and we nearly lost each other over it."

I will never forget how still Nick looked then as the train rocked around us. He simply stood rooted to the spot, fighting with whatever was burbling inside him. His hands clenched and unclenched.

"Bex cannot have your baby," Nick said. "I don't think we can survive it."

"And yet she can't *not* have it," Freddie said. "And you know it. Do you really think we can survive that, either?"

My mouth tried to form words. Any words, any at all, from the cloud of them swarming my head. The thousands of logical objections to this. The countless reassurances that they were both overreacting. The pleas to sleep on it. The promises that we were tough enough that none of this could touch us. But I couldn't figure out which of them would be the truth. Instead we sat there, silent, each of us breaking in our own ways as the train kept hurtling through the dark.

ACT FOUR

When my journal appears, many statues must come down.

—The 1st Duke of Wellington

CHAPTER ONE

A re these the amber waves of grain, or the fruited plains?" Nick asked, staring out at the low land on either side of the car, dotted with only the occasional farm.

"Both," I said. "Mostly the former. And corn. Lots of corn. If you ever wondered why I'm corny, here it is."

The harder we tried to start a family of our own, the more I wanted to show Nick a little bit more of what mine had been like. He'd never seen me on anything approximating my own turf—a gaping hole in his mental Library of Bex that I couldn't just fill with Twinkies and Cracker Jack and tales of the Coucherator. If we did end up having kids, a jaunt to Iowa would become harder—double the heirs, double the stress—so Nick and I got permission from Eleanor to spend Christmas with my mother. At long last, I was taking him to a corner of the States that truly belonged to me.

There are airfields near my small hometown, but they aren't trafficked enough for us to slide into Muscatine without anyone noticing, so Nick and I flew to Des Moines with our baseball caps pulled low, and Margot rented a white Ford Focus for the two-plus-hour drive to my house. We cruised out of the capital and through Iowa City, past the Herbert Hoover presidential home and library—Lacey, an *Annie* fan, had once proudly vomited there from carsickness—and then down Route 38.

Eventually the fields along that rural road gave way to white clapboard houses, roads with more stop signs than stoplights, and the modest two- and three-story square brick buildings that made up Muscatine's business district.

"That's Pete's Hardware," I said, pointing to a sun-faded, green-and-red-striped awning over an old metal cursive sign. The decal in the window had been scrubbed away years ago by some local teen idiot so that it only read P HARD. Pete had left it that way, figuring a reaction would only encourage more local teen idiots. Pete was now running for Congress. "Oh, and Joey's Tacos. Joey is famous for his bread taco, which is, wait for it, meat and toppings inside a shell made from a piece of bread that he's folded into a U shape and deep-fried."

"So...a sandwich," Nick said. "Oooh, can we go to Pizza Ranch?"

"Ironically, I've never liked their ranch dressing," I said.

"I love it here," he announced. "Let's relocate. We can be Knitwear Nick from Nick's Knitwear and Pottery Bex from Bex's Pottery, and eat bread tacos forever and ever."

"Nick," I said, "I love you, and I love your Demi Moore in *Ghost* fantasies of pottery wheels..."

"Mmm," he said dreamily.

"But we would go broke if we had to rely on selling your knitting."

He straightened up. "You laugh now, but wait until everyone in Iowa is wearing my creations."

"*Creations* is a good word for them," I agreed.

We pulled up to the two-story converted farmhouse my parents had bought when Lacey and I were eleven, tucked in a spread-out section of what qualified as Muscatine's suburbs. I hadn't been back since my father's death, and the loss hit me again as I saw only my mother bang open the screen door to greet us on the porch.

"Honey!" she called out, scurrying down the stairs to fold us both into hugs. "Nicholas! Welcome to Iowa." She drew back and scrutinized him. "That mustache is very Young Tom Selleck."

"I'm itching to take it off. Literally," he said.

Mom grinned and shouldered my weekender as we followed her inside. We had experienced a lifetime of highs and lows since my father died, so it was irrationally surprising to see the house much as I'd left it: the wood-paneled entryway, the Coucherator in front of the TV, the framed Olan Mills photos of me and Lacey lining the staircase. Even the Christmas decorations were all the ones I remembered from my childhood, a collection Mom and Dad had steadily built without ever eliminating any of it; they'd simply shifted all the handcrafted abominations from our elementary school years onto a short fake tree that sat in the dining room, leaving the tall one with the white twinkling lights for the nicer orbs and commemorative ornaments, like the ones I'd sent them from Windsor as a thank-you for helping Nick make Thanksgiving happen, or the year I bought them Henry VIII's six wives.

"What is *this* supposed to be?" Nick asked, pointing to a plastic-looking puddle on the kids' tree that said *X* on it.

"It was a Shrinky Dink project that they did in kindergarten," Mom said. "Bex's melted. Also *X* was the only letter she liked."

"It marks the spot," I defended myself. "There's always treasure under it."

I watched Nick delightedly prod at all the cockamamie projects of our youth, then move on to Mom's shadow box full of thimbles from every place she'd ever visited. He fit here in my past as if he'd always lived in it. But not everything was as easy. Framed photos of our lives had been scooted aside to make room for memories of events where Dad should have been, but wasn't: Our engagement celebration in my London apartment after I'd pulled the Lyons Emerald out of a Cracker Jack box; our wedding; Lacey's wedding; Danny's christening. And it would be endless. There would be no photos of Earl Porter's beefy hands cradling his grandchildren, sitting them on his belly, or—as I had photos of him doing with us—sneaking them a surreptitious sip of beer and then watching with glee as they screwed up their noses in disgust. Both his presence and his absence felt huge.

"I don't understand how I can be used to this, and yet it will never feel right," I said softly. "Wasn't it just yesterday that he sat me down over there and told me to pull it together and go back to England?"

"I know, honey," Mom said, putting an arm around my waist. "I know."

We stood there like that, facing our memories and the empty spot in our future, for a long time.

"What about this one?" Mom asked me, handing me a dog-eared book whose hardcover spine was peeling away from the binding. "*A Bargain for Frances.*"

"Of course we need this one!" I yelped. "Wait, wasn't this Lacey's?"

"You may be right." Mom frowned. "I do recall buying this because she'd developed a habit of wanting whatever you'd gotten more than anything she had."

"This book made me want a china tea set," I said, riffling through the pages. "I'll take it. She had her chance."

Mom grinned. "That's the spirit."

She and I were sitting in my old bedroom, rooting through boxes of things she'd pulled out of the attic and from my closet and under my bed—remnants of my childhood that she'd been storing in rooms that still looked remarkably like when we'd last lived in them. When Lacey got pregnant, Mom had summoned her to Iowa to sort through the memories. Now it was my turn. Even though my baby was still theoretical.

"I'm also obviously taking all of the Frog and Toad books," I said, scooping those over to my side of the floor. "And Sweet Valley High."

Mom laughed. "Those were used when we bought them," she said, holding up a tattered copy of the one where Regina Morrow's heart explodes from snorting cocaine. "Now they're disintegrating. They're relics."

"But I need them!" I clutched the one where Enid gets in a plane crash to my chest. "How else will my kids learn never to date Bruce Patman?"

"Try basic parenting."

"I'll be too busy teaching protocol and posture and how to wave." I looked around my room, and noticed that the knob was still missing from the top drawer of my dresser. "Being here reminds me of how free we really were. How much room I had to be messy and figure my shit out. I don't know how to raise a monarch."

"Neither did I, and it turns out I raised one anyway," Mom said. "Honey, no one really knows what they're doing when they have a baby. You'll make mistakes, either with the baby part or the monarch part, or both, but everyone does. I still think about the day your dad and I brought you and Lacey home from the hospital. We were terrified. I put your diapers on backward more than once. Don't even get me started on how bad he was at cutting your baby nails."

I glanced at a framed photo of Dad and me in our matching Little League uniforms. We'd been assigned to be the Yankees that year. We'd been so mad about being forced into those uniforms that I think we won the championship halfway out of spite.

Mom glanced down at a box and smiled, then withdrew a grimy softball and tossed it from one hand to the other. "My point is, you both turned out well, regardless, and so will your kids," she said. "Nicholas will be a much different father than the one he had. I hope you know that."

"I do." But my voice was querulous.

"Where is all this coming from?" Mom asked. "You haven't put yourself through all these medical procedures if you're gun-shy about having a baby. Are you having second thoughts about Freddie?"

I buried my face in my hands. "I don't know," I whispered. "Maybe."

That night on the train, I had sat by myself in the lounge car after Nick and Freddie retreated to their cabins. But at a certain point, I'd let him percolate long enough. I'd found Nick sprawled on his narrow bed, his head on one of two riotous plaid pillows, palms over his eyelids. I closed the door and clicked the lock, then turned toward the bed, right as the train hit a curve and all but tossed me at him.

"I'm flattered," Nick had teased, but there was strain in his voice.

"Talk to me," I said, arranging myself at the foot of the bed.

"About what?"

"Cute."

He lifted his palm to look at me. "We could do what you said and get a random donor and not tell anyone."

"Too late."

He made an indecipherable sound. "Then I suppose a fake pregnancy and secret adoption are out of the question?"

"I assume you're joking," I said.

Nick made a face. "Like 90 percent."

I kicked off my shoes and crawled over, snuggling up against his long body. "When Dr. Akhtar brought up sperm donation, I shut her down. Maybe I shouldn't have done that, but I knew the idea of using Freddie would pick open old scabs," I said. "And I was right."

He wound a strand of my hair around his finger. "I've been thinking about it nonstop since I came back in here. Would I always look at that baby and see every horrid scenario that played out in my head when I found out he'd kissed you?" He closed his eyes. "It's starting already. It's a bad movie I can't pause."

Hearing that had been enough for me. We'd gone back to Dr. Akhtar and tried another round of IVF, with Nick's sample. No dice. Of course.

Now, my hands poked at my stomach, which had stretched and deflated from hormones more times than I cared to count.

"I always imagined our kids having a blast with Uncle Freddie," I told Mom. "Like having two dads for the price of one. But now..."

"That idea is a bit closer to home than you thought," she finished for me.

"I'm definitely afraid we're wrong not to use Freddie," I admitted. "But what scares me more is pushing Nick to do it, and then finding out his instinct not to do it was right."

"And how does Nick feel?"

"We haven't talked about it again," I said. "The last IVF is too raw. Also, I don't know how to..." My voice cracked. "What if they look like him? What if we lose Freddie forever because he can't ever look at our child, or children, without seeing a person that he and I made?"

Mom frowned. "I agree that's an awful lot to process," she said. "But it seems like you're hanging on to Freddie more than you ought to be. Is there something else we need to talk about here?"

"I can't believe you're asking me that!" I said. "I love Nick. I fought to be with Nick. But I don't want to live without Freddie, either. And I'm scared this might make that inevitable. We've always had a connection." I let out a harsh laugh. "The idea of it becoming umbilical, too, is...a lot."

Mom looked at me in silence for a moment. "Bex, I think the time has come for you to do a little work on your own behalf here," she said. "You have to let go. You have to let *him* go."

"This would not be letting him go," I pointed out. "It would be either bringing him too close, or shoving him away."

"Unless he offered to be your donor as a way of forcing the kind of space he knows he needs," she suggested.

"No way," I said. "He wasn't thinking clearly. He cannot really want to do this."

"He's an adult," Mom said. "At a certain point, you have to take him at his word."

I curled up on the floor and rested my head on her lap. "I can't believe it's come to this," I moaned. "Freddie thought he was my only way out once before, and now what if he really is?"

"I can't tell you what to do, honey, but I don't think you should say no to his offer out of fear. That's all." Mom pulled the ponytail holder from my hair and started combing it out with her fingers, just like she did when I was younger and came to her for advice about stuff that seemed every bit this important. "I think we all need to stop looking backward at what we've always loved, and milk whatever joy we can from the time we have left."

"Holy shit, Mom," I said, sitting up to stare at her. "Are you *dying*?"

She smacked my knee. "No! I was trying to be profound," she said, laughing. "You're ruining it."

"I always wondered where Bex got her propensity for whacking me in my limbs," Nick said, then he rapped twice on the doorjamb. "Knock, knock. Sorry to interrupt. Nancy, do you, ah, know anything about knitting?"

"A little," she said. "What's the problem?"

He held out a gnarled mess of yarn. "I'm wondering about my next step here."

Her brow furrowed. "Is it...an intestine?"

Nick looked at it. "Perhaps it is now," he said. "It meant to be a sweater."

Mom snickered. "Maybe we all have something we need to let go," she murmured to me. Louder, she said, "Come downstairs and let me dig up some of my mother's old books. Join us, Bex?"

I shook my head. "I'm going to marinate in here for a bit," I said.

"Don't stay too long," Nick said. "Your mum made a tuna noodle casserole and I've no idea what that is but I can't wait."

"I'll be down in a minute," I said.

As their footsteps faded, I lay back down on the floor and stared up at the ceiling, which still had some of those glow-in-the-dark star stickers that stop working almost immediately and yet never let you peel them off. Lacey and I had invented a game where we shot rubber bands at them for points; you could still see some faint scuffmarks from our misses.

My hand groped around and closed on the ponytail holder on the carpet beside me. I cocked it with my fingers, closed one eye, and zeroed in on the smallest star in my roof galaxy.

"For the win," I intoned, and let it fly. It glanced off the target and dropped gracefully to the floor next to me.

"Bull's-eye," I said. "Still a killer marksman."

Killer. There he was again. He would always be there.

But then my hand fell onto my stomach, and a wave of emotion knocked my eyes shut. Nick's face, when the last round hadn't worked, was absolutely ashen. And a few days later, while hunting for a phone-charging cable, I'd found those same chipper pamphlets in his bedside table. He'd been to Dr. Akhtar on his own. He was curious.

Maybe he was having second thoughts, too.

CHAPTER TWO

The rest of the holidays in Iowa were, by and large, idyllic. We had a huge dump of snow on Christmas Eve, and Nick made two snowmen that he decorated to look like me and Lacey. We ordered takeout from some of the restaurants we'd passed on the way into town—the bread taco was a huge hit—and did puzzles, played games, and watched an endless string of *Jeopardy!* and *Wheel of Fortune* (Nick developed a real fondness for the phrase *Potent Potables*). It was as screamingly American as we could make it, relaxed and festive and fun—but as our departure date inched closer, our moods slowly darkened around the edges, as if we knew we were fighting off an inevitable sorrow.

Nick curled up and slept for most of the flight home—or at least, I assume he did, because he donned an enormous sleep mask that made him look like Kanye West during that one really bad eyewear phase. I stared out the window and tossed around every possible way I could think of to tell my husband that we might need to take his swimmers out of the pool. (I had rejected that exact phrasing.)

In the end, I didn't have to. We arrived home, jet-lagged and unkempt, and immediately padded into our expansive yellow kitchen. The staff was still on holiday, so Nick made himself a peanut butter sandwich and then stood at the marble island, staring at it, his face unspeakably glum.

"I want this family so badly, Bex," he blurted. "I always imagined us having an entire houseful of kids. Four or five of them, running around and screaming and sliding down the banister. Playing loud games. Eating peanut butter sandwiches I'd made them on picnics. Breaking antiques. Chasing the dog."

"We don't have a dog," I said.

"And we don't have the children, either, and it hurts," he said. "We've tried so hard. I want to be the one. I want it so much. I want them to be mine, but..."

I came around the kitchen island and hopped onto the barstool next to him. "All of our children will be yours," I said. "One way or another. You know that, right?"

"I do, and I don't, and I do," he nattered, picking up the sandwich and then putting it down again. "I've never felt more hamstrung in my life. We can't keep on as we have been, but the alternative..."

"If the alternative makes you unhappy, then we can totally keep on," I said. "Maybe one of them will take."

"No," Nick said. "Your body has been through too much for us to keep doing things we know will fail. You're a person, not a broodmare. It's not 1592."

"But apparently 1592 isn't that different from now, in this one specific way," I said. "There are rules."

He picked at the crust. "I wish we could tell them all to stuff their rules," he said. "Or pack everything and leave. For real, not just to faff about in Scotland in wigs until something forces us back. Have a baby or not. Adopt five kids. Live in that Von Trapp house in Sweden. I'd get a whistle, and you'd learn the guitar."

"It's a really great fantasy," I said gently. "But it is a fantasy."

He pulled up a barstool and sat, poking a finger rudely into the center of his sandwich.

"I thought about this a lot, too, over our break," I admitted. "I was pretty messed up about it when we first got there, actually. But Mom and I had a big talk, and it changed my perspective a little. Like, we wouldn't think twice about this if all...*that*...hadn't happened, right? We'd have used Freddie in a heartbeat."

"But all that *did* happen," Nick said. He sounded so tired. "And it finds a way to keep reminding me that it happened. I've tried to have perspective. I've tried to remind myself that this baby would be made out of our love even if it's not out of our genes. If you borrow a cup of sugar from your neighbor to make a cake, that doesn't make it *his* cake. I'd be the one rubbing lotion on your belly and massaging your feet, and holding your hand when you're in labor, and getting up in the middle of the night, and changing diapers, and walking that baby to her first day of school. I would be Dad. Freddie would just be helping us figure out how to get her here. I know all of this is true, but..." He gulped air. "I've recited those things to myself every day since the last try didn't work. But I'm not sure yet if I believe them."

"You are one of the most loving people I have ever known, and, not for nothing, we are both stubborn as hell," I said, twining our fingers. "I do not see us letting all that psychological shit win. I really don't."

"You seem awfully confident," he said. "I wish it could be that easy for me."

"Do you think this is easy for me?" I asked. "Because it's not. It's brutal. But this is a tipping point, Nick." I caught his gaze and held it. "We will always remember this conversation. We will always remember what we decided tonight. If Eleanor's rules are writing this story, which ending can you live with?"

Nick poked another finger into his sandwich, then prodded at it until the first two had a frown arcing underneath them. Then he stared at me, and in that look, his melancholy gave way to a sort of determination.

"I want to believe in myself the way that you believe in me," he finally said. "Call him."

Nick and I were coming home from a meeting with Bea the following month when Freddie came running up to us in the courtyard, flushed but handsome in a blue suit.

"Hi," he said. "I saw you out my window. Do you two have a moment to talk? It won't take long."

Nick and I exchanged glances. We'd begun the day at Dr. Akhtar's office, where I'd had another of what felt like an endless series of blood tests—this time to see if Freddie had been able to get the job done where Nick had not. Sometimes it seemed like I must have given all the blood I'd ever had in my body.

"You can't go back on it now, mate," Nick said, with a jocularity that sounded forced to all of us. "It's a done deal. We're just waiting to see if it worked."

Freddie flushed hugely. "Right, right. I lost track of the timing there a bit." He nodded aimlessly. "But I, um. It's not that. It's about me. I mean, I know that's also...sort of. Anyway, it's not about the baby."

"Why don't we go inside?" I suggested.

"Yeah, this isn't a conversation I really want to have in the courtyard," Freddie said.

"You're making me nervous," Nick said as we clattered up the steps and into Apartment 1A, as neat as a pin and smelling like cinnamon rolls.

"No, no," Freddie said. "It's not bad news! Is there somewhere we can be private? I don't want the staff to overhear any of this."

"Of course," Nick said, shooting me a quizzical glance. The conversation I'd had with Freddie formally asking him for his help had been brief, and kind, and a bit fraught, all adjectives that could describe every chat we'd had since. I had no idea where this was going. Not even a hint.

We stepped into Nick's office, cozy and warm. Someone, in preparation for our return, had lit a fire in the grate, and it crackled in welcome. Out the window, I could see that it looked like snow.

Freddie closed the door tightly and turned to us.

"You should sit down," he said.

"Why all the cloak-and-dagger?" Nick said as we took spots on his sofa. "Are you going back into active duty?"

Freddie gave a wry smile. "In a sense." He picked up a poker and prodded the fire, then hung it up and turned in our direction, without actually looking at either of us. "I wanted you to be the first to know—well, actually, the second and third, or rather, the sixth and seventh, if we're really being specific about order here, *eighth* if you include me, which I hadn't been..."

"Fred!" I clapped my hands. "Get to the point!"

"I've asked Daphne to marry me and she's accepted," Freddie said, in a rat-a-tat rush.

I felt as if I'd taken leave of my own body and was watching this conversation from somewhere twenty feet above the three of us, next to one of the lions carved into the paneled wood ceiling. Nick said nothing. Freddie looked between us both, back and forth, over and over, and said nothing.

"You're not kidding," Nick said. It wasn't a question.

"Deadly serious, Knickers. It's my turn to marry the heir," Freddie said, attempting levity, but faltering at the crushed look on Nick's face.

"Is this because of Father?" Nick demanded.

Freddie looked taken aback. "What? No. Of course not. Why would it be?"

Nick spread his hands out, as if this should be obvious. "Father started all this, back at the state dinner. I'm sure he's delighted, but you can't live your life to impress him, Freddie, he doesn't care about anybody but—"

"It's not Father," Freddie interrupted. "That's absurd."

"Then what?" Nick asked, standing up, then sitting down again. "Is it me? Is it *this*?"

He gestured at me, and I saw his lip tremble.

Freddie paled, but his smile didn't falter. "No," he said. "Absolutely not. It's *me*. I chose this. It's what I want. Clive got his scoop after all, in the end." He laughed, but it was hollow.

"Clive," Nick barked, "is absolutely the wrong reason to do this."

"Leave it out, Knickers, it was a joke," Freddie said. He started worrying at his tie, finally managing to loosen it. "This is good news. I thought you'd be happy."

"Good news? This is *madness*," Nick said.

"No," Freddie said firmly. "It's sensible, is what it is."

"*Sensible*," Nick repeated. "How romantic."

"The pressure of royal life is never going to be too much for Daphne," Freddie continued. "My family is never going to be too complicated or too overwhelming or too confusing for her. This"—and here, he mimicked Nick's gesture at my body—"will never confuse her. It's easy. It's so *easy*."

"King of the Netherlands," Nick said softly, shaking his head.

"King consort," Freddie corrected him. "Prince consort? I'm not sure how the Netherlands works."

"Which is why this is an absolutely ridiculous notion," Nick said. "Of all the women to marry in haste, a crown princess seems like the recipe for the biggest possible disaster." He rose again now, and started to pace.

"It's hardly haste. We know each other very well, and occasionally we've..." Freddie flushed. "You know. It's not out of nowhere. I've thought it through. I've done nothing but think about this for ages."

"You can't have done, or else you'd have seen reason," Nick said. "Don't do this. You don't need to do this."

"It's done," Freddie said quietly. "Hax gave me his blessing last night." He smiled joylessly. "Daphne was person number three to find out. Lax had been eavesdropping in the next room. You should've heard her shriek."

Nick barely seemed to hear. "You swore we wouldn't lose you," he said. "Is that not as important to you?"

"It's vital to me." Freddie's voice was strained.

"But you've chosen the path most likely to make that happen, and for what? Someone you don't even love?" Nick asked. "You'll be gone. You can't live here and live there. It'll have to be there."

"I realize that."

Nick looked at me, then back at his brother. "Did you know you were going to do this when you agreed to help us? Is it why you agreed?" He looked down at the floor for a moment. "I'm so sorry, Freddie. I know what you want me to say but I just can't do it."

Flustered, he turned on his heel and left. Freddie ran his hands over his face, then flopped into the tapestry-covered wing chair by the fire. "That went brilliantly. How about removing my wisdom teeth without anesthesia next?" He frowned at me. "You could've backed me up there, you know."

"I was not about to butt into that," I said.

"Are you going to butt in now?" he asked huffily.

"Hell yeah," I said. "Come on, you must have expected this, or you wouldn't have been so wigged out about telling us. You kept saying the two of you weren't even dating!"

Freddie picked at a loose thread in the chair. "What even is dating in this day and age?"

"Are you seriously making jokes right now? You asked her to marry you!" I squawked. "What is that even based on?"

"Fine," Freddie said. "Officially, you're right, we never had any kind of Define the Relationship conversation before now, and we haven't seen each other *regularly*, exactly…"

I made a skeptical noise in spite of myself.

"*But,*" Freddie continued pointedly, "what we have been doing is lovely. She is lovely."

I covered my face with my hands. "Lovely isn't love. It's not even lust."

"But lovely is stable," Freddie said. "Lovely is sustainable. Lovely is safe, and that's how we make each other feel."

"This is crazy, Freddie. You're only thirty years old. You can't marry someone out of pragmatism!" I told him.

Freddie threw his hands up. "The entire bloody monarchy is based on pragmatic marriages," he argued. "Besides, it's Daphne. We like Daphne."

"But *you're* supposed to *love* Daphne." I balled my hands into fists and kneaded my thighs. "This is unfair to her. Even if you don't think you deserve more, you know she does."

Freddie leapt out of the armchair. "More than what? More than horrid old me? More than my fidelity forever? More than my willing-ness to give up my entire life here?" he said hotly. "She knows where I stand. She chose me anyway. She knows that I mean it when I say that I'll devote my whole self to making her happy."

"At the expense of your own heart," I said. "Freddie, this won't work. It never does."

"With all due respect, Bex, how the hell would you know? You've never had to try it."

We stared at each other for a beat.

"I would have done this even if you'd had seven babies without my help," Freddie continued, more calmly now. "It will give me my own family, children, a purpose. That should be more than enough for my heart. Besides, if you think about it, I've been in training for this my whole life."

"To be the de facto king of the Netherlands?" I asked.

"To support the heir to the throne," he said gently. "If there's anything I have experience doing, it's that." He drew a shaky breath. "I loved you, Bex. I may even still love you. I will probably always love you. But I learned the hard way that my brother is the real love of my life, and I think we are all fooling ourselves that he'll have an easy time of it if you turn out to be pregnant and I'm right here. Gran called that an elegant solution, and I've found a way to go one better. We can all win." His voice quieted. "Me included."

Desperately, I grabbed his hand and looked up at him pleadingly.

"It's not too late," I begged him. "Hold out. Find a love that shakes your world."

"I tried that, Bex," Freddie said. "But there is a finite amount of you in the universe." He dropped his eyes. "Please, Killer," he whispered to the floor. "Just this once, I'd like to get the girl."

I dropped his hand like a hot potato.

Freddie turned and grabbed his jacket, swinging it over his shoulder. He paused as he walked past me, and then, as if for the last time, bent down and kissed me on the top of my head.

"Good luck, Bex," he said. "I hope we all get what we need."

He left, and I sat there, staring out the paned doors onto the garden and beyond. Worrying about Nick. Worrying about Freddie. Wondering if Daphne, Freddie's insistence aside, knew that she'd said yes to being someone's safety pick. Wondering if, in the end, it even mattered. When the phone buzzed on the arm of my chair, I didn't even look, just lifted it to my ear in a trance. I don't remember saying hello. I don't remember what, exactly, Dr. Akhtar said. But when we hung up, my arm fell to my lap, my phone tumbling to the floor.

"I'm pregnant," I said, to the empty room.

CHAPTER THREE

A nd *then* the makeup artist got powder all over my beard," Freddie said. "I looked like a very sad Santa impersonator."

"Poor thing was mortified," Daphne said, sticking her head into the FaceTime frame and giving me a little wave. "Her hands were shaking so hard."

"I have that effect," Freddie said. "I can't help it. I'm magnetic."

"Obviously," I snorted.

"We took one like that for posterity," he said. "If we draw a little hat on it, it could be our Christmas card."

"Always thinking ahead," Daphne said. "But turn your phone around and show Bex those paintings, Freddie. She'd much rather see the art than our faces."

"Nonsense, you *are* the art," he said theatrically. "My beautiful bride."

Daphne beamed at him moonily. Freddie was really committing to this. And thank goodness for that, because tomorrow, the press and the public would find out that Prince Frederick had placed King Hendrik-Alexander's mother's engagement ring—an orange tourmaline evoking the Dutch national color—on the Princess of Orange's finger. The UK's third in line to the throne now essentially belonged to the kingdom of the Netherlands.

I leaned in to try to see more details over their shoulders.

"Your palace is stunning, Daphne," I said. "How do you not spend all day sitting in the middle of the floor? I wish I could climb through the screen. It makes me want to paint *right now*."

Daphne grabbed the phone from Freddie and turned it on the Huis ten Bosch ballroom. The paneled walls and arches of the odd-shaped room were covered floor to ceiling with seventeenth-century paintings, with an octagonal viewing gallery in the center designed to let in light from the heavens. It was incredible, like living inside every piece of art all at once, and it was largely unknown because it wasn't open to the public—but it would go down in history now as the site of Freddie's and Daphne's engagement portraits.

"We'll sneak you in when you come for the wedding," Daphne said. "If not sooner, perhaps? I suspect my parents will be planning a ridiculous number of events."

"Lax loves a good party," came Freddie's voice from off camera.

"And why one, when there can be ten," Daphne joked.

"When will you both come back here so I can hug you?" I asked.

"Daphne's here for the foreseeable," Freddie said. "But I'll darken your doorstep on Wednesday. I'll be going back and forth for ages, trying to reassure all my patronages that I'm not pissing off into the sunset forever."

"No one thinks that," I said.

"From your lips to Knickers's ears," Freddie said, then he caught himself, and blanched. "Please tell me he's not standing off camera."

"He is downstairs knitting something undefinable that you should both hope is not a wedding present," I said. "But if he knew you were going to call, he'd have come up to say hi. We're both impatient to celebrate with you properly."

Nick had actually started to walk in, and then walked right back out when he heard Freddie's voice. I'd let him. His Aggressively Pleasant face had been getting a workout lately and it was due for a rest; he'd been feeling his brother's daily absence even more keenly than when Freddie was in the military—this was less deadly, yes, but potentially more permanent. But after a few perambulations around our garden the day Freddie told us, he'd gone in search of his brother to express his support and erase some of the sting of his first reaction. Especially in light of Freddie's huge favor to us.

"The last time I buried my real feelings about Freddie's decision making, it poisoned us all," he'd told me. "I'm glad I was honest. But now I have to make sure he still feels his family in his life, so that no matter what happens, he knows he'll always have a home here." He'd shot me a helpless look. "If you'd told me as a boy that my relationship with Freddie would be the one that demanded the toughest balancing act, I'd have told you to get stuffed."

Daphne brought me back into the present. "Have you had your appointment yet, Bex?" she asked, affixing a look of casual interest onto her face. "That's today, yes?"

"Ah, yes, it's, um, in about twenty minutes actually," I said. "I didn't know you—"

"Of course he told me," she said. "We're getting married. No secrets."

I opened my mouth to let fly a sarcastic rejoinder, but thought better of it, and bit it back. Daphne wasn't a sarcastic person. She couldn't have meant that as a jab at my own premarital skeletons. Her tone was pleasant, but I could see tension at the edges of her eyes, and then I felt guilty. This situation was emotionally complicated for her, too.

"I'll let you both know how it goes," I said. "Talk to you soon. Have fun today."

I disconnected the call and stared at the blank, dark screen, in which I could see a faint reflection of myself. It reminded me of the windows that night at The Shard, when Eleanor had first fallen ill, and again on the train, where I had stood staring fruitlessly out into the growing dark as hidden scenery sped past us. So much gazing into the unknown.

Maybe I had been going about this all wrong. In judging Freddie's rapport with Daphne, I'd been searching for a familiar love in his face—a heat and a depth of yearning that resembled the way he'd looked at me, as if that were a benchmark by which all his feelings should be measured. But that passion had also been peppered with guilt and torment, a pleasure that could only also bring him pain. None of that was in his eyes with Daphne, because it didn't exist with her. She didn't come with the dark side. Their relationship was fresh, untarnished, uncomplicated.

Heat is wonderful, until it burns you.

⁂

The nurses at Dr. Akhtar's clinic knew me well by now. Cycle after cycle, I'd come in every two days to get my egg production checked, to make sure everything was proceeding according to plan. We'd made small talk. I'd learned about their own kids, their spouses, the one who was in a complicated throuple with her former neighbors. They treated me like I was a regular person, rather than some fancy royal personage, and were masterful at making me feel their support even when they couldn't explicitly say it. But when Nick and I walked into the office that afternoon, all the greetings were strictly professional. No one met our eyes.

I knew why. My blood draws had shown the pregnancy hormone level was rising the way it should have, but we'd had this happen once before in our long string of attempts, and the egg that had burrowed into me turned out to be an empty circle. Another victory turned into a loss. Nobody wanted to trade in false hope.

I got undressed and draped my bottom half in the weird half-ply tissue paper they use at doctors' offices. It scrunched and crunched underneath me as I scooted back onto the examination table and put my feet in the stirrups, Nick assuming his familiar position near my head. I stared at the industrial ceiling. One panel was stained, as if someone crawling around in the vents had spilled a coffee.

"I'm scared," I whispered. "I don't feel pregnant. I'm not peeing all the time. My boobs feel fine. What if there's nothing there?" A tear rolled down my cheek. "I don't know if I can take that."

His hand found mine. We didn't say another word. Not when the tech came in, not when the wand for the vaginal ultrasound went in, not when the photo of my womb filled up the screen.

It wasn't empty.

Far from it.

Within seconds Dr. Akhtar burst in, as if she'd been waiting on the other side, and grinned broadly when she saw the monitor. "Will you look at that," she said.

"Twins," I breathed.

"Identical ones, it seems," she said, zooming in. We could barely make out two little zigzags inside. "There's a membrane between them, but they're sharing a placenta." She took control of the wand from the tech. "Do you want to hear them?"

"So soon?" I stammered.

"Occasionally," she said. "Let me just...ah, yes, there." A wet pulsing sound came through the speakers. "That's Baby A," she said. "And that..." She moved, and the noise was replaced by another one. "Is Baby B. Two babies, two heartbeats."

"Double trouble," Nick said, gazing in awe at them, then at me.

I covered my mouth with my hands. "Hi, babies," I cooed. "I hear you. Loud and clear."

"Get used to loud," Dr. Akhtar said. "It's going to be the norm for pretty much the rest of your life now." She took a few screen grabs and then hit print. "Congratulations. You'll come back every two weeks for a bit to make sure everything looks good in there, and then we'll turn you back over to an OB. But for now, after we take your blood again, you can go home and put your feet up and look at your first baby pictures."

She handed us a stack of small square black-and-white images from the printer. One of them, magnified perfectly, showed the tiniest margins of bodies, curled up and facing each other like minuscule versions of me and Lacey when we'd crawl into one bed and whisper to each other by flashlight when we should have been sleeping.

The door clicked behind Dr. Akhtar, and Nick helped me off the bench and wrapped his arms around me. His tears fell in my hair.

"Are they good tears?" I whispered. "Are *you* good?"

Nick pulled away, beaming. "I am so good," he said. "I wish I'd had more faith in myself. The minute I saw them on the screen, all cuddled up, I couldn't imagine how I ever thought..." His voice thickened. "We did it. We're going to be parents. *We* are," he said pointedly.

Relief flooded me. "We're going to be really awesome parents," I said.

We stared at each other for a moment, dumbstruck smiles on our faces, then simultaneously reached out and knocked on the faux wood panel on the exam table. Then we both giggled.

"Superstition," Nick said. "I can't help it."

"I know. But I love you," I said. "I love them. Let's be hopeful this time. And I really need to put my pants back on, because my butt is getting cold."

Nick laughed. "We'd better make a note to give Freddie a spectacular wedding gift. A silver chafing dish is not going to cut it."

"Would he like a house in Sweden, do you think?" I wondered, doing up my pants very carefully over my stomach, as if the babies (the babies!) might be disturbed by an overly aggressive zip. "I guess he's going to end up with a lot of houses, though."

"We can percolate that," Nick said. "But there is one fairly serious thing we do need to do first, and right now." He held open his arms. "Rebecca Porter, may I, at very long last, have this twirl?"

I felt my face crumple in on itself, but this time—maybe for the first time—it was with joy. Tears streamed down my cheeks as Nick tenderly picked me up and spun me once, twice, three times, before setting me back gracefully on my feet.

"There," he said, taking my face in his hands and kissing me, before smoothing away my tears with his thumbs. "Now it's official. We're having a baby. Two babies."

"Two down, three to go," I joked.

Nick laughed. "I knew you'd come around," he said, then tugged at my ponytail. "Come on," he said. "Let's take the three of you home."

The reaction to Freddie's betrothal was—predictably—gigantic. Bloggers were instantly obsessed with Daphne; a new fashion site had already been started called Daphne's Diary, and the teal dress she wore for their engagement photo shoot sold out in six and a half minutes. It wasn't surprising that everyone had caught, as *Vanity Fair* had put it, "Tulip Fever": On paper, Freddie and Daphne were the platonic ideal of a sweeping love story, the wayward prince and the reclusive princess bringing each other out of the darkness. Daphne looked fragile but beautiful in the pictures, and Freddie looked dashing and strong, like he'd just parked his white stallion around the corner.

Of course, *The Sun*'s headline two days after the announcement had been BITTER BEX BANS DARLING DAPH FROM PALACE. Clive's accompanying article—while smugly reminding readers who'd nailed the scoop in the first place—speculated that Nick was enraged because once the wedding took place, Freddie would outrank him, at least until Nick took the throne himself. Quite a few reporters had made note of this technicality, in fact: Freddie *was* leaping up from "spare" status, and while Nick was not fussed about having to deploy a bow now and then to his younger brother, Freddie was overwhelmed by the pace of his own version of my duchess training.

"I don't know how you did it, Bex," he said, flopping onto our sofa one afternoon and clanking his feet up onto the coffee table. He was back in London after a few weeks of whirlwind events and meetings in The Hague. "It's endless. I wish I'd paid attention in school when we learned about the Netherlands."

"At least you don't need to be taught how to get out of a car without flashing anyone," I said.

"Yes, but you weren't asked to learn a totally different language," Freddie retorted, patting at his breast pocket, and eventually taking out his silver-plated cigarette case. "Dutch is impossible. So many Js."

"*Still* smoking?" I asked. "How stressed are you?"

Freddie tapped the cigarette case against the pile of art books on top of the coffee table. "It helps me study. Don't worry, I won't smoke in here."

"I should hope not," I said, pointing at my slightly distended belly. At just shy of twelve weeks, I definitely didn't look pregnant yet, as much as like I'd eaten several more doughnuts than usual. Although that was also true. "How long are you back?"

Freddie's eyes went to my stomach and then back down at the art books. "Forty-eight hours," he said. "Cilla's been run ragged trying to get me in with as many of my patronages as possible. Apparently, Bea was on at her about being very clear that I'm not—how did she put it? Totally abandoning my country."

Bea's reaction to Freddie's engagement had mirrored ours: abject shock, smothered by appropriate congratulatory words and then a lot of frowning.

"I always assumed he was going to run off with a cocktail waitress," she had confessed to me. "I don't have a binder for this one."

To Freddie, I cracked, "Lady Bollocks is gonna Lady Bollocks."

He shook his head, looking suddenly tired. "No, I can read between Bea's lines. She's cross," he said. "I'd hoped she'd be happy for me, even if I did fire her. She willed this into existence, after all. I made a correct woman out of her." He scratched his head. "At least Cilla and Gaz are on my side."

The sound Gaz had made when Freddie told him was the exact same one you make when your friend who was supposed to bring drinks to the party shows up with nonalcoholic beer, and I was glad it had escaped Freddie's notice. "Everyone is on your side," I said. "We're just going to miss you."

Freddie nodded. "I'll miss you, too," he said, and the nakedness of it washed over his face for a second before he almost literally shrugged it off. "The Netherlands is beautiful, though. Far less air pollution."

"Says the man holding cigarettes," I noted.

"Well, I've got to ease my poor lungs into it, you know," he said. "Can't go cold turkey on deadly particles." He smirked at me. "Though there are loads of other legal things over there that are probably terrible for me."

I laughed and tossed a velvet pillow at him. "Don't be childish, Frederick."

"Excellent," Freddie said, plucking the pillow deftly out of the air and tucking it behind his head. "You already sound like a mum. Do another one. Tell me not to sniff glue or something."

I threw another pillow. "Too late, I think."

"Cripes!" He ducked. "How many pillows do you have over there?"

"We bought an arsenal because we knew she'd need something to hurl during Cubs games," Nick said, strolling in from the foyer. "And, of course, at idiots."

Freddie smiled tentatively. "You'll have to have Gaz over twice as often once I'm gone to keep your throwing arm from atrophying."

"Or, you could visit often."

We all let that sit there. Nick loosened his tie and bent over my lap.

"Hello, babies," he said. "How's Tuesday treated you so far? How many pancakes have you eaten today?"

"About seventy-four," I said. As someone who generally preferred waffles, this was a very surreal pregnancy side effect.

"You can't call them *babies*. You need to try out names," Freddie said. "Like…Fred and George, after the Weasleys."

"What if they're girls?" I asked.

"Fredwina, then. Beautiful name," he teased. "Ooh, or even better, sell the rights to a charity. Meet Her Royal Highness the Princess British Equine Veterinary Association and her sister the Princess Shark Guardian."

"Helpful as ever," Nick said. "I thought you were at The Hague learning about the Dutch parliament."

"I'm bicoastal," Freddie boasted. "Or, bi-country, at least for a bit longer. But I'm here on official business." He leaned forward and placed his elbows on his knees, and I could see him go tense. "I know it's expected that you'll stand up with me at the wedding, Knickers, but I don't want you to be there just for ritual. It would mean a great deal to have you there with me, and so I would still like to ask, officially, if you would do me that honor."

Freddie looked so nervous, as if he thought Nick might actually say no. Instead, I watched Nick all but melt at the thought that his brother—after all this—thought he'd ever tell him to go it alone.

"Of course I will," he said, sticking out his hand in the manner of a dude who isn't sure if it's hugging time or not. "I'd turn up next to you even if you hadn't asked. There is nowhere else I'd want to be."

As they shook, Freddie's face flooded with relief, and he pulled Nick into a hug.

"Thank you," he said. "The whole thing is very nerve-racking. Fortunately, all I really have to say in Dutch is *ja*," he said. "It will be a little odd to be married in a ceremony I cannot totally understand. Good thing they're all pretty much the same, right? Love, honor, etc. Various pledges of troth."

Nick and I exchanged a glance, which Freddie intercepted. "Don't," he said. "That wasn't me being blasé. You can't second-guess everything I say about this for the rest of my life."

"We know, we promise. You're right." Nick pulled at his hair. "You wouldn't be spending hours with a Dutch tutor if you weren't serious. You didn't even do your schoolwork when you were in actual school."

"*Dank je*," Freddie said. "That's Dutch for 'thank you.' See? I'm very committed to this. We need to get it done before the babies arrive."

"Freddie," I said, "I'm not going to be housebound forever after the babies come. Or, worst-case, Nick can hold up a big iPad and FaceTime me in."

"No," Freddie said. "I don't want to wait any longer than I already am. What's that old line from *When Harry Met Sally*? When you figure out the rest of your life, you want it to happen as soon as possible?"

"Since when are you watching *When Harry Met Sally*?" I asked.

Freddie shrugged. "Marj and I watched a lot of rom-coms over the years." He stood up and stretched. "Right, I'm off to talk to Father about boring logistical issues regarding what I have to give up and what I don't. Anyone want to join?"

"Tempting, but I've got to make breakfast for dinner," Nick said. "I can't tell if they're real cravings, or whims."

"As long as that's healthy for my nieces and/or nephews," Freddie said, crossing the room to squeeze my shoulder on his way out. "Little Prince Sun Pat Peanut Butter and Prince Flora Margarine."

"What happened to naming them after charities?" I asked.

"More sponsorship money in corporate Britain," he said, and with a jaunty wave, he strolled out and banged shut our front door.

All this engagement fuss did give me a convenient shield from public scrutiny as I waited nervously for a safe end to my first trimester. The only people who knew about the pregnancy were Lacey, my mom, and Freddie and Daphne. The Porter side of the equation had been rapturous; Freddie and Daphne had been vocally and facially and in all other outward ways relieved and pleased, the former probably in part because he didn't want to give any more samples than necessary, and the latter . . . probably for a similar reason. But as the twelve-week mark drew nearer, Nick and I began to feel guilty keeping a secret this big from the one person who was the most obsessed with what it meant to history, even if we knew that same person would gloat mercilessly about how she'd solved the problem. So we invited ourselves to tea to give the Queen the news in person.

When we arrived, though, we found Eleanor's door closed and guarded by Richard's chief of staff, Barnes. He was holding a rolled-up copy of a newspaper in his hand, and his toupee was a tad askew.

"We have an appointment with my grandmother," Nick said.

"You'll need to wait," he said. "His Royal Highness and Her Majesty are having a private conversation."

" . . . need I remind you that you are still married?" came Eleanor's voice through the door. Even Barnes raised his brows. "You are not legally free to be cavorting about London with some gold-digging socialite."

Nick's eyes were wide. "What's going on?" he asked Barnes.

In a wordless huff, Barnes handed Nick the paper. I peered over Nick's shoulder at the front page of the *Evening Standard*.

ROYAL ROMANCE IS CONTAGIOUS

Freddie's Not the Only One Catching Feelings

Prince Richard has been bitten by the love bug.

As his younger son prepares to marry the Princess of Orange, the Prince of Wales's customary Range Rover was spotted idling outside The Goring Hotel, where it picked up socialite Jane Archibald-Jones and drove them to a private dinner at Soho House. She returned to her hotel in the early morning hours, alone, after a lengthy stop at Clarence House.

Archibald-Jones, 58 and thrice divorced, had been living on the Continent until the dissolution of her last marriage. Richard himself, troublingly for the Palace, is still wed; this marks the first time romantic rumors have surfaced about him since it was revealed that his wife, Emma, Princess of Wales, has been debilitated by mental illness. It's not known how or when Prince Richard and Jane connected, but royal watchers of a certain age will recall that Jane's daughter was one of the young brides-maids in the Prince's wedding to Emma...

"I was not cavorting. We simply ate dinner," Richard boomed as we read.

"Yes, and then had a very leisurely nightcap, it sounds like," Eleanor said. "We all know what that means, Richard."

Next to me, Nick closed his eyes. "I wish we'd gotten here fifteen minutes later," he said.

The door to her quarters burst open and the Queen herself stuck her head out into the hallway. "Stop lurking, Nicholas, and come in."

"I really can't see that this is any of their business," Richard said, from his spot on the silk sofa. Both his arms and legs were crossed.

"I'm not going to leave them skulking about the hallway," Eleanor snapped as she sat back down in her armchair. "Besides, luncheon is about to arrive. I thought perhaps sushi?" she said, peering at me. "Some very soft Brie?"

"Sounds great," I chirped. There was no way Eleanor had ordered sushi. She once told me that the idea of placing raw fish in her mouth was as appealing as being forced to catch it herself.

"I should be off, then," Richard said.

"No," Eleanor said, turning back to him. "We're not through discussing this."

"There is nothing to discuss," Richard said. "The last time I checked, it's completely acceptable to have dinner with whomever I like."

Eleanor picked up her own copy of the *Evening Standard* and peered at the photo they'd run of Jane. She was attractive in an earthy way, and was apparently an accomplished equestrian. She'd also been nicknamed Pain Jane for the amount that men and women alike were drawn to her despite their other attachments.

"She's always been trouble," Eleanor said. "Didn't her previous husband work for Putin?"

Richard rolled his eyes. "No, Mother," he said. "Pucci."

Eleanor shrugged as if this were mostly the same thing.

Richard stood up. "I cannot believe you're angry about my having dinner with an old friend," he said. "This is controlling even for you."

"She's an addict. She can't help but shop," Eleanor snapped. "It's one thing to socialize with her at an event, but this cozy public dinner, then taking her home with you? Ending up in the paper? It's unbecoming."

Nick flinched with his whole body. I found myself pretending to be entranced by a figurine of a shepherdess on the side table to my right.

"Unbecoming?" Richard echoed. "I've never done anything unbecoming in public in my life. I never even tried to remarry because you said it was inappropriate with the boys so young. Then you said it was inappropriate after we told the truth about Emma. *Then* you told me it was inappropriate after the wedding, when Christiane was supporting me during the trauma this one caused." He pointed at me.

"The Greek monarchy disgraced itself," Eleanor sniffed. "You can't be part of that."

"And now Christiane is engaged to be married to that prat who keeps saying he's descended from Napoleon, and I"—and here, he had the good grace to look melancholy—"am still married to a woman who hasn't spoken to me or recognized my face for half my life."

"You said it, Richard," Eleanor said. "You *are* still married."

"Then let me divorce."

"Never," Eleanor said.

"Gran—" Nick interjected.

"Absolutely not."

"Twenty-five years without a partner," Richard said, "is a bloody long time, Mother, and I think the public might support me. Did you ever think of that?"

Eleanor sighed deeply and pressed on her closed eyelids. "The public," she said slowly, "does not want its future king drooling around the singles scene like a bulldog in heat. It invites scrutiny, and it will diminish the monarchy if you have an active personal life playing out in front of them like a tawdry little television drama."

Richard's color was high. "You would prefer I had flings in dark corners? You are colder than I thought."

"What you do in private is your affair," Eleanor said. "Carrying on in public…"

"*Dinner is not carrying on,*" Richard said, an octave higher than usual. "Why are you doing this? Is it because you're bitter that you've lived so long without affection, and so you're consigning me to the same fate? Well, congratulations. You wore the crown alone. Let me know when history gives you a medal for that." He angrily buttoned his blazer. "But I'm not a priest. And I'm certainly not celibate. You may not have needs, but I do."

"Please no," Nick muttered.

"Neediness is a fatal flaw," Eleanor said stubbornly.

"I have always done what you've asked. And all it's ever brought me is more demands. I'm tired of it," Richard said. "Go bother Agatha about using Tinder to date half this town, and leave me alone."

And with that, he stormed out and slammed the door.

"My word," Eleanor said. "I thought sixty was past the adolescent tantrum stage." She pushed a minute silver bell wired to the coffee table. "I need a glass of wine, don't you?"

"Gran, perhaps he's right," Nick said.

She fixed an eye on Nick. "You want him to divorce your poor mother?"

"Please don't use her mental state against me," Nick warned. "She'll be my mother forever, but she hasn't been his wife in a long time."

The door opened. Eleanor held up a hand to Nick as two footmen rolled in a square dining table outfitted with three silver-domed place settings. They lifted the cloches to reveal three individual shepherd's pies in ceramic ramekins.

"What, no sushi?" Eleanor sang at the footmen, who both looked alarmed, because this was the absolute first they'd heard about it. "Ah well, this will do nicely, thank you ever so much."

Nick and I exchanged small grins, which we smothered when Eleanor turned her attention back to us and picked up her delicate gold fork.

"And you two," she said. "How are you?"

"We're great," Nick said, scooping some mashed potato and meat into his mouth.

"Super," I added. "I got a weighted blanket and I've never slept better. I feel so rested."

"You do look good," Eleanor said. "Glowing, even."

"New face serum." I swallowed my bread with an innocent smile. "I'm really racking up my Boots points."

Eleanor blew out a breath through her nose. "Why is everyone being so recalcitrant with me today?" she said. "Are you pregnant or not?"

"Gran!" Nick said. I could tell he was trying not to laugh.

"What?" she said, a look of studied innocence on her face. "I've a vested interest in this, especially now that you've taken my suggestion regarding Frederick."

"He has the biggest mouth. I can't believe he told you that!" I said, dropping my fork with a clatter.

"He didn't," Eleanor said, dabbing at her lips with a cloth napkin. "But you just did. Goodness, you're a bad secret keeper, Rebecca."

"I don't know about *that*," I said, "considering I kept almost my whole first trimester from you."

Eleanor pointed her fork at me. "Don't you dare toy with me, Rebecca. I am an elderly woman."

"And strong as oak," I said. "But you can exhale. It's true."

Eleanor set down her fork and beamed at us. "Congratulations, my darling," she said, the picture of sincere delight, relief, and self-satisfaction. "I knew we could do it."

"And how," I said. "We got a real bargain. Two for the price of one."

She froze. "Twins?"

"Surprise." I could barely contain my glee. "Didn't expect *that*, did you?"

Eleanor blinked very, very slowly, and then picked up her glass of Chardonnay and tilted it toward me. "Bex," she said to me, my nickname sounding so right and wrong all at once on her lips. It was the first time I'd ever heard her say it. "You, my dear, have been nothing but surprises."

CHAPTER FOUR

The first thing I saw at the construction site was a giant sign that read CONGRATS ON YOUR NEW PROJECT next to a photo of two people in construction gear onto which they'd pasted Nick's and my faces. It was hilariously homemade, and heartfelt, and my own heart skipped a beat. It had been a long time since anyone had made such an enthusiastic hand-drawn sign for me in London; maybe since the day of the wedding.

"Are you *crying*?" Eleanor asked, next to me. She was wearing a hat that looked like a purple octopus, and her expression was alarmed.

"No," I said. "Ish. I'm not in control here. You must remember how pregnancy hormones are."

Eleanor eyed me coolly. "I can assure you, Rebecca," she said, "I was always in control."

Rather than breaking out the bullhorn at the more standard twelve weeks, Nick and I let things cook a little longer—partly out of paranoia, partly to let Freddie's news breathe—before announcing that we were expecting twins. The world welcomed this news with wild enthusiasm (and a heavy amount of betting on both gender and names; the current front-runners were Albert and Arthur). Even the online haters had to admit that, no matter how derelict a mother I was destined to be, it was nice when people had babies. We were riding a tidal wave of public warmth, and with Freddie haring off to Europe, Richard and Eleanor doubled down on putting me on display to reassure the United Kingdom that it still had royals putting down roots here. I had wanted more work, and I'd gotten it.

The car door opened and Eleanor slowly disembarked, raising a hand to the assembled masses as a cheer went up. I scooted out behind her as quickly as I could, given that I was four months along and yet already felt like I had a beach ball filled with sand stuffed up under my dress. We walked to a neat construction site ringed with workers in orange jumpsuits, their white hard hats respectfully in hand, the merry sign—onto which someone had also added a baby in a hard hat—waving around behind them.

"Your Majesty. Welcome to the beginning of the Eleanor Line," boomed the mayor of London, an imposing, bloviating sort with hair that looked like it had been cut with a chain saw. He fumbled through the protocols with Eleanor and then shook my hand. He had a surprisingly limp grip. "And, Your Highness, you look just like your portrait," he said. "Spitting image."

I smiled. "Yes, aren't I fortunate?"

"Er, not that I've properly seen it," he admitted. "Popped by the gallery, but it was out for cleaning."

"How thoughtful of them," Eleanor said sweetly, resolutely not looking in my direction. I'd shown her the postcard, listened as she shrieked, watched as she tore it in two.

"Yes, well, you'll want it in tip-top shape for those lovely babies to see someday, eh?" the mayor said. "Oh, that reminds me," he added, summoning a worker, who stepped forward tentatively with two onesies. They bore the unmistakable Tube logo with CLARENCE written where the stop name would be.

"How marvelous!" I said, taking them and holding both over my stomach as best I could. *Click, click.* A perfect sidebar photo for tomorrow's *Daily Mail.* "Thank you!"

"Twice blessed," the mayor said.

"Indeed," Eleanor said. "We are thrilled. Now, tell me more about the Eleanor Line. Will it be the best of them, do you think?"

I bit back a grin and tucked the onesies under my arm. Eleanor never did like to be upstaged, not even by the heirs she'd been so aggro about me providing. But I was outpacing her in gifts, for once in our lives. Since we'd announced my pregnancy, every event I'd done—and I'd done a lot—had come with a trinket, in duplicate, for the forthcoming princes or princesses. Tiny socks, little T-shirts, loads of bibs and blankets and knit caps, almost all of which we would covertly donate to charity, unless they were personalized, in which case we'd tuck them away for posterity (officially—there was no way I wasn't getting photos of the kids in Paint Britain hats, especially now that Richard had brought me back into the fold there and let me be its primary patron).

"These are unreal," I said to Nick, marveling at the canopy and large wheels and brass handle of the matching baby carriages parked in our foyer—a gift from the entire board of the Clarence Foundation. "This feels like something Mary Poppins would've used."

"The Banks children were far too old by the time she got there," Nick said, bouncing one of them up and down as if a real crying baby were inside to soothe.

"Use your imagination," I said. "Margot and Steve would look amazing pushing these through Kensington Gardens."

"Too conspicuous," Nick said. "Also these can't be up to code."

He crouched down and poked at one of the spoked wheels. Nick had read an unending stream of baby books since that first ultrasound, and had taken to doing things like moving me away from air-conditioning vents, in case they were circulating secret asbestos, and making his own binder of baby safety tips and product ratings. It was sweet, and sweetly annoying.

"No, sadly, these will probably end up in a basement waiting for a made-up museum exhibit of things we once used," he said, straightening to a standing position. He started vrooming one of them around in a circle. "Perhaps we could have a bit of fun in the halls with them first. Twin races."

"You're on," I said, grabbing the other one and darting down the corridor. "Last one to the kitchen forfeits naming rights."

"This is a practice round," Nick yelled after me. "Are you supposed to run that fast?"

"Damn right," I called back. "Technically I have six legs now."

Jokes aside, the more *actual* the twins felt, the more I nested, which I had thought was an old wives' tale until I spent an entire afternoon arranging the onesie drawer in the room that was meant to be their nursery. Getting the house ready for the babies, everything folded and tucked in just so, was deeply soothing. All the questions that needed to be answered were nice ones, with no wrong answers—what color would be most restful in their bedroom? Did we want duckies or puppies for the wallpaper trim?—and because we'd decided not to find out the twins' gender (so as not to blurt it out to the press, but also because it seemed like one of the last, great surprises a person might experience), I spent a lot of time in a pleasant haze of lemon yellow and pistachio green.

One afternoon, Nick and I were up in the Den of Secrets, him knitting and me rooting through Georgina's things to see what I could add to the babies' growing bookshelves besides her *Little Women* volumes and the tomes I'd brought back from Muscatine.

"I was sure I saw a Beatrix Potter anthology in here somewhere." I stood back and squinted at the room's uppermost shelves. "I bet I can see up there if I stand on her chair."

"Absolutely not," Nick said. "I cannot take you to the ER and explain that you fell because I was watching my pregnant wife climb up a bookcase in our sex den. I do not even need a baby book to know that."

He put down the nubbly hat-adjacent object he was knitting and pulled over Georgina's desk chair, carefully standing on it and running his finger across some book spines way at the top of her shelves.

"Oooh, *The Adventures of Tintin*," Nick said. "Baby Pret A Manger and Baby Masala Zone will need these for sure." He tossed them down to the ground, where they landed with a dusty thud. "Aha, here's your Potter, poppet."

"Thank you," I said, leaning into the shelves on the left side of the room. "Look, Georgina has a hardback Betsy-Tacy anthology! She really didn't throw anything away."

"I wonder why she kept all her childhood books up here," Nick said, hopping down and scooting the chair back to its home.

"Who knows why Georgina kept anything anywhere. Oh, *The*

Bobbsey Twins on a Houseboat!" I shrieked, ripping that off the shelf. "This is great. When we were kids, all my parents' friends gave us Bobbsey Twins books because, well, I guess that's the joke you make when someone has twins. They're pretty bad and I love them." I hugged the book to me. "Thank you, Georgina. Hoarding wins again."

Nick flopped back down on his pillows. "Promise me you won't carry any of these downstairs by yourself," he said. "Those stairs are treacherous enough without a pair of precious eggplants, or whatever size the babies are now."

"Cauliflower, I think." I knelt and opened the cupboard under the shelves. "Wait, I've done this one. It's where I found her diaries." I pursed my lips. "There's still some other random shit in here, though."

I reached in—the cupboard was deep; my arm went in up to my shoulder and I still barely grazed the back—and scooped out the various books and loose papers still rustling around in there. A complimentary 1984 wall calendar from the Royal Ballet had gotten caught on the shelf's back corner, so I leaned in until I could grab it with the tips of my fingers and ease it out. As I withdrew my hand, I grazed it on something sharp.

"Ow!" I said, jerking my hand to my mouth and sucking on the wounded knuckle of my thumb. Something had poked me.

"You okay?" Nick asked.

"Just a scrape. There's something back there. I can't..." I reached in more carefully and felt along the sides of the cupboard until my fingers hit a metal circle on the right-hand wall.

"Is your tetanus shot up to date?" Nick wondered.

I ignored him as I felt the contours of whatever had bit me. It had a jagged ridge in the middle.

A keyhole.

I sat back hard and looked up at the bookshelves, which were designed to look like three separate cases side by side, but were actually a built-in single wall unit. Each section had multiple shelves up top, and the lower right and left sides had cupboards, while the middle section between was merely decorative.

Or so I'd thought.

I turned around frantically until I saw the pillow I'd been using as a treasure chest. My hands shook as I unzipped it and fished around for the letters. The key was still there, folded up tight inside them.

"Nick," I said, holding it up. "What if...?"

He squinted at it and then brightened. I reached inside the cabinet and felt around until I could position the key against the lock. The key slid in and let me turn it with a neat click.

"Nothing happened," I lamented.

"Oh yes it did," Nick replied.

I pulled my head out of the cupboard and saw that the allegedly decorative panel had popped open like a giant file drawer. It was crammed full of stuff, typical for Georgina. There was a huge photo album, overstuffed with what looked like news clippings and pictures, and an old Chanel shoebox with a photo taped to the top of it. I lifted it out and recognized its subjects immediately: In a room I couldn't identify, Georgina, probably in her early twenties, sat on a stool, the sort of industrial metal number you'd see in chemistry labs, smiling widely at the camera in a slinky black cocktail dress. Behind her, holding what looked like a remote trigger for the camera in his hand, a handsome young man gazed down at her with absolute naked adoration. His other hand was smoothing a wayward piece of her hair with undeniable intimacy.

"Grandfather," Nick whispered.

The lid came easily off the box. It was full of papers and some curling old photographs. Nick and I read them, traded them, consumed them in total silence. Finally he grabbed at my arm.

"Freddie," he said, sounding strangled. "Bex, we have to get Freddie."

CHAPTER FIVE

My love,

I hated leaving you in tears like that, knowing it may be the last time we're alone. I couldn't stand the thought of today's words being the last private ones we ever share. We said so much in anger and in sorrow, and I'm afraid you won't remember all the things we also said in love. And I do love you, Georgie. I will love you until they bury me.

The moment you kissed me, all those years ago, I was gone. I wish it hadn't happened when it was too late. I wish I hadn't been too weak to do the right thing. I've always been weak. That isn't artful self-deprecation, or an excuse for my infidelities (unfaithful to Eleanor in my heart and in our marriage, unfaithful to you because I dutifully go back to her bed every night). You knew I was weak even when you were a child, and I wonder if that's what ultimately drew you to me: my need to be warmed by your fire. You are so strong, so brave, so ready to seize what you want; you make even someone like me feel like a warrior. But my weakness has ruined you, ruined me, ruined us, possibly even ruined Eleanor (as much as she can be ruined; she'll outlast us both). I can't ruin our child as well.

I know it must kill you to see him in Eleanor's arms. I can't look at him without seeing you, and what was stolen from you—from all three of us—and I know it must be exponentially worse for you because, unlike me, you're forced to keep your distance. All I want is to take our son and run with you to the edge of the world. But that would collapse the whole house of cards, a house built by no less than the ruling family of this country. We could never outrun it. Richard would grow up with it haunting his every move.

But we also can't keep up this dual life. Hiding in windowless garrets behind wardrobes, consuming each other under cover of darkness, stealing seconds alone in palace halls... I'd have done this forever, selfishly, if I hadn't walked in on you today and seen you crying. It made me realize that it's my turn to be the strong one. And that means letting you go.

Get married, Georgie. Have more babies. Live big and loud, the way we wish we could have. There is happiness in the world for you. Please let yourself find it, let it sustain you; that's the only thing that can sustain me. And then, someday, possibly when we're both gone, our son will be king. And that is bigger than us all.

Always yours,
Henry

Freddie put the letter down, his face waxen. "Fuck," was all he said.

Nick's color wasn't much better. He'd been green since we unearthed it, his hand shaking so badly when he tried to dial Freddie that I'd ended up having to do it. With a pang of guilt for adding yet another lie about my father-in-law to this morass, I'd told Freddie that Nick was really struggling, and that he needed Freddie to help defuse tensions with Richard in person. It was enough to get Freddie on a private jet, but not so much that he'd go rogue and phone Richard on the sly. It wasn't even that far from the truth. Technically, Nick *was* having a hard time with Richard—it just wasn't, for once, Richard's fault.

Freddie had turned up at our door six hours after I called.

"Where's the fire?" he joked.

"We need to go someplace private," I said, and I'd led him up the stairs into the master bedroom and opened the door to the Narnia closet. He'd stood there, blinking, confused.

"This is unutterably kinky, Bex," he'd said, but he did as I asked, climbing up into Sex Den with deepest trepidation. "I've heard of safe rooms, but this is another level of— Oh."

He'd stopped short when he saw Nick, ashen, clutching the sheaf of love notes we'd unearthed in the box along with some photographs of his great-aunt, presumably taken by Henry, that would have been better left unseen by anyone but them. Nick had handed Freddie the most revealing note of all, and we'd watched as the life drained out of him, too.

"I had to breathe into a paper bag after I read it," Nick said to his brother now.

Freddie peered at it, as if proximity would change the words somehow. "Is it possible we're not reading this correctly?"

Nick slid down the wall and into a sitting position. "Our grandfather and Georgina were in love, she got pregnant, and Gran raised the baby as her own," he narrated. "And that baby is our father. Is that how you're reading it?"

"Fuck," Freddie repeated, covering his face with his hands. "Fuckity-fuck."

Nick's eyes were wild. "And if this is true," he said. "Which…it must be. I mean, why would Henry Vane lie in his own love letter? But." He gulped. "This means…"

"Father's not the heir," Freddie blurted.

"And neither am I," Nick said. His hands were shaking. "None of this is ours. This whole life, all of it, everything we've been raised to do and say and believe, has been a lie. Our lives are a fucking lie. Our past. Our present. Our future. All lies. And we have babies coming who will make the lie bigger and bigger."

His breathing sped up again. I made a move toward him but he waved me off, inhaling a huge, slow stream of oxygen. One of the twins nudged me in the ribs. My hand went to the spot where I felt it, and I thought about what Nick had said. This wasn't just about the brothers; this unraveled everything about all of our lives. I wanted to put it back in the box, and cursed the nosiness that had caused me to dig into a life that was none of my business. No wonder Georgina was a hoarder. She was burying the truth of her life in stuff. She had probably hoped it would fill the space left by the things she had lost.

Freddie turned his face into one of the floor pillows and yelled into it. Then he jerked away. "This is their little place, isn't it?" he gasped. "Father might have been conceived in this very room. I can't. This is madness. Are we *absolutely certain*...?"

He pulled the box over to his lap and started sorting through the knickknacks Nick and I had already seen. Georgina had hung on to everything, from shards of paper scribbled with hasty words of longing to lengthier missives written in Henry's sloping cursive, waxing rhapsodic about how long he'd loved Georgina from afar, and how agonizing it was to play out their dreams in hiding, how they dreamed of a different future.

It brought new clarity to the collection of family photos. In many of the early ones, Henry stood between his wife and his lover, all three of them smiling, Eleanor more primly and Georgina as if she held a dazzling secret. Which, of course, she did. I imagined her and Henry's pinkies secretly touching, connecting them, the way Nick and I would sometimes try to do. But in photographs after Richard, they were as far apart as possible; Eleanor's smile a bit more assured, Georgina's strained and missing its light.

"Right," Freddie finally said. "We're pretty bloody certain."

Nick was staring at a small black-and-white photo of Henry and Georgina, close up, slightly blurry—the focal inaccuracies of trying to take, in essence, a selfie in the non-digital age—in which they blissfully nuzzled. "*These* are my grandparents," he said. "Imagine what would've happened if..."

He picked up one leather baby shoe, which must have belonged to Richard. I tilted my head back and looked at the books. Of course she kept all her girlhood favorites hidden away up here. She'd saved them in secret for him. Or for someday. My free hand drifted to my belly as I tried to imagine what it would be like to hand the twins over to Daphne to raise, knowing that I would have to pretend for the rest of my life that they were not mine, that they didn't grow in my body, under my heart; that I hadn't built them out of love for their father and brought them into this world myself. Thinking about it made my skin sear.

"Poor Georgina," I said. "No wonder she stayed away."

"And we never bothered to come find her," Nick said, rubbing at his face. "I feel awful. She had grandchildren who treated her like a weird old bat. I can count on one hand the number of times we spoke."

"We wouldn't have if we'd known," Freddie said.

"But that's just it," Nick said. "Someone could have encouraged us to reach out to her, to make sure she had any semblance of a relationship with us. Gran or Great-Gran could have found a way for us to know her. But they never did."

"I don't know," I said. "Her reclusiveness seems like a choice. Maybe it hurt too much for her to be any closer to you than she had to be."

"So many choices, and none of them ours," he said.

"I feel responsible for this," I admitted, rubbing my temples. "Georgina hid all of this away for a reason and I should've let it stay there."

Freddie shook his head. "No," he said. "This isn't your fault."

"How could you have known?" Nick said, spreading his hands wide. "We just thought she was eccentric. And if you'd stopped and let things molder up here, we'd never have found out."

"We were never *supposed* to find out," I argued.

Nick chewed on his fingernail. "Do we think...is there any chance Father knows?"

We fell quiet. I searched every interaction I'd ever had with Richard. He was nothing if not dutiful to the Crown; it sometimes felt like he was more attached to The Firm than to his family. I had never really thought about why; it was just the way he was. Was he driven by the need to earn a place he knew wasn't his, or by the desire to earn the one he thought *was*? There was no way to tell.

"All we can do is guess," I said. "I doubt there are any answers up here."

Freddie pulled out his vibrating phone, the lit screen revealing an unanswered string of texts. "Daphne," he said, dropping it back onto the pillows.

"She's going to worry," I said. "She already is. You should answer her."

"What can I even say?" He let fly an angry laugh. "*Hey, babe, turns out we're all Lyons bastards! Surprise!?*" He picked up the phone and scrolled through her messages, then shook his head. "I can't even write a complete sentence right now. God, Nick, it could have been so different. *We* could have been so different."

"You could have been career military, if you'd wanted," Nick said.

"And you could have been..."

"Someone who knows what the end of that sentence ought to be," Nick said very quietly.

"No pressure to be anything other than ourselves," Freddie said. "We could have been normal."

Nick pressed his fists against his forehead. "I don't know how to unpack this," he said, his voice rough with emotion. "How do we even begin?"

"Well," Freddie said slowly. "Bex is right about one thing. All we have left are questions, and most of the players aren't around anymore for us to ask them."

"Except for one," I said.

We'd had to call ahead to see if Eleanor was even at the palace, and her equerry Murray must have alerted her to a strain in Nick's tone because we walked into a very careful presentation indeed. The Queen was at her dressing table, wearing a quaint tweed skirt and a blouse under a woolen pink cardigan, tucking the last of her hair into some curlers. No jewels in sight, not even secretly meaningful ones. I knew how Eleanor's mind worked: She was trying to look as gentle and grandmotherly as possible. She had to be concerned.

"We need the room," Nick said curtly to Murray, who was hovering nervously by Eleanor's side. "Now." He cleared his throat. "Please."

"Nicholas, my word, what an entrance," Eleanor said from her velvet stool, the very place I had sat when—several years ago—she'd more or less conned me into giving up my American citizenship. I wondered how many other cons Eleanor had run in this room.

Murray looked from Nick to the Queen, clearly unsure of his next move.

Eleanor patted her curlers. "I suppose you may go, Murray," she said.

When the door shut behind him, she turned to us and folded her hands in her lap, making a bit of a show of arranging her right one with her left, as if reminding us she was mortal. And perhaps to convince us that she was weak.

"This is a strange surprise," she said pleasantly. "And Frederick, back from the land of the windmills. What a treat."

"You might not think that when you find out why I'm here," he said, glancing from me to Nick and back to me again, before taking the letter out of Nick's white-knuckled hand, and stepping toward her.

And we watched as Eleanor read the truth of her life—the other side of it, from the point of view of the two people who were supposed to love her the most, but who had loved each other more. The Queen rarely looked like anything other than the picture of self-control, but I could see the cracks begin to open.

"My, my," she managed. "Georgina's fantasies were even more elaborate than I imagined. I did tell you, Rebecca, that she was trouble."

"This letter is from him," I said.

"An elaborate forgery," Eleanor said. "She never did anything by halves. It's sad, really."

Nick shook his head. "I cannot believe," he said, his voice vibrating with anger, "that we came to you in good faith and you're still bullshitting us."

"Nicholas! I simply won't stand for that language," she said haughtily, her chin high and strong. "Frankly, *I'm* offended that you would believe the scheming of a sad and jealous—"

"The letter isn't all we found," Freddie said.

Eleanor's features sharpened. "Oh?"

"There were photographs," he said, turning beet red. "Intimate ones."

She pointed at me. "I *told* you that Georgina made a play for him."

"And a baby shoe," Nick added. "A front page, folded onto itself, from Father's birthday. A lock of what looks like baby hair, in an envelope. Shall I go on?"

Eleanor's breath caught. She looked back down at the letter she was holding—a photocopy we'd made on Nick's printer; after she'd destroyed Lacey's phone, we weren't stupid enough to hand her any originals—and her fingertips traced her husband's signature, light as a kiss on a sleeping person's cheek. Her face crumpled.

"I did wonder," she said, so softly I had to crane my neck to hear it, "whether there was anything more."

"It's true, then." It rushed out of Nick in a heavy breath. "I was trying to have some sympathy for you. Then we came here and you told more lies, upon the mountain of others."

"And do you blame me?" she asked. "You've been given a window into an old woman's worst heartbreak, at the hands of her own sister, which she had to bury in public and in private for a lifetime. I'd have thought you, Nicholas, of all people, would understand that."

Nick fell silent. Freddie looked like he wanted to drop through the floor.

"I suppose I'm Georgina in this situation, then," Freddie said. "You must really loathe the sight of me."

A look of tenderness crossed Eleanor's face.

"My dear boy," she said. "Never. You forget—I know what it's like to lose."

"Yes, you do," Nick said, and he was calmer, but still steely. "You know everything, apparently. And we know nothing."

"Clearly not," Eleanor said, lifting the papers. "You know this. What more is there?"

"Those are the facts," Nick said. "I want the story."

"It is what it is, Nicholas. My sister had a baby with my husband. Your father is not my natural-born child," Eleanor said, her voice rising. "Plumbing the hows and whys, opening myself to the bone, won't make a damned bit of difference."

"It would to me."

We all turned toward the door as the color drained from Eleanor's face.

Richard.

CHAPTER SIX

I had seen Richard walk into rooms. I'd seen him storm out of them. I'd seen him circulate in public, yell at his sons in private, and even deliver flowers to his incapacitated wife. Through it all, he'd remained very much the picture of the man in the papers: sleek, tall, ramrod straight, every inch a person who identified as a prince. But I had never seen him as I did in that moment: slumped against the doorframe, airless, small. Judging by his expression, the Prince of Wales had not known he held the title through false pretenses.

"You don't think," Richard said, "that this is information I should have had?"

Nick quickly crossed the room to him. "Father," he said. "I'm so sorry, we didn't—"

"Not you," he said, pointing a shaky finger at his mother. "*Her.*"

"Now, now, don't be melodramatic," Eleanor began, but her voice lacked its usual assuredness.

"Melodramatic," Richard repeated. "You're right. Melodrama is inappropriate. I'd say *raging bloody dramatic* would be a more appropriate response. I've just walked into a room to confirm three separate wedding travel plans for you and me and Nicholas, to protect the direct line of succession, and learnt that we aren't technically even *in* it."

"As far as the world knows, you are," Eleanor said.

"The world," he said, "is not my concern right now."

"It should be," she said. "Perception is reality."

"Then please, correct my *perception* that my *reality* is a cruel prank," he said. He slumped into the room, shaking loose his necktie. "Tell me a story, Mummy," he said sarcastically. "You certainly didn't do much of that when I was a child, so it's nice to get one in while you still can."

Eleanor stared at him, then again down at the letter. "I am not sure I know how, exactly," she admitted. "I haven't talked about this in..." She looked at Richard. "A lifetime."

I edged toward her. "You told me some of it," I said. "You left out a *lot*, obviously, but maybe start there?"

"Please," Nick pleaded. "This didn't just happen to you. It happened to them, and now it's happening to all of us, and I just... *we*... want to understand. Help us understand, Gran."

Eleanor peered up at us, her four confessors, positioned around her now almost in a semicircle. She seemed diminished somehow, frail, and almost fearful. Finally, she gestured for us to take a seat.

"You came here for answers," she said. "And there aren't any short ones."

I sat obligingly down in the armchair opposite her, Freddie taking the one next to me. Richard leaned slightly on the bed, as if in need of support but unwilling to sit and cede his height advantage. Nick kept pacing.

"Eleanor," I said. "How much of what you told me was real?"

"That depends on your perspective," she said. Nick made a noise of disbelief and Eleanor straightened a little. "Georgina had everyone wrapped around her finger, and she milked it. Daddy adored her. The press delighted in her. Our family friends flocked past me straight to her. Even Grandmummy thought she could do no wrong, while I was nothing but a disappointment. She got to go away for school, make friends, see a bit of the world, and have the sorts of life experiences that are thrilling for a young girl, but which were deemed too common for me. I had to stay home, locked away, preparing for my life of duty. All I gave was effort, day in and day out, and it was never enough. But Henry looked out for me, first as my tutor then as my friend. And when I lost..." She stopped and covered her mouth.

"Her first love," I filled in for her to the others. "Her parents sent him away, and he died."

Freddie paled. "That's awful."

"Henry was a girlhood crush, but Robert...Robert was real." The last word was almost inaudible. "He was undone by it all, and drank too much and was flattened on a road in Wales. They didn't find his body for three days, and when they did..." Her eyes closed. "I fainted when they told me, can you believe it? Like something in a silly film."

None of us dared move. Eleanor stared into the fireplace, visibly fighting to compose herself. "When you're my age, of course, you realize that people can recover from anything. But I didn't understand that then. My heart didn't feel like it would ever work properly again, and I told myself loving anyone that much was too painful a risk to take twice. But then Henry put me back together, and I realized I'd already reinvested myself in him. Trust. Affection. Love. And *need*. I did not think I could do this job without him.

"Then one day I found him out in the gardens playing croquet with Georgina, and there it was. I saw the way she looked at him, and I saw it start to have an effect on him. The same effect she had on everyone, our entire lives. That old Georgina charm," she said. "I hadn't thought she would bother with Henry. He was very nearly too old for *me*, and she was only seventeen. But seventeen felt more mature back then, I suppose, and Georgina certainly always thought of herself as sophisticated. I remember looking at them and thinking, *I cannot lose him. Not to her.*

"I never let on that I'd spotted anything. When she went back to school, I wrote, telling her all about Henry's attentions to me, his tenderness, his kindness, what a fine partner he might make for me as I navigated all of this." She waved a hand at the trappings of the Crown that sat around us. "I thought she'd accept that and move along. To this day, I still don't know if she loved him for him, or because I told her how I felt and it made her want him for herself."

Her tear ducts filled. "But I saw it in his face, whenever her name came up. His eyes always gave him away." She blotted at her own. "I suppose I undertook some manipulations of my own. I told Henry she'd met someone while she was at school, and was practically betrothed, that it was very hush-hush. A clandestine romance."

"You stole him," Richard said.

"He wasn't hers to steal, and I took nothing he didn't freely give," Eleanor snapped. "Georgina was no saint. Anything that came to me, she wanted. Toys. Clothing. Attention. Even the Crown itself. I did everything I could to impress Grandmummy, to make my father proud, to ready myself to take this on. I prepared. I behaved. Georgina had charm, but she didn't realize how much of that was because she had the freedom to be charming. When my role increased, and attention shifted necessarily to me, Georgina became barbed with me in a way she wasn't before. They prioritized me, for *once*, and she never forgot it, even if it was because there was never a real choice in the first place."

"That doesn't mean she went after Henry as revenge," Nick argued.

"She would have hurt him, or tired of him. Both, once the intrigue was over," Eleanor said vehemently. "And I never would have. I never *did*. Despite all of this."

"She thought the world of you, though," I said. "She looked up to you. It's all over her diaries."

"The ones you read. You didn't see the rest of them. Things changed between us. She changed them," Eleanor said. "She made herself the star of her own romance. But this is my story."

We all exchanged glances, and sat back, waiting.

"Henry believed me, and seemed to let her go. He and I began spending more time alone together," she said. "He looked at me differently, touched me differently, a lingering hug here, a brushed hand. He knew the demands being made on me. And he was the only one who ever really listened to me. We could talk to each other. My parents paraded other dreadful titled men past me, and each was more grasping than the last. None of them saw me as an actual person. Only as the Crown. A prize for them to possess. *The* prize.

"And then Grandmummy fell ill, and everyone panicked. The old bat ended up living another two years, of course. Sometimes I wonder if she was faking it to move me along."

Nick, leaning against the fireplace, snorted at this, and Eleanor glared at him.

"Regardless," she continued, "it began to feel as if time were of the essence. Henry took me out on the lake one afternoon in the spring, and we agreed we should get married."

"Romantic," Richard said sarcastically.

"I think maybe it was," I said to him, before turning to Eleanor. "You told me before that Henry wouldn't necessarily have chosen this life for himself. He did it for you."

"I needed him. And he needed me. I shielded him against his family's disdain for his academia and lack of political ambition, and he shielded me from my family's lack of affection or concern for my well-being. He *did* love me," Eleanor said stubbornly. "Passion is not everyone's endgame. A person can contain many kinds of love, and none is more valid than the other."

My eyes flicked to Freddie, who was staring at the flames in the hearth. I forced them back to Eleanor.

"What happened when Georgina came home?" I asked.

Eleanor's jaw tightened. "The specifics, I'm afraid, died with her and Henry," she said. "I thought it was over before it began. Georgina was still Georgina, maddening but my best friend, all at the same time. Henry and I got married. We had Agatha. We were happy." Her voice caught. "I *believed* we were happy."

Richard tapped his fingers against the bedpost. "Until I came along," he said.

Eleanor looked up at him, half a century of sorrow all over her face. "Yes," she said. "And no." She pursed her lips. "Henry was a terrible liar. He could never hide anything, even if he tried. And he did try. But I told myself I could live with it. I told myself I didn't need all of him; I told myself I had parts of him she never would. I was, after all, his wife. I was stronger than this. Until..."

Richard pushed off the bed and walked to the window, leaning against it and staring into the gardens. The evening sun set them aglow, as if they, too, were burning.

Eleanor took a deep breath. "Agatha had just turned a year old," she said. "She'd had her bath, and the nanny had brought her to me for some hugs before bedtime. Mummy marched Georgina right in, practically shoved her at me, and that's when my sister told me she was four months pregnant with Henry's child. While I was holding mine. I will never..." She put a hand to her chest. "She told me with so much hope in her face that she and Henry had been in love for ages, and that my wedding had been a regrettable mistake. A *mistake*, she called it, in front of *my* child that had come from it." Her voice dripped with emotion. "Georgina actually took my hands and begged me to let them be together. *The way it was meant to be*, she said. And I will never forget how she sounded. As if this were such a fair suggestion. As if it would be so reasonable for me to step aside and give her what she wanted. You can't imagine how it felt. It was—"

"Like the air was gone from your body," Nick finished. "Like you were a ghost and you might blow away."

"I have never felt... *less*," Eleanor said thickly. "She was the spare by birth, but I was the spare in every other way. The extra part. The backup."

"Quite," Freddie said. I had to stop myself from reaching for his hand.

"Mummy put a stop to that silly fantasy, of course, with help from my grandmother," Eleanor barreled on. "Queen Victoria II was legendary for many reasons. One of them was that her disapproval, when it came, and it came often, was crushing. I still want to shrivel into myself when I think about how she looked at Georgina after we told her. I think if she could have left her in a nunnery for eternity, she would have. But instead she told us that Georgina would have the baby, and Henry and I would raise it as ours. *It is the royal child of a princess and a duke*, she said, *and it shall remain so*.

"Georgina came undone, naturally. She screamed, and collapsed as though someone had cut her off at the knees. And our grandmother walked up to my sister and pulled her up off the ground and said, *Foolish child. It is already done.*" Eleanor snapped her fingers. "Just like that. As if I were being given her bedroom, and not a child."

"This is insanity," Nick said.

"It did feel it, in the moment," she allowed. "But in 1957, this was not entirely uncommon among aristocratic women who found them-selves pregnant outside of wedlock. Georgina was never going to be allowed to keep him. It would have ruined her reputation. Especially given that the baby's father was..." Her voice trailed off. "It was an elegant answer to an inelegant problem."

"Our specialty," Freddie managed.

Nick looked doubtful. "You really got no say? In taking on another *child*?"

"What was I meant to say?" Eleanor shot back at him. "The Crown is bigger than I. It is bigger than you. It was bigger than Georgina and Henry's supposedly grand romance. Do you really think my grand-mother would stand for the future monarch to be abandoned? Not to mention in service of her husband disappearing with her sister? Every one of those details is unbearably tawdry, even for an ordinary family."

"And what was Henry Vane's reaction to this?" Freddie asked.

Eleanor glanced at his photo beside her bed. "I wasn't there. Mummy and Grandmummy spoke to him," she said. "When he came home that night, he put his arms around me and said, *Thereto I give thee my troth*. From our wedding vows. That was all he said, and it was all I needed to hear. We were bound together by those, and now by this lie. So I said nothing." She sighed. "I regret that now. We should have spoken. I should have thrown a vase at his head. But I kept thinking, *He's not lost. He always comes home*. And I needed that to be true. So I let it go."

"I can't fathom how you pulled this off," Nick said. "With not even a palace mole in sight."

"It was easier to fake a pregnancy in my day," she said. "There was no internet. No way for people to scrutinize me in slow motion. No message boards for crackpots to exchange clues. I was only third in line at that point, so the public wasn't as fussed about me yet. We limited access to my quarters to one trusted and well-compensated maid, and the few times I did need to go out, we used padding. Georgina didn't start to show much until she was almost six months along, so she did extra appearances while she could, and then claimed she was nursing me through medical bed rest for my last trimester."

"I don't understand why you didn't make Agatha the heir," Richard said.

Eleanor glared at him. "I tried," she said. "It was a different time. Changing the primogeniture laws was not something people took seriously in the fifties. Once Agatha was born, people simply thought, *Well, she'll have a boy eventually*, and to change them when I allegedly had another baby coming who *might* have been a boy...that would have raised too many eyebrows." She gestured at my belly. "It's a new world now, so that's done and dusted for Nicholas's children. But back then, we just hoped that you would be a girl."

"And what a disappointment I was," Richard said. He half turned. "Is that why nothing I do has ever pleased you? Is that why I hunted and pecked for every scrap of affection? Because you never wanted me? Because you were forced to pretend to love me as yours, and forced to put me in line for a throne I didn't deserve?"

"You were not a disappointment," Eleanor told him urgently. "And I never had to *pretend* to love you. When they put you in my arms, a son, a king in waiting, you didn't belong to her or him or me. You belonged to the United Kingdom, and you were perfect. Untouched by all of this, innocent in a way none of us were. I was determined to make you stronger than your father. Better than your mother. You would never be weak, or needy. You would rise above the mess of your birth and the wreckage it left behind."

"And if I didn't want that?" he asked.

Eleanor threw up her hands. "It was done," she said. "The play had been performed."

"And Georgina...what, left town?" I probed.

"Not immediately," Eleanor said. "She moved into 1A. Kept to herself. I thought we had put it behind us, but once again, I was wrong." She curled the letter in her fist slowly. "He'd been sneaking you over to see her," she told Richard. "For a year. He took the child I agreed to raise as mine, and the three of them played house, an afternoon at a time. Georgina and I had a roaring fight when I found out. She told me he wanted to leave me, that she was waiting for him, that all this could end if I would only see reason. And I looked her square in the face and told her she had him all wrong. That the man who hadn't even had the courage to acknowledge his love child to me, his wife, would never upend his life for it. *Stop fucking my husband, and go find your own*, I told her."

Freddie let out a gasp. Swiftly Eleanor threw the balled-up paper into her fire.

"Yes, it was quite an exit," she allowed. "And I presume what followed between the two of them resulted in this letter. But in the end, I was right. Henry lacked the strength to follow his passion any further than a few kilometers down the road. He came back to me, as I knew he would, and we had Edwin, and he never saw Georgina like that again. We had peace, for a time." The sadness in her face deepened. "We tried. He loved his children. I even had that portrait painted—the one you three unveiled. It was from a photo he took of me. He was so proud of it. But Georgina grew increasingly erratic. Every year on your birthday, Richard, she would call, sobbing. Mummy even had her hospitalized once in Switzerland. And it tore at Henry. He'd go riding. All day. The year you turned five, it was blustery and wet, and I begged him not to go. He didn't care. And he got pneumonia, and..." She drummed her fingertips on her knees. "He gave up, I think. Georgina didn't speak to me for a year, and then she became...what she became. Traveling around the world, trying on different men, too, trying to outrun her past. But then Richard had her grandchildren, and it was just too much. She completely shut down. I suppose history comes for us all, eventually."

"Would it have, though?" Nick wondered. "This secret stayed dead with them for so long."

Eleanor tapped her open palms on the wings of her chair. "Everyone has a weakness," she continued. "And paranoia is mine. When she died, I let myself into her apartment on the pretense of identifying the more obscure heirlooms, and I tore it apart. I found piles of diaries, everywhere. I'm amazed she had time for all those men, with the amount she wrote." She smiled coldly. "It was the last fire ever lit in her hearth."

A memory flashed across my mind of the first day we walked

into Apartment 1A, and noticed that even the fireplace hadn't been properly cleaned. "The ashes were still there when we moved in," I said, disbelieving. "You literally sent history up in smoke."

"Yes, I bloody well did," she said. "And you'd do the same. If Nicholas had been journaling about you, and Freddie, and the parentage of those babies…"

"Leave our situation out of this," Nick snapped. "It is not the same."

"But it is, in so many ways," Eleanor said. "Consider the things you've already done in the name of changing the narrative. Imagine knowing there was written proof of your worst secrets. Imagine it falling into Clive's hands. Or anyone's."

Nick turned pale and said nothing.

"Precisely," Eleanor said. "But then Rebecca started jabbering about some journals she found, and I realized I might not have been as thorough as I thought. I needed to know more. I needed her to want to tell me."

"So, you played me," I translated. It was my turn now to feel a twisting in my gut. She was an incredible manipulator. In another life, she could've been Britain's greatest trial lawyer. "You wanted me to trust you, so you pretended we were developing a relationship. You acted as if you liked me, and wanted me around, and like a goddamn fool I ate it up."

"God bless you, Rebecca," Eleanor said. "You've never come across a juicy bit of intel that you kept to yourself. I told you selective truths when I needed to, in the hopes that you'd stop digging, and after a time I thought I'd won the day."

"This isn't *a game*," Nick said desperately. "This is our lives. Father and I have been driven toward a throne that isn't even ours, and which I don't even want, all in the service of a lie."

"Don't be childish, Nicholas," Eleanor clucked. "Why on earth wouldn't you want to be king?"

"That's the part you forgot, Mother," Richard said harshly. "You said it yourself, how you sacrificed so many opportunities to prepare for this. Wouldn't you have preferred free will? With this, or with that, or with anything? Everything I've ever done has been colored by my destiny to give myself up in service of Crown and country. And it isn't even mine. It was never mine. It was for nothing."

"It most certainly was not for nothing," Eleanor threw back at him. "You have been raised to be king, and king you shall be. I'm sorry you had to find out about this, Richard. I would have taken it to my grave."

"That's why you told Marta you'd never forgive her," I said. "Because she helped manipulate you into a situation that tainted everything that came after it, and you hated her for it. How could you do the same thing to them?"

"My dear," Eleanor said, not unkindly. "I've told you before that I learnt at her knee. People can bend. The key is knowing how to trust which ones won't break."

"You may have backed the wrong horse there," Nick said hotly. "Every time you scolded us, or used my birthright and protocol and duty to get your way, you were using something you knew didn't belong to me. It makes me so angry I could scream it from the rooftops."

Eleanor made a fist, then flexed it. "But you won't," she said. "This news will die with all of us, one by one."

"Or, we'll stop lying to the British people, and the throne can pass to Edwin, where it belongs," Nick said.

"Don't be fools," Eleanor said, but she sounded worried.

"He's right," Richard said. He had begun pacing in time with Nick. "If you love this country, how can you bake a deception like this into its DNA?"

"Not you, too," she said. "Right, would you like me to give the throne to King Edwin, then? He doesn't even take himself seriously. How could he possibly represent the United Kingdom with the kind of dignity that I have for nearly sixty years?"

"Because it's his birthright. Not ours," Nick argued. "Perhaps he'd surprise you."

"Richard," Eleanor said, turning to appeal to him. "You surely understand. You are of royal blood. You were raised for this. You are passionate about duty and—"

He held up a hand. "Stop it, Mother," he said. Then his lips curled. "*Mother.* A word I'm not sure you deserve."

That hit her in the gut.

"You may not have been my child, but you are my son," Eleanor all but whispered. "I fed you. I changed you. I gave you a family. I am the one who came when you called. That is all that matters."

"That's just it, Your Majesty," he said, stopping by the doorway. "I'm not sure it is anymore."

Seconds later, the door slammed behind him.

CHAPTER SEVEN

Richard did not simply leave the room. He left London. He might have left the country. The only person he spoke to before he vanished was Barnes, and if that toupee knew anything, it certainly wasn't talking. But he must have been given instructions, because the day after Richard's disappearance, we were delivered a note on a silver tray—not a formality that was customary in our house—that read simply, *You had yours. Now it's my turn.*

"His turn to *what?*" I asked.

"Disappear, I suspect," Nick said, tapping the note against his left hand and then abruptly ripping it into pieces. "The tit-for-tat would be funny, under other circumstances. What if he doesn't come back?"

"He will," I said. "We did."

"Out of duty," Nick said. "And concern. I'm not sure he's too sprung on the former right now, and if Gran has another health incident, he likely won't bother with *that* either at this point."

Freddie's take was blunter.

"All those times we wished for Prince Dick to piss off," he said over a full English, "and he's gone and done it the *one* time we needed him not to."

"I'm going to text him again," Nick said, picking up his phone. "I really thought he might be at Mum's, but Lesley hasn't seen him."

"Maybe he's with that what's her name," Freddie said. "That socialite he was . . . seeing."

Nick finished typing and plonked his phone next to his breakfast plate. "Thank you for not saying whatever verb you were actually thinking."

"It's too early for that verb," Freddie said, spearing a sausage link more aggressively than was strictly necessary.

"What did Daphne say?" I asked.

Freddie pointed at his mouth, then chewed exaggeratedly before washing it all down with some orange juice. "She said she's very excited for me to get home and rescue her from conversations with Lax about her honeymoon trousseau," he said, wiping his mouth with the back of his hand.

"You're really not going to tell her?" Nick asked. Next to his coffee cup, his phone buzzed, and we all peered at it. "Gaz," he said. "He wants to bring over cake. Ugh, I could use some cake right now, but he'll know the instant he sees our faces that something is going on."

"And yet you're still surprised I haven't told Daphne?" Freddie asked.

"We aren't engaged to Gaz," I pointed out.

"Don't tell Gaz that," Freddie joked, but he wasn't smiling. He rubbed at his temples. "I will tell Daphne when or if there is something to tell."

"You're saying there isn't enough to tell her already?" Nick asked. His eyebrows were very high on his forehead.

"Daphne's not in this, the way we are," Freddie said. "There's a lot of backstory here that's very private." He held up a hand. "I know she's my fiancée. I know. But this is personal."

"So is being married," I said. "She thinks you have no secrets."

"They aren't my stupid secrets to begin with." Freddie kicked at the table leg. "Besides, how's she going to find out?"

"That depends on us, I suppose," Nick said. "Or on whatever Father does."

"He's not going to blow this up," Freddie said. "Is he? No . . . ?"

The three of us could only shrug at each other. Richard had a ticket out if he wanted it. But not one of us knew the truths of Richard's inner workings, and whether he'd ever wished for even a second—as Nick and Freddie had—to be free of all this.

"I'll deal with Daphne then," Freddie eventually said, stabbing his waffle. "If I have to."

Nick's phone buzzed. He picked it up and stared at it, confused.

"Is it Richard?" I asked. "What did he say?"

Nick flipped his phone around to show us. His text to Richard had been kind: I know that conversation was terribly hard. We'd love to talk to you about it. I hope you're all right. Richard's reply was a GIF in which Jeff Bridges's character in *The Big Lebowski* fishes a pair of sunglasses out of his cardigan pocket and jams them onto his face. That was it.

"What does *that* mean?" I asked.

"I have absolutely no idea," Nick said, taking his phone back. "How has he even heard of that movie?"

"I didn't think he'd heard of GIFs, either," Freddie said. "So, wherever he is, he's drunk, right? That's the only explanation for this."

"It's 9:45 in the morning!" Nick said.

"It's five o'clock somewhere," Freddie said, "and we don't know where he is."

Nick rubbed at his face. "At least we know he's alive."

"This doesn't seem like the response of a man who's ready to have a serious conversation," I said.

"It's not even the response of a man who wants to have a non-serious conversation," Freddie said.

"He must be freaking out," I offered.

"We're all freaking out," Nick said. He shook his head and started chuckling. "I'm sorry," he said. "It's not funny. But he was so cross with me and Bex for skipping town, and now look at him. He really has done the exact same thing."

"At least you left *after* your wedding," Freddie said. "Mine's in a month. What am I supposed to do? GIF him to death until he sends back his RSVP card?"

After a beat, we started laughing. It was tinged with hysteria, but the release felt good.

Nick drummed his hands on the kitchen table. "Edwin is supposed to be king. Can you believe that?" he said, still in the grips of the gallows humor. "*His* Henry, whom I once saw pick someone else's nose and eat it, should be the new me."

"That Henry is only seven years old, so don't write him off yet," I said.

"Perhaps if we go public with this, they'll chuck the lot of us, and go so far down the line that Penelope Ten-Names becomes Queen," Freddie said. "GIF that, Prince Dick."

"At least we know she likes us," I said. "Besides, we can always seek refuge with you. They can't boot *their* future king."

Freddie shook his head. "Prince consort," he said. "Assuming Daphne doesn't dump me over this."

"Is *that* why you're not telling her?" Nick asked, concerned. "She would never."

Freddie stood and started gathering our dirty dishes, something he had not done before in my presence and possibly not in his life.

"I finally found something that makes sense. And it makes sense to her, too, and to them. They want me. They're so excited to have me," he said. "I don't know if I can take finding out it's only because of my connections, and them turning around and saying, *No, thank you, never mind.*"

"Freddie, I'm sure they love you for you," I said. "Daphne definitely does. Tell her."

"No." He dropped the plates in the sink. "I'd rather not know if you're wrong."

"I could kill Father," Nick said, staring at the ceiling in frustration. "We're in no-man's-land because he's chosen to pull a runner and fall into a vat of daiquiris or something. Am I meant to GIF him back? What do I send?"

"Rihanna rolling up the car window," I said. "No, wait, Angela Lansbury eating popcorn."

Freddie nibbled on his thumbnail. "That look on his face. I can't forget it," he said. "What if he really *doesn't* come back?"

Nick took a long sip of his coffee. "I have no idea," he said, as he put his cup down with a clatter. "I have absolutely no idea what to do about anything."

I have never thought of myself as an actress, but over the course of the next month, the three of us may have outdone everyone performing on the West End. The public had never loved me more—being pregnant seemed to have absolved me of allegedly banging my husband's brother—so Nick and Freddie and I were deployed steadily to draw attention away from the otherwise potentially glaring absence of their father. Our three-person act, honed out of necessity, worked like a charm. But the void he left inside The Firm was gaping. In addition to the wedding itself, Hax and Lax had planned a gala celebratory dinner that week, as well as some kind of variety show at a local soccer stadium, and it was a challenge to be evasive about whether the father of the freaking groom would be in attendance.

"Where's Dickie?" Agatha wondered at one of our logistics meetings.

"Nagging chest infection," Freddie said.

"Migraines," Nick said at the same time.

"Both," I said quickly. "All that coughing."

"He's recuperating at the country house," Nick said, "but he said we should keep meeting here so that, ah, Barnes and the staff wouldn't be inconvenienced."

"He must be awfully ill," Edwin said. "I sent him one of those cute little videos where it turns your face into a doggie, and he didn't even tell me to get stuffed." He frowned. "It's so unlike him."

"Is it a sex bender, dear?" Lady Elizabeth asked me. "You can tell me. We've all been there. Eddybear once sprained his—"

"He'll be fine," said Eleanor, and we all scrambled to our feet as she entered. Her rubber-tipped cane dragged on the carpet; I hadn't known she was back to using it, but then again, this could have been a bit of theater to evoke sympathy. "I spoke to him this morning and he's keeping his distance so as not to infect Frederick. The groom is the one person this wedding can't do without, after all. Now. Where are we?"

Nick put a hand on the binder in front of him. "I'd been running things while Father is, er, out," he said, glancing at Eleanor. "Would you like to take the reins?"

"I'm sure you're doing a wonderful job," she said with extra sweetness. "It's good practice for the heir, eh?"

"Perhaps you'd like to give Edwin a go," Nick said innocently. "He went to the trouble of showing up today, and all."

We looked at Edwin, who was mugging into his phone. "Oooh, darling, I look dishy as a kitty cat," he giggled to Elizabeth.

"Absolutely not," Eleanor said, and sat down. We followed suit.

"Eddybear gets anxious around binders," Elizabeth told us, patting his knee.

"Right, I'll keep this, then," Nick said smoothly. "Okay. Hax and Lax have got the chap who just won Eurovision to headline the variety show—"

"A scandal. It was a terribly dull song," Eleanor sniffed.

"And we're meant to send a British musician as well, though Lax politely requested that we not send any of *ours* who were at Eurovision," Nick finished.

"Let's send Elton," Edwin said. "Or Paul?"

"Seems rather like overkill, Uncle," Freddie said.

"It's a royal wedding," Elizabeth pointed out. "At least consider it. I love a good sing-song to Elton."

"I'll have Cilla prepare a list," Nick said. "Let's move on to the dress code for dinner..."

When the meeting ended and Eleanor gave us leave to stand ahead of her, everyone dispersed in a hurry—Nick and Freddie in particular—leaving Eleanor sitting in contemplation, staring up at the painting on the wall. The unfinished one of her had been rotated back in, and she was studying it with an air of sadness.

"I feel a bit like that portrait today," she said. "Incomplete. As if I'm slowly fading to white."

"Did Richard at least say where he was when you talked to him?" I asked. "Has he decided anything?"

"I'm surprised you believed that, Rebecca," Eleanor said. "I've not spoken to him at all."

"I guess I assumed you wouldn't add another lie to the pile," I said. "You're right that I should know better by now."

"It didn't occur to me that there would be anything for anyone *to* decide. Only to cope with," she said quietly. "The longer he stays away, the more I worry about what he's thinking."

"Not everyone can live a lie," I said.

Her head snapped up to me. "Could you? Could Nicholas?"

"I'll let you know."

Eleanor sagged a little before catching her own posture. "You truly think one of them would walk away over this?" she said. "Over this matter of choice? How do they not realize that not *having* to choose can be a blessing?" She ran her hand along the ornately carved edge of Richard's conference table. "We are surrounded by so many incredible historical objects. *We* are historical objects. We are lucky." She cocked her head and looked at me. "How can they hate that? Do they hate it? Do you?"

"When I accepted Nick's proposal, I knew what came with him," I said. "They didn't have that option about themselves. I think anyone would at least wonder what they might have been, if they hadn't had their future prescribed to them."

"I never did," Eleanor said. "I saw entire rooms of people bob in deference to my grandmother. I saw people weep at her funeral, at my uncle's, at my father's. I saw my family commanding rooms full of world leaders and politicians and diplomats and commoners. I saw the world change and our family stay exactly where it was, and I thought, *That's what I want.*"

"To be adored?" I asked.

"To be respected," she said. "That's far more powerful. Far more lasting. I wanted the legacy." She gripped her cane, but did not stand. "Perhaps I was being naïve in assuming my son and my grandson felt the same."

Her eyes fell upon every now vacated chair in the room, in turn. "I've watched Edwin grow up to be a gadabout, and a shirker," she said. "I've watched Agatha care more about the symbols of the monarchy than the monarchy itself. Richard has always been the person who took it seriously. Dedication is in his nature. He'd have been dutiful to the core no matter what his place was. I believe that." She pursed her lips.

"The throne is only weak when the wrong person sits on it. A direct line matters less than a solid one."

"That's great, but you've had decades to make peace with the idea," I said.

"Accepting something does not mean making peace with it," she spat. "This was a nightmare that I was called upon to make the best of, and I did that. Largely alone, and for Richard's benefit." She pointed at me. "If he doesn't see that, make Nicholas."

I spread my hands. "They have their own minds, Eleanor. We just have to wait."

"Wait," she repeated emptily. "To find out if a lifetime of agony was for nothing." A note of desperation crept into her voice. "He will come around. They all will. They have to."

"Why?" I asked, leaning forward. "For you, as a person, or for the Crown?"

Eleanor did struggle to her feet then, and looked down at me. "Rebecca," she said. "You should know by now that there is no difference."

"Darling *moeder*!" gushed Queen Lucretia, gliding over to me and cupping my now very pronounced bump with a featherlight touch. "The miracle of life is the most powerful sunshine! I am overcome."

She kissed me three times, twice on the right cheek. She was resplendent this evening in a royal-blue strapless gown with a beaded bodice and a simple cape; this was not a tiara event, but some truly bananas diamonds hanging from her earlobes had a pretty similar effect. One of them bonked me on the cheekbone when she came in for the second kiss.

"It's wonderful to see you, Your Majesty," I said, trying to rub at it subtly. The last thing I needed was to be at Freddie's wedding with a shiner.

"And Prince Richard looks wonderfully well," she said, clasping my hands. "I did fret. It seems every time we are to cross paths, illness mars the day. But he is tall and strong. A statue!"

Lax gestured absently toward the carvings over our heads in the Royal Palace's Citizens' Hall, a vast, high-ceilinged space bedecked with sculptures looking down upon us—of the Amsterdam Maiden, of the planets and the elements, of Atlas. Daphne's family was based in The Hague but used the impressive Amsterdam palace for official functions, its two-story sandstone façade somewhat evoking Buckingham Palace, but crowned with a cupola and a ship-shaped weathervane. Richard had kept us guessing about his whereabouts right up until the minute his car arrived outside. I glanced up at Atlas, the world on his back, and thought how apt it was that we were all here circulating underneath the very symbol of how it felt to carry something bigger and heavier than you are.

In my case, it was doubly true. I'd been cleared to travel by private jet for the wedding, though at thirty-three weeks pregnant with twins, this had come on the condition that we bring two doctors and keep Lax's obstetrician on call—in addition to the fact that Cilla would be lurking on the fringes of the wedding, ostensibly helping Freddie, but also watchdogging me. My swollen feet and ankles were ably concealed by an emerald lace gown that matched my engagement ring; my discomfort, I'd been told, was about on par with a woman nine months pregnant with one fetus, and I sent up a prayer of thanks that the afternoon's public pre-wedding variety show had always only been planned for Freddie, as a way for his new country to welcome him into its arms. I only had so much stamina, and the stress of wondering whether Richard would show his face had drained me of a fair bit before the rehearsal dinner had even begun.

"Poor thing," Lady Elizabeth had said to me as we walked into the hall for cocktails. "I remember when I was about that pregnant with my first. I felt like my undercarriage was going to explode. Which of course it did, in a way, but—"

"Father," Nick had blurted out.

We had all jumped a little and turned to see the Prince of Wales, looking tanned and handsome, striding in with Eleanor on his arm. The hush that blanketed the room was nearly palpable, as the band whipped up "God Save the Queen" as a sign of respect. Even in a non-Commonwealth country, as guests of another monarchy, Eleanor carried a special kind of majesty and gravitas—and incited genuine deference, even from other rulers. She'd been queen for as long as nearly everyone in this room could remember, and I think she represented, to them, the best of what our lives as royals could be: devoted to service, beloved by country, and a living symbol of history.

"I don't envy them," Elizabeth had said to me, nodding at Richard and Eleanor. "*Everyone* wants their ear. No room for an extra tipple or a spot of mischief in a dark corner." She smirked. "Eddybear would burst if we couldn't steal away for a snog. Oh, look, he's already giving me the tug on the ear. No rest for the wicked."

Once she flitted off, I sidled to the bar and sucked down a very large glass of ice water, and took stock of the rest of the party. It was nice not to be the center of attention for once; lurking at the bar, people-watching, I felt like the old Bex for a flash, although she probably would have been drinking a beer. Nick was stuck in a conversation with a clutch of diplomats, but when he spied me eyeballing him, he winked. Across the room, Daphne glowed in an orange silk dress and diamond hair combs, with no outward trace of the nervous woman she'd once been. But the way Freddie kept her so close, a protective hand on her at all times, looked more like a bodyguard than a doting bridegroom. Eleanor's voice floated into my head, reminding me that love doesn't look the same for every two people, so I blinked my inner cynic away and squeezed through the crowd to the nearest bathroom. It was occupied. I eased myself into a brocade chair in the hallway and waited.

"Bex!" came Daphne's voice as she rounded the corner into view. "Is everything all right? Are you feeling well?"

I gestured at the closed door, which now was rattling in such a manner that I suspected Elizabeth and Edwin were the occupants. "I'm waiting for the restroom. My bladder is the size of a pea lately. I think one of the twins is using it as a pillow."

Daphne frowned at the door, then took my hand and helped me stand. "You forget, this is technically one of my houses," she said.

I followed her down the hallway, past the room where the party was, and up a winding back staircase.

"I hope I don't get stuck in here," I joked as I carefully navigated the narrow turns.

She laughed. "Not ideal, perhaps, but it seemed faster than expecting you to get across that room without being stopped to talk," she said. We emerged into a wide corridor. "Here we go. My office is this way."

She opened the door into a room done in cream and gray, with a few pops of color in the form of picture frames, and throw pillows on her low, modern couch. A large window overlooked Dam Square; across to the right I could see the line still forming outside Madame Tussauds, where a wax Freddie and Daphne had appeared a week ago.

Daphne gestured to her private powder room, and I gratefully availed myself of it, then came out to find her gazing at her engagement photo, framed and sitting in her bookcase. It was the one with the makeup in Freddie's beard. He was staring at the camera and giving his best parody of Blue Steel, and she was cracking up. It was freaking adorable.

"I remember so well the day we met, Daphne," I said. "You were a ball of nerves, and look at you now."

"You were so direct with me, at a time when so few people were. I'll never forget it." She reached out and touched Freddie's face in the photo. "My eyes are open, you know," she said. "I know I am not the love of his life. Not yet. He's protective of me. He cares about me. I think he can fall in love with me, in time. And I truly believe he will never hurt me." She looked back at me. "I can give him understanding, and loyalty, and a place of his own. A place where there are no shadows." Here, her glance went to my stomach, then back to my face. "He needs it so badly. I hope you support that."

We held each other's gaze, and then I drew her in for a hug, awkward though it was over my bulk. I wanted to tell her that Eleanor had felt the same thing, once upon a time; that she had clung to the idea that she could love her husband enough for both of them, and it hadn't worked out. But history had repeated itself more than enough for one era.

"Freddie has never once doubted this," I said instead. "It's what he wants. So it's what we all want."

"I'm so glad we understand each other." She kissed my cheek. "Let's get you back. Someone is probably upset that we're both gone, and it won't do for this party to turn into a manhunt." She grinned. "Goodness knows where they'll find Edwin and Elizabeth."

Our laughter bounced raucously around the stairwell as we descended.

L❧

"I should have stopped at least one negroni ago," Nick moaned, sliding onto the sofa in our guest quarters. "Those bartenders had heavy hands."

"I'll take your hangover if you'll take my feet," I said, tearing off my nylons and putting them on the table. My entire life since I married Nick felt like a series of events where I was just waiting to get home and take off my hose. My poor feet looked like sausages with five other sausages sticking out of them.

Nick sat up and took them into his lap. "I cannot believe he showed up," he said, beginning to rub my left foot. "I mean, I can. But it was obnoxious to cruise in on Gran's arm like we haven't spent all month wondering what the hell he means when he sends us a GIF of Leo and Kate on the prow of the *Titanic*."

A knock came at the door. "Ooh, brilliant, I asked if someone could send up snacks," said Nick, scooting out from under my legs to answer the door.

"Did you talk to him?" I asked, leaning my head back and closing my eyes.

"No, not yet, but—oh."

I opened my eyes to see Richard standing in the doorway to our suite. His tie was off, and his hair was mussed; he seemed tired. He looked at both of us emptily.

"May I?"

Nick opened the door wider and gestured for him to enter. Hax and Lax had arranged for Freddie's immediate family to have guest rooms at the palace, after concluding that it was the wisest place to stash me in case the babies decided to upstage everyone and be born early on foreign soil. Lax even ordered me a scooter to traverse the long palace hallways. Nick had used it three times already.

Richard shuffled in and sat down, and I saw that he had a bottle of scotch in his hand. Nick closed the door and wheeled on him.

"Do you have something to say for yourself that isn't in moving pictures?" he asked.

"I apologize," Richard said. "I've already spoken to your brother."

"You left us twisting in the wind," Nick snapped. "Did it not occur to you that we might have wanted or needed to talk about what happened?"

He glared at Nick. "Perhaps skipping town when faced with a complex emotional issue is genetic," he shot back.

"But didn't *you* want to talk about it?" I asked. "This was a huge thing that happened."

Richard's lips twitched, and he took a sip of scotch from the bottle. "It was, and that's precisely why I left," he said. "I keep my own counsel. I am not accustomed to doing it any other way. I admit, it was not ideal, but I needed distance and space to think."

"And we needed you," Nick said.

"For that, again, I apologize." Richard sounded very weary.

"You're here now, though," I offered.

"Indeed," Richard said. He tapped the bottle absently. "I can see why you stayed in Scotland as long as you did. It was freeing, having no one to please but myself. And coming back feels like giving Mother a victory I don't want her to have. I know she didn't start this. But she did finish it, and when I think about the marks this lie made on me, on my *childhood*..." He took a drink, and rolled the whisky around in his mouth before swallowing hard and wincing.

"Once Henry was gone, Mother started treating me as if I were fifteen and not five," Richard continued. "Was I representing her properly. Was I standing up straight enough. Was I informed enough, was I being too silly, was I allowed to want to read comics and pretend to fly planes in my own nursery. She certainly seemed to think not. Anything fun, I did in secret. I was anxious all the time. I never seemed to live up to what she wanted me to be, yet also never knew quite what that *was*. And then I grew up into…into this." He spread his hands, the bottle in the right one sloshing. "I made the wrong choice of partner, because I had no one to guide me. I was a distant father, because I knew no other way, and the Crown came first. I handled your mother and her illness poorly. I lived one lie by my own choosing and it made my life lonely, and it turns out I've been living another one this entire time, and it's ruined me in its own way, too."

He swigged again. I had never even seen Richard drink out of a soda can, much less a bottle of booze. It was disorienting. The perfectly controlled Prince Richard, letting his grip slip.

"I was young when my father died, but I have memories of him," he said. "He was kind to me, I know that. But even at that age I could tell something was missing, like he wasn't truly there even when he was. I wonder what would have been different if he'd been allowed to raise me with…*her*. Or…" He shook his head. "The more it all sank in after I left, the more I thought, *I wish they'd sent me to some other family*."

Nick let out a low whistle.

"This felt like *it*. A chance to break out and be my own man, at last, the one Georgina might have helped me to be," he said. "My position brings with it great privilege, but it has also been an albatross, and in these last few weeks I have wanted so badly to throw it off and never look back. The throne isn't meant to be mine, so why take it? Why not, at last, be free?"

He and Nick stared at each other for a long moment, bleary and laid bare.

"I came so close, Nicholas," Richard whispered. "But Georgina made this sacrifice so that I could live free of the taint of their scandal. She never breathed a word to me. She never even hinted. She watched me from afar and went to her grave believing her son would be king, and if that sustained her at all in life, then I cannot take that from her even after death. Abdicating would be a slap in the face to Mother, but also to…my first mother, and I cannot bring myself to do that."

"So you're staying," Nick translated. "And I assume you're going to ask us to, too, and to bury this the same way Gran did."

Richard ran his free hand through his hair, in a gesture that reminded me of Nick. "Edwin vanished for forty-five minutes with his wife this evening, then wandered around downstairs for about that long with his fly undone. I am hard-pressed to think the country would be very well off with him on the throne," he said. "We may not have much to do by way of actual decision making, but we still carry a thousand years of history on our backs. It's impossible to untangle that from this one very sordid chapter in the books. I still feel beholden to it. The monarchy may well not last. It may be deemed outmoded and swept aside someday. But if that does happen, it cannot be because I threw it away. That, I truly cannot live with."

He scooted to the edge of the chair and leaned in, coming alive a bit. "But I wouldn't fault you for coming to a different answer for yourselves."

Nick blinked. "Wait. What? What are you saying?"

"If you and Rebecca decide you do not want to be part of this, I will fully support you," Richard said. "I would only ask that you not reveal the reason for vacating your positions."

"But succession...?" Nick said. "You would have to remove us completely. My children, too."

"Succession can be sorted," Richard said. "Make this decision based on you and your family alone."

Nick's eyes filled with tears. "All this time," he marveled, "and it never occurred to me that there was another choice besides go public, or don't. I...I'm afraid I don't know what to say."

Richard heaved a giant sigh. "That's partly why I said nothing at all for so long," he said. "The first thing I felt about all this was utter agony that I could have lived such a different life. Been a different person, made different choices."

"Me too."

"But neither do I hate the person I am, or what my choices have led to," Richard said, more gently.

This time, Nick smiled a little. "Me too," he said. "Again. But if I feel *this* betrayed at having the wrong life thrust upon me, how can I keep quiet and thrust the wrong life on my own children?"

"It's a lot to contemplate," Richard agreed. "But I meant it. You are not bound by my decision. I won't trap you in this life, in this lie. I won't deprive you of choice."

Nick wrestled with what to say for long enough that I interjected.

"Thank you, Richard," I said. "This means a lot to both of us."

"It feels good," Nick added, choked up, "to think that we understand each other. At last."

Richard stood, and they shared an awkward handshake that Nick abruptly turned into a hug. Richard seemed shocked, for a second, and then relaxed into it and patted his son's back. They pulled apart, and Richard turned to include me.

"We have a wedding to celebrate," he said. "Sleep. Enjoy tomorrow. Take that time for yourselves, and for Freddie. The future can wait at least that long."

CHAPTER EIGHT

The wedding of the Princess of Orange and Prince Frederick of Wales was to be a two-part affair: first, a civil ceremony performed by the mayor in a very dressed-down exhibition space, and then a religious one immediately thereafter at the more ornate Nieuwe Kerk next to the palace. It was a lot to handle even with a full night's sleep, which neither Nick nor I had gotten. My mind would not be stilled, and neither would the babies tap-dancing on my bladder. It felt like the entire world yawned before us, and I didn't know where to look. Worse, Eleanor's dark secrets, dragged into the light, had overshadowed the fact that we were about to encounter a massive shift in the relationship of the brothers to each other, and me to Freddie. Now that day was here, and we hadn't done any of the work to get ready for it.

"Freddie always lived down the hall, or around the corner," he said at breakfast, morosely prodding his uneaten sausages. "Even when we were fighting, I knew he was *there*. I feel like we lost so much time together over the last few years and we'll never get it back and now he's leaving." He sighed. "It's been generations since a prince of the realm has gone off to claim another country's throne. What if it turns sour and he feels there's nothing left for him back home?"

"There will be," I had said. "*We* will be."

And yet I, too, felt fidgety all morning, worried that this moment wasn't getting the gravitas it was due, that we were about to let it pass us by like any other wedding, like he was any other man. I wanted to wish him one last goodbye, and put a period on the run-on sentence that was Freddie's and my curious relationship to one another.

I'd had a little something made for him, so while Nick finished the exacting process of getting his military insignia right, I tucked the gift into my purse and told Nick I'd meet him downstairs.

"Takes me half an hour extra just to get down there," I'd cracked.

"Try the scooter," he replied from the dressing area. "It'll change your life."

Grinning, I scooped up my trusty navy suede pumps—I was not going to wear them a second longer than I had to—and padded down the hallway to rap on the door to Freddie's suite. The valet they hired for him opened the door, then goggled a little before pulling it together and waving me inside.

"Ah!" Freddie said. "*Het is mijn favoriete…* duchess," he finished lamely. "How'd I do, Jan?"

"Flawless," said the kid.

"You're lying, but that's why I like you," Freddie said. "Why don't you head off? Bex can escort me downstairs."

Jan bowed deeply and retreated into the hallway. When the door shut, I turned and drank in Freddie in his uniform, exuding a preternatural calm, and immediately burst into tears.

"No, no, none of that," Freddie said, plucking two tissues from a box on the table and walking them over to me. He rubbed my back as I blew into them. "Although I will miss your honking noises."

I wiped my eyes. "It's stupid to cry. You're only a flight away," I said. "I'm hormonal."

He gave me a sidelong squeeze. "Maybe you are," he said. "But I feel it, too."

"The crew back in England sends its regards," I said, muffled by the tissue. "Even Bea, in pretty much those exact words."

"She wouldn't be Bea if she sent a florid goodbye," he said. "I hope they didn't mind not being here. But it would be harder to cope with leaving London if I saw all their faces today. Cilla said Gaz couldn't even look at the invitation without wailing."

"Yes, I think everyone agrees it was for the best." I welled up again. "I'm not much better, though. I swear I didn't come in here to cry all over you."

I popped open the clasp on my bag and dug around for his gift: a tiny pin composed of two flags, the Union Jack and the Dutch tricolor one, crossed at the poles.

"I have one like it with my own flags," I said as I dropped it into his palm. "Nick gave it to me a very, very long time ago. It always helped me feel connected to my first home, and like I had a place in my second."

Freddie stared down at the pin, and when he finally looked up at me, his eyes were swimming, too. "It's perfect," he said. "Listen, Bex..."

"This had better not ruin my makeup," I warned him.

"I think it's too late for that," he said. "I just wanted to say thank you. I know you and Nick have had your doubts. Thank you for understanding that I needed this. Because..."

He reached out then, haltingly, and placed his hands so gently on my belly. We said nothing, until he let out a long slow breath and dropped his hands. "It is ever so hard to go, and that's why I have to."

"Freddie..."

"Our bond has never just been about sex, or love, for me," he said. "I've been so emotionally dependent on being able to *talk* to you, to have you in my family and in my life. Not very many people have known me as well as you do. Maybe no one has. But it can be hard to untangle all those things, so even though that chapter is behind us..."

"It still has to change," I finished for him. "I know. Daphne has to be that person for you now."

Freddie nodded. "But you never do forget your first," he said.

He pulled me into his arms for a long hug.

"Thank you for making me want to reach for more," he whispered.

"Thank you for all the times you held me together."

"And thank you for not having any pointy bits on your hat or else I'd have just speared myself," he said. "And then Princess Persil Liquid Detergent and Princess Duracell Batteries will have to be told I'm a pirate."

I snorted and we pulled apart, smiling. "Okay," I sniffled. "I need to clean myself up so we can go marry your ass off."

Freddie chuckled, and then carefully wiped a finger under one of my eyes. "There. Beautiful," he said. "Have you and Knickers decided what to do yet?"

"No," I said. "We only talked to Richard last night. I know you did, too."

"It was a good conversation," Freddie said. "He told me what he planned to say to you. I hope you know I'm behind whatever you and Nick decide."

"Even if it involves living in your guesthouse?"

"Especially then," Freddie said, smiling. "You can earn your rent by doing odd jobs. I'm a very untidy person and I always did think Knickers would make a wonderful maid."

"Awesome. He already has the costume," I said.

Freddie guffawed at that. "Right, my girl," he said. "On that note, time for the tripod to become...a tuning fork? Perhaps you were right to try to use cycles as the analogy." He offered me his arm. "After all, a bike runs very well on its own without the extra part."

I put my hand in the crook of his elbow, and we walked out of his room and down the stairs and into the new life that waited for him. For both of us.

⤬

"Bex," Nick said, the sound coming at me distantly, as if through a haze. "You did it. You made it."

My eyes fluttered open. "Wow, I really conked out," I said. "But it's *done*. I can't believe it."

"You did wonderfully," he said, stroking my hair as I struggled to sit up. "I know you were really in pain there at the end."

PPO Stout came over and opened my car door, reaching in a hand to help pull me to my feet. Cilla and Nick and I had flown back from the wedding as soon as the festivities ended, and they blearily followed me out of the car and each took an arm to help me hobble up our front steps.

"I should have bought bigger shoes for this," I said. "And my back is killing me. I feel like one of those people who chains themselves to monster truck tires and pulls them around, except they do that on purpose. For fun."

"No more lugging anything for you," Nick said. "We're home now. Nothing to do but rest until Mars Bar and Toffee Crisp decide to—"

"WELCOME HOME!"

Nick stiffened, but I fully shrieked. And then we relaxed at the sight of Gaz, Bea and Gemma, and Lacey and Olly and my mother, who was staying with us in the countdown to the twins' arrival, waiting for us in our foyer. Gaz bounded over and folded Cilla into his arms as Lacey rushed to hug me.

"You almost broke my water!" I scolded, but I was laughing. "Where's Danny?"

"My sister's watching him," Olly said as he shook Nick's hand and patted him on the opposite arm. "We didn't think you'd be up for his brand of chaotic energy after such a big weekend."

"Sorry for the to-do," Gemma said, nudging in for the next hug. "Gaz wanted to bring you some snacks, and we decided to have a bit of fun with it."

"I didn't want to have fun with it," Bea said. "*I* wanted to bring over some legal paperwork to do with the hospital and birthing suite and all our logistical arrangements, and *they* thrust the fun upon me."

"Pastries are in the living room," Gaz said. "In exchange, of course, for wedding gossip."

"I told you, it was blessedly gossip-free," Cilla said. "Also, that nondisclosure agreement was quite draconian."

"You look so tired, sweetie," Mom said, taking my hand. "Sit down and let us wait on you while you tell us all about it."

"I've been poring over the papers," Gemma said, trailing me into the living room. "Daphne looked stunning. Everyone is going to be wearing that neckline now."

I heaved myself down onto the couch with an unladylike grunt and took the copy of the *Mail* she'd brandished. The front page bore the formal portrait of Daphne and Freddie in a drawing room at the palace, beaming at the camera—him in his uniform and her in an ivory silk Valentino with a high, gentle cowl neckline and three-quarter-length sleeves, her sixteen-foot lace-edged train curling around in front of them. Down in the bottom corner, there was a photo of me and Nick entering to take our seats for the religious ceremony.

"I look like the broad side of a barn," I moaned.

"A very beautiful, stately barn," Nick said, sitting next to me and placing my feet in his lap so he could untie my sneakers.

"You looked great," Lacey said loyally, handing me a plate loaded with baked goods and a slice of quiche. "Also, no offense, but no one will remember what you wore to this."

"How was Freddie?" Bea asked as Gaz bustled around loading everyone else up with carbs. "Happy?"

"Did he not look it?" Nick asked, rubbing my left foot.

"No, he did," Gemma said. "But it's hard to tell on TV what's real and what's acting."

"He is definitely devoted to Daphne," I told the room.

"That's super." Gaz looked mournful as he handed me a cup of tea. "I mean it. I'm not rooting for it to all collapse on itself, but I am going to miss having his furry mug around."

"Everyone will," Mom said. "Earl and I hated having the girls so far away, even just when they were at Cornell, but we had to let them go. Change is the worst part of life." She smiled. "But it's also the best part. Your bakery is going to be beautiful, Gaz. And Bex and Nick have the twins coming, Danny is yelling NO at me every two seconds, and Gemma and Bea are…" Mom stopped short.

"Getting hitched, actually," Gemma said. She waved her left hand, revealing a wide gold band, overlaid with a platinum filigree detail.

"SHUT UP," I blurted.

"Ever the American," Bea muttered.

"This is fantastic!" I said. "If I could move, I would hug you."

"I'll handle it," Nick said, leaping off the sofa and diving onto the other one, the better to wrap his arms around Bea and Gemma at the same time.

"Make it a foursome," Gaz said, trotting over and tackling them from the other side.

"Going for five," Cilla added, piling on with a giggle.

"Sentimental twaddle," Bea said, her voice muffled by so many arms. "But yes. None of us is getting any younger. It seemed well past time to make honest women of the both of us."

Gaz backed out of the embrace and scratched his head. "I have loads of ideas about wedding cakes," he said. "Not that I would ever assume you'd turn to me for yours. But if it tips the scales, I've done some very interesting things with marzipan lately."

Cilla elbowed him. "Please don't make this moment about you."

"I'm *not*," Gaz said. "I'm being helpful."

"I'll put it in the back of the wedding binder," Bea said, but she was smiling.

⟢

By the time everyone left, it was late, and my back was killing me. I'd also eaten more buttery bread products than was strictly reasonable, plus we'd ordered Indian because I'd gotten a real yen for samosas. I was stuffed, and my stomach was unhappy with me, so I waddled upstairs and took a quick shower and then crawled into bed. Nick was on his side, flipping through the news channels on the TV.

"Oooh, look, there you are," he said, over a shot of me walking around outside Freddie's wedding.

"I look even crazier in motion," I said. "It's like I shoved a really big beach ball up my dress. I can't believe the press hasn't accused me of faking it."

Nick laughed. "You are so hard on yourself," he said. "You look amazing, both in that dress and also in this...robe?"

"It's a caftan," I told him. "And men are required to say that to their uncomfortably pregnant partners."

"That doesn't mean it's not sincere," he said. "You are a very sexy pregnant lady."

"Thank you," I said. "If I weren't so physically uncomfortable and exhausted, I'd put the moves on you right now."

"If I weren't so exhausted, I'd let you," he said. "I'll settle for a rain check. Also, what is my face doing right there?"

He pointed at the TV; the news was now showing footage of Daphne and Freddie leaving the church after their religious ceremony, over a very benign story about famous well-wishers who'd popped onto Twitter with their congratulations. As Daphne and Freddie stepped out into the sunshine, he had pulled her into a swoony kiss, to the delight of the crowd that had gathered outside; behind them, Nick appeared to be wincing.

"I was trying not to sneeze!" he insisted now. "That's going to be the shot on the cover of *People* next week, you watch. Freddie and Daphne looking romantic, and me, lurking behind them like a skeptical creep."

"Frame it and give it to Freddie. It's the wedding gift he'll love the most," I said. "Way more than the Dutch oven we got him."

"That's such a good pun, though," Nick said.

I slowly—so slowly—maneuvered myself into an upright position. On the TV, Penelope Ten-Names was standing in front of Nieuwe Kerk, interviewing the mayor. The press that traveled to Amsterdam to cover this happy ending—the proper fairy tale Nick and I had failed to deliver—still had stories to file, even though the VIP guests had already escaped. Freddie and Daphne were en route to a villa in the Maldives with ten days to do, as Lady Elizabeth had so sensitively put it, nothing but each other.

My stomach was gurgling—that samosa was not sitting well with me—and a weekend in Amsterdam, on full display, had worn me out way more than I thought. I lay back on my pillow and groaned.

"What can I do for you?" Nick fretted.

"Nothing. I'm just anxious and need to sleep," I told him. "I would love to put off finishing the conversation Richard started, but it's the only thing I can think about."

"Me too," he admitted. "This whole thing is rather a mindfuck."

"Are you tempted?" I asked.

"Aren't you?" Nick chewed on the inside of his cheek. "Picture it: a cottage in the UK somewhere, raising up the kids in peace, walking them to the village school. Having crumbling headstones in a church-yard in fifty years where our children could always find us and scatter rose petals on our graves and recite poetry and cry. We could even get jobs." He sounded wistful in the way that only a person who'd never had a proper office job would sound.

One of the twins gave a very aggressive kick. My stomach lurched. "Ow," I said, touching the spot of impact.

"Do you think that was a vote for or against?" Nick asked. He leaned toward it. "Hello? BBC Two and ITV, do either of you have a thought?"

"Here's one way to look at it," I said. "I've led a normal life. I can go back to that and be perfectly fine. But can you do it? Do you really know what it *means*?"

"If I could snap my fingers and make it so that I had *never* been royal? I'd do it. I really think I would," he said. "The idea of being able to live in a quiet hole somewhere, being unremarkable, is a dream."

"But you can't, and that's the problem," I said. "The closest you ever got was Wigtown, and even then, we were being protected and bankrolled by your family. That's not real life."

"Do *you* not want to give this up?" he asked. "Is there any part of you that would feel differently about being married to me if we chucked all this?"

"That is mental and you know it," I said. "You're stuck with me until the end of the road, buddy, no matter which one it is. I'm just trying to be practical."

"I know the baked-in fancy part of my personality is the crux of my sex appeal," he joked. "Be honest, you've never been able to resist a man with his own heraldic flag."

"No, the real draw was your family history of syphilis," I said. "That, and your forearms."

Nick grinned. "It is a relief that even in complicated circumstances, we can still be glib."

"I would never be glib about these," I told him, grabbing his arm and giving it a messy kiss.

He brought his knees to his chest and hugged them. "My entire life I've been complaining that I've never been given a choice, and now that I have one, it's paralyzing." He drummed his fingers on his shins. "To go, or not to go. That is the question. Which, by the way, you haven't answered yet, either."

I shifted again, trying in vain to feel better, and pictured myself as I was before. That girl who only wore jeans and hair elastics—in a ponytail with no extensions enhancing it—felt very far away from me now, and it was alluring to imagine jumping off the hamster wheel of being a public figure and getting reacquainted with her. But there was more than a decade between her and me, and what if—

Suddenly, I felt a telltale wetness underneath me. "We have to go."

"It was that easy?" Nick looked at me, puzzled. "No indecision?"

I gestured to my stomach. "To the hospital," I said. "I think my water broke."

The shock of it immediately sent me into denial. I wasn't even at thirty-four weeks yet, and everything had progressed normally to date; surely this wasn't real labor. *It's not that much water. Maybe my bladder quit on me? I think I have food poisoning actually. I should call the doctor, but first I'll get back in the shower and shave my legs. I forgot to do that. Then I might feel better.* And on and on it went, calmly, stupidly, until Nick took the razor out of my hands and told me the hospital was ready, and my Go Time bag was in the boot of the waiting car.

"Oh, okay," I said, and then I threw up in the sink. "I think I ate some bad cheese, Nick."

"Whatever gets you downstairs," he said.

My cramping was getting stronger. I concentrated on breathing and on not vomiting all over the back of PPO Stout's car, which we were taking to the hospital's private entrance. When we got there, I was hustled into a wheelchair, pausing once to puke in a waste bin near the elevator.

"I mean, okay, it probably is labor, but I *also* might have had bad cheese?" I said hopefully, as a kind nurse handed me a gown and instructed me to change and lie down in our very posh hospital room that I hoped we did not actually need yet. I did as I was told, while Nick finished filling out some paperwork and called my mother.

"Let's check to see what the situation is here," the nurse said, delicately turning up the gown as Nick jogged back in the room. She nodded thoughtfully. "Right. Well. Do not push, love," she said.

"Hell no. I am not pushing until I have had all of the drugs," I said.

She smiled at me. "We're too far along for that, I'm afraid."

"I'm sorry, what? No," I said. "We cannot have missed the drug window."

"You are ten centimeters and most definitely in labor," she said. "These babies are coming now."

"Now?" I said, looking from her kind face to Nick's ashen one. Panic gripped me. "Like, *now* now?"

"Now enough that I can tell you Baby A is not bald," she said. "Your doctor is on the way."

"No. Sorry. I'm not done being pregnant yet," I said nonsensically. "I've only just started being able to rest a full dinner plate on my bump. We haven't decided on names. We haven't even *talked* about names." I grabbed her hand. "Please. I'm freaking out. We could do a couple of drugs. I won't tell anyone."

"I would also like some drugs at the moment," Nick said, disentangling me from the nurse. "But I don't think it's going to happen. Take a deep breath, Bex. It's going to be okay. This is all absolutely under control, right..." He peered at her name tag. "Brenda?"

"Absolutely, Your Royal Highness," she said.

Nick shook his head. "No titles," he said. "No formalities. We're Nick and Bex, and we're proper frightened right now."

Brenda pulled out a machine and did a quick scan of my belly. "Solid heartbeats," she said. "That's very promising."

She scurried out to get an update on the whereabouts of my medical team, leaving me and Nick clutching at each other, pale.

"Did you call Mom?"

"Yes."

"Lacey?"

"Yes."

"And I have a meeting with Bea tomorrow, you need to let her know I can't come to work."

"I'll sort it," Nick said.

"And call Cilla."

"Roger that."

Brenda popped her head back in. "Good news on the drug front," she said. "You're going to do a C-section. The doctor thinks it's safest since we don't know why the twins have decided to come early. Sir, er, Nick, go scrub up, and you'll meet her in the operating theater."

"I love you," Nick said to me hastily as he was pulled away and disappeared from my eyeline. Things were moving very quickly—too quickly—as Brenda wheeled my bed out into the hallway, where a few other nurses helped pull me toward the room where I would meet my babies for the first time.

"I've never been early for anything in my life, Brenda," I babbled. "This doesn't make any sense. Is this because we went on a plane? Should I have stayed home?"

"No, luvvie," Brenda said firmly. "You can't go blaming yourself for what biology decided to do. Twins are early *all* the time. They're probably eager to meet you, and soon enough, they will."

She parked my bed in a small OR, where they erected a curtain across my chest that obstructed my view. The anesthesiologist got to work with my IVs, and I stared at the ceiling, blinking in time with one of the fluorescent lights that was flickering. Brenda turned it off and on again, and it steadied. My breathing did not.

Nick hurried in and sat down beside me, putting a hand on the top of my head. I reached for him, my chest starting to rise and fall with increasing vigor.

"It's been a long road to get here," he said. He was very pale. "Can you believe these are the last few minutes that it will be *just us*, ever again?"

I shook my head as much as I could. "It's too soon," I said, strained. "They're too small. This shouldn't be happening."

He met my eyes. "I know. I'm scared, too." Then he leaned down and whispered, "When I went to call Cilla, my hands were shaking so hard that I hit 'Clive' instead. Hung up in a flash, but that was quite a jolt."

I giggled in spite of myself. "Oh God. That would be all we needed."

"I know," he said. "One more big scoop for our old friend, eh?"

I heard a bustling on the other side of the curtain, and then my obstetrician's head appeared along with a face I didn't recognize.

"Right, my dear, well, this is not the last time your children are going to ignore your best-laid plans," he said. "Consider it their first tantrum, eh?"

"First of many," Nick said, and I could hear the tightness of his throat.

We waited. The doctors worked. Nick smiled at me, tight-lipped. I could tell that he was frightened but trying to remain calm for me. I felt a little pressure, and nothing else. It was mostly silent until Brenda bent down and narrated, "She's out."

"She?" Nick and I looked at each other. "It's a girl?"

Still silent.

"Why can't I hear her?" I asked.

No one answered. I held my breath. The quiet was deep and it was suffocating and it was shredding me into a thousand pieces. *It's too soon. They're not ready.* I'd thought that about us when we got pregnant the first time, by accident, and now here I was freaking out about timing all over again. And with a life on the line. Again.

Then, there it was, a pitchy yelp, followed by a flood of tears as my body released everything I'd held in since my water broke. The rest came in a blur: Her little bruised face was brought onto my shoulder for a split second before she was whisked away; then, another cry, and a laugh when her sister apparently urinated all over the table. And suddenly Nick was pulled away to accompany our daughters to the neonatal unit, and I was left being stitched up by two doctors who chatted casually, calmly, with each other and with me about what a surprise this all was. Whatever muscles I could still feel, I clenched, wondering how my children's little lungs were working, whether their hearts were strong, whether they or Nick needed me. I found out later there had been twenty people in the delivery room that I couldn't see, one full team for each baby, ready for the worst.

When the last stitch was done, Brenda took me into recovery, where I waited in agony for Nick to come back to me. He finally did after about fifteen minutes, glowing with glee and adrenaline.

"That Baby A is a cracker," he said, leaning down and giving me an enthusiastic kiss. "Tiny as a doll, but she ripped out her feeding tube two seconds after they got it in. We're in trouble."

I made as if to sit up, but Brenda glared at me, so I stayed put. "And she's okay?" I asked.

"She's perfect," Nick crowed. "They both are. Baby B needs a bit of oxygen, but they're not worried. They're feisty and wrinkly and a bit red, and Baby A is bruised from your pelvis, but it's already started to come down. I've taken loads of photos already." He sat down hard. "They're real," he said, reaching out and taking my hand. "They're here. They're wonderful, Bex."

I burst into tears. "I thought I'd messed it all up again," I sobbed.

Nick scooted toward me and brushed the hair off my forehead. "You never messed up anything," he said. "And you grew two strong little girls. Maybe you also made them nosy, like their mother, and they decided they were too bored to stay in there. But they're fighters, and I'm so proud of them. And of you."

"I need to see them," I said. "And not in a picture. I don't think I'll feel okay until I see them with my own eyes."

I could swear I heard Brenda, her back to me, sniffle. "It so happens," she interjected, "that there's a shortcut to the elevator that passes through the neonatal unit. That might be the most, er, *private* way to get you back to your suite."

Half an hour later, Brenda was steering me into the NICU, where I heard a disembodied array of beeping until I was parked neatly between two incubators.

"Bex," I heard Nick say. "Meet your daughters."

I turned my head to one side, then the other, to see two pink babies in pink knit caps lying snugly on their backs, with IVs and ID bracelets and narrow feeding tubes and any number of other alarming-looking things connecting them to their monitors. But the beeps were steady. The nurses were calm. And the girls had matching scowls on their faces as they scrunched their eyes closed, like they were desperate for a nap and very annoyed by all the fuss.

"Hello, babies," I said to them, placing a hand on the clear plastic side of each incubator. "Welcome to the world."

CHAPTER NINE

There you go, bug," I cooed, taking my daughter from the nurse and nestling her against my chest. "Snuggle up for a nap."

I had unbuttoned my shirt enough to rest her face against my skin. Nick was doing the same with her twin sister next to me, tipping his head back against the rocking chair and smiling in ecstasy.

"This is therapy," he said. "I could do this all day."

"Pretty soon you will, sir," said the nurse on duty. "They're thriving. They'll be home before you know it."

Once Bea knew the babies were safe, she'd sent out word of the premature delivery. Even though we wouldn't have our girls in tow to show them, we'd agreed to speak to the assembled press and well-wishers when I was discharged. That had been two days ago. When I saw the ensuing footage of that appearance, it almost made me cry; Nick and I had looked like dazed, lovestruck fools when we walked out of the hospital's glass double doors.

"The staff here were marvelous," Nick had said as we stood there in front of over a hundred reporters from all over the world—all of whom were smiling directly at us, a detail I clearly remember because it had never happened to me before. "They had two terrified first-time parents on their hands, and they were strong and steady and calm, even when I tore my gown the first two times I tried to put it on by myself."

A gentle laugh wafted through the crowd. I looked up at the building across from the hospital and realized that every window was crammed with people looking down at us, and before I could help myself, I waved up at them. Every one of them waved back.

"And the babies?" asked Penelope Ten-Names from her spot in the front. "I understand we'll get names in a few days. Any hints?"

"Once the shock wears off, we'll let you know," I had said with a grin. "After we have an audience with the Queen."

"They're doing brilliantly, though. Small, but mighty," Nick had said. "Like Britain herself."

This was now day three of our new schedule of NICU visits, and the press so far was keeping a respectful distance, making it an oddly peaceful time. Focusing only on these minuscule beating hearts, without fear that we'd leave the hospital through a throng of people trying to get a shot of me lactating, made it easy to shove the outside world away for as long as we could manage it.

My phone vibrated on the table next to me. I shifted as carefully as I could, so as not to wake my daughter.

"Gaz," I told Nick. "Now he thinks we should name one of them after Saint Wulfhilda of Barking, who got…" I squinted at my phone. "Fired from the Abbey for being too hot."

"*He's* barking," Nick said. "Should we tell him, and put him out of his misery?"

"No way," I said. "His misery is way too entertaining."

The baby grabbed Nick's finger. "Yeow," he said theatrically, tickling her nose. "First you rip out your feeding tube, and now you're trying to pull off my finger. What two-kilogram baby can do that?"

"A fighter, that's who," I said. "In a spiritual sense, but mixed martial arts would be an interesting twist."

Nick laughed. "I'm not sure that's in the cards."

"Maybe not," I said. Nobody was around us—they'd put us in a private area—but I still lowered my voice. "We should probably talk about what is in the cards, though."

He knew what I meant. His eyes scanned the area.

"The fantasy of leaving is so, so alluring," he said quietly. "But now I'm not so sure I can do it."

"I wondered if you'd land there," I said. "It would be...such a shitshow."

"It's not even that," Nick said. "I mean, it *is* that. But it's so many other things, too. I keep thinking of my grandfather. He said in his letter that running off wouldn't actually let him and Georgina escape anything. That the scandal would always chase their family. We're in a similar position, and now that I'm seeing these two in front of me, flesh and blood, I don't know if I can do it to them. Is that crazy? If I have the choice that I have always wanted, is it madness not to take it?"

"Deciding to stay is a choice, Nick," I pointed out.

"But not my choice alone," he said. "What do you want to do?"

I leaned back in my padded rocking chair. Nick had painted such a nice picture of what our alternate future might be. A simpler life, with simpler jobs, and simpler choices. Years ago, I told him I fell in love with a person, not a prince. But they don't exist separately. They will always be one and the same.

"No holds barred?" I asked him.

"None."

"There is no clean exit for us," I said. "It might be different if there were. But something will always be chasing us."

Nick gazed pensively at the daughter in his arms. "Gran said that when she first held Father, he seemed so pure, and all she wanted was to raise him strong enough to face his destiny. All I can do is make my best guess at which path is right for them, and ultimately, being infamous won't be any easier for them than being famous. It could be rather worse."

He gestured with his chin in my direction. "And imagine the teenage rebellion when she finds out she could've been the bloody queen," he joked. "I'd better double down on this now."

"Like a vow renewal, of sorts," I said.

"If I've learnt anything from all the Real Housewives, it is that renewing one's vows is a death knell for any relationship."

"Too true," I said. "I'll think of another metaphor."

Both babies began to wriggle and mewl.

"What's the matter, poppet?" Nick cooed. "Did luncheon go down the wrong way?"

But the energy in the whole room had started to shift, and maybe the girls sensed it. I craned my neck and saw, in the distance, the doctors and nurses exchanging frantic expressions, then scurrying over to form a line toward the door. I heard the water at the scrubbing station turn on, and the tear of the plastic around another sterile pre-soaped brush, before a very specific voice drifted through the NICU.

"This soap smells ghastly," we heard Queen Eleanor say. "How dreadful that these poor babies start life thinking that the world reeks of loo cleaner."

Nick and I exchanged *holy shit* looks, and shortly thereafter, the Queen appeared in front of us wearing a lavender coatdress and matching hat, smiling and nodding and politely thanking the staff for taking such wonderful care of all the babies. "And particularly mine," she said, stopping in front of me. She leaned down and poked at a little foot that had come free of its swaddle. "Hello, madam," she said. "It's your favorite relative."

Everyone scattered, having paid sufficient respects, and the three of us were alone in our corner of the NICU. One of the nurses, as she left, pulled the curtains around us for privacy.

"They're so tiny," Eleanor marveled.

"Would you like to hold one?" I asked. Eleanor shrank back a bit, nervous, so I added, "Like all the women in this family, they're tougher than anyone thinks."

Eleanor looked pleased, and sat in the nearby empty glider. I carefully handed over the baby in my arms, who blinked with interest up at her great-grandmother.

"Look, Nick," I said. "A pair of queens."

She whipped up her head, more surprised than I'd seen her before. "Are you implying what you seem to be implying?"

"Yes," Nick said. "You've had enough traumatic chapters in your life. We're not going to be the authors of another."

Eleanor took a deep breath. "I know all too well that it's one thing to make a decision but quite another to live with it," she said. "As someone who had to do that for a very long time, I can tell you, at times the pain made me wonder if the alternative would have been easier." She looked up at Nick. "Are you ready for that? Do you think you can live out this choice without regrets?"

Nick gazed at his grandmother, his smile rueful but resigned. "No one lives without regrets, really," he said. "But when they surface, and I'm sure they will, I just have to remember that I'm doing this for something bigger." He glanced at the baby in his arms. "And something much smaller. The same way you did."

"My darling, darling boy," she said. "Thank you."

She looked over at the baby Nick held, and then down at the one in her arms. Then she cleared her throat and turned to me. "Rebecca, there's something I need to tell you," she said. "I realize I abused our relationship by telling you a very specific version of the truth, but it's important to me that you know the relationship itself was not a lie." She took a moment, and cleared her throat. "You matter to me very much."

I smiled at her, there in her signature dress and topper, holding my firstborn daughter, her latest-born heir. "I love you, too," I told her.

"Also, no one else is interested in my thoughts about the Cubs bullpen. Murray simply *cannot* grasp it," she said, sounding put out about it. "We need to get these babies home and start teaching them about managing your middle relievers."

"Yes, it's high time we all moved forward," Nick said. "In that vein, Gran, Bex and I have decided to pack up Georgina's writings. All of them. We'll have Bea personally deliver the box this week."

She blinked. "Aren't you afraid I'm going to burn them?" she asked.

Nick shrugged. "They're yours, not ours. It's your story, yours and Father's. Neither one of you got to write the beginning of it. It only seems fair that you be allowed to write the end."

The baby reached out and grabbed Eleanor's finger. Eleanor cooed at her, then pursed her lips. "Whether or not the proof dies with me," she said, "the truth doesn't have to. When these ladies are old enough to understand your decision, you have my blessing to offer it to them. Although I would certainly hate to deny the world..."

She looked expectantly at me and Nick. I glanced at him, and he nodded.

"Nick is holding Margaret Eleanor Mary," I said.

"And you, Gran, are holding our future queen, Georgina Emma Victoria," Nick said. "It felt right. I hope you agree."

Eleanor's lips trembled. "It is absolutely right." A tear trickled down her cheek. "History has all but forgotten her. Perhaps now, it never will."

She gently began rocking the chair, then looked up with a start as Georgina burped in her face. Eleanor's expression relaxed into a chortle, and Nick joined her in it, both of their faces at peace in a way that had been missing since we'd opened that box. Georgie was named both for the beloved queen that was—whose death during World War I gave all the Lyons heirs their name—and for the one who never got to be, who'd loved her child enough to let a secret tear her to shreds. Maggie bore Eleanor's name as a tribute to the strongest woman I have ever known, a talisman to help her navigate the twist of being born second—one slender minute that would someday feel monumental to them both. They carried everything and yet nothing at all on the shoulders of their five-pound bodies.

As I watched them nestled in the arms of a queen and of a king in waiting, I sent up a fervent wish that they would lean on each other for the rest of their lives, the way Georgina and Eleanor couldn't. Unlike the heirs and spares before them, though, they would always have us. Nick and I had taken some blows, self-inflicted and otherwise, and somehow emerged unbroken—forged in fire, fiercely in love, and ready to fight for our daughters. These girls, these women in waiting, wouldn't repeat history. They would make it.

TURN THE PAGE FOR A PEEK INTO GEORGINA AND HENRY'S STAR-CROSSED LOVE STORY

GEORGINA'S STORY

1956

His hands caught my attention before anything else did. Not his eyes, not that jawline, not even the disobedient lock of hair that always flips out of place, kissing his forehead the way I cannot. No, as usual, I saw Henry Vane's strong, elegant hands before I even heard his voice. They rested on my sister's shoulders, guiding her into the room, with a gentleness I could close my eyes and feel from memory.

I loathed him. And I loathed how much I loved him.

But I had to wipe the spite off my face, at least until I was alone. Usually, I enjoyed attending Trooping the Colour. Even though it technically honored Queen Victoria II's birthday, the spotlight was spread about such that we could all be forgiven for believing the sun shone that day specifically to illuminate each of us. Those with military stylings, honorary or not, would dress in full regalia and join the guards' horseback procession and act extremely haughty and important. Though my job, which consisted of sitting in a carriage and waving and looking pretty, resulted in exactly as much adulation but without the smelly horses and prescribed frowning. Then we would all converge on the palace balcony for a flyover that yielded a front-page-news photo every year and nearly always threatened to snatch somebody's hat. When I was just old enough to understand birthdays, I thought they were all celebrated like that, and threw the most vicious tantrum when Mummy denied me the parade I believed was rightfully mine. Eleanor never let me forget it, though the teasing felt different once we established that one day it *would* be rightfully hers.

And now Henry had ruined it for me, with the simple fact of his presence. It is hard to revel in being on display when you are fighting to keep a façade in place, and the mere sight of him with Eleanor still tempted my stomach into rebellion. I did not want to invite the remains of my lunch to the party, so I pasted on a vacant smile and determinedly looked elsewhere as the high-ceilinged room filled up. Those who'd been on horseback were always the last to arrive, their towering bushy black hats having been set aside so that every hair could be combed back into place, every medal straightened. The clack of their boots on the polished parquet floor was quickly drowned out by the chorus of greetings from waiting relatives—and the nannies tending their offspring—who were too far removed from succession to be invited to watch the flyover from the balcony, but were allowed to stand at the windows framing it. I'd invented an excuse to arrive in London late the previous night and been as tardy as possible that morning, lest I be forced into displaying a social grace that I definitely did not feel. It worked—making the tongue-lashing from my mother worth it—but now I saw Eleanor start to scan the room for me, so I hastily positioned myself on the other side of a tall gilt planter bearing a robust bouquet of English roses. The absolute last thing I wanted was to be drawn into conversation with Henry and my sister. My years in finishing school had seemed like dismal exile until I realized they provided the perfect excuse to keep my distance from the happy couple, and I'd been hopscotching Europe on a self-prescribed Educational Refinement Tour ever since. I hadn't seen them at all since their wedding, during which I had spoken a grand total of five words to the groom. It was much easier to ignore Eleanor's bliss from the safe distance of Switzerland.

From only half a room away, however, it was impossible, and I could barely breathe. I knew without looking where Henry was and what he was doing: standing with Eleanor near the door, indulging distant relatives in the social currency that was expected of the future consort to the eventual Queen, while most likely hating it for the obsequious behavior it was. I badly wanted him to notice the slim cut of my new dress, yet preemptively bristled at him for the way I knew his gaze would inevitably shift back to Eleanor like it was nothing, like I was nothing. Like we had never been anything to each other.

"Georgina. Join us here on earth."

My eyes flicked a few degrees to the left and landed on my grandmother's shoes. I raised my head as she heaved herself up off a nearby silk settee.

"I'm sorry, Your Majesty," I told her, sweetly. "Just dreaming of the Alps."

The Queen tut-tutted. "I sent you to Château Mont-Choisi for some polishing, not to have you return a daydreaming twit."

"Then you ought to have sent me to a hideous hole someplace in deepest Siberia," I said. "A rare strategic mistake, Grandmamma."

"Quite." She smirked despite herself, and leaned in for a double kiss. Up close, the bags under her eyes were poorly hidden. Last year's illness had sapped much of Queen Victoria II's energy, but none of the stubbornness that led her to deny she'd been all that sick in the first place. "At least you look quite lovely. You outshone your mother and Ingeborg in your carriage. The bloom of youth," she added, with an expansive gesture.

"Yes, I liven up these dreary proceedings considerably," I said, theatrically fluffing my hair. Grandmamma shook her head with affection. It was easy for me to delight her, possibly because I was so inconsequential to her. Unlike her sons and my sister, who represented her legacy, I required none of her brainpower or emotional energy. I would never be sitting on the throne; I existed simply to look beautiful and marry well and be a source of amusement for the people she thought truly mattered, herself included.

"Georgina!" Ellie's voice cut across the room. "Welcome home!"

I felt Henry's gaze land on me before I even turned my head.

Twisting my face into something that could pass as pleasant, I stepped around the flowers and opened my arms to Ellie as she hurried into them. Henry stayed right where he was.

"*Eleanor*," the Queen called out sharply as she shuffled away to harass her sons. "A monarch does not scurry nor does she hug." She tutted. "Disgraceful."

My sister tensed, and a rush of tender protectiveness took hold of me. None of my heartbreak was her doing. I could (and did) wish every night for Henry to flush himself down the loo and never be heard from again, but she was still my Ellie, and she needed me. I looped my arm through hers and turned us as subtly as possible toward a wall, away from our grandmother's judgmental eyes.

"I didn't think a monarch was meant to look like a walking coral reef, either, but there she goes in that hat again," I whispered.

Ellie's giggle was gratifying, but short. "You mustn't make me laugh, or I'll get in more trouble. I already got a tongue-lashing for not sitting up straight enough on my horse during the procession."

"From what I saw, you were marvelous," I said. "It's Her Majesty's head that's crooked."

"Don't be cruel," Ellie admonished. "She's trying to help. She's preparing me for my turn."

"Your turn," I scoffed. "You're fourth in line for the throne. She's acting like they're all three going to kick off tomorrow."

Ellie shuddered. "Don't say that," she said, gazing up at a very large, dark portrait of King Albert holding a stag's head. He looked glum. "I should like a bit of time with my husband and baby before..." She flicked her head toward our dour ancestor, whose left foot rested on a velvet stool that read REX NON POTEST PECCARE. "*The king can do no wrong*," she translated with a frown.

"What a load of codswallop." I nudged her playfully. "For one thing, I believe we've already covered Grandmamma's hat."

Ellie smiled in spite of herself. "I am glad you came home," she said. "You've been abroad forever. Henry is altogether too cowed by Grandmamma to help me deflect her at dinner." She grabbed my arm. "And you must meet Agatha, since you missed the christening." Her expression turned in a way I could not parse. "Rubella, you said?"

"I...yes, I was bedridden for ages." It was a carefully told truth, as I had in fact spent the weekend between the sheets, albeit with a handsome French baker who thought my name was Noelle and made outrageous baguette jokes. "There's no time to meet her now, though, we're due out on the—"

But my sister had an iron grip to match our grandmother's will, and she was already dragging me into the exact scenario I had dreaded: finding myself face-to-face with Henry Vane.

Eleanor and I had both admired Henry in our girlhood. In retrospect, it was inevitable; as the son of trusted and sufficiently posh family friends, he was the only young man we even *knew*, let alone were allowed to spend time with unsupervised. When the fog of war lifted, he'd remained in our lives as both our tutor and a sympathetic ear, our first and best example of deep thought and deep thoughtfulness. Unlike anybody else in our lives, he paid heed to us as actual people, not just as princesses. Whenever Eleanor grew anxious about the role she was being groomed to assume, he'd bring her a tome about a particularly scandalous ancestor of ours, to remind her that perfection was not a typical monarchal trait. And he was the only person who ever gave me fresh blank books to use as diaries, likely because he was the only person who ever noticed I *kept* diaries. Ellie and I agreed privately that he was precisely the sort of person we ought to marry one day, never entertaining the notion that he was a person either of us actually would.

Then two things happened at once: I learnt Ellie had been carrying on a secret romance with the son of a household employee, and that he had died in an accident. I shall not soon forget the sound that burst out of her when she heard—right before she fainted, something I thought happened only in novels. Even in tragedy I wanted to admire her for keeping such a dramatic affair to herself, but instead it unsettled me to know how coolly easy it had been for her to live an enormous lie. Even more, it terrified me to watch her fall apart. I had never seen her unmoored, and these foreign textures to my sister's life were so confusing that I couldn't sort out how to be what she needed. But Henry did. With no heirs from Uncle Arthur, we all knew what her place in history was going be, and Henry might have been the only who surmised that she would not bear its weight if she did not properly heal.

And thus began Henry's sweet, scholarly staying power. He was patient. He was gentle. Attentive, intuitive, kind. Eleanor's misery wore on him, but he persisted, nurturing her like a recalcitrant bud that finally couldn't help but open to the sun. Of course our parents began plotting. And of course, right on cue, Eleanor fell for him. Who wouldn't want to place her life in the hands of the man who'd brought her back to it?

But I had fallen first. And I knew in my bones that, while Henry had been the one to revive her, it was I who enlivened him. Mine was the shoulder he sought when Eleanor's emotional burdens became too heavy. Mine were the eyes he held too long, whose hand he "accidentally" brushed, whose company he found excuses to keep. Mine. *Me*.

Somehow, it had not mattered. And now, as Ellie marched me closer to him, the room seemed to close around me, boxing me in with all the things it took so much effort to pretend didn't affect me: his proximity, his scent, and worst of all, the baby in his arms that served as incontrovertible human proof that Henry Vane had chosen Ellie instead.

I set my jaw and looked into his face, warm and inquisitive and with no hint that this might be ripping him up the way it was me.

He rejected you. He did not want you. It never meant anything.

He is not yours.

"Why, if it isn't the Duke of Cleveland," I said, as lightly as I could manage.

"Hello, Princess," he said, using his childhood pet name for me. "You flew in from... Paris this time, was it? How is France?"

"*Très* French."

"Is that a compliment?"

"Anything but London will do," I said, a touch too acidly.

Ellie poked me. "You mustn't be like that, Georgie," she said, looking around the room. "Not in your position."

"Oh, pish, I don't have a position," I said. "You know what I mean. On the Continent, I can flit from Switzerland to Italy to France eating bread and cheese and chocolate, and drinking too much wine and flirting with anyone I like, and there are no dreary stuffy relatives nearby to tell me it's unseemly."

"You never did mince words," Henry said.

Was I imagining a softness in his tone?

"Georgina," Eleanor said, a trifle impatiently. "Look. Agatha." She sighed contentedly. "We're a wonderful little family now."

Her uncharacteristically saccharine tone would have nauseated me even without the issue of Henry. With gargantuan effort, I bent my head over the wriggling infant in Henry's arms. *Agatha*. A name for a fully grown busybody, not a baby. I saw Henry in her serious face and resolved to hate her forever, too—until she smacked her palm against my cheek and laughed delightedly, and suddenly there was Ellie. I couldn't resist giggling with her.

"She is sweet," I admitted. "Highly corruptible, of course. I shall take that job very seriously. Oodles more fun than being a godparent."

"I did try, on that front," Ellie insisted. "But Grandmamma had a list of aristocrats she wants in her debt, and Mummy made us cut out anyone unmarried."

"And I'm an unrepentant heathen. A spinster and loving it," I quipped.

"Didn't *Tatler* just call you the most eligible girl in England?" Henry furrowed his brow and I tried to find it ghoulish but could not. "I'll wager there are titled lads all over the country who'd bend the knee to you."

"I don't need them. I've a rollicking parade of lovers in France alone." I summoned the courage to level him with my direct gaze. "I can't imagine giving that up for *one* boring old British git."

The tips of his ears reddened just a touch.

"Georgie, my goodness," Ellie admonished. "I thought finishing school was supposed to turn you into a lady. You're certainly old enough to hold your tongue a *little*."

"And apparently *you're* old enough now to have grown into Grandmamma's mouthpiece."

My tartness was a trifle unfair, but I resented being rapped on the knuckles in front of Henry like an unruly child when I was doing such a bang-up job of neither kicking him nor kissing right there in front of the whole family. Before Eleanor could respond, we got the signal to file out on the balcony, and she motioned for Henry to hand over the baby.

"Don't have too much fun over there," she said, settling Agatha in her arms. "One of these days you may never come back, and then where will I be?"

She took Henry's proffered elbow with her free hand, and he hesitated for the barest of seconds before extending me his other one. Ellie was busy with Agatha, and stupidly, I let myself meet Henry's gaze. We held each other there for what could have been a moment, but which felt like an eternity.

"Fancy a grand entrance with the B-team today, love?" said my uncle Arthur, coming up behind me with Aunt Ingeborg's hand clasped tightly in his. Henry and I smoothly disconnected, as if it had never happened at all, and he swept Eleanor out to their adoring public. I gratefully gave Arthur an extra kiss on the cheek. It was impossible not to like Arthur. He had his mother's generous physique and his father's generosity of spirit—as loose and friendly as my own father was uptight. Next to each other today, in their military finest, Arthur had still looked like an unmade bed in comparison. Even Father's mustache had somehow stood at attention.

"The next king is hardly the B-team," I said.

"Tell that to *her*," Ingeborg said, nodding at the Queen's back, but her tone was not bitter; it was resigned. She wore sadness as thoroughly as her own skin. Hers was an exhausted beauty, worn down to a nub from years of being pressured to bear a child she and Arthur simply couldn't conceive.

"Perhaps I shall," I said, grinning as best I could. "I do enjoy seeing how far I can push her."

Arthur winked. "That's the spirit," he said as the three of us made our way outside and to our own end of the balcony. Below us, the crowd spread far and wide—well beyond the Victoria I memorial and down the Mall. "I'll tell you, my girl, it's a slog being the one they're all fussed about," he went on. "Enjoy your freedom before they realize they've forgotten to clip your wings."

"I should like to see them try," I said as the roar of the jets reached our ears. Excitedly, I tilted my face to the sky. The force of the flyover was a bracing, exhilarating shock even when we knew it was coming; as the jets tore through the sky, their churning wake ruffling my hair and imperiling my hat, I clapped a hand to my head and let out a squeal of glee. I heard Henry do the same, and, like magnets, our heads turned toward each other. The look on his face put the planes' wake to shame. I had been prepared for it to be hard today. I had been prepared for it to hurt. But I had not readied myself for what I saw in Henry's eyes before he remembered to blink it away.

Regret.

The apartment set aside for me at Kensington Palace was freshly painted and completely empty. Mummy had shoved the key into my hand and me into a chauffeured car, clearly hoping the prospect of my own palatial dwelling would tempt me into forgoing Europe in favor of finding a husband, moving in, and having what she viewed as emergency babies lest the line of succession once again turn left. My parents—and, for all her tolerance of me, the Queen herself—had grown tired of thirdhand gossip about my travails abroad, hopscotching between old money acquaintances and undoing all the good my schooling had supposedly done. Uncle Arthur had been correct: It was easy and convenient to brush me away while they groomed Ellie, but with her increasingly sorted and stable, The Firm would soon take a concerted interest in me. My liberty was on borrowed time.

But as I wandered through the cavernous Apartment 1A, it felt no more mine than any of those borrowed apartments or country homes overseas. The vast space felt chilly and hollow, like an empty gallery instead of a loving family home. Especially as I could not currently foresee having the loving family, or even just the love, to fill it. The only room that spoke to me was the library, a dark-wood jewel of a spot with a tall rolling ladder and a generous window into the garden. It would have let in abundant natural light, but right now, I left the thick curtains drawn. I wanted the darkness. I wanted the memories I knew it would bring, like picking at a scab I knew I shouldn't.

The summer I fell in love with Henry, I'd kept it between me, my diary, and the eighty-four pillows stacked on my canopy bed, into which I would cry nightly at the inevitability of my loss. I had to go back to Switzerland. Eleanor would be alone with Henry to stake her claim, and she would win. Eleanor always came in first, and I, second. Genetics said so.

But as I lay there, tears running into my ears as fast as the thoughts flew through my head, I began to see a difference. All of Eleanor's seemingly infinite advantages came down to the randomness of conception. But that did not mean life also owed her Henry. In this, at least, I surely had a voice. And so I used it: I poured out my heart onto two pages of perfumed stationery, which I guarded in my room like a state secret. It was no longer what to say, nor whether to say it, but when.

Cruelly, I had no chance until the night before I was due to return for my last months of arduous Swiss finishing. Ellie caught a real corker of a head cold that kept her home from a dinner party at the Vane house, and while I had outwardly oozed sympathy, inside I thrilled to the knowledge that I would get Henry alone. I tucked the tightly folded letter in my brassiere, and waited.

It was agonizing to watch him all night, my declaration of devotion pressed against my skin, but my patience paid off. Every meal at the Vanes' crumbling estate was chased by a pretentious cigars-and-port story hour among the Old Etonians, a ritual I saw for what it was: Henry's blowhard father grasping at the prestige that had since eluded him, while the women in the room pretended to be interested in stories they'd heard a hundred times. Henry loathed it and always escaped as soon as the group got too blotto to notice. I gave him a respectable head start, then abandoned my perch in the window seat and stole after him.

I found him in his usual spot: the library. The room smelled like scotch and cigar smoke, disrupted only by the chilly breeze coming from the door he'd opened to the garden. Henry stood there gazing at the sky through a pocket telescope, and I crept closer as quietly as possible, enjoying a rare, uninterrupted chance to stare at him.

"You don't miss a trick do you, Princess?" He swiveled to smile at me as I let out a gasp. "Yes, I'd know those footfalls anywhere. You're as stealthy as the Blitz."

"Fortunately, I have other talents." I felt myself flush, so I laughed rather too hard as I drew level with him. "You've the right idea here. They're all being hideously boring. As usual."

"Perfect visibility of Saturn," Henry said, handing me the telescope. "Let's see. Have they told the one about how Wibbles pranked the Head Boy by putting glue in his toothbrush?"

"Oh, they're long past that," I said, putting the instrument to my eye. All the twinkling spots looked the same to me. "When I left, Father was deep into the story about the time what's-his-name fainted on the rugby pitch because he thought he'd lost an ear, but it turned out to be an odd-shaped toadstool growing in the grass, or something."

"Or something?" Henry teased. "You mean you don't know verbatim? Your father saw it and said—"

"Don't you dare make me listen to it again," I said, smacking my hand over his mouth. "I did not escape that room for you to be just as tedious."

As he chuckled, his lips tickled my palm. Goose pimples spread up my arms, and I yanked my hand back and returned to the planets.

"I apologize for my own lack of stories about secondary-school idiots," he asked. "According to Father, I'm an enormous disappointment in that regard."

"Henry," I scolded, poking him in the chest with the telescope. "The only disappointment here is that I might need glasses, because everything up there looks like a sparkly freckle to me. Perhaps if your father associated with fewer idiots, *he* wouldn't be the idiot from a political family who only works *near* Parliament."

"You always know how to make me feel like less of a pillock," Henry said, throwing his arm over my shoulders and squeezing me appreciatively. His arm felt so right on my body that I shivered with joy. He misread this, and started rubbing my shoulder for warmth.

"You're lucky, in a way. Mummy barely notices me enough to call me disappointing," I prattled, trying to hide my delight at his touch. "I'm just the spare. The extra set of kidneys in case Eleanor's turn to rubbish."

"No," he said. "Perhaps I'm nobody's disappointment, but you? You're definitely nobody's bloody spare."

We fell quiet. The rubs to my upper arm became slower, almost absent-minded, as if we did this all the time and it were the most natural thing in the world. I luxuriated in how it felt to stand there with him—two invisible, inconsequential people who were neither of those things to each other. I held myself as still as I could, desperate not to break the spell, but eventually my longing took over and I nestled closer, tucking my head under his chin.

I felt something graze my hair—his lips?—before he gave a start, then leapt toward the open door. "Gosh, it did get awfully chilly in here."

"No, Henry, it's all right."

He fumbled with the door latch and then turned and leaned against them. "It won't do to get you sick, too. My apologies, Princess."

But he wouldn't look at me.

"Henry," I said, taking his hands. "Don't be afraid of this."

His color got higher and hotter as I pulled him toward me until our bodies met. I reached up and touched his lips, first with my fingers, and then with my own mouth. He let out a ragged breath and succumbed, scooping me practically to my tiptoes. We lost ourselves for several minutes until he spun me and leaned me against the windows, his hand traveling to trace the line of my bodice. I moaned, and he froze.

"Dear God, what are we doing," he said, to himself as much as to me.

"We're doing what we want to be doing," I insisted, reaching for him again, but he sidestepped me.

"Georgina," he breathed. "I can't. Eleanor . . . I think she expects—"

"Forget about Eleanor. She's not here."

"You're so young," he murmured, closing his eyes.

"I'm old enough."

"And I'm so much older."

"Twenty-six is hardly a withered husk."

"It might as well be," he argued. "I'm almost too old for your sister, much less you."

"Stop talking about my bloody sister." I took his face in my hands and forced him to look at me. "Not everything is about Eleanor. This is about you and me."

"There *isn't* a you and me, Georgie. It doesn't make any sense," he said.

"Are you trying to convince me, or yourself?"

"This is a crush. Crushes fade."

My hands dropped to my hips. "What trite excuse will you try next? That I am too young to know my own heart? Because that is nonsense, Henry. I know it all too well." Frustrated, I plunged my hand into my dress, noticing he could not help watching me do it. I retrieved the folded square of paper and pressed it to his chest. "I've bungled this. You were supposed to read my letter first. Please. You *must* read it."

I could feel his heart pounding as he reached up to cover my hand, and the letter, with his. He didn't push me away, and the last barrier burst in me.

"I've loved you for ages. It has been agony watching my sister fall in love with you, too, because I knew it meant speaking up would break her heart. But I do have to speak," I said, hardly pausing to breathe. "You said it yourself, I'm nobody's bloody spare. I want you, Henry. And I want you to choose me."

"If you're wrong," he whispered. "If it passes, if you change your mind...I can't, Georgie, it will ruin me. My family..."

I stepped into his body again and felt his breath quicken. "I won't change my mind, and I am not wrong," I avowed. "And I will wait as long as it takes for you to believe it."

I kissed him again, pouring everything I had into him as if I could drown out his doubts. Then I took a step backward and saw a man who was hopelessly drunk on me, and I knew I had won.

"Read it," I repeated. "And come to me."

He never did.

It was the last time we'd touched.

I inhaled deeply in my own future library, so like that one, then walked to the window and pulled aside the curtain to press my palm against the glass. I could feel the Vanes' French doors against my back as surely as if I were still splayed against them, ready to take what I had been positive would be freely given.

"What happened?" I wondered aloud, not for the first time. My breath fogged up the window.

"That is a fine question," a voice said, and I screamed, my hands flying to my open mouth as I whirled around.

Henry shrieked, too, at my reaction, and then we both laughed with embarrassment. "Turns out I'm a damn sight stealthier than you ever were," he said, blushing a bit.

The old longing flared up in me. I swallowed it as best I could. "How in the world did you get in here?"

"There's no staff, which is why it's a terrible idea to leave the front door hanging open," he replied. "Honestly, I mostly came in to make sure you hadn't been robbed or murdered."

"There's nothing in this old mausoleum to steal," I said. Then I narrowed my eyes. "And how did you know where to find me?"

Henry tapped his fingers against the hat in his hands, and then walked deeper into the room, setting it on a dusty oak desk barely two meters from where I stood.

"I thought," he began, "that we should talk."

"It's a bit late for that."

"You avoid us like the plague."

"Can you blame me?" I spat.

"This was all your doing, Georgina!"

"Yes, pardon me for being honest with you," I snapped. "Where *were* you? I waited for you, Henry."

He snorted. "For what, ten minutes?"

Bile rose in my throat, and I marched over and slapped him before I could stop myself. "How dare you. I bared my soul to you, and you ignored me. Did you have a good laugh at the silly child's love note? Did you even bother reading it before you threw it in the bin?"

Henry rubbed his cheek, then appeared to wrestle with himself before reaching into the interior pocket of his trench coat. He pulled out an unmistakable square of paper and placed it on the desk between us. It was folded less tightly now, soft at the edges from use.

"I don't understand." I blinked at it. "You would have come to me, Henry. You can't have read it."

"I read it the second you left the library," he said. "I read it every day. I still do. I read it this morning, even though I knew it would be agonizing."

My lip trembled. "Agonizing," I repeated. "Agonizing for *you*? What about me? I was humiliated. I heard nothing from you."

He rubbed his jaw. "Georgie—"

"Nothing," I repeated, shoving him a little. "I told myself you had gone silent because you were getting your affairs in order, to avoid a scandal, so that everything would be set when I returned. I waited, and waited, and what was my reward when I arrived home? Your ring on *her* finger. Without a word to me, you faithless bastard."

Henry threw his arms wide. "What was I meant to do? Fly over and challenge someone to a duel?" he asked. His voice cracked a bit at the end. "Eleanor had told me about...well, about all of them."

I frowned. "All of whom, exactly?"

"Don't pretend," he said. "The boyfriends you'd been amassing overseas. The gondolier, the painter, the literary genius, most of them at the same time. I'd never have fit into that picture. If I'd gone to you...I almost blew up all of our lives. Thank God she told me."

"And you believed her?" It stung as much as if he'd slapped me back. "You had my heart right there in your hand, and you took her word for it instead of mine?"

"Why would I doubt her?" he countered. "Eleanor has never lied to me."

"There is a first time for everything, then, because that is exactly what she did," I said. "There had been no gondolier, no painter, nobody. Only you."

"That can't be." He rubbed his forehead. "She must have misunderstood. Or else..."

I thought of the expression on Eleanor's face today when she'd asked about my phantom bout of rubella. About her insistence I fawn over

Agatha. The way she herself had preened so baldly about them being a family.

"She knew," I said aloud. "She deliberately drove us apart, because *she knew*." I pressed the heels of my hands into my eyes, as if to shove my tears back inside. Eleanor didn't deserve them. "And you let her. Why did you let her?"

"*Let* her? Hearing that tore at me."

"Even if I *had* taken six lovers, so what? I'd told you that you were the one I wanted, and you chose to recast my love as some sort of parlor game," I said. "Do you really think so little of me?"

He sat down hard on the desk. "I suspect it's more that I think very little of *me*."

"As you should."

"Touché."

But I could not remain petulant in the face of the tortured look on his. A rueful smile crossed my lips, and Henry clocked my gentler mood before he continued.

"My family has always made it clear that I am mundane. Small. Eleanor's interest in me is the only thing that's ever made me larger in their eyes, but even now, they think she chose me for practicality rather than passion, because being a prop is all I'm good for." He swallowed hard. "I sat down to write you every day, and each time it seemed increasingly absurd that stodgy old me could be enough for someone who had all of Europe at her feet. I lost my nerve."

"Or you let Eleanor lose it for you."

His shoulders crumpled. "I am a coward," he told the floor. "It was far simpler to believe her than to trust the impossible dream of a life with you. You are passionate, you are brave, you are all that I am not. The memory of that kiss will sustain me forever. Eleanor simply held up a mirror and showed me a man who could never sustain you in return."

"The truth is quite the opposite," I said, a tear disobediently escaping. "You see, there *was* a painter. Eventually. And several others. Even a gondolier. But all of them came after you got engaged, because every time Ellie wrote me about how deliriously happy you were, it sliced me into pieces and I was desperate to feel admired and desired and needed.

But not one of them drove you out of my heart. Why do you think I stay away?"

Henry slid nearer to me, ostensibly to smooth the tears from my cheeks. "And why do you think I cannot?" he whispered. "I pointed you out to Ellie today, hoping she would bring you closer. I kept trying to talk to you during the wedding week. I can't stand not being near you, even though you no longer want me."

"Of course I still want you, you thick twit," I said, exasperated. "I've never stopped."

We gazed at each other, woozy, our faces dangerously close. His tongue flicked over his lips, and mine parted, expectant and welcoming. When he dipped his head and kissed me, it was with ten times the electricity of our first, amplified by desperation, lust, and lost time. We stopped only when we needed more air than we had allowed ourselves, and as we took delirious, hungry gasps, he smoothed my hair and nuzzled the soft side of my neck.

"Now what?" he whispered.

Anger rose in my heart like a fountain bubbling to life. Eleanor. My Ellie. I'd been her protector. She'd been my betrayer.

I stepped back and slowly began unbuttoning my dress. "Now, we take what's ours."

He said nothing, only watched, until it was more than either of us could stand. We consumed each other, savoring every minute of a union we'd both given up hope would ever happen, until we lay quivering and sweaty atop the pile of garments we'd torn off our bodies—and in some cases, torn full stop. I wondered idly how I'd get a change of clothes.

I felt reinvigorated. Born again. The bleakness that had taken hold of me lifted, and my head lolled sideways with a loopy grin. "That gondolier has a lot to learn."

Henry's face clouded. "I know what you want me to say, but I cannot talk about Eleanor that way."

I rolled my eyes. "Believe it or not, Eleanor was the last thing on my mind. Frankly, I don't want to talk about her ever again. Or *to* her, if I can manage that."

Henry propped himself up on his elbow and ran a finger down the length of my torso, then back up, over and over, until he finally cupped my breast in wonder. Or was it something sadder?

"Henry," I said. "You touch me as if it will be our last."

"It is," he said. "It has to be."

I stared at him. "She stole from us, Henry. She stole us from each other. She stole time, she stole love," I said. "Are you not infuriated with her?"

He leaned over to kiss me lightly. "I am so angry with her," he said, "that I can only breathe because I am holding you. I don't know how I'm going to look at her. I don't know how I can possibly lie with her. But I don't know if I can lie *to* her, either."

"Pity she didn't have the same compunctions," I said. "Eleanor brought this on herself. She knew what she was doing, and now I know what *I* am doing, and neither of us should care."

"But it's too late, Georgie," he said. "Carrying on will make a bad situation worse."

"Wrong. I think we both already feel better."

"You need a partner who can love you openly."

"Wrong again."

"You say that now," Henry said. "But you weren't raised to be any man's mistress."

"That's three ticks against you, sir," I said, kissing his shoulder. "Because I think I'd be quite good at that, and God knows there's a rich history of it in the monarchy."

The side of Henry's mouth twitched up briefly. "I do so love you, Georgina," he said.

"Then be with me," I said. "Or else, yes, you're right to take a very good long look at me, because this one memory will have to last you forever."

He sat up then, leaned back on his knees, and traced me thoroughly with his eyes. For one horrifying moment I thought I had lost him. But then I saw in his face the same need and devotion I had spied years ago. The difference here was power: This time, I actually had it.

"You and I both know this won't be our last," I said, sitting up and kissing him deeply. "Do not treat it like a mistake, and do not *make* the same mistake. Choose me the way you should have back then."

He wrapped his arms around me and buried his face in my hair. "I'm terrified, Georgie. I'm not strong enough to say no to you, but am I strong enough to say yes?"

"I shall be strong enough for the both of us," I promised, leaning back and putting my hands over his heart. "You have me. I have you. Nothing else matters, nothing else can touch us. I will not let it."

This time when I kissed him, he returned it. "Then yes," he whispered. "I choose you."

He is mine, I thought. *He was always mine. I hope we bring Eleanor to her knees.*

ACKNOWLEDGMENTS

It's a lucky thing to write a book, luckier still to have someone read it and not hurl it at a wall, and an absolute blessing when people finish it and want to spend more time with its characters. We are so grateful for you, the readers, who took Bex and Nick and Freddie—and Gaz, always Gaz—into your hearts and didn't let go. It was your requests that made us sit back and wonder if we could pull off a sequel, and you who inspired us to push ahead to actually write it. We hope *The Heir Affair* rewards both your waiting and your faith. Without you, it would not have existed.

On a practical level, this book never would have become tangible without the efforts of our dear friend and agent Brettne Bloom, and the support of the rest of the wise, wonderful women at The Book Group, especially Hallie Schaeffer and Dana Murphy, whose early enthusiasm buoyed us more than we can say. Likewise, we have many people to thank at Grand Central Publishing who worked tirelessly on *The Royal We* after we'd already turned in those acknowledgments, including Emily Griffin, Caitlin Mulrooney-Lyski, and Fareeda Bullert. This go-round, huge thank-yous go out to our brave and brilliant editor Maddie Caldwell (that edit letter was a thing of beauty), Jacqueline Young, Staci Burt, Tiffany Sanchez, Angelina Krahn, Mari Okuda, and Elizabeth Turner Stokes (who produced another perfect cover)—and surely a whole lot of other talented folks whom we'll end up thanking in our next book.

The Wigtown Airbnb in chapter one is a fictionalized version of a real place called The Open Book. We have not been there, but we gratefully thank Melissa Joulwan for bringing it to our attention and helping inspire the beginning of *The Heir Affair*. Check it out, everyone, and if you go, report back. Also, of course, the book itself is a fictionalized version of things that may bear a resemblance to real people or events. We wrote *The Royal We* long before an American actually did marry into the royal family; we outlined *The Heir Affair* in 2018 and finished the first draft—with no material plot changes—in November 2019. No parts of this book were altered as a commentary on or reaction to subsequent or current royal events. So what we're saying is, thanks to the universe for giving us a royal psychic hotline, and also, can someone please teach us to channel our predictive energies toward other things?

No writer works in a vacuum. We are lucky to have each other—thank you, each other!—but we are also so grateful to Amy Spalding, Gretchen McNeil, Liza Palmer, Jenny Han, Robin Benway, and Jasmine Guillory for their kindness, support, and advice. The invaluable Eliza Hindmarch once again answered our endless nitpicky questions about Britishisms with patience and love; any errors we've made on that front are all our own, and in good faith. Tiffany Brown, thank you for helping to keep *Go Fug Yourself* running smoothly; you're the reason it still runs at all, in fact. Go Sparks.

We deeply appreciate our ride-or-dies Carrie Weiner, Lauren Shotwell, Jen Pray, and Catherine Gelera for the laughs and the love and the sushi and *Big Brother/Bachelor/Survivor* hot takes, and letting us hold a bunch of Emmys. We're grateful to Jason and Erin Oremland for helping with emergency playdates, among many other things. Thanks to Jenn Carofano-Rosen, Diana Aizman, Corinne Murphy, Lee Broekman, Tina Sanchez, Julie Kaplan, and Moksha Bruno—the Roscomare fam—for being perfect just as they are, for bringing love and levity when it was needed, and for their equally excellent partners. (Double thanks to Moksha and Lincoln Bruno of Linc Imagery for making us feel like queens ourselves in our author photos.) Thank you to Marissa Gluck, Grant Rickard, and Morgan Fahey for always being an invested ear and an interested party. Michelle Dornfeld, BBBFF, thanks for all of it, black belt and beyond. And Rachael Gerstel, to whom all good things should come, you are a blessing. And thank you, Evil Witches. You know who you are.

Last is never least. Our families are the best. Thanks to Susan, Jim, and Elizabeth Morgan for their constant love and enthusiastic interest and support. Maria Huezo, you are a treasure, and the only reason sanity ever prevails. Thank you, Kevin Mock, for always being present even when physically you could not be; you are an exemplary human and husband. Dylan Mock and Liam Mock, the beans, the best of us: You are both brilliant and loved beyond measure, and your hugs are our sustenance. Love always to Kathie and Alan Cocks, Alison, Mike, Leah, Lauren, and Maddie Hamilton (you are all 3, 2, 1, amaaaazing); and Julie, Colin, Nicholas, and Claire O'Sullivan, whose faces are terribly missed, as are those of the rest of the Mock clan.

And Fug Nation, you are the wind beneath our wings. Nowhere else would we say, "Read the comments." Thank you, as always, for being there.

ABOUT THE AUTHORS

Heather Cocks and **Jessica Morgan** are the creators of the internet's wittiest, longest-standing celebrity fashion blog, *Go Fug Yourself*, which made *Entertainment Weekly*'s Must List and the *Guardian*'s list of 50 Most Powerful Blogs. They are the authors of *The Royal We* as well as two young adult novels, *Spoiled* and *Messy*, and have written for publications ranging from *New York* magazine to *Vanity Fair*, the *New York Times*, the *Washington Post*, *Cosmopolitan*, *W* magazine, and *Glamour*.